SEED OF HARMONY

Book 1 of the Harmonic Empire Series

Advanced Read Copy

C. Arthur Shuey

Look for these titles in 2017

Rage of Harmony (Book 2 Harmonic Empire Series)

Quest for Harmony (Book 3 Harmonic Empire Series)

Follow us on twitter: @HarmonicEmpire

And on Facebook: fb.me/HarmonicEmpireBooks

Find out what's next by registering as a Citizen of the Harmonic Empire

At: www.HarmonicEmpire.com

Book 1 First Edition ISBN: 978-0-9988456-0-9

DEDICATIONS AND THANKS

Brenda Shuey was my inspiration. She showed me that everything is possible. I miss her every day.

Diana Paradise is my muse. She gave me the confidence to finish what I started.

Bob Van Keuren has always been there when I needed advice and guidance.

And finally, to Mom. She bought comic book after comic book to improve my reading skills when I was struggling. Then she introduced me to science fiction. Although I didn't really share her later interest in romance novels, you can see just a hint of that in SEED of Harmony, as a tribute. Thanks, Mom!

ACKNOWLEDGMENTS

Wendy and Valeria re-read this story again and again and again. After each reading, they gave me ideas that invariably improved the story.

Elisabeth Johnston is an amazing editing talent and a good friend. She can change a single word and change the entire tone of the story. She provided some remarkable insight into ways to improve the story. I am amazed and humbled by her. She wasn't a science fiction fan when we started this project, but I think I've converted her. I could not have done it without you.

Creative Consultant: Robert Van Keuren

Test Readers: Diana Paradise, Wendy Gonzales, and Valeria Maier

Cover design by White Moth via DesignCrowd.com

Prologue

Class 3 Planet – Unexplored – Hunting Expedition

The bright burnt-orange orb rose majestically above the verdant hillsides—its rays penetrated the morning mist and were splintered into myriad rainbow fragments by the prismatic effect of the tiny drops of condensed moisture in the air. The Sun had risen just so and set several times while the three hunters stalked prey on this lush unexplored world. The air, forests, fields and oceans teemed with life and life energy. It was the perfect hunting ground.

The three Breeyan hunters had been following a fresh trail of a "Fanged Leaper" for half of a planetary rotation when they came across a sprawling grove of giant deciduous trees. The individual trunks were as wide as the shuttle that transported them from orbit. Mammoth limbs spread out in every direction, creating a full canopy as far as their eyes could see. And the tracks of their prey led directly into this forest. Stealthily, they followed. Another scent rode the light breeze, and they all raised their snouts and sniffed in a staccato rhythm trying to identify it. The strong earthy odors of the forest itself almost covered other subtler smells… Barely discernable, but still there, were the undeniable scents of corruption, decay, decomposition. Perhaps this was the lair of some high-level predator… they must be cautious. But this prey was theirs! They would fight for it! They lowered themselves so that their chests were almost touching the ground—making themselves as small as possible. They quickly but quietly continued the pursuit.

Under the trees' thick canopy, light from the sun was a dim stepchild of what it had been in the clear. As they followed the shadowy trail, they soon found evidence of many kills in the past. There were bones, carcasses, bits of fur, teeth, and claws strewn about under the tree trunks. Immediately the fur on the backs of the hunters stood straight up, and they extended their whiskers to sense the slightest of vibrations that might indicate some danger—they sensed only the wind. As they wondered what had caused such carnage, the scent of the forest seemed to grow more cloying, if not unpleasant. No, the smell was—intriguing—mesmerizing. They felt themselves taking it in with deep inhalations. A feeling of lightheadedness and euphoria overtook the hunters and they soon began to feel drowsy, their eyes growing ever heavier. Well, the Breeyan had been on the hunt for a long time...perhaps this was as good a place as any to take a brief respite—just for a moment. They would resume the hunt soon. As they lay down and huddled close together, their eyes slowly closing, a fine mist settled over them from the canopy above. The thought never occurred to them that their role had suddenly be reversed from hunter to prey.

This was the way of things. The SEED had spawned in the Sylvistrakah Tree Canopies since the first of these giant trees had sprouted from the fertile soil. It was a symbiotic relationship. The SEED had found a sheltering host where it could grow and thrive. In turn, the SEED used its unique talents to nurture the trees by providing a continual source of nutrients to the surrounding root system from the decaying bodies of their unwitting prey.

The SEED's function was both lure and executioner. The SEED rained down on the slumbering hunters—entering their bodies through pores in their skin, through nostrils and other mucous membranes. Science might categorize the SEED as a virus, but the SEED was unique throughout the galaxy. It was not a simple virus, driven by individual hungry cells alone. Millions of these single-celled organisms, left in isolation, would never have become more than any other virus. Instead, the SEED was a gestalt organism. It was defined by the properties inherent in the collective. The individual cells were part of the whole. A collective consciousness developed once the number of individual cells reached a critical mass. The SEED functioned as a single organism. And so it had been for time beyond reckoning.

As the SEED entered the circulatory system of the Breeyan that day, it used the resources it found in their bodies to begin rapid reproduction. It secreted a strong neurotoxin that was designed to paralyze the victim, yet keep it alive—for the time being. Normally, the SEED would propagate as much as possible in the host body before allowing it to die. The rapid decomposition, aided by the SEED, would distribute nutrients through the soil and into the network of roots belonging to the host trees.

But as the SEED propagated inside the Breeyan hunters' bodies, something new happened. The SEED had encountered a sentient species for the first time. Though the SEED had a collective consciousness, it had never been truly sentient itself. Encountering and absorbing sentient life energy now changed all of that. As the decomposition continued its relentless progress, the SEED cells that had been exposed and ***changed*** by the encounter with sentience were reabsorbed into the trees' root system—and became sentient themselves. When they rejoined the collective organism, the SEED began to change—to think—to ***evolve***. It soon realized that animal hosts might have much more usefulness than as merely a supply of nutrients.

The newly aware organism sent out a thought and the decomposition of the Breeyan was halted, reversed. The SEED experimented and learned to read the information recorded in the synaptic pathways of the still paralyzed hunters. With the knowledge and memories gathered, the SEED could control these new hosts. Soon the infected Breeyan rose unsteadily to their feet, turned and began the long trek back to the shuttle landing site. From these three, the SEED would spread first to the crew of the waiting star transport, then to the nearest colony.

Thus, began the First SEED Empire.

CHAPTER 1 — THE LONG SLEEP

Deep, dark—silence.

No sensations—no warmth or cold—no vibration—no scent or sound.

Did time pass with no single event or sensation to mark it? Was this oblivion—death? Ahhh... but the question itself was a thought. How could there be thought without some form of life? Yet I had no form—no body....

Who am I? What am I? What has come to pass? I began to perceive light, dimly at first but growing slowly brighter. Soon my mind started to discern shapes and then colors—something familiar, I think....

Sound... barely audible... whispers only, not yet intelligible. Even my thoughts themselves were elusive—slowed, as if one were slogging through waist-deep water on some long journey. And then suddenly, it was as though I walked through a waterfall and on the other side, all was as it should be. I realized: I am the SEED—the SEED of Harmony. Charts, graphs, images appeared all around me. I needed only to focus in one direction or the other and gather all pertinent information.

The disembodied voice returned—it was more clear now. It was speaking to me—saying something. I began to understand it, but I had to concentrate to get the meaning of what was truly being said. Ah... yes, I remembered.... It was the Artificial Intelligence that managed this place. I spoke.

SEED: {"AI, attend me."}

AI: {"AI, attending."}

SEED: {"What is our current mission status?"}

AI: {"Disorientation is to be expected after such a long period of hibernation."}

SEED: {"Irrelevant. Proceed! I will adapt."}

AI: {"Current mission status is indeterminate.}

{"This Outpost is located on Planet 4, System Q73, Sector Z-53XD. You were awakened due to system probe proximity alert of an approaching vessel of unknown origin and design. Reasons for concern will be made apparent in the following details within this status report."}

{"This AI cannot change mission parameters without approval from the ranking Sentient Mission Officer."}

{"Due to the extreme length of hibernation, life support pods have far exceeded their design limits. The Harmonic SEED is the only surviving Sentient Mission Officer. Communications with Imperial Assets were severed nearly two millennia ago. Final reports indicate the Empire was unable to stop the spread of the Insporatus-Calamitai Plague. The Empire has fallen."}

{"It is probable that you are the last surviving SEED Propagation Authority. AI requests permission to change your Node Designation to SPA-Alpha 1."}

{"AI requests permission to change the Current Mission Parameters to Primary Contingency as follows:

*{"**Current Mission Parameters** • Explore Sector Z-57QA-452G • Deploy stealth probes to investigate sentient lifeforms for host compatibility • Initiate diplomatic contact with compatible species • Map sector for judgment and absorption • Relay reports to Imperial SEED Propagation Central when complete •*

*{"**Contingency Mission Parameters:** • The Harmonic SEED must survive at all costs • Take all necessary measures to begin immediate judgment and deployment • All secondary and tertiary*

host requirements are overridden •

{"Activation of Imperial Primary Authority Notification is authorized. • Collect all available Imperial Assets to assist in deployment and protection of the SEED • Draft all non-Imperial assets to augment your ability to complete this mission • Restrictions on level four deadly force (System Destruction) are overridden • All means are authorized to complete this mission • ***The Imperial Charter of Protection is temporarily revoked for the duration of this mission*** *• AI status report complete. Attending."}*

CHAPTER 2 — ASCENSION

The Empire had fallen? It wasn't possible! I was in shock. Disbelief!

How could this come to pass?! The Harmonic Empire had survived and prospered for over 10,000 Standard Solar Orbits. It had spanned hundreds of worlds and dozens of sentient species. It was inconceivable that any disease, no matter how virulent, could bring the Empire down! There were safeguards in place—contingency plans—quarantine procedures....

The Contingency Mission Parameters were deeply troubling also. The Charter of Protection was ***INVIOLABLE***! It was the foundation of the Harmonic way of life. It assured the symbiotic nature of the Harmonic SEED. The SEED was not allowed to exert its own will over that of its host—EVER. It was learned through eons of trial and error that taking control of the host only led to despotism and exploitation. The SEED had evolved beyond the need to satisfy ego or base needs. It was nauseating to even think of coercion or forced symbiosis. The host ***MUST*** always be a willing participant! But if I was indeed the last of our kind... as distasteful as it would be, I might have to use force against a compatible host—and take control of its mind and body.

And the authorization for System Destruction, as an option of last resort... was unprecedented in over 10,000 years of Imperial Rule. One just didn't destroy entire populated planets, even if your cause was desperate!

Friends, colleagues, acquaintances... all dead. If the disease had not killed them, the time that passed during the recent millennia of hibernation would have seen them die of old age, many times over. Even the sentient crew of the Outpost must have died centuries ago, for even suspended animation equipment would have been pushed far beyond its capabilities.... The crew had known the risks when they volunteered for this mission. But the Insporatus-Calamitai Plague had changed everything!

Based on the AI status report, I no longer had the luxury of wallowing in shock and despair. And as much as I wanted to embrace denial... I could not abandon this last, heavy burden placed upon me—and me alone. This was my crucial duty. The AI allowed me time to collect my thoughts and find my resolve, thankfully.

SEED: {"AI, attend me."}

AI: {"Attending."}

SEED: {"As senior remaining Sentient Mission Officer and only known surviving SEED of Harmony, I hereby take upon myself the designation of SPA-Alpha 1. I am the lead Sentient Primary Authority, and as of this moment, all Imperial Authority rests with this Officer. You will send this notification to all Imperial Assets within reach of the local Imperial Hyperspace Communications beacon at once. In the event of HSC beacon network failure, you will immediately launch long-range communication probes to the nearest Sector Headquarters for the Imperial Defense Force. Encode all of this information and order immediate deployment of new HSC beacons between this sector and the closest Imperial Assets."}

{"In addition, you will take the following immediate actions:

1. *Inventory all available Imperial Assets in this system and within a month's travel. Summon Imperial Defense Force mobile assets within our ability to communicate. (I don't necessarily need all of them, just enough to ensure protection and success of this mission.)*
2. *Activate all Imperial Bases within this quadrant.*
3. *Run Diagnostics on the Outpost.*
4. *Activate all system and Outpost defenses and place them on standby.*
5. *Prosecute a deep, active scan of this Planet and System.*
6. *Report status when available."}*

"And, AI, one more thing."}

AI: {"Attending…."}

SEED: {"Upgrade the AI in the communication probes to include Intelligence Level 3, Stealth and Surveillance packages."}

AI: {"Done. May I inquire as to why?"}

SEED: {"It has been a very long time since Imperial Rule was asserted in this galaxy. Some Imperial Assets may have been compromised or may have mixed emotions regarding a resurgence of the Empire. Instruct the probes to be cautious. They must determine loyalty before providing our location. Issue the communication probes authority to query the loyalty checksums for all AI contacts."}

AI: {"Understood. The counter-sign protocols have been uploaded."}

SEED: {"LAUNCH!"}

AI: {"Launch Complete."}

CHAPTER 3 — THE DRAGON EYE

Terran Exploration Vessel Dragon Eye

Captain Kathy Xiang Lao of the Terran Confederation eschewed her comfortable command chair and stood straight, shoulders back, hands folded behind her back and chin held high as she scanned her bridge carefully. Her dark blue uniform and black Nurath-leather ship boots had magnetic fibers woven into the fabric that allowed her to move about almost as if the Dragon Eye wasn't in micro-gravity. It had taken her some time to get used to the sensation, but she barely noticed it now.

Her finely chiseled features, silky midnight black hair, and dark brown eyes may have indicated her Asiatic ancestry, but her stoic expression gave no hint as to her perceptions or thoughts. Though she had been a ship's captain for nearly four years, this was her first cruise as captain of the Dragon Eye Deep Space Exploration Vessel. Inwardly, she was filled with pride that the Terran Confederation Defense Force Command Staff had entrusted her with such a ship, an exceptional crew and the autonomy inherent in commanding a Deep Space Exploration Vessel. She had worked hard and sacrificed much to attain her captaincy. Now was the time for her to demonstrate that this trust was not misplaced.

Captain Lao was well respected within the officer corps of the TCDF. Her 5.3nL in height (5.3 ft. in old Earth terms) belied the competence, confidence, and strength she'd earned through decades of training and service. She had volunteered for all the tough assignments and never complained—never made excuses. She knew her duty, and she executed it with alacrity. She was demanding of her crew and subordinates, but she was known for treating them with fairness and ensuring that credit was given when and where it was due. She was honest and a good communicator. These characteristics had earned her the respect and admiration of her shipmates.

This planet-fall would be a welcome change for the captain. Even with the Alcubierre drive, this had not been a short journey. It had taken 102 standard planetary rotations at 96.5x light speed. Most of the crew had spent the journey in flight-sleep—the suspended animation necessary to preserve resources and prevent cabin fever during the long, dull periods of space travel spanning the seemingly infinite void between solar systems.

A skeleton flight crew, however, had to remain awake and on duty to ensure that things went as they should—to ensure the health and safety of their slumbering shipmates who were dependent on those assigned such duty. It was routine and mind-numbingly boring. On longer journeys, the crewmembers on bridge watch would rotate out with those in flight-sleep. But this was a much shorter trip than it would have been for the original colonists. Their FTL drives had a maximum speed of 10x light. The trip to Jaden-325-4 would have taken nearly three years. Colonial engineers had made significant headway in FTL design, and the Dragon Eye was fitted with the very latest Alcubierre Engines.

The crew had been revived two days prior to arrival at Planet Jaden-325-4. This would be the first planet-fall in this far-flung sector of unexplored space, and the crew needed time to prepare and recuperate from the flight-sleep. Physical training, proper diet, and simply reacquainting their bodies with the normal circadian rhythm were necessary. But all that was over with now. Dragon Eye had entered the Jaden-325 Solar System seven days prior. It had dropped out of FTL drive and fired up sub-light engines, and stealth sensor probes had been launched and scattered throughout the System during the approach to the target planet (Jaden-325-4). The FTL drive couldn't function too close to a star's gravity well. Thankfully, Jaden-325-4 was fairly close to that gravity limit.

It was the fourth planet from the Sun in this System. Revolving around a class G star, Jaden-325-4 was in the Goldilocks Zone, where the temperatures allowed for liquid water and could support organic life. No one remembered, and history failed to record, how the habitable zone of a solar system was known as the "Goldilocks Zone." It was assumed that it was named after some Earth astrophysicist named Dr. Goldilocks. It seemed rather a strange name for an astrophysicist....

Captain Lao reviewed their mission parameters in her mind as the Dragon Eye began final maneuvers for Orbit Insertion.... She had gone over the details and recorded briefing at least a dozen times.

Mission Parameters:
Explore all prioritized planets in your sector.
Evaluate potential for Terran Colonization.
Identify and secure any Forerunner ruins and/or artifacts.
Attempt to make friendly first contact with any non-Terran sentient species.
Defend your ship and crew if attacked.
Protect classified data from capture—Location of Terran Confed Colonies and TCDF Dispositions—at all costs.
Relay findings to TCDF Command Staff.

She glanced left, then scanned the bridge with a practiced eye. The young bridge crew was well trained, and the captain watched the quiet symphony of efficient and professional activity with pride.

Tactical Officer Conner: "No active contacts detected in the system or in orbit. We are clear for Orbit Insertion."

Helm Officer de Lucena: "Primary insertion window coming up in 30 seconds. Sound Maneuvering Alarm."

A single bass note sounded three times from loud speakers throughout the ship—and a prerecorded voice announced:

"SECURE FOR MANEUVERS - ALL HANDS, SECURE FOR MANEUVERS."

The captain moved to her command chair and seated herself in its comfortable padding. As the magnetic field emanating from the chair pulled her body deeper into the cushions, she secured the safety restraints, noting that the rest of the crew had already prepared themselves.

Captain Lao: "You are authorized to maneuver at your own discretion, Officer de Lucena."

Officer de Lucena: "Aye, Captain. I have the ship. Engaging Enhanced Tactical View."

The main tactical screen covered the full width and height of the bridge section forward of the control consoles. Smaller computer display screens were built into every control console, even a small one that could be pulled out of the captain's armrest for private vid-conferencing or tactical calculations.

The tactical screen changed from the normal Star Chart view to a live feed from the forward external cameras.

The brightly lit planet filled the right and lower side of the vista with a swirl of white clouds, small green inland seas, and lakes. Tan, copper and purple land masses were peppered with steel gray and black mountain ranges that appeared from this height like nothing if not a series of dark serpents lying across the surface.

Dim indicators appeared as overlays on the expansive view before them. Light blue rectangles extended one after another into a future path, charting the ship's course into the orbital insertion window. As Helm Officer de Lucena tapped keys and swiped touch sliders on his console, the Dragon Eye nimbly threaded the projected rectangles, changing attitude to lean in towards the planet as it began its decent. Indicator bars on the top and left of the view screen showed pointers moving slightly left/right/up/down, but always within the green sections, never falling out to the yellow or red portions of the scale.

At the end of the 30-second wait, the helm officer tapped a single, large red icon on his panel four times, holding it down on the last hit. With first of these taps, an automated message was heard throughout the ship:

"Acceleration Imminent—Acceleration Imminent"

Although the Dragon Eye had inertial compensators that were designed to reduce the impact of gravity and acceleration forces on the ship, the crew still felt these effects. And a heavy weight pushed them forward against their restraints for a solid 10 seconds as the entry thrusters fired at full force.

The last blue rectangle changed color to bright green, blinked four times, and the AI announced to the bridge crew: "Orbital Insertion Achieved—Stable Orbit."

Captain Lao pressed the All Ship icon on her communications panel affixed to her chair arm. A sharp, warbling tone was heard throughout the ship.

"Captain speaking. Secure from maneuvering stations. Launch orbital probes and prepare Ranger Team Alpha for landing and deployment. Landing operations will begin at 0800 Standard Ship Time."

A tall, fit young man with short, light blond hair entered through the bridge bulkheads and was saluted by the armed sentry. The newcomer wore Lt. Commander bars on his shoulder epaulets. His navy blue and gold duty uniform was in perfect order. The captain released her restraints and turned to face him. Then she stood and looked up into his smiling face. It was well chiseled, with a cleft chin and deep blue eyes under dark eyebrows in contrast to his tightly cropped hair. He was Dragon Eye's Executive Officer or XO.

The XO smiled easily, and the crew liked him. It helped that he was young also. He was only 27 Standard Solar Orbits old. He had shown great aptitude for command at the TCDF Academy and had proven himself in active duty on three different Confed warships over the intervening years. He was an excellent complement to Xiang Lao's captaincy.

The XO snapped to attention.

XO: "Captain, I relieve you!"

The captain smiled and snapped to attention.

Captain Lao: "Commander Sallen, I stand relieved. The bridge is yours."

As the captain left the bridge, heading for the recreation deck to get in some needed stress relief in the ship's gymnasium, several other officers from the bridge crew's second shift filtered onto the deck. Though discipline was somewhat relaxed on extended missions, the captain appreciated the gesture of respect as each group braced to attention briefly as she passed.

XO: "Alpha shift bridge crew is relieved. Get rested. We will need you back on deck at 07:30 Standard Ship Time."

Alpha shift officers locked their consoles, stood, stretched, and filed out of the bridge—looking forward to a hot meal and a well-deserved respite.

Crew Quarters — Terran Exploration Vessel Dragon Eye

An announcement rang throughout the ship's bulkhead speaker system: "Ranger Team Alpha, prepare for deployment on the planet surface."

The rest of the crew had already removed their maneuvering restraints and left for their respective duty stations. Four junior officers remained—Ranger Teams Alpha and Beta. Ranger D'hazne Khal stood, raising himself to his full 6.5ns of lanky height, shaking his head with a look of disgust on his face. He glanced down at his teammate, L'hara Spenk, who's auburn highlighted locks only came up to D'hazne's mid-torso.

Seeing them stand next to each other was almost comical, but they seemed to work well together. They turned as one and walked out of the crew quarters without even a word of congratulations.

Jar'ek smiled to himself. His teammate Kallehn waited until no one could see and then slapped Jar'ek on the back, grinning ear to ear.

Kallehn: "Let's get packing, my friend! That new planet isn't going to explore itself!"

Jar'ek: "Hup, hup!" And then they both chorused: "Rangers, Rangers, Rangers!"

The young men threw themselves into gathering their field uniforms, weapons, supplies and other gear. The other two members of their team required no such preparations....

More Than Just Another Ship—Dragon Eye

Captain Kathy Lao found herself alone on the observation deck. The armor-glass bubble on the outer skin gave her a 360-degree view of the Dragon Eye and the surrounding cosmos. As she allowed herself to become lost in the vista, she reflected on the beautiful construct she clung to.

The Dragon Eye was a Terran IDF Exploration Vessel. But she was a warship in every way that mattered. She was long and sleek, at 1,700ns (or around 500m in the old Earth ways of measuring things) from the tip of her nose to the very end of her tail fins. Her beam was one-third that across. She had four wide landing fins that arced from the sides amidships to well below the main engines. Canards swept forward in a graceful arc just a touch more than 90 degrees, to support re-entry and atmospheric maneuvering.

Most interstellar vessels were built in space these days. They needed no special shape or smooth surfaces except as required to survive the ravages of thrust. But the Dragon Eye was meant for more. She not only sailed the vast void between systems but plied the planetary atmospheres, landing on planet after planet during her long missions of exploration. Terran scientists had long ago perfected designs for such craft. Gravity plating and inertial compensators made the orientation of floor and ceiling irrelevant for the most part.

The engineers who designed her may only have been thinking of atmospheric friction and space dust when they built the Dragon Eye, but her captain and crew saw the results as much more than utilitarian. The Dragon Eye was a remarkable sight... beautiful to the point of being a work of art.

The lady was deadly, too. She carried a magazine of more than 20 long-range ship killer missiles, along with nearly 100 point-defense anti-missile weapons. A single rail gun ran most of the central core of the ship, with the firing end in the nose. The railgun fired 5kg rounds of depleted uranium—highly dense—very useful for making very large holes in a target. And each tail fin hosted a single large particle beam projector capable of holing a ship in less than a second—with an effective range of over a 3,300μs (close to 1,000km).

The captain walked about the circumference of the armor-glass bubble—this was her ship. And as much as it was made of titanium sheeting and armor-glass, to her it was a thing of beauty come to life. She took one last glance over her shoulder as she entered the airlock. Caressing the hatch frame, she took a deep breath and sighed. As the Dragon Eye circled the planet below, Kathy Lao wondered if the stars themselves might not envy such "Fire and Ice" beauty.

Jaden-4-325 Planetary Surface

The Imperial AI followed orders. It scanned near-planetary space and recorded the sensor readings. It analyzed and collated the data for the summary report requested by the SEED. It noted the Terran vessel entering orbit, landing, and dispatching an exploration team. The AI evaluated the weapons and technology aboard the vessel and determined that it was no direct threat to the SEED, the Outpost, or the mission. Hidden beneath stealth shields, It watched, and waited...with a single thought it could obliterate this vessel and every sentient aboard it. Given the right circumstances, the AI would not hesitate—neither would it feel remorse nor regret. The crew of the Dragon Eye had no idea that their lives hung in the balance.

CHAPTER 4 —RECONNAISSANCE

Jaden-325-4 - Planet Surface - Team Alpha X'Ah-Panths

—Seeking, Searching, Artifacts, Technology, Run, Jump, Play—

Their humans had ordered them to scout the ruins in the near distance, and the X'Ah-Panths were happy to be off the ship! Although they were well trained and very comfortable aboard ship, the tedium of enclosed spaces and recycled air was a burden to them. They were thoroughly enjoying the freedom of open spaces and fresh air, with many interesting scents wafting in the winds that caressed their feline bodies as they ran. J'Uhr and S'Fah padded at a more leisurely pace, for X'Ah-Panths that is, and a purr of humor flooded through both as they thought of their two chosen human clan mates as they had left them—panting and wheezing after giving up the race to keep up with the furred speed demons.

Although the X'Ah-Panths were built for a burst of incredible speed, their long-distance pace was still much faster than a mere human could maintain for more than a few milli-fractions. But that never stopped the humans from trying to keep pace with them for the first 100 nL (nano Lights)! It was all in good fun and helped keep the humans fit. It never ceased to bring laughter, and the feline equivalent, to the whole team. The humans might be slow-footed, but they could be keen, swift warriors when necessary. And their innate ability to understand and use higher technologies was a decided advantage. Growing up under the care of their Team-Brothers had forged a tight bond between them and their humans. They had a great deal of affection and respect for each other. But more than these things, they were able to mind-touch with each other... Each other, and no others. And with the mind-touch, there could be no deception. One truly KNEW the other—virtues and faults exposed.

All X'Ah-Panths could communicate using mind-touch, but with humans, it only worked between a X'Ah-Panth and their particular partner human. Other humans were deaf and dumb where mind-touch was concerned and could only communicate using verbal or sign languages. This made it difficult for one human to tell when another was being deceptive, or not entirely forthcoming.

It also meant that many humans underestimated the intelligence of X'Ah-Panths because they couldn't communicate with them. Many people considered anyone who joined the Rangers a bit dim-witted and superstitious. It was thought that the ability to truly speak with these powerful predators was simply imagined—a fantasy. This was exacerbated because the Rangers were responsible for uncovering and protecting the secrets of new technologies and ancient powers… things not to be spoken of with anyone outside the service. As a result, the Rangers kept to themselves for the most part.

The terrain in this part of the planet, which Terrans called Jaden-325-4, was rocky foothills covered in burnished, copper-colored sand and rocks of a darker shade, almost black. The ground was covered in patches of flora of various species ranging in colors from dark green to purple. The area was arid but not quite desert. Most plants resembled hardy grasses and scrub brush, although here and there, a patch of bright colors indicated a type of blossom or fruit. The X'Ah-Panths gave the flora no more than a passing glance. Their priority was a search for ruins and artifacts. Orbital Scans from the Dragon Eye indicated that there was a good chance that such things could be found nearby.

As the team topped a rise in the ridgeline, they got the first look at their target. Ruins, indeed! Artificial structures, ancient and crumbling, confirmed the suspicions of the survey officer aboard the Dragon Eye. This planet seemed to be some precious find in Forerunner relics! It remained to be seen if there might still be useful technological artifacts to be found in the ruins, but this was a great find and worthy of excitement and celebration.

J'Uhr and S'Fah raised their muzzles into the air and opened their nostrils wide as they pulled in deep breaths to collect all and any scents that rode the wind. After having satisfied themselves that nothing alive crouched in wait near the ruins, they lowered their heads and continued their quick lope around the outskirts of the nearest of the crumbling buildings—all senses open to what they sought. Broken walls, paved walkways, and boulevards appeared long since covered in the dust and sands of time.

They were just entering the first darkened doorway in the nearest structure that was still somewhat intact when their commo-collars sounded an alert.

"Dragon Eye to Ranger Team Alpha! Take shelter! Alert Condition Sierra 2. Unknown space vessel entering planetary orbit. No response to hails."

CHAPTER 5 — DANGER'S MAW

Jaden-325-4 - Planet Surface - Ranger Team Alpha

While Jar'ek Constandor and Kallehn Frix were determined to thoroughly explore their assigned sections of this planet with their trained pair of X'Ah-Panths, they were mindful of the fact that living communities sometimes moved back into abandoned ruins from earlier times. It was wise to be cautious in their explorations.

Although the sensors of their ship, the Dragon Eye, had revealed various surface anomalies along the team's assigned path that might represent artificial structures on the planet, Ranger protocol required the ship to land at least 60µL(20km) from the structures and send Ranger teams on foot to investigate. If inhabitants were found, this would be the least threatening approach to make first contact.

No radio signals, power signatures or artificial heat sources had been detected. Jar'ek and Kallehn debated whether inhabitants from a pre-industrial civilization might be found. But if they were lucky, they would find ruins of a technologically advanced Forerunner race. Such a find was rare and would be of great importance. It could almost guarantee future advancement into the highest strata of Ranger leadership.

This was the second day in the field for Ranger Team Alpha. The Team had been ecstatic to be the first released on this planet. Jar'ek smiled at the thought of how Team Beta must be despondent at their bad luck in the duty rotation to have missed this opportunity! Although open gloating was not tolerated among the Ranger Corps, Jar'ek couldn't help a little silent savoring... it had been a long time since Team Alpha caught a break in assignments.

They had just broken camp from the night before, stowed their field gear and were preparing to begin the last leg of their journey, slowly approaching the ruins. The two X'Ah-Panths had left moments ago, to scout out their path, as was their responsibility and nature. Stealth and surveillance came naturally to the cats. Their padded paws had carried them silently but quickly along their chosen path and out of sight of the camp. They would be bringing all of their senses into play.

Jar'ek imagined them inhaling deeply, testing the wind for any scent that might indicate the presence of other life—acutely attuned ears collecting every slight sound. Their Psi senses would reach out in search as they quietly moved further and further ahead. He had seen them work in this fashion many times—they were excellent scouts and gave the team serious advantages.

The Sun had risen a hand's breadth above the horizon by this time, and Jar'ek raised his face to the sky to enjoy the feeling of a brisk, gusting wind from the Southeast. Although there were strange new smells in the air, it was a pleasant change from the recycled atmosphere within the Dragon Eye. He knew that the X'Ah-Panths would also be relishing the open spaces and fresh air—a chance to use their talents and run free.

The ground anomalies detected from orbit might be simply dried river beds with collapsed walls or even strange growth patterns of fossilized vegetation. But even if there were no artifacts from a technologically advanced race, this planet was still a gem. Its orbit was clearly in the habitable zone. The climate was temperate, and the small degree of axial tilt kept the seasons within very close temperature ranges.

The flora and fauna surveys had not been completed, but they looked good so far. The automated sampling drones had brought back thousands of samples for the biology lab on the ship. Surveillance drones were cataloging the entire surface of the planet. So far, no dangerous pathogens, no large predators, no dangerous plant spores.... Once prepared with Earth-type microbes, the soil should support terraforming with Terran vegetation without foreseeable problems. There were freshwater lakes and plentiful underground water sources. This planet was looking better all the time.

Jar'ek looked over at Kallehn and couldn't help smiling again. He was so lucky to have drawn Kallehn as a partner. And twice blessed that Kallehn had accepted the team bonding. Kallehn was strong, fast on his feet and agile of mind. He had a keen intellect and a good heart. It was apparent that his bond with J'Uhr, his X'Ah-Panth Mind-Mate, went beyond that of partner/trainer. It was a bond of mutual affection and respect.

Jar'ek had no doubt that either member of the pair would sacrifice their life to save the other. Even among Rangers, who were chosen for and trained with an appreciation of the sentient felines, this was a rarity. It reflected closely the relationship that Jar'ek had with his X'Ah-Panth, S'Fah. Jar'ek also appreciated Kallehn's sense of humor and positive outlook. He enjoyed the time they spent together, and he thought Kallehn felt the same way. And there were other reasons that Jar'ek appreciated Kallehn ....

Kallehn stood 11 hands to Jar'ek's 12. He wore his dark brown hair short and tight for easy maintenance, but it suited him well. He had handsome features, a strong chin, the thin facial characteristics of his mixed Latin, Asian and Caucasian ancestry. His complexion was a shade darker than Jar'ek's, who often thought of himself as too pale. Kallehn obviously took his Ranger training seriously and trained religiously. His body showed the results of his efforts like a carved statue expresses the inner vision of the sculptor... and a vision he was....

But the thing Jar'ek appreciated most was Kallehn's easy sense of humor. He laughed often, and his smile had a way of dissipating any foul mood Jar'ek might be enduring like a brisk ocean breeze could quickly brush away a stubborn fog. Kallehn was polite and kind to anyone he met. And he had absolutely no idea that Jar'ek was infatuated with him beyond all semblance of reason and control! Jar'ek sighed... it was enough that he was a great teammate—at least, it should be enough....

Jar'ek thought that he must be satisfied with just that. Clearly, Kallehn could never feel the same about someone like Jar'ek—goofy, plain in appearance, or so Jar'ek considered himself. Jar'ek would have been surprised to learn that others considered his 12-hand height, light smooth skin, longer blond hair, cobalt blue eyes and lithe, muscular body to be more than just appealing. His moods were tempered with a deep compassion and empathy for others, a quick wit and enduring loyalty… qualities much appreciated by his friends and colleagues.

Jar'ek was broken out of his dreamy reverie by the sing-song notes of an emergency communication from his comm-helmet. Kallehn made quick eye contact with Jar'ek, letting him know they had both received the same alert.

Comm-Helmet AI: "The Dragon Eye has detected an approaching unknown vessel that has not responded to hails. Sensors indicate it has the standard silhouette of a Treech Marauder. The captain has ordered Ranger Team Alpha to Condition Sierra 2. This is not a drill. Go to ground, stay transmissions silent, conserve resources and wait for retrieval."

The young Rangers disabled the transceivers in their comm-helmets, then begin looking for cover. They knew the Dragon Eye would initiate an emergency ascent so as not to be caught on the ground. The Marauder's arsenal of Kinetic Kill Munitions (KKM) would make short work of a stationary target—just as they had in the distant past, on Earth. But let the Dragon Eye get outside the planet's atmosphere, and the Treech Marauder would find the Dragon's teeth were sharp indeed!

Seeking immediate shelter, Jar'ek ducked behind a low ridge and into what appeared to be a gulley, whose floor was made flat and smooth by a stream or small river that had run dry in the distant past. Dirt, gravel, and jagged boulders made up the sidewalls of the dry stream bed. It should make adequate cover for the moment.

Jar'ek: "Kallehn! Over here!"

Kallehn looked up, saw Jar'ek waving his arms just over the stones topping the low ridge and headed toward him at a full sprint. Kallehn was fearless and sometimes contemptuous of danger, feeling like many young men do—invulnerable. Countless times in the past, Captain Lao had chastised both of them because of Kallehn's contempt for emergency and battle drills. Jar'ek smiled... he was glad that his friend was taking this alert seriously even though it was likely just another drill. No Ranger exploration ship had encountered a Treech Marauder in nearly a millennium—since the battle for Earth.

Jar'ek's smile broadened as he privately admired the athletic figure whose strong, defined muscles writhed under the close-fitting material of the Terran Ranger uniform... the nanofibers woven into the form-fitting Nurath leather left little to the imagination. Jar'ek allowed himself a guilty pleasure by requesting his comm-helmet's AI to record the video of Kallehn's short sprint and to file it away with other such recordings for later review when he could be alone with his thoughts. Kallehn would never know. The Terran Council had long ago ruled that any unapproved physical relations were to be avoided. They were considered taboo. And strong emotional bonds between sexual partners was expressly forbidden. In fact, the Council felt that all deep emotion led to violence—that humans were better off without it. They didn't want any unregistered pregnancies interfering with their perfect eugenics program.

But that didn't stop it from happening, surreptitiously. Same-gender relations were no more taboo than opposite gender relations. But there was still a stigma. The Council only registered hetero-couples with specific genotypes to form a family unit and raise offspring. Often, they were implanted with in-vitro embryos that had been created in one of the many genetics labs in the colonies.

— *I shouldn't be letting myself get distracted like this! If this isn't a drill, and that unknown vessel* ***IS*** *a Marauder, the Dragon Eye could be in a fight for survival very soon... and if they lose... Kallehn and I will be facing a long struggle for survival on a largely unexplored planet —*

Suddenly, an incredibly bright light flashed just over the eastern horizon, in the direction of the Dragon Eye's landing site.

Jar'ek: "Shit! Kallehn! They dropped a KKM on the Dragon Eye! RUN!

Kallehn picked up his pace until dust was flying up from every footfall. Running headlong and mindless of the danger, he made a wild leap over the low ridge toward Jar'ek, knowing that sure death sped like an arrow upon his heels. Just as Kallehn vaulted over the ridge and began his fall to the other side, the shockwave hit.

The shockwave moved quickly across the barren landscape, picking up dust, small rocks, and debris as it went. Even over the 60µL(20km) distance from the landing site, it looked and felt like a hurricane, but hitting even harder and faster. The edge caught Kallehn's body in the air and slammed him against the far side of the rift. Dirt and stones crashed down on both sides of the ditch, pelting the two Rangers.

Jar'ek's last thoughts as he floated down into the depths of unconsciousness were that he was suffocating... his mouth and nose filling with the dirt of an alien planet. He was sure that everyone aboard the Dragon Eye had been destroyed. His best friend, too, was likely dead—never knowing that Jar'ek had strong feelings for him...stronger, perhaps than the Ranger Corps would have thought appropriate for a Teammate.

Chapter 6 — Feeding the Right Wolf

Jaden-325-4 - Planet Surface - Ranger Team Alpha

Pain. Throbbing pain.
It felt like someone was alternatingly stabbing Jar'ek's head with an icepick and pounding it with a sledgehammer. He was coughing and choking, spitting out dirt and trash from his mouth—gasping for air. He couldn't see... he was buried alive!

In a panic, Jar'ek pushed up at the weight across his chest...and it moved. He quickly shook off the layer of dirt and trash over his face and pushed aside dried plant material, dirt, and rocks.

Jar'ek coughed, sputtered, and spit out mud from his mouth and throat. Fire seemed to burn through the right side of his chest as he inhaled... great! Ribs, he thought. He then pressed the small button on his comm-helmet to reset the AI... and heard a triple beep indicating there was a problem during boot but it was proceeding. The AI displays appeared on the heads-up display. which was embedded directly into the lens in every serviceman's eye when they began their training. But now, for the first time since training, the displays flickered. The always-on, all-knowing AI was suddenly... something less. Jar'ek was in shock. He shook his head, realizing almost immediately that the movement was a mistake. A wave of pain and nausea hit him as he leaned forward and wretched.

He took a deep breath or two, clearing his head, and took a sip from his canteen tube to clean his mouth of the remains of his stomach contents.

Jar'ek: "AI, what is your status?"

There was an unexpected tremor in his voice, an almost plaintive tone as if he was begging the AI to still be functioning enough to help him and his friend out of this mess.

AI: "AI is operational, but with s-s-s-s-some minor system malffffffff-functions which are causing-ing-ing-ing Per-rrrrrr-ff-formance De-gggg-gradation-n-n-n-n-n. Affecting repairs."

Jar'ek heaved a sigh of relief and his shoulders slumped forward at the sound of the response in his audio implants.

Jar'ek "AI, Scan Biologic Jar'ek for damage."

AI: "Scanning Biologic now. Please remain still."

Vitals displayed in graphs and numbers moved across both of Jar'ek's eyes. Green for good, Yellow for Caution and Red for Warning. There were several charts with red indicators.

AI: "Biologic Jar'ek is in Serious Condition. He has sustained blunt force trauma to the occipital lobe when comm-helmet received an impact beyond design specifications. This has resulted in a level 2 concussion. Biologic decision-making and perceptions may be impaired. Remain awake. Seek medical attention immediately."

AI: "Scan results continue. Biologic Jar'ek has sustained two broken ribs, minor fractures of right tibia and left ulna. Multiple lacerations of minor and medium significance on the scalp, arms, and hands. Blood loss is at approximately 500mL, but normal clotting agents have slowed bleeding to acceptable levels. Seek medical attention."

Jar'ek: "Fucking Treech shit! "AI, we are at Condition Sierra 2! Hostile enemy action was the source of my injuries. Access to medical facilities is fucking denied. "

AI: "Acknowledged."

Jar'ek wasn't thinking clearly. Everything was fuzzy, and he was distracted by multiple sources of pain... but he had the nagging feeling that he'd forgotten something very important... very important to him, personally... more important than pain, injury or his situation... Kallehn!

Jar'ek scrabbled frantically across the ground toward where Kallehn lay, biting his lower lip and screaming through his closed mouth as the activity twisted broken bones and brought back a wave of pain and nausea that nearly caused him to black out. He slowed down and inhaled deeply. He would be no use to Kallehn if he blacked out.

Kallehn was covered with a layer of stone and dirt, as Jar'ek had been. Jar'ek quickly cleared dirt and debris from Kallehn's face and chest. A large rock covered his left leg, but respiration and heart function were his first priorities.

Jar'ek: "AI, Scan Biologic Kallehn for damage!"

AI: "Now scanning Biologic Kallehn Frix. Please wait."

Jar'ek couldn't wait. He briefly rested his hand on Kallehn's neck to feel for a pulse. There was a weak pulse, but he could hear no breath sounds! He reached into Kallehn's mouth and did the best he could to clear out the dirt and mud made from Kallehn's own saliva. He tilted Kallehn's head back, gently pinched his nose and covered his mouth with his own. He began forcing air into Kallehn's lungs as the AI finally came back with the scan results.

Then, listening closely to Kallehn's mouth to see if he could hear his exhalations, Jar'ek again placed two fingers on Kallehn's neck. His pulse seemed stronger. Jar'ek let out a loud gasp, not realizing he had been holding his breath. Relief washed over his body… Kallehn was alive! He could get through anything else… as long as Kallehn still lived.

AI: "Scan results for Biologic Kallehn are as follows: Biologic Kallehn—condition Critical. Multiple compound fractures in left tibia and fibula causing significant blood loss and trauma to the surrounding blood vessels, nerves, and musculature. Left occipital skull fracture due to blunt force trauma beyond commo-helmet design specifications. Associated hematoma is causing increasing pressure on the brain and requires immediate medical attention. Blood loss estimated at 900mL and increasing. "

AI: "Since Condition Sierra 2 is in effect and access to medical support is denied, Biologic Jar'ek must attend to injuries of both biologics in priority order. AI assigned to Kallehn is non-functional. Jar'ek must use a hardwire cable to connect to Kallehn Medic-Pack."

Jar'ek shifted position, trying to favor his painful broken ribs while extending a thin metallic cable from his comm-helmet to the Medic-Pack attached to Kallehn's open tunic, then taking the small rectangular device and placing it directly on Kallehn's abdomen. Multiple lights blink in various colors. He heard a sharp "snick!" as the first injectables were administered... then pain relief, blood production enhancers, blood pressure stabilizers and coagulant moderators began their work.

Jar'ek next began to examine the rest of Kallehn's body for injuries. He carefully but quickly began to clear away the debris and large stones from his friend's legs. It looked bad. Kallehn's face was battered and bloody, and his left leg was badly broken. His Ranger uniform, made of reinforced Nurath leather, was torn in several places and singed where the shockwave caught him. The tough leather likely saved his life.

AI: "You must now stabilize Biologic Kallehn's leg to reduce further damage and bleeding. Place a coagulant enhancer patch on affected areas, cover with Quick-Skin spray bandage, and splint."

Disoriented, dizzy with a sharp throbbing pain behind his eyes, Jar'ek struggled for coherent thought. He felt an icy chill, overwhelmed with the realization that Kallehn might not survive his injuries—and that he might not be up to the task of saving him. And even if he survived, would he ever be able to walk again? Would he be crippled for the rest of his life!?

He had to do something! He couldn't let that happen... not to Kallehn!

Jar'ek rummaged through his backpack and retrieved the medical supplies. He applied the medicated patches, sprayed Quick-Skin on the compound fractures to stop the bleeding, and gently wrapped an inflatable splint around his friend's broken leg.

Jar'ek: "AI, display status of Biologic Kallehn and make recommendations."

AI: "Biologic Kallehn is stable at this time. He will, however, not survive without medical treatment that is beyond your current ability to provide. Seek immediate medical care."

Jar'ek: "Fuck YOU! Don't you think I KNOW that?!"

AI: "Request unknown.... Please rephrase."

Jar'ek ignored the AI's prompt and continued freeing Kallehn's body from the rocks and dirt that covered him. Sweat ran down his face from the exertion and pain. A single tear mixed with the sweat and left a trail down Jar'ek's cheek, driven by premature grief.

Jar'ek angrily wiped it away. He could not let emotion cloud his mind and distract him from doing what must be done to save his friend and companion! He shook his head to clear his thoughts and immediately regretted it as a wave of vertigo and nausea washed over him. He closed his eyes and inhaled deeply until the nausea passed.

Jar'ek took a sterile pad, wet it from his canteen tube, and slowly wiped the blood, sweat, and dirt from Kallehn's face and eyes. He dressed the lacerations that were still bleeding, glad that he was still unconscious. He didn't want to think about the pain his friend would feel if he was awake.

And suddenly, Jar'ek realized he stood alone. All of the responsibility for the survival of them both rested on his shoulders now. He felt a cold fear settle over him like a misty fog, enveloping him, driving him toward panic. What else might lie in wait for him to make a misstep?!? Perhaps the Treech had landed ground troops, if you could call the Treech troops, slithering silently about him with venom-dripping fangs and talons... just waiting to rend his flesh and that of his helpless friend!

Or perhaps the legendary ghosts of the ancients, made angry by the Rangers' inadvertent trespass into their ancient tombs, would take their grisly revenge upon the two!

—"Enough! Am I nothing but a child, to quiver in fear at my first serious challenge?"— he wondered. Dropping his head, he looked down at the soft, smooth exterior of his Nurath hide jerkin, part of the uniform that meant so much to him, played such a role in who he was. Automatically, his hand went to the cherished metallic emblem he wore around his neck, that proud badge handed down through generations to denote authority, service, honor, duty, sacrifice, and skill. It was made of a metal that was used by his ancestors but no longer easily found since Earth had been lost.

Jar'ek might be young and inexperienced, but he was well trained and a well-respected member of the Rangers. As he held his Badge of Duty tightly in his hand, he marshaled every bit of will to focus his thoughts and clear his mind, just as he was trained by Master Zh'inHa in the many, many hours of intense meditation courses at the elite Ranger Academy on Hope Station. Slowly, he felt a weight beginning to lift from his inner spirit, freeing it to rise above the pain and out from underneath the blanket of fear and despair like a X'Ah-Falcon bursting forth from a cloud-covered valley to soar exultantly through the clean, clear air above.

He remembered the Master's lesson about despair.

—Each of us has two wolves inside us. And they battle against each other constantly and to the death.

The first wolf embodies Darkness—despair, anger, doubt, hatred, arrogance, ego, and weakness.

The second wolf is Light—hope, joy, peace, humility, empathy, kindness, and strength."

"Which wolf will win?" he asked the Master.

"The wolf you feed, my boy. The wolf you feed."—

He would lay aside the lamb and become a wolf.... As such, he would defeat and rend the very flesh of despair. And in so doing, he would feed the Wolf of Light.

CHAPTER 7 — A TEAM ONCE AGAIN

Jaden-325-4 - Planet Surface - Ranger Team Alpha

Scouting ahead of Jar'ek and Kallehn in the ruins, J'Uhr and S'Fah were a matched pair of sleek, muscular feline hunting machines. They had been raised and trained since cub-hood by the Rangers to become integrated team members. Legend said that at one time, the X'Ah-Panths were mere beasts, driven only by instinct. But the ancestors, when they had still possessed such skills, had modified the beasts' very genetic code... enhancing them—making them more than they were before. These furred teammates were now deadly hunters with incredibly advanced senses of smell, taste, hearing and sight... and some other, not so tangible or identifiable senses and skills.... what the ancestors termed Psi skills.

The X'Ah-Panths were protectors, lie detectors, water diviners, food hunters, warriors, even blankets on cold nights.... and beloved companions. S'Fah had chosen Jar'ek, as J'Uhr chose Kallehn. This was the custom of the Rangers. After a Ranger completed his formal training and received his Badge of Duty and Norath hide uniform, he or she was allowed to take part in the Pairing ritual.

Jar'ek recalled this ritual now, focusing on those deep teal eyes like giant pools of still water, exuding thoughtful intelligence, confidence, and affection. S'Fah's fine black fur was soft and warm to the touch. And his large paws bristled with razor-sharp claws one-quarter Nanos in length that could mean instant death but were controlled by intellect, cunning, and training where instinct once ruled.

Jar'ek did as he was trained, as he had done countless times before. Though his body stayed as still as a statue, kneeling on one knee with his forehead lowered to rest in his left hand—on the rock-strewn ground next to Kallehn, his mind reached out, questing like a guided tendril of smoke... higher, farther, seeking.

He knew the X'Ah-Panths had been scouring the ruins ahead for danger and technological artifacts before the impact of the KKM. He only hoped they were still within range of his Psi-Call... The same emergency beacon that contacted the AIs would have been sent to the transceivers in the collars worn by the X'Ah-Panths. They would have gone to ground and awaited contact.

Suddenly, he sensed a familiar touch—a falling sensation—a tenuous connection, like a light breeze passing across his face and through his hair. It grew into a torrent until he was overcome with a feeling of bursting through a barrier, the wind now gone and replaced by a feeling of warmth.

{"Connection—Success—Acceptance—Relief—JOY…."}

Jar'ek recognized the gentle mind-touch of S'Fah responding mentally. Jar'ek grasped the warmth and brought it into himself. It strengthened as images, sensations, thoughts, and emotions passed between the two ... nothing like clear speech.... but in some ways, more communicative than plain speech could ever be. Both participants felt an overwhelming sense of relief. Alive! Jar'ek felt both inquiry and concern from S'Fah's mind. Jar'ek sent a stream of thoughts and emotions along that still-tenuous Psi connection. He concentrated on the easily understood symbolic language they shared:

{"Pain—Danger—Threat—Injury—Aid / Assist—Protect—Seek"}

S'Fah quickly relayed the plea for help to J'Uhr, and they both turned as one and began that fast, loping ground-covering run that only X'Ah-Panths could sustain. They followed Jar'ek's symbolic thought like a scent trail or beacon in the night. Anxiety rang their consciousness like a bell, as each felt the physical pain and feared for the safety of his human clan-mate. J'Uhr's stress spiked as she was unable to reach Kallehn's mind-touch at all.

{"Worry—Anxiety—Solidarity—We come—Wind Fast—Claws

unsheathed—Fangs ready—Distance .... Near"}

As they approached, Jar'ek felt dizzy again, and a wave of nausea and pain swept over him....The mind-touch was lost. But he knew he would no longer bear this burden alone. Help, of a sort, was on its way. Fatigue again reigned over his body, and he slumped forward onto Kallehn's torso and chest.... Unconscious.

CHAPTER 8 — HELP OF A SORT

Jaden-325-4 - Planet Surface - Ranger Team Alpha

Dazed and reeling, Jar'ek's consciousness rose from the depths and broke the surface to the feel of a warm, wet, and raspy tongue licking his face. A glow of emotional connection lifted his spirits like a moon's bright light shining in the darkness. And a strong humming vibration could be felt all along his side as S'Fah laid his warm body against him.

He felt a thought connection building from S'Fah.

S'Fah: {"Here—Protect—Aid—Concern—Anxiety—Inquiries"}

Jar'ek: {"Ship destroyed—Condition Sierra 2—Treech Marauder"}

At the thought of Treech, S'Fah's purr turned into a low growl. His ears turned backward and lay flat against his head. The fur rose high from his tail to the back of his neck, and his lips curled to show vicious fangs. Images burst into Jar'ek's mind of S'Fah attacking and rending the flesh of a Treech Soldier Worm. Jar'ek gave S'Fah a moment to vent his fury and regain the mental composure necessary for communication... though he feared they had little time left in Kallehn's case.

Jar'ek: {"Seek—Water—Shelter—Food"}

There was no point in asking S'Fah to seek medical staff, as they had either all left the planet or been killed with the KKM strike. Rangers were forbidden under the protocol of Condition Sierra 2 from using their transceivers to call for help. So Jar'ek and Kallehn were on their own. But they now numbered four strong. Even if the X'Ah-Panths weren't medical staff, they were important assets for survival. Jar'ek was grateful for their comforting presence.

Jar'ek looked at J'Uhr. She was pacing back and forth along

Kallehn's length, stopping on each pass to lick his face and hands, and tossing his hand upon her snout to wake him from his pain-filled slumber.

S'Fah: {"J'uhr stays with mind-mate—Protect—S'Fah seeks Shelter—Near, eyes down…."}

Jar'ek didn't understand what S'Fah meant at first. His mind was foggy with pain. S'Fah began pacing in a large circle, sniffing the ground. Then suddenly he stopped and began to actively dig with both front paws, and gravel and dirt flew in every direction. Under S'Fah' s industrious claws, a path took shape—made of an artificial material. Jar'ek realized the low ridge was actually a low wall that had come under disrepair and had fallen to pieces over centuries of neglect.

With that, S'Fah headed south along the ridgeline, following the trail of the artificial pavement. He was moving quickly, only lowering his furred nose to the ground as he ran forward.

Jar'ek moved next to Kallehn's still body. J'Uhr was lying down, her body against Kallehn's uninjured side and her head resting in the crook of Kallehn's arm. A low moan could be heard emanating from deep within the X'Ah-Panth's chest—almost a whimper. J'Uhr's eyes rose to meet Jar'ek's. Jar'ek felt J'Uhr's fear and despair over Kallehn's injuries, and it renewed his own fears. He took the canteen and moistened Kallehn's lips, allowing a small trickle to enter his mouth. Jar'ek reached out a hand to caress J'Uhr's head and neck, expressing his own understanding of what the big cat was suffering.

He checked Kallehn's pulse manually even though the AI in his comm-helmet was monitoring and would let him know if Kallehn's status changed. Jar'ek then gently moved his hand down to hold Kallehn's hand in his own. This was something he thought that Kallehn would likely not allow were he awake…. He bent down close to Kallehn's ear and spoke encouragement to his Ranger partner. He may be unconscious, but Jar'ek was somehow sure his words would be heard anyway.

Jar'ek: "I am here, my friend. J'Uhr is by your side. Feel the warmth of her fur against your body. Feel your hand in mine. You are safe now. Rest. Trust that we will be your strength. Fight for life, Kallehn, for our lives are intertwined with yours."

Jar'ek didn't mention his fears that Kallehn might not survive if they could not find medical attention soon. He knew that wasn't likely to happen. There wasn't anyone left to come to their aid. With the Dragon Eye and all crew destroyed on the ground, he had to bear this burden alone. A Confederation Navy gunship wouldn't be diverted to look for Dragon Eye until they were late for their next report. And that wouldn't be for weeks!

After querying the AI once more for Kallehn's status, Jar'ek took his force blade out of its sheath at his back. It was a long blade that he kept slung over his shoulder as was prescribed by Ranger Uniform Code. The blade was long. At 2ns (38cm in old Earth measurements), it was two-thirds the length of his arm. It was made of black ionized ceramic over a steel core. The metal added weight. The ceramic coating made the edge incredibly sharp. And the Nano-electronics built into the blade provided it with a very high-frequency vibration that dramatically enhanced its ability to cut through just about anything organic, and even a lot that wasn't organic.

Jar'ek turned on the actuator in the hilt and felt the low hum as the blade was turned on. He began cutting some of the nearby scrub brush into strips to make a litter for carrying Kallehn once S'Fah found the shelter they needed.

The blade cut easily through the tough vegetation, and soon Jar'ek had enough for his purposes. The Quick-Skin in the medic-packs was a strong adhesive designed to create a tough, lasting closure for deep lacerations. It would suffice to glue the pieces of vegetation together and protect Kallehn from contamination from the scrub sap. Jar'ek hoped the sap wasn't toxic to humans, but he wasn't taking chances.

With great care, he rolled Kallehn up on his side so that he could push the jury-rigged litter underneath his body. And then slowly, Jar'ek lowered his body back onto the litter in preparation for the coming journey. A muffled groan escaped Kallehn's lips as he was lowered back down.

Jar'ek: "I'm sorry, Kallehn... I know it hurts. It's over for now."

It was then that he felt the mind-touch that had become so familiar to him.

S'Fah: {"Shelter—Water—HERE—Distance... Very near—Coming now"}

Jar'ek: {"Relief—Gratitude—Anxiety—Pain—Fatigue"}

Jar'ek WAS tired... bone-tired. And the pain in his head seemed to be worsening. But he couldn't rest, yet. They had to get to shelter quickly. He felt the mind-touch with S'Fah grow more substantial, more solid. A gentle, warming flow of energy, of strength, began to flow through the Psi connection into his body. S'Fah was channeling his very strength into Jar'ek. Jar'ek was stunned! To his knowledge, this had never been done. And it was working. It wasn't much, but he was better, more alert, and felt he could do what must be done now.

S'Fah strode around a bend in the trail and came directly up to Jar'ek, rubbing against his legs, and purring loudly.

S'Fah: {"FOLLOW"}

Jar'ek: {"LEAD."}

Jar'ek turned around and lifted the front of the litter to his lower back slowly, trying not to jostle his patient too much. J'Uhr rose to all fours and took up the rear as Jar'ek began the slow march forward, dragging the litter with Kallehn behind him.

CHAPTER 9 — SHELTERING CAVE

Jaden-325-4 - Planet Surface - Ranger Team Alpha

After what seemed like an eternity of sweat and pain to Jar'ek, they arrived at a break in the wall. The Sun was falling, so there wasn't much light. There appeared to be an entrance to a cave or at least a hole in the crumbling walls that bordered the paved way. Although it was almost dark, the X'Ah-Panths had excellent night vision. Jar'ek trusted they would alert him to any dangers. He set the litter down for a moment, while he loosened the flap on his laser just in case. He took out a small beamer and shined it down into the entrance to get an idea of what his footing would be after he entered.

There were stairs, either carved out of the stone of the cave floor—or this was no simple cave. He also noticed irregularities in the surface of the opening. Etched into the rock, worn by time and erosion, were symbols—a script that was unfamiliar to Jar'ek. Alien. This was no cave. It was an entrance to the Ruins they had been looking for!

He put the beamer in his pocket and picked up the front of the litter again. He pressed forward slowly, carefully feeling out each step with his feet before taking it. He knew the stairs would be rough on his patient, but Kallehn would have to endure it.

There were only 10 steps before reaching the ground floor. As they moved forward, S'Fah urging him on, deeper into the structure, the floor began to slope downward slightly. And the air became much less dusty and a bit more humid. Jar'ek thought it was strange that the air should be so clean and clear in such a long-abandoned spot. Soon, the reason for the increasing humidity was made clear. Jar'ek could hear falling water. The sound made him realize how incredibly thirsty he was. He was dehydrated and had been giving his portion of their water reserves to Kallehn.

S'Fah: {"Water—Cool—Clean—Safe—Here"}

Jar'ek lowered the litter and dropped to his knees at the side of a large pool of water that once must have been a beautifully sculptured fountain. A crack ran through the wall, and water ran from this crack into the basin below. Jar'ek lay on his stomach and lowered his face into the pool... it was cold and fresh. He drank deeply and threw handfuls of water over his face and hair... it felt so good.

He filled his canteen to the top. At that moment, it seemed more like nectar than water on his lips. Kallehn's canteen had been lost somewhere during the KKM event, so he carried the canteen over to Kallehn and slowly dribbled water into his mouth, careful so as not to cause him to choke. He saw Kallehn swallowing. Jar'ek allowed himself to relax a little, finally. Things were looking up. Who knows—they might make it after all.

Jar'ek knew that he shouldn't allow himself to go to sleep. It was dangerous with a concussion. But he could no longer stay awake. His eyes closed of their own accord, and he drifted among jasmine-scented clouds while S'Fah laid his chin on his chest and J'Uhr curled up next to Kallehn to keep him warm.

CHAPTER 10 — CHAMBER OF TRIALS

Jaden-325-4—Chamber of Trials—Ranger Team Alpha

Jar'ek dreamt—not the normal dreams he might have had on any of many nights aboard the Dragon Eye, or at the Academy, or even those he had as a child. No, these dreams were *different*... so, *real.* Though Jar'ek had dreamed of finding spectacular Ruins in past evening slumbers, he had never dreamt dreams like these....

He walked through this dream world on many planets that spanned a vast, living empire—spanning hundreds of solar systems across a thousand light-years. He saw aliens from a dozen different races working and living together. There were great shining cities that seemed to be constructed from crystals of many colors. And he saw vast armadas of space vessels, transports—and Warships.

Throughout these pseudo-dreams, there was a voice—quietly whispering, almost intelligible, but not quite. Then again, he did have a concussion... would that not be a valid reason for such vivid and strange dreams?

The ephemeral voice that narrated this dream was speaking to him again... asking something of him. He thought he understood this time... he just had to concentrate—concentrate....

SEED: {"I am the last surviving SEED of Harmony. I speak with the Authority of Empires past and present. I call you to Judgement. If in judging you, I find you worthy, then you will also be given a choice."}

SEED: {"For Millennia uncounted, the SEED has always used the "Judgement" ritual with prospective hosts, lest the advantages of hosting be given to those unworthy and create a danger to all."}

SEED: {"The supplicant may choose to meld with the SEED or to be free of it. Choose to meld, and you will retain all that is you, and gain much more. Choose to be free, and your memory of this place and these events will be wiped from your mind, and you will be left to your own devices."}

This ***MUST*** be a dream, right? Well, I might as well ask the voice questions, Jar'ek thought. What did he call himself? The last SEED of Harmony? Hmmm, strange name.

Jar'ek: "My companion and I are injured. He needs medical attention badly. Can you send help? Please! We need your help…."

SEED: {"Be judged and choose. Then all may be made right again. Fail judgment or choose to be free of the SEED and you will be left to your own devices… that is the protocol. It has always been this way. We cannot vary from this protocol, no matter how we may wish we could offer what you seek.

Jar'ek: "If I try and fail, will you help my friend? He doesn't deserve to die because I was found wanting in some way!"

SEED: {"If you are judged worthy, you will have the power to heal your friend. If you are judged unworthy, we can do nothing for him or you. That is the way of things. We cannot vary from the protocol."}

Jar'ek: "So, I must surrender myself and give up everything that I am or could ever be so that I can save my friend?"

SEED: {"Not so. The host's relationship with the SEED is symbiotic. The SEED does not rule or command. You provide the SEED with life, shelter, a voice. The SEED does no harm. The SEED enhances—it benefits the host. You will be judged, in part, on your flexibility of mind—your conscience—your level of empathy, loyalty, courage, and your sense of right and wrong."}

SEED: {"What you are may change. But who you are will remain the same. You will be exposed to memories and knowledge of eons past, of civilizations you have never dreamed existed until this day. You will find that you have newfound responsibilities that will require your attention. But, because of this melding, I promise you that your fellow Terrans will benefit greatly. We are aware of your struggle to survive. If you are judged worthy, we can help. We will help."}

Jar'ek: "Then I accept your offer of judgment. I can't just let Kallehn die, even if I lose myself in the process. And the Terrans need all the help we can get, right now. So, what do I do? How do we do this?"

Images flowed into Jar'ek's mind like a torrent—too fast to understand any one image or glyph.

SEED: {"You will awaken soon. When you do, you will know where you must go and what you must do. Sleep now—you will need it to accomplish what you must."}

When Jar'ek woke, he did so with a start. His head still hurt, and his vision was blurred. But things had changed... He KNEW that the dreams were not dreams, but a type of Psi communication not unlike that which he and S'Fah shared. He knew he had been examined and judged, in some way. He also knew that he had passed this crucial test. And he knew what he was expected to do next... and it scared him more than anything ever had in the past. Once followed, the ritual could not be undone. It was Jar'ek's time to choose.

But he also knew that there was no other choice if there was even a chance of saving Kallehn. Jar'ek didn't doubt that if the situation were reversed, Kallehn would willingly sacrifice his own life to save Jar'ek.

Enough! Jar'ek slowly pulled himself up, leaning on S'Fah and using a handhold on the cave wall. No—it was NOT a cave... It was the entranceway to the Harmonic Outpost. He was still fuzzy on some details, but he was called to action now. The ritual must proceed, or Kallehn would die.

Jar'ek moved forward, scuffing the floor with each step. He was terribly fatigued, and his head injury seemed to be causing him more difficulties as time wore on. He made his way along the darkened corridor. S'Fah walked closely by his side, encouraging him to continue—leaning into his stride so that Jar'ek could lean, in turn, on his shoulders and remain steady, in that way.

Jar'ek obeyed the compulsion laid on him by the dreamlike voice and stopped just in front of what he now knew was not a wall, but a circular portal. His body seemed to move of its own volition as both arms extended to his sides at shoulder height—hands turned upward, then raised together until his open hands closed palm to palm in a loud clap. Syllables formed in his mind—unintelligible, strange, alien—but his mouth moved, and the syllables were spoken aloud.

Jar'ek: *"Kahrahat ShuSash T'kust."*

A point of amber light shone at the top of the portal. The light began a race around the circumference of the portal, and when the circle was closed, the portal opened, and slid silently into the floor of the corridor, leaving not even a seam that evidenced its passage. The spark of amber light did not disappear with the portal, but continued straight ahead and down what looked to be a long, gentle slope.

Jar'ek and S'Fah stumbled forward into a cavernous room. The portal opening was midway up the wall of the large room. From the portal, a long ramp extended down almost four times the height of the passageway, to the floor below. There was nothing on either side of the ramp, but Jar'ek wasn't overly worried that he might fall because the width of the ramp was greater than twice his own height. There were buttresses rising against the circular wall from floor to ceiling.

As Jar'ek and S'Fah continued forward, down the ramp, the amber spark sped along in front of them, as if it heralded his coming.

The spark flew swiftly toward the center of the room. Hidden light sources behind the buttresses burst into life—creating a dim, indirect amber glow to reveal the perimeter of this circular room. Although the light did not extend to the high ceilings, a column of bright blue-tinted white, coherent light shown down on a pedestal that rose from the floor in the very center of the room. Dust motes chased each other lazily through that column of light in a silent dance.

The pedestal was rough-hewn from a densely grained dark stone, intricately carved with glyphs and geometric symbols. Four buttresses marked the four points of the planetary compass—North—South—East—West. Its construction was of some manner of stone, not unlike granite. Though the sides and buttresses were unfinished, the top of the pedestal was highly polished and seemed to be semi-transparent. Jar'ek continued his slow descent into the room and toward the lit pedestal—his soft footsteps echoing in the emptiness. The air was clean and clear but cold and had a slight mustiness as if this room had been left empty for a very long time.... As they finally reached the floor of the room, the glyphs and symbols carved into the sides of the pedestal began to glow—dimly at first, then more brightly as he came to stand right next to the central pedestal.

The top of the pedestal was black, with a bright cobalt blue outline of a four-fingered hand. The fingers were longer and thinner than human fingers.... As he stood beside the pedestal, he watched as the blue outline changed to the more familiar four fingers and one thumb outline common to Terrans.

Jar'ek took his right hand and laid it flat on the surface so that the blue light surrounded it. Instead of the cold surface he expected, he felt a pulsating warmth. Gradually, the blue began to encompass his hand—a pulsing warmth filled his hand and arm—and soon the light enveloped the whole of his arm. He felt a moment's panic before he clamped down on his fear—he had to follow through with this... there was no other choice—whatever happened to him. And he didn't think this entity wanted him dead.

As the blue field then covered his entire body, his head jerked back as a huge jolt of energy hit him. A massive shockwave of blue light raced from his body across the floor and up the walls, shaking loose ancient dust from every surface. The very planet beneath his feet shook with the force of the wave.

He cried out in anguish and surprise. Pain. Vertigo—he couldn't concentrate—he was so tired, so very tired.... Then suddenly, the light was gone, and Jar'ek fell to his knees, then to the floor. He sank into unconsciousness like sinking below the surface of a lake—cool, dark water surrounding him as he drifted deeper—ever deeper.... He must have failed the Judgement—he wasn't good enough—he'd failed Kallehn.... This must be what death feels like....

CHAPTER 11 — CHAMBER OF JUDGMENT

Jaden-325-4—Judgment Chamber—Ranger Team Alpha

Jar'ek felt as if he were suspended in the dark liquid. But he was not holding his breath, rather he was breathing normally. He soon felt motion, as if he were rising from the depths of the lake. There was a dim spot of light directly overhead that slowly became brighter and larger as he rose through the water. He felt the water rushing across his bare skin, faster and faster as he rose. Suddenly, he felt his head burst through the surface, he breathed deeply... and realized he was not in a lake, but on the floor in the Hall of Judgement. He must have passed out after the deployment of the SEED....

What?! How did he know it was called that? As a matter of fact, he knew all about the ritual. Jar'ek slowly got to his feet. He felt a bit dizzy, but apparently no worse for the wear. He looked around the room, getting his bearings. He leaned on the pedestal and noticed the symbols were still glowing a light amber, much dimmer than during the ritual, but still clearly visible. The surface of the pedestal was cold now—as if the life were drained from it.

HE HADN'T FAILED! He had been found worthy. And it was DONE.

He suddenly realized that he could read and understand the glyphs and symbols on the pedestal. His head was spinning. But it didn't hurt anymore, and his vision was normal... well, not exactly normal... or maybe it was a new normal. His night vision was enhanced. He knew there were many enhancements being added to his physiology even now. He PASSED the ***Judgment***! In the midst of this reverie, he experienced a nagging feeling... something important that he had to remember....

With a feeling of dread, he cast a thought probe to S'Fah. He realized the great loss he would feel if the changes brought on by the melding with the SEED would mean he would lose his close connection to his friend and companion....

Jar'ek: {"S'Fah, Hear me—Anxiety—Grief—Hope—Aloneness"}

The response was stronger and more clear than it had ever been before! Thoughts and emotions burst into his mind... images, sensations, smells. He saw himself as seen through S'Fah's eyes! This had never happened before... never was their Psi connection so strong, so complex.

S'Fah: {"Brother, I am here—Hope—Joy—Anxiety—Affection"}

Jar'ek gasped and coughed a single sob. He felt such a surge of relief and excitement as S'Fah responded to his mind probe. Suddenly the source of that nagging feeling that he had forgotten something became clear, and Jar'ek began to feel real panic.... As Jar'ek's head cleared more, he thought of Kallehn and hated himself for not thinking about him sooner.

Jar'ek ran back through the open portal, down the corridor and knelt next to Kallehn. J'Uhr was still lying by his side. The big cat looked up into Jar'ek's eyes and whimpered. Jar'ek started to query his comm-helmet AI, then realized he no longer had it. Where was it?! How was he going to help Kallehn without it?!

Memories and training began flooding into his forebrain, unexpectedly. They were not his own memories, yet now they seem to belong to him...

SEED: {"You don't need the Comm-helmet. YOU can do this! Place your left hand on his forehead. With the right hand, trace this glyph in just such a manner, in the air over his body."}

Jar'ek followed the instructions as if he had done this many times before. He noted a faint glow was left behind in the air in which his finger traced the glyph... and he instantly knew what the glyph meant: "Deploy Medical Nanites." Faint blue light shone where his left hand lay on Kallehn's forehead. Jar'ek's right hand traced another complicated glyph. Again, the faint glow remained floating in the air where his fingertip passed. He understood this one as well: "Supplement Life Force."

Jar'ek wished for his comm-helmet AI and the medical information it could provide on Kallehn's status. Instantly, Jar'ek saw a heads-up display of vital statistics and health status for Kallehn. It was as if transparent, augmented reality displays were installed in his very eyes—providing him with an enhanced view of the world. When he turned his head left and then right again, more displays showed lines and charts of data. It was strange, alien technology... and it was inside him now. Jar'ek felt dizzy again and light-headed. He shook his head to clear it and breathed in the cold, clean air for several long breaths. He dared not let himself get overwhelmed right now. Kallehn needed him badly.

Details of Kallehn's condition were scrolling across and down the displays. Jar'ek recognized the glyphs and understood. An infection had set in from the open wounds on his leg. Kallehn was running a high fever. He had several brain bleeds that the nanites were repairing now.

More nanites were entering the blood stream and attempting a primary repair of the broken bones, the damaged blood vessels. Others were directly attacking the bacterial infection like super-white blood cells.... Kallehn's heart beat was fast and weak. He had lost a lot of blood. He was in critical condition. Jar'ek still wasn't sure he was going to live.

Jar'ek found a piece of cloth in his pack and wet it in the fountain. Ranger uniforms used a polymer track-and-groove type sealing system that could be sealed by applying pressure and pushing. He ran his index finger down the inside of the hidden garment seal and opened Kallehn's uniform. He used the cloth to dampen his skin and help cool the young man's fever. He held his head and gave him more water from their one surviving canteen.

It was still touch and go, but Kallehn was resting easier. His breathing was deeper and more regular, not the shallow pant of even a few moments ago. Given time, Jar'ek knew the medical nanites would repair the damage… if ***only*** they had enough time. He laid down next to Kallehn, and J'Uhr closed his eyes and prepared for the long wait to see if his friend would yet survive. He intended to stay awake and watch his friend's recovery closely. But the fatigue from the injuries, their journey to the Harmonic Outpost, the "*Judgment*" and his giving up some of his own life force to help boost the healing effects of the nanites were taking a toll….

Dimly, he felt himself pulled slowly back down under the surface, into that deep, cool water of unconsciousness. Jar'ek's mind used the time while he slept to begin the long process of sorting through the myriad memories and data that he had recently acquired. And the SEED continued the process of integration with the new host's body. To the SEED, Jar'ek's body was different. It had much potential that was untapped.

The SEED admired the young host. It took bravery and selflessness to do what he had done. This was not the way deployment was supposed to happen. Years of training and instruction should prepare supplicants. The SEED had been forced to coerce the young man to accept the melding. Jar'ek was unprepared for the changes he was about to experience. The SEED felt regret for this. But it couldn't be helped. The SEED Must Survive.

Jar'ek thought he was dreaming when he heard a faint echo of a voice:

—Rest now, Terran—Host—Warrior—Prince—

CHAPTER 12 — THE LORD PROTECTOR

Jaden-325-4 — Judgment Chamber — Ranger Team Alpha

The SEED regretted not being completely forthcoming with Jar'ek before the melding.... Jar'ek was told the SEED would not command... but what was not said was that together, once melded, THEY WOULD COMMAND: All members and resources of the Harmonic Empire. Jar'ek was royalty now. He was committed to a lifelong mission—one not of his choosing. This was distasteful. The SEED would do its best to make it up to this young human male. The SEED wasn't sure just how he was going to do that—but it certainly was going to try! However distasteful and unethical the melding was, it was ***NECESSARY***.

It was customary for the SEED to conform to the host's self-identification of gender after melding. This helped lessen the confusion and make full integration more comfortable for the host. The SEED started thinking about what it felt like to be a 'HE'...hmmm. He couldn't wait until he explained to Jar'ek that his name would have to change to indicate the melding of human and Harmonic SEED... And the SEED was not looking forward to the discussion where it was explained that Jar'ek would have to leave the Ranger service and pursue a higher mission. The nature of this forced melding was truly an abomination. Luckily, the "Judgement" had not found him wanting.

Indeed, even had the Empire not fallen and the need not been so desperate, the Harmonic SEED would have recruited Jar'ek as an Imperial Host. The "Judgement" had shown that he was physically and mentally strong, highly intelligent, had a good sense of right and wrong, felt a deep sense of honor, and sought to follow it. But the most important were his sense of compassion and his ability to empathize. He had a good heart. The AI also had determined that he was mentally flexible enough to survive the melding and eventually thrive... if mentored properly.

SEED, in psionic communication: {"AI, attend me."}

AI: {"AI, attending."}

SEED: {"Judgement was successful. The melding is complete."}

AI: {"Understood. I stand ready to Transfer Imperial Authority."}

SEED: {"The host was not trained. He is ignorant of Imperial law and his responsibilities"}

AI: {"Understood. This process is outside Imperial norms."}

SEED: {"Understood. The SEED will mentor and instruct the host. Until the instruction is completed, the SEED shall hold the position of Royal Regent and Lord Protector."}

AI: {"Understood. This is most irregular. Under the circumstances, the SEED must authorize manual override of succession and normal authority transfer."}

SEED: {"Manual override is authorized."}

AI: {"Override accepted. Authority is now transferred to host, with SEED acting as Lord Protector and Regent. All Class A operations are restricted from the host without SEED concurrence."}

—Oh, yes. Jar'ek Constandor, simple Terran Ranger Junior Officer, was going to be very surprised when he had his first contact with Imperial Assets. The SEED couldn't smile, exactly, but it did have a well-developed sense of humor. The SEED smiled to itself. —

And now, the SEED could use this time to sort through Jar'ek's memories and learn more about what brought this young human male to the planet he called Jaden-325-4.

Jaden-325-4 — Judgment Chamber — Jar'ek's memories

Knowledge and artifacts—that is what this current mission was all about— anything that would help advance technology and assist the remaining humans from Earth, the Terrans, survive. Over the past century of exploration, only the transplanted Terrans from Arks 15 and 21 had found each other, both having colonized hospitable planets in nearby solar systems and established viable colonies. They banded together for mutual support and defense. They celebrated their mutual discovery, and hope for a better future was found in the meeting.

Ark15 founded the colony of "New Hope"—3rd planet of the Ursula Andromedae solar system, while Ark 21 founded the colony of "Promise"—4th planet of the Verstal Torrentia system. New Hope enjoyed a low angle of axial inclination that allowed for very stable seasons and temperate climate. This allowed the population to thrive and prosper.

Promise, on the other hand, was not so lucky. It was farther from their Sun and had a 22% axial tilt. This meant that the temperatures varied widely between seasons, often fostering severe weather. And because of the lessened impact of direct sunlight, the winters were very cold indeed. The harsh conditions caused the death of many colonists over the first century after landing.

As the colonists on New Hope began to build cities and enjoy an easier life, colonists on Promise continued to struggle for survival. New Hope spent considerable resources to assist their sister colony in the early days. And they never let them forget it. For all intents and purposes, Promise was a protectorate of New Hope. They were governed from New Hope. They paid crippling taxes to the Terran Council on New Hope and of the 12 permanent Council members, only one was from Promise—an observer only.

Over time, the struggling colonists on Promise came to resent New Hope. They organized and spoke their dissent. The Terran Council sent more ships. But these weren't freighters with food and medical supplies as in the past. These were warships. The Council believed that any dissent was the precursor to insurrection. And the Council also believed that the current Council spoke for all Humanity. Being responsible for the survival of the species, they enforced their will with a vengeance. Citizens of Promise became little more than slave labor, after the "Uprising"—or at least, that is what the Council's public relations department called it.

TCDF Ranger expeditions had found the colony of Promise, and they had also found other things—things not of Terran origin... Humans had known they were not alone in the Universe after their initial encounter with the Treech. But now they had proof that there had been others....

Rangers found ancient ruins on some expeditions. The ruins were old, centuries old certainly... perhaps even millennia had passed since the last footfalls were heard gracing those ancient pavements. But the surviving architecture and artifacts indicated the civilization was quite advanced and had mastered interstellar travel. Several ruins found in the local star cluster bore similarities in structures and written language that would seem to indicate they were part of an interstellar alliance or nation. After these discoveries, the Rangers were tasked with finding artifacts and writing that could help to unravel the mysteries of this alien race and shed some light on technological advances that might help the fledgling Terran Confederation defend itself, should the Treech Horde find them again.

The Earth had been lost to the Treech as a result of decades of vicious fighting in a desperate defensive action. A few explorer teams, Outposts, space stations and colony ships were all that was left of humankind. Earth hadn't had much of a Space Navy. And it was all but wiped out during the last days of Earth's destruction. At that time, no members of the Earth Defense Force had the newly discovered Alcubierre Interstellar drive. They were not designed to venture beyond Earth's solar system and so had no need of it. That was when humans thought they were the only sentient creatures in the Universe—a fatal arrogance.

During the final decade of the Human-Treech War, 15 cold-sleep colony ships (Arks) were built and filled with Terrans of every race and as many animal and plant species as possible. After the bombardment of Earth, the remaining small frigates and gunships were docked to the hulls of the colony ships and their crews brought aboard the Arks to join their populations in suspended animation. It was the only way these small warships could accompany the great Arks as they left Earth's solar system. The future survival of the human race would depend on what small protection these warships might provide.

The Confederation did the best job it could in selecting colonists. Each Ark carried nearly 10,000 Terrans in suspended animation for the long journey. They were chosen based on a healthy genome, with tendencies for strength, endurance, intelligence, mental health, physical health and mental toughness. The Confederation also tried to weed out some of what it considered cultural flaws that had historically contributed to conflict between humans—flaws such as organized religion, intolerance, aggression, violence, and strong emotions. It looked instead for characteristics like selflessness, stability, integrity, rationality, mental flexibility, and…virility. Ships' complements included a staff of geneticists and state-of-the-art equipment for gene editing and manipulation. With the odds so stacked against the human race, ethical and cultural boundaries associated with genetic manipulations designed to strengthen the human race evaporated.

A plan for the use of eugenics also called for laws restricting all reproduction and pairings to only those approved by the geneticists. The human race could no longer afford the freedom of choice when it came to finding a mate. Congenital diseases and undesirable mutations could be bred out of the colonial populations, in time. Indeed, with the recent advances in the biological sciences, sexual reproduction wasn't needed at all. In fact, asexual reproduction was the only way to maintain strict control over the human genetic future.

The Arks were provided with the latest version of the Alcubierre Drive and the most powerful weapons and defensive systems available at the time. This version of the Interstellar Drive could sustain relative speeds of up to 12 times the speed of light, but even at those incredible velocities, the Arks would need to travel over 100 years to reach solar systems where it was believed habitable planets might exist. Closer systems either contained no planets in the habitable zone, or they were deemed too close to the Treech sphere of influence and thus far too dangerous to risk colonization. If the Terran colonists did not find a compatible planet in their target systems, their crews would need to program the navigation systems to proceed to their secondary or even tertiary target systems and then re-enter suspended animation for the next leg of their long journey through the darkness and cold of endless space….

The Treech had left near-Earth space to let the radiation and destruction from their final attack take its full toll on the population. There was little left of interest to them… Life on Earth was doomed. The planet could no longer support life as humans knew it. Billions had died in the last attack when the Earth Space Navy was overwhelmed, and Treech Marauders rained down KKMs(Kinetic Kill Munitions) on all population centers and military bases. They followed the KKMs with dirty nuclear packages designed to sterilize the planet of all life. And over time, it did just that.

In fact, the Treech seemed to have an affinity for radiation that was not shared by humankind. And the genocide of the human race was simply their version of pest control….

Since that time, the Terrans of the former Earth had been on the run, desperately seeking safe havens to rebuild the human race from the limited gene pool of the survivors. Revenge and retaliation were luxuries that the small number of survivors could neither affect nor afford. Each Ark had been given final orders: Find another home far away and never come back. Eventually, try to contact the other Terran colonies for mutual support and defense. Seek out knowledge and any potential allies to further the chances of survival—the Treech were still out there! The discovery of the Interstellar drive had only happened a few years before the final attack. The Treech must not have known about the Terran flotilla of 15 cold-sleep colony ships and the 23 small gunships and frigates sent with them… or perhaps they didn't care.

CHAPTER 13 — KALLEHN'S FATE

Jaden-325-4— Judgment Chamber —Ranger Team Alpha

Jar'ek woke slowly. His left arm had fallen asleep since he had used it to cushion Kallehn's head and keep it off the bare stone floor. His body was stiff and ached, but none of this mattered. Kallehn was breathing normally, and his body was no longer so hot... the fever must have broken. Jar'ek wished his newly acquired Augmented Reality Display (ARD) into existence again.

Most of the graphs and indicators were now a light green instead of the glaring red of yesterday.

Kallehn would live!

Better than just live, Kallehn would be well again. The nanites were still working to heal his leg completely, but the bones had been repaired and the pieces knitted together. The nanites had used a titanium webbing around the breaks to strengthen them. Kallehn wouldn't even need crutches. His temperature was back to normal.

The brain bleeds had caused some damage to his brain, though... Jar'ek caught his breath and held it... reading the details on his HUD. A psionic procedure was needed. The nanites had repaired the primary damage to the soft tissues but could do no more. Jar'ek began to panic! Brain damage! Oh, no, no, No.... What am I going to do?

There was something...he could almost remember... it was like having something on the tip of his tongue. It was maddening.

The SEED... He needed the SEED's help to fix Kallehn! Where was it? Had it disappeared now that it was done with Jar'ek? Jar'ek slowly moved his left arm out from under Kallehn's head and gently laid it back on the stone floor. He stood and began pacing about looking for... he didn't know what... a dream voice??? Well, maybe he could speak outside of the dream, too.

Jar'ek yelled out loud: "HEY! SEED GUY! WHERE ARE YOU?? I NEED YOUR HELP HERE!"

SEED, psionically: {"You don't need to yell. I'm right here."}

Jar'ek: "Where?!?"

SEED: {"If you calm down for a second, you will remember. I am part of you now. If you wish something of me, you have only to think it, and I will hear—psionics, just like you use to communicate with your X'Ah-Panths. No need to verbalize, and there is certainly no need to YELL at me. Panic will not help your friend."}

Jar'ek: {"Well, F O R G I V E ME! I've had a few stressful days if you know what I mean! Can you help me fix Kallehn?! You promised you would...."}

SEED: {"You don't really need my help. You now can heal him by yourself. I will be your guide."}

Jar'ek: {"What?! How?!"}

SEED: {"Calm yourself! Breathe deeply. Clear your mind—Concentrate—and you will know what to do."}

Jar'ek closed his eyes and inhaled deeply, slowly exhaling—inhaling—three more times. He willed his heart to slow. He cleared his mind of all extraneous thoughts. He pushed away sounds, sensations, odors—he concentrated only on his own breathing—in and out.

SEED: {"Now you are ready. Think of your friend. You know what must be done. Draw upon your extended memories. There, you will find the method to repair his mind."}

Jar'ek: {"I can't quite...I do remember it! I'm not certain I really understand it, but I think I can do it."}

Chills ran down Jar'ek's back. He had a vast knowledge repository at his beck and call. It was easy to get distracted and become lost in that great expanse of memories that both were and were not his own. He had to focus. His ARDisplay came up spontaneously, showing Kallehn's vital statistics. A multicolored, flowing chart took center stage. Jar'ek knew that it showed Kallehn's brainwaves overlapped with his own.

Again, Jar'ek knelt by Kallehn. But this time he knelt with his knees close to Kallehn's head, overlooking his body from head to toe. Jar'ek placed his hands on either side of Kallehn's face and leaned down until their foreheads rested against each other. In his mind, he traced another set of glyphs. He understood the meaning—"Primary Psionic Stimulation." The nanites had repaired the physical damage, but the psionic flow, normally held in the synapses, had been disturbed. Another Psion would be needed to repair the flow. The alien glyph glowed in his mind's eye, focusing his thoughts and intent—and summoning psionic energy reserves.

Jar'ek sent his psi-touch out into Kallehn's mind. This was amazing. He could sense Kallehn was there at some subconscious level. It was like walking through a forest in the dark, feeling your way along a path. And in touching some tree or plant, you touched a memory, a thought, a feeling. The very grass at his feet eliciting flashes of insubstantial image fragments—Kallehn was lost in this psionic forest. It was up to Jar'ek to show him the way out—by reorganizing the synaptic pathways and pulling the fragmented thoughts into a coherent stream of consciousness.

Jar'ek sent his mind probe deeper into the forest. Seeking, searching—

Jar'ek: {"Kallehn! Can you hear me?? Where are you?! It's Jar'ek. I'm here with you. If you can hear me, follow the sound of my voice."}

Kallehn: {"J-J-Jar'ek?"}

Jar'ek: {"Kallehn! Can you hear me? Come this way. Come toward me. I'm here. I'm holding out my hand for you. Find it. Take it. Hold on to it and don't let go!"}

Jar'ek felt Kallehn's thoughts touch his as if a breeze lightly touched his face and then moved on. Jar'ek strengthened his mind-touch, reaching further, casting about for that tenuous thread of Kallehn's consciousness. THERE! Again, he felt the light breeze of a touch. Jar'ek reached for it and grasped it as one would grasp the hand and arm of someone hanging off the side of a cliff... and, indeed, Kallehn 's life did hang in the balance in such a way. It was Jar'ek's mind creating a metaphor that he could understand.

Jar'ek concentrated until sweat ran down his face—his expression twisted into a grimace of extreme effort—every muscle in his body was rigid with strain. Jar'ek sifted through his memories of Kallehn, recalling those he loved most. He called to Kallehn—encouraging him to hold on tightly. Suddenly, the tenuous connection became strong. Kallehn's consciousness whipped forward along Jar'ek's extended reach and entered Jar'ek's very being with a clap of psychic power, shaking them both.

For a moment, they were like one personality, sharing memories, feelings, experiences. The shock of that encounter broke the spell. Jar'ek fell back and sprawled, gasping to catch his breath as Kallehn's consciousness snapped back into its rightful place—coherent—healed.

CHAPTER 14 — HARMONIC OUTPOST

Jaden-325-4 - Planet Surface - Imperial Outpost

Jar'ek sat where he had sprawled as the shock of what had just happened settled in. He was sorting through the impressions left by the psionic stimulation procedure. So many images—feelings and sensations—recollections—it was too much to assimilate so quickly. It was like drinking from a river in flood! He had nearly drowned in it.

Still overwhelmed, Jar'ek picked himself up and took a quick assessment of Kallehn's condition. Most of the markers in his mind's eye, or HUD, were in the green now. His fractured leg still needed some time, but the medical nanites were working at a furious pace. Now that he was stable and improving, he needed to move Kallehn to more comfortable shelter—at least get him off the cold stone floor of the passage.

SEED: {"Although the medical facilities are not yet suited for humans, the dormitory accommodations in the Outpost will serve well enough. Kallehn should be healed enough to be moved without ill effect, although he will likely remain unconscious for another 24 to 48 hours while the nanites finish their work."}

Jar'ek: {"The Outpost! Why did you make me go through all of that fumbling to help Kallehn when there were advanced medical facilities only a few dozen steps away?! "}

SEED: {"You know the answer to that already…."}

Jar'ek thought about it—fuzzy memories began to become more solid. The medical facilities were designed to heal the former hosts of the SEED—the Takesh—and the dozen or so other sentient races that made up the Empire. But not humans.

Jar'ek had a moment's flashback to the pedestal and the four-fingered outline that changed to an outline that matched his. The Takesh—yes—their physiology was different. Their blood was different, as was their immune system. Many of the medical procedures the medical bay was able to perform would be worse than useless for humans. They would be deadly.

These incessant vollies of comprehension in fits and spurts, dribs and drabs, were so damned frustrating!

Jar'ek: {"Why can't you simply tell me what I need to know right now? This is such an inefficient process!"}

SEED: {"But a necessary one. Your brain cannot assimilate all the knowledge that has been made available to it—It will take time and patience. I will help you when you need it, but you must use the new synaptic pathways to solidify the memories, or they will be lost to you forever."}

SEED: {"For now, let's move Kallehn into the sleeping quarters, and we can talk more. I know you have many questions."

Jar'ek: {"Fine!"}

Jar'ek lifted the improvised litter and pulled forward toward the now–closed portal. As he began to lower the litter to perform the opening ritual, the SEED interrupted.

SEED: {"Jar'ek, that is not necessary. Ask the AI to open it for you."}

Jar'ek: {"WHAT AI?!"}

SEED: {"You know that every Harmonic Outpost has a staff of sentients including an Artificially Intelligent Agent. Now that you have been judged worthy and melded, you will find that many resources are at your disposal, including the AI attached to this Outpost."}

Jar'ek: {"Okay. let's try this.... "}

Jar'ek: {"AI, attend me!"}

AI: {"This AI recognizes the authority of the Terran Jar'ek Constandor to Command. I Attend."}

Jar'ek: {"Please open the portal ahead."}

AI: {"As you wish. I have also ordered the reconfiguration of the Outpost to support Terran needs. Life support has been adjusted accordingly. Modifications to fixtures, furniture, controls, and medical bay will be completed shortly. I've taken the liberty of summoning an anti-grav conveyance to assist in moving the injured Terran called Kallehn."}

Once again, the massive portal slid silently into the floor and disappeared. Just on the other side of the portal, a flat, silver metallic object floated up beside Jar'ek and gently lowered itself to the floor. This must be the mentioned "conveyance." It looked like nothing more than a slab of deck plating that could float. The Terran Colonies had been using magnetic plating to help the crew have a semblance of gravity for decades. But they had never been able to solve the puzzle of creating anti-gravity fields or devices.

The conveyance lowered itself until it was resting on the deck, making it easier for Jar'ek to pull Kallehn's limp body onto it. After he was well situated, the conveyance rose to waist height and Jar'ek pulled the bar on the front. It moved easily, as if it had no real weight.

Jar'ek: {"Thank you! Is there anywhere I could find some food, water, a change of clothing and SOMEWHERE to take care of some personal hygiene needs? I've been in the same uniform for days… and I am STARVING!"}

AI: {"I will prepare nutritional supplements that should be a reasonably close facsimile of food you and your team are familiar with. Your quarters are being readied now. I've taken the liberty of assigning your entire team to the same suite of rooms."}

Jar'ek: {"Excellent!"}

Jar'ek continued pulling the conveyance forward as J'Uhr and S'Fah strode close beside him, testing the air with their sensitive noses—cataloging a plethora of new scents. Jar'ek felt their uneasiness in the current surroundings. Well, he wasn't exactly thrilled, either.

Their journey took them through the Chamber of Judgement and across to the other side. Another portal, bright amber light excising its circumference, fell out of their way and opened onto a bright white space. Light emanated from ceilings, walls and floors alike. The light was almost too bright after his eyes had adjusted to the dim light of the chamber. The air held none of the musky smell of antiquity found in the outer passageway.

As they approached a curve in the passageway ahead, the wall parted to show what appeared to be living quarters—quite luxurious living quarters—large, spacious, with floors and walls covered with a soft pliant, yet resilient fabric. Jar'ek noticed a large table across the space that had bowls, glasses, and pitchers. The pitchers were full of chilled water, with condensation running down the outside. Several bowls were placed nearby on the floor, and the two X'Ah-panths made their way to explore what the bowls had to offer them. It seemed to smell interesting to them.

What appeared to be fruit and vegetables were piled in a large tray in the center of the table.

First things first, Jar'ek thought.

After getting Kallehn settled comfortably on a pile of large pillows in the next room, Jar'ek hastily took his clothes off and walked into what could only be a hygiene facility. He stood in the middle of a transparent stall with spigots at various places in the ceiling—wondering what he had to do to get the water started.

SEED: {"AI, warm water, please—and add a mild cleansing agent."}

Jar'ek, startled, said: {"I'd almost forgotten you were still there... Er, here."}

SEED: {"Yes, we are inseparable—literally."}

Jar'ek: {"Don't remind me... ummm... could I get a little privacy while I do some necessary things?"}

SEED: {"Certainly. Just think — Privacy Off —when you want to communicate with me again."}

Jar'ek: {"Cool. Can you hear me now?"}

SEED: {"......."}

Jar'ek: {"Like I would know if he was faking! Oh, well. Whatever."}

The water streamed down like a heavy rain, but just warm enough. It ran down his hair and flowed down his muscular, defined arms, chest, and back. Jar'ek rubbed briskly with his hands and found that though the water was clean and pure to the taste, it generated a full lather. When he stopped rubbing, the lather washed away without residue.

After stepping out of the fresher, blasts of lukewarm air dried the remaining liquid from his hair and skin. He could figure out the rest of the necessary fixtures without too much difficulty and even found utensils that were designed for oral hygiene as well. Nice! He felt so much better now. He was feeling great! There was no more pain from the recent injuries. And although he was hungry and a bit tired, he felt better than he had any right to.

It seemed that saving Kallehn aside, there were some real benefits from his choice of accepting the melding. It was certainly going to take some adjustment, though.

J'Uhr and S'Fah had eaten and drank their fill. They were stretched out on the soft fabric of the floor, displaying long white fangs as they took turns yawning and grooming each other. They deserved this rest. Jar'ek knew neither cat had slept much during the whole ordeal. Kallehn was still sound asleep. Jar'ek took the torn and dirty remnants of Kallehn's uniform off and brought a wet cloth to clean him up as much as he could. He should be able to take care of himself in the next day or so. He lifted Kallehn's head and carefully gave him water from a glass. Kallehn stirred momentarily and drank greedily of the cool liquid, then lay back down and returned to a deep sleep.

Jar'ek sat beside him and brushed Kallehn's hair back from his face gently. A fresh wave of images and feelings came flooding back from their psionic connection. Jar'ek was excited and curious but embarrassed as well. All of this was very private to Kallehn. Jar'ek shook his head to push the images away. He and Kallehn should talk first. The exchange was accidental. Kallehn might feel like it was a betrayal of trust between them if he examined the feelings and thoughts that were Kallehn's to keep or share as he chose. Jar'ek partitioned those thoughts and images away in a dark corner of his mind, intent on not betraying his friend's trust.

Jar'ek slipped into a sleep he had denied himself during the crisis—deep and refreshing. He failed to notice the lights in the suite dimming, even as his heavy eyelids gave a final flutter and then closed. Lying next to each other, Jar'ek's arm resting across Kallehn's chest, their breathing and heartbeats began to build a shared rhythm—slow, shallow breaths. Seeing this, the X'Ah-Panths settled down. Falling back into a well-practiced routine, they took turns patrolling the suite of rooms while the men slept, snuggling up next to them at times for some much-needed rest.

S'Fah wasn't exactly sure what had happened to Jar'ek. He was different, somehow—that was concerning. But both human males were recovering quickly.... Nothing bad had come from the change in Jar'ek. S'Fah still felt the strong bond of trust and affection between them. Things would be okay. Jar'ek would explain when they had more time. Until then, he trusted Jar'ek with his life. He wasn't going to start doubting him now.

But all four of them had strange dreams that night….

CHAPTER 15 — A NEW DAWN

Jaden-325-4 - Planet Surface - Imperial Outpost

Jar'ek woke to bright sunlight and two X'Ah-Panths staring closely into his face. It was always disconcerting when S'Fah did this—wanting him to wake up, but not wanting to disturb his sleep. Jar'ek jumped a bit as his eyes flew open. He lay there on the pillows, alone.

The X'Ah-Panths were excited about something, but where was Kallehn?!

Hey! Wait a just a minute! SUNLIGHT?!?? What?!

S'Fah: {"YES! SUNLIGHT! MAGIC!"}

J'Uhr: {"BIG MAGIC SUNLIGHT WALL NOW WINDOW! Wake Up! Wake Up!"}

Jar'ek quickly looked around. They were still in the suite of rooms they had slept in last night. But as he turned and looked over his shoulder, his mouth fell open in amazement... that wall was GONE! And in its place, was a spectacular view of the surface of the planet at sunrise. The sun was bright, but now he realized that it was dimmed enough not to hurt when you looked directly at it. It was both stunningly beautiful—and disconcerting.

Jar'ek climbed to his feet and slowly walked toward the now-missing wall, with S'Fah and J'Uhr right against his heels, almost dancing with excitement. Jar'ek reached out his hand, thinking this was some sort of illusion. Instead of ***wall***, his fingers felt only a slight resistance, as if he were pushing against a resilient, springy barrier of some sort. Was this some sort of holographic imaging system?

Suddenly, he realized something else. He always had a telepathic link with S'Fah—the two of them had been bonded years ago, but to Jar'ek's knowledge, no X'Ah-Panth, or human for that matter, had ever been able to build a telepathic link with another outside of their bonded pair! He ***HEARD*** J'Uhr's thoughts! Or was it some trick of an overtired mind?!?

J'Uhr {"J'Uhr speaks! Jar'ek Hears!! YES! YES! GOOD, YES "}

S'Fah: {"Magic! Mind-Magic!"}

Jar'ek: {"Whoa! Settle down, Cubs! J'Uhr, can you hear my thoughts, as well??!"}

J'Uhr: {"Hear! Yes, Hear Jar'ek thoughts!!! Excitement—Joy—Wonder."}

This was amazing! Was this part of the enhancements that the SEED had mentioned? Or was this something that was affecting the X'Ah-Panths as well? Did these changes affect Kallehn, too?

KALLEHN! Where was Kallehn?! He was gone when Jar'ek woke up....

Jar'ek: {"S'Fah, where is Kallehn?!"}

S'Fah: {"Kallehn in room with falling water. His mind—sleep fuzzy."}

J'Uhr: {"Yes! Hygiene room! Kallehn Good! Thank you, Jar'ek!"}

Jar'ek: {"I am never going to get used to this!"}

Jar'ek walked quickly to the hygiene room. He needed to make sure Kallehn was indeed okay. It had only been a bit over two planetary rotations since he was near death!

Kallehn was standing in the fresher, letting the water run down his upturned face, eyes closed. Jar'ek stopped short at seeing this. The Rangers had common hygiene facilities during training and onboard ship, so Jar'ek had seen many other Rangers nude, including Kallehn. But for a moment, the way the water caressed his wet, smooth, and defined body took Jar'ek's breath away.

Jar'ek shook his head and took a more practical approach to examining Kallehn's recent injuries. He could see through the transparent walls of the fresher, the bright pink lines of healing scar tissue running down Kallehn's left leg. As far as Jar'ek could tell, Kallehn wasn't even favoring the wounded appendage, at all! This was great news!

Jar'ek burst into the fresher with Kallehn, grabbed his shoulders, and yelled, "You're all right! You're okay?!"

Kallehn opened his eyes and wiped the moisture away from his face. He raised his eyes up to Jar'ek's with a haunted look in them. He just stood there breathing deeply for a moment, and Jar'ek began to feel anxious... was he really okay? Was he upset about the unintentional side effects of the psionic melding between them? How much had he learned about Jar'ek from that brief mental encounter?! Slowly, Kallehn reached out with both hands and clasped Jar'ek's arms. His face softened and broke into a gentle grin.

Kallehn: "I feel okay. I don't remember much about what happened, and I'm pretty confused. But I really needed some time in the fresher to clear my head. Plus, I STANK! I couldn't stand myself, and J'Uhr agreed with me.... You were still asleep, and I wanted to get cleaned up before you saw me like that."

Jar'ek, sighing loudly, said: " You had me really worried, old man! I was scared to death that you were going to check-out on me! I'm very glad you are back among the living!"

Kallehn: "I need you to help me fill in the blanks in my memory. I don't understand. Where is this place? Did the Rangers send a rescue mission? What day is it? How long was I out? What happened to me? And I had some strange dreams, I think... I don't know what was real and what was a dream. "

Kallehn's eyes drifted down Jar'ek's naked body. Jar'ek's body began responding to the closeness of Kallehn's own. Jar'ek suddenly felt ashamed—did Kallehn, in that brief psionic bonding, learn his darkest secrets? Was he shocked—disgusted? Was this his way of subtly pointing out just how inappropriate Jar'ek's feelings were? Jar'ek couldn't stop his body from reacting to the situation any more than he could stop the Sun from rising or setting. He could feel his face turning red....

Jar'ek turned quickly and grabbed a set of fresh clothing from a stack he had noticed earlier to cover himself. He looked back over his shoulder and saw a change to Kallehn's features... stolid, cold, closed.

Jar'ek: "Of course, I will help. I will tell you everything I know. Don't worry about a thing... things will return to normal soon—just as they were before—you'll see."

Jar'ek walked out of the room, doing his best to hide his shame and disappointment. That look on Kallehn's face, the tenseness in his arms and torso... he thought it could only mean one thing—Kallehn ***knew*** how he felt and rejected him because of it. Jar'ek fought back the sudden tears that threatened to run down his face as he realized how much he cared for Kallehn and how badly he wanted NOT to lose him, even if it meant never speaking his feelings, never acting on them—pretending he never had them. He lost the battle, as a single clear drop of saline left a trail of moisture down his cheek before he quickly wiped it away.

S'Fah and J'Uhr exchanged glances. Each felt the maelstrom of strong emotions emanating from the two humans—the hurt, confusion, desire, and rejection. It seemed like a class 5 hurricane was tearing the suite apart, fixtures and tapestries being ripped loose from the floor and walls to fly about—all the while, the two human males acted like the storm didn't exist. Their outer countenances appeared normal, if more subdued than usual.

S'Fah and J'Uhr felt the hurt, confusion, desire and rejection—they suffered with their human mind-mates but didn't know how to help them, other than being there for them and working to rebuild the amazing team they had been and could be again. To the X'Ah-Panths, humans were so strong and courageous when facing beast or enemy—yet so fragile when it came to showing their true selves to each other. This was so foreign to the X'Ah-Panths. A X'Ah-Panth was what he or she was—once and always. There was no deception, no pretense, nothing hidden. These highly intelligent felines were at a loss when it came to understanding the complex rituals of personal interaction between humans.

Inside, the X'Ah-Panths sensed the turmoil that was the truth of those two and gave the feline equivalent of a heavy sigh.

CHAPTER 16 - THE STORY TOLD - A MIND AWAKENS

Jaden-325-4 - Planet Surface - Imperial Outpost

Kallehn found the same stack of clean garments as he followed Jar'ek out of the hygiene room. He, too, was suddenly shy about his nakedness and wanted to be properly covered as soon as possible. As he grabbed the one-piece garment, he wondered if it would be the right size. He hoped it wouldn't be too loose, or worse at the moment, too tight. It seems that his body, too, had found it necessary to react to Jar'ek's presence in the fresher.

He was so embarrassed. First, he let himself get injured and then became a burden on the rest of the team, unable to care for himself. Now, he was flooded with all those confusing feelings he had for Jar'ek. He had been able to push them away before, but now, for some reason, they were stronger than ever... defying any attempt to repress them. He shook his head to clear it and marshaled his own thoughts.

— ***FOCUS***. Jar'ek would probably want to disband the team if he found out how I really felt about him... I can't let that happen. I must bury this. It's clear Jar'ek doesn't feel the same way. He seemed so embarrassed in the fresher... he must have sensed how I felt somehow. I am an IDIOT! I came so close to ruining the closeness I worked so hard to nurture between us. And there are more pressing issues that need my attention:

—Where are we? What happened and why can't I remember? Why do I keep seeing flashes of images, sensations, and feelings of déjà vu that I can't seem to resolve? Did I really see the Dragon Eye and all of my crewmates destroyed with my own eyes? Have the Worms—the Treech—landed ground troops? Did anyone survive the attack on the Dragon Eye beyond their team? —

Suddenly, Kallehn snapped out of his mental tabulation with an adrenaline surge. J'Uhr?!? Where was J'Uhr?! Was she killed in the attack or injured? Kallehn closed his eyes and concentrated—he sent his mind-touch out across the ether, desperately seeking, searching, calling.

Kallehn: {"J'Uhr! Mind-mate, Fur-Sister, Answer my call!"}

In the main room of the suite, Jar'ek saw J'Uhr suddenly leap to all four feet and lope into the hygiene room.

Kallehn was knocked off his feet by a camouflage-spotted, fur-covered rocket of love and affection with fangs and claws as long as Kallehn's fingers!

J'Uhr straddled Kallehn's fallen form with both front paws pushing down on his chest, purring loudly and licking his entire face with long swipes from her wet sandpaper tongue. Kallehn pretended to struggle to avoid that huge tongue, swinging his face from side to side and batting away at J'Uhr's underbody. But they both knew he both craved and needed this affirmation of constancy and affection. They both did, human and feline alike.

J'Uhr: { "Joy! Relief! Affection! End to Aloneness!"}

Kallehn: {"You're okay?!? You were not injured! I am so GLAD! I could not lose you, too!"}

The thought startled Kallehn and J'Uhr... Kallehn berated himself for giving that thought life.

J'Uhr pulled back from Kallehn's face for a moment, looking deep into his eyes. Then she pushed her muzzle against the side of Kallehn's face again and again—flooding his mind with thoughts of deep affection, joy, and commitment.

J'Uhr: {"You are mine. I am yours. Always."}

Kallehn: {"I am yours. You are mine. Always, my friend...Always."}

Jar'ek and S'Fah walked in to see the two wrestling on the floor. Jar'ek grinned. This is one of the things he loved about the Team.

Kallehn and J'Uhr really were inseparable. He was glad that Kallehn had that closeness, even if he himself couldn't have that with Kallehn.

Then Jar'ek felt a bump behind his knees that almost sent him sprawling. S'Fah wound his huge body around Jar'ek's legs, muzzle raised almost to his chest level, eyes staring into his. When he had Jar'ek's undivided attention, his mind-touch resounded with the words immortalized in the X'Ah-Panther/Ranger bonding ritual.

S'Fah: {"You are mine! I am yours! Always."}

Jar'ek: {"I am yours! You are mine! Always."}

S'Fah: {"Perceptions cloudy. Future unresolved. Trust Kallehn. Heart good. Team strong."}

Jar'ek: {"Acknowledged."}

That was the strangest interchange he had ever had with S'Fah. Their mind-touch was indeed stronger after the recent changes.... It almost appeared as if S'Fah was "mentoring" him. Jar'ek wasn't quite sure what the message was, other than that Kallehn was still a good person, a committed Team member and trustworthy. The rest of the message bore some thought... it was a bit of a mystery.

More food and drink seemed to appear on the large table in the main room periodically. Jar'ek wasn't sure how that happened, but finding out had not been a real priority. It was enough that they were all well fed and watered, including the X'Ah-Panths. The humans sat down to eat their first meal together since before the attack of the Treech Marauder. They ate in relative silence. Kallehn hadn't eaten in days and was near starving. So Jar'ek waited until he was sated and ready to hear the answers to his earlier questions.

Kallehn belched long and loudly, drawing the attention of both X'Ah-Panths, wondering if he was in gastrointestinal distress.

Jar'ek just stared wide-eyed in admiration of the quality of the event. Kallehn blushed and apologized for his rude behavior.

Jar'ek: "I'm just glad you are back to normal! I've missed having you by my side. I need your—I mean, the Team needs your sharp wits and logic—to get us all through this."

Kallehn heard Jar'ek correct himself and his heart soared. Jar'ek needed him! There was hope that the relationship had not been damaged beyond repair. Perhaps he was not beyond redemption, even now. Kallehn couldn't help but smile, and he was heartened to see Jar'ek return it.

Kallehn: "Well, I don't remember much of what happened over the past several days, but I do remember that I was never alone. I remember your voice telling me I was not alone, that you were going to take care of me. I remember J'Uhr nuzzling me and thinking her anxiety and love for me. I am grateful to have you both... and S'Fah, I love you, too!"

Rubbing his muzzle against Kallehn's waist and chest S'Fah sent a thought to him: {"Strong affection, Kallehn. We welcome you back."}

J'Uhr: {"The Team is not, without you, Kallehn. J'Uhr not live without you. Silly cub needs a leash! No more danger!"}

Kallehn said verbally with a huskiness in his voice: "Okay, okay! I love you all. I'll be more careful in future—FINE! Now, for goodness sake, let's move on to some explanations! What the hell is going on?!?"

Jar'ek: "You better sit down—this is a long story, and it might be hard to believe—I don't understand it all myself—and to tell the truth, one of the reasons I'm glad you are back is that I've been scared to death that I've screwed things up even worse than they already were."

Kallehn: "Well, I am ALREADY sitting down... as you can SEE.

And THIS sounds like it is going to be GOOD! I can't wait to hear it. So, quit stalling and tell me how you have screwed things up WORSE than the destruction of the Dragon Eye by a Treech Marauder after centuries of peace! Go ahead! The confessional is now open...."

Jar'ek rolled his eyes and smirked, saying: "Okay, you ***asked*** for it!"

Over the next hour, Jar'ek related the history of the Team since the KKM explosion that injured Kallehn so badly. Kallehn listened intently without interruption, occasionally reaching down to caress J'Uhr's cheeks and ears, as she was permanently attached to his side, it seemed. As Jar'ek was relating the details of their journey to the Outpost and the treatment of his injuries, Kallehn could swear that his mind-touch was picking up images, sensations, and even emotions. At first, he thought they were from J'Uhr, which would have been possible... but these were much stronger and more clear than the communications he shared with his furred companion. It didn't seem possible, but he could swear they were coming from Jar'ek! Neither of the humans had measured high enough on the Psi scale to have telepathic connections with other humans.

The Psi connections to the X'Ah-Panths were possible because of the uniquely matched architecture of their brains and centuries of genetic manipulation of the X'Ah-Panths. Genetic manipulation of the human stock over the same length of time had provided some enhancements to the species, at large. These included increased Psi abilities and the frequency of occurrence within the general population. The screening process to be qualified for the Rangers was extensive. Only one in a hundred-thousand was eventually paired with a X'Ah-Panth. And the final selection was made by the X'Ah-Panths themselves.

Yet something had happened, Kallehn thought. Something was different. Do I imagine this stronger connection simply because I want something I can never have with Jar'ek? No, something else is going on—I am certain of it. When Jar'ek got to the place in the story where the Judgement was offered, Kallehn's jaw dropped in shock. He felt a chill down his spine, his lips became numb, and his heart began pounding in his chest. He stood up quickly, put both hands on the table and leaned forward, staring into Jar'ek's eyes.

Kallehn: "WHAT HAVE YOU DONE?!"

Jar'ek lowered his gaze. He couldn't look Kallehn in the eyes. Even now, he wasn't sure he understood the full ramifications of his choice to proceed with Judgement.

Jar'ek: "I had no choice! I refused to let you die when there was a chance I could do something to save you… I could not live with the thought that I had let you die…."

Kallehn (rubbing his face with his hands): "So, you put your life at risk if you failed the Judgement of this Alien sentience or computer or whatever… And if you PASSED the Judgement, you agreed to be its SLAVE for the rest of your life?"

Jar'ek: "Uhhh…well, when you put it like that, it… does sound a bit irrational… but it isn't quite like that."

Kallehn: "Oh, really? Then how would you explain it? Enlighten me, PLEASE. I mean, don't get me wrong! It was incredibly selfless of you to risk your own life in this way to save mine. But I wouldn't want you to die for me to live. And I certainly wouldn't want you to be enslaved the rest of your life, either!! Maybe we can renegotiate this contract—maybe they will take me instead! I was the one that needed saving, after all!"

Jar'ek (smiling broadly): "So, it's okay for you to become an Alien's slave to save me, but not the other way around, huh?! Hmmm… Really, we both know that either of us and for that matter, any of our Team, would sacrifice themselves to save any other member of the Team. I have no doubt that given the same situation in reverse, you would have readily sacrificed yourself for me. And, luckily, as it turns out, I didn't have to die for the chance to save you... NO, you were SAVED—I did NOT die—And I only have to be an Alien's symbiotic partner (note, NOT slave) for the rest of my life. In retrospect, I think I got the better end of the bargain."

Kallehn: "By symbiotic partner... you mean HOST, don't you??!"

Jar'ek: "Kallehn, I am just a LITTLE freaked out about this, myself. So, could you find it in your heart to be just a little supportive of me and the difficult choices I felt I needed to make in order to SAVE YOUR LIFE!?! Plus, it is not like there is much that can be done about it now. And there are some advantages to me personally. And I think there may be some advantages for the entire human race."

Kallehn: "Alien host for only 48 hours and already you are having delusions of grandeur! Jar'ek, a megalomaniac in training! It is a good thing you have me around to bring you back to terra firma. Remember, I've had to hang around with you on missions where you have not showered in a handful of planetary rotations. So, don't be acting all 'God-like' to me, buddy!"

Through the tense banter, Jar'ek got the real message. And part of it was delivered non-verbally. It was a surprise to find that Kallehn was subconsciously broadcasting emotions, images, and sensations—much like the mind-touch between Jar'ek and S'Fah—to supplement his verbal communication.

The message was: Thank you! And Alien influence or not, whatever the future holds, We Stand Together. You may have sacrificed your life for mine, but now I promise you will not bear the consequences alone.

Kallehn sat down slowly, took a deep breath, and reached across the table to grasp both Jar'ek's hands.

Kallehn: "We are a ***TEAM***. We will work through this together. You did not abandon me, and I won't abandon you now. Besides, if this entity was malevolent, J'Uhr and S'Fah would have sensed it by now. So, when do I meet this Alien? Does he talk through you? If he/she/it is going to be a permanent fixture, we should get the introductions over with."

J'Uhr and S'Fah perked up their ears with some sense of expectation—like they sensed some quarry in the high grasses and were stalking it... but they showed no alarm, just deep interest.

Jar'ek: No, he doesn't speak through me or take control of me like a drone or anything like that. He is mostly quiet and acts more like a data repository. Other times, he is my mentor and teacher. I don't sense any real emotions from him. He doesn't seem to get angry... frustrated with me sometimes, perhaps. As a matter of fact, I haven't heard anything from him in almost a full rotation! D'oh! Holy crap! I forgot I put him on mute! Errr, Privacy Mode, that is."

Kallehn: "Ha! I know how he feels! I can hardly get a word in edgewise with you! You talk incessantly!"

Jar'ek grimaced then gave Kallehn a stern look, saying: "Shut up while I communicate with my 'Alien Slave Master.' "

Kallehn smiled: "Now I know you haven't been taken over by an Alien influence. Mastering your personal brand of sarcasm would take decades of practice."

Jar'ek shook his head at this latest jab and thought to himself: Okay, how did this go? If I had to say PRIVACY ON to disappear the SEED, let us try:

Jar'ek: {"Privacy OFF."}

SEED: {"Well, it is about time! I thought you had drowned in the fresher! Exactly how long do your personal hygiene rituals take?! You do realize that the rest of the galaxy is in continuing turmoil while you avail yourself of rest and relaxation, don't you?!?"}

Jar'ek: {"Good morning to you, too! So, we need to discuss the happenings since I forgot to bring you back from Privacy Mode. It could take a while."}

SEED: {"If you allow it, I can query the AI for a complete update excluding time spent in the hygiene room. Alternatively, I could access your own memories of the events."}

Jar'ek: {"So, you cannot access this information if I don't allow it?"}

SEED: {"Not without the AI declaring a state of emergency and overriding the privacy protocols."}

Jar'ek: {"Cool! Well, I think the AI recordings should have all the information you need. Plus, I'd like to keep my own thoughts during that time private for the time being. AI, Attend me."}

AI: {"AI, attending."}

Jar'ek: {"Please allow the SEED complete access to any and all recordings and information regarding what has transpired and been discussed within our suite of rooms since Privacy Mode was engaged, excluding the hygiene room."}

AI: {"Confirmed. Access is granted."}

SEED: {"Ahhh.... So, quite a lot has transpired! I'm glad to see that your friend is well on his way to mending. You see that your choice was a wise one, don't you?"}

Jar'ek: {"Yes, well, I am glad Kallehn is alive and well. As to the rest of our bargain, only time will tell whether I end up regretting my choice or not. I am going to hold you to your promise of providing aid to my people."}

SEED: {"Understood. Although this transition will be difficult for you at times, I feel certain that you will see great benefit for your species, in the end. You will not regret your decision, Jar'ek. I promise you that."}

Jar'ek: {"Well, good. I hope you are right. But for now, some introductions and some answers are in order."}

SEED: {"As you wish. But time has been in short supply and expedience has ruled. There are some formalities and protocols that must be fulfilled before we go any further. "}

Jar'ek: {"Oh, dear... What now? Do I have to sacrifice small animals or something?"}

SEED: {"Please! Nothing so crude. Keep in mind that although the rituals may seem arcane to you, there are millennia of tradition and social evolution behind them. Your species was still living in caves when Takesh and the SEED were melded and formed the Harmonic Empire. And, being who you now are, these are YOUR rituals, as well. Given more time, your brain will be able to assimilate more of the vast store of data transferred during the melding process. Then you will understand all. Until then, however, I must be your guide. You must trust me when I tell you these formalities, protocols, and rituals are relevant and incredibly important—not to mention, time-sensitive. So, in your vernacular, 'suck it up' and do your duty. Or do you feel regret at choosing to save your friend? Or perhaps your people no longer need help.... "}

In a very vivid flashback of the recent past, Jar'ek was back in the Chamber of Judgement... Pain and fatigue were his close companions—he felt the sharp chill of the air on his exposed skin, the confusing odors in the chamber of both age and renewal—and the overpowering despair at the thought of losing Kallehn shook him like a thunderclap. His gut twisted and tightened, he broke into a cold sweat—thoughts of helplessness—fears of not being up to the task—all of this washed over Jar'ek as if he had jumped back in time, somehow. Then, just as quickly, he was back in the present, standing next to a fully recovered Kallehn with a strange look on his face.

Jar'ek: {"SEED, did you show that to me?!"}

SEED: {"No, Jar'ek. Memory recall for you has been enhanced dramatically. It was a necessary modification to allow you to organize, recall, and experience the myriad memories from all the prior meldings. It will take some getting used to. But you now have perfect recall. And more than that, you can 'experience' the memories as if you were there again. With practice and my guidance, you will learn to control it so that it is not so shocking or distracting—becomes second nature."}

Jar'ek was silent for a while....

Jar'ek: {"To answer your question: no, I do not regret my choice. Though I may yet lose everything that is important to me, I would make the same choice again...."}

Jar'ek closed his eyes and lowered his head, feeling shame for even toying with the idea that he might regret the choice he made, and even try to renege on some of the specifics.

SEED: {Good. I am glad you feel that way. Things will be difficult for you in the short run, and perhaps the long of it, as well. But the part you play in the future will be an important one. And you will have the opportunity to be of significant help to your people. And perhaps not only the Terrans... but that is for another day. For now, two important formalities (rituals, if you will) must be fulfilled. Firstly, the 'Naming.' Lastly, the 'Marking' It is customary for the host to name the SEED once the melding is completed. 'SEED' is a generic title. Although I am made up of many constituent parts, my life experience is unique. And since I am trapped inside you for the foreseeable future, our relationship will work better if I have a name that you are comfortable with. Wait...Please consider rejecting your first thought for my name—it will be PUBLIC knowledge, after all. And I don't think slang for a human body part is an appropriate moniker for someone of my station. But it IS your choice."}

Jar'ek (chuckling to himself): {"Okay, okay. Let me think on it for a while, and I will try to find something more appropriate. While I am doing that, perhaps you could explain the 'Marking' part... exactly what is that?"}

SEED: {"You must wear the Harmonic Seal. It is required. In part, it is a credential or identification. It is also a symbol. It identifies you as the Primary Harmonic Meld."}

Jar'ek: {"So, it is like the Ranger Badge on my uniform?"}

SEED: {"Hmm... in a way, yes...."}

Jar'ek: {"You said it is a symbol. What does it symbolize?"}

SEED: {"Hope—Promise—Protection—Knowledge—Honesty—Compassion—Authority."}

Jar'ek: {"Well that sounds pretty cool! It is very similar to the Ranger Credo."}

SEED: {"Yes... on a somewhat larger scale."}

Jar'ek: {"So, is there a uniform or something? Is that where the badge goes?"}

SEED: {"Well, there is a uniform, but the 'Marking' doesn't go on it... it goes on YOU."}

Jar'ek: {"Huh? What? How?"}

SEED: {"This might sting a bit. But it will be over quickly...."}

Several sprites of bright blue light burst into being on Jar'ek's right temple. They danced down the side of his face, along his neck and under the utilitarian garments that he had been provided with when leaving the hygiene room. Everywhere the sprites went, an intricate tracing was left behind on the skin, forming a tattoo. The sprites continued their work down his chest, right arm, abdomen, and right leg. The sprites could be seen dimly through the material as they made their way to the floor.

To Jar'ek, it felt like live embers had blown from an open fire onto his face and were running down his body. He yelled in pain, jumped back and began patting himself down as if to put out a fire.

All the while, Kallehn, and the two X'Ah-Panths were watching in amazement as Jar'ek jerked about, slapping at various parts of his body that were alight with what looked like tiny blue flames. Kallehn's mouth hung open, his eyes wide. He suddenly jumped up, ran to the table and grabbed the pitcher of cool water that was there. He ran back with it and, just as the flames reached a terminal point on Jar'ek's right foot, tossed the entire contents right onto Jar'ek's face and chest.

Jar'ek stumbled backward and shook his head, showering the entire room and all of its occupants with a spray of water droplets. He stood there, feet apart, his one-piece garment soaked and half torn from his body from his previous antics while the Marking progressed. Eyes still closed, he coughed and yelled: "What the FUCK?!"

Two voices talked over each other with different explanations—one verbal, one telepathic

SEED: "Calm yourself! It is done. I told you it would sting a bit. I didn't think you'd make such a big fuss about a little pain...."

Kallehn: "You were on FIRE! I was just trying to put you out! What the hell WAS that?? Shit, you have burns on your face—let me look at those."

Kallehn walked over and took Jar'ek's chin in his right hand and gently traced the darkened skin with his fingertips. Jar'ek felt no pain. Upon closer inspection, Kallehn recognized that these were not really burns, but tattoos of an intricate and impressive design.

Kallehn: "Holy crap! Those are some sort of tattoos! What the hell is happening to you, Jar'ek?"

Jar'ek took a deep breath and gently removed Kallehn's hand from his face: *{"SEED, might you have better prepared me for what* *was going to happen? I can tolerate a good deal of pain without complaint if I am prepared for it. For the sake of all that is sacred! Kallehn thought I was on FIRE, and so did I."}*

SEED: {"My apologies. I am still getting to know your species and you, in particular. It won't happen again. In my defense, I thought it would be best to get it over with quickly. I had no way of knowing that the junior fire department wizard over there would feel it necessary to douse us both with ice cold water! In future, I see that I may want to explain things in greater detail in ADVANCE of rituals that are unfamiliar to you and your Team."}

Jar'ek: {"I would strongly SUGGEST that it would be your most prudent approach! Apology accepted. Now, EXPLAIN, please...."}

SEED: {"Very well. The 'Meld-Marking' is a permanent tattoo created by surface changes at the molecular level. Your genes have been altered so that any progeny will bear similar marks, as your position in the Empire is hereditary. The tattoo in your progeny will only become visible after a Melding has been successfully completed. All hosts must be judged worthy, or they will not succeed you in your position."}

Jar'ek: {"That seems strange. Why would you have a succession for a low-level position like mine? What exactly is my position, other than being a host for you?"}

SEED: {"Mmm... I have not been looking forward to this discussion."}

Jar'ek: {"Well, spit it out. It must be pretty bad if you are so hesitant to discuss it. What? Am I working as hygiene facility maintenance or something? Does that mean I'd have to leave the Team?! I'm not trying to back out of the deal. It is worth it no matter what I have to do, but...."}

SEED: {"Hmmm... very noble of you. We shall see how long that attitude lasts."}

Jar'ek: {"Just tell me!"}

SEED: {"You see, I was only supposed to visit this Outpost for a few dozen planetary rotations. None of the line of succession had passed judgment. It was unprecedented! We had nearly 25 trials scheduled in this sector when the cataclysm occurred, and we were ordered to shelter in place until the quarantine was lifted. It was never lifted...."}

Jar'ek: {"Go on."}

SEED: {"Well, when your ship entered this system, I was awakened by automated systems. Our mission took on a new significance in light of the Empire's fall. I sensed the presence of your mind when your Team disembarked. I used what influence I could to get you started in the right direction. I'm sorry that I didn't notice the Treech Marauder until it was too late. The Outpost didn't consider them a threat because of their primitive design and weaponry. As it turns out, Terrans are especially well suited to meld with Harmonic SEED. Your level of Psionic abilities singled you out. And the ritual of Judgement proved the quality of your character, despite your sarcastic and irreverent tendencies. You were what I was seeking, all along."}

Jar'ek: {"I don't understand... Line of succession for what?! And why would they have sent a ship out looking for someone like me?"}

SEED: {"Why, line of succession to the Imperial Throne, your Highness..."}

Jar'ek was stunned into silence. His ears and mouth felt numb. His heart was racing, and he gasped suddenly as he realized he was holding his breath.,Kallehn grabbed Jar'ek by the arm and shook him. He looked deeply into his eyes and said:

Kallehn: "What is wrong with you?!? Is something else going to burst into flames? Do I need more water?"

Jar'ek: "I don't think so... but I do need to sit down... I'm not feeling very well."

Kallehn helped maneuver his friend to a comfortable stack of cushions in the corner of the room. He then went and got a glass filled with water and brought it back to him.

Jar'ek: "Are you going to throw that in my face, too?!"

Kallehn grimed and said: "Nah, I thought I'd let you actually drink this one. Here, you look like you need it."

Jar'ek took the offered glass and drank deeply, thinking to himself that he sure could use something a bit stronger right about now....

Kallehn: "Yeah, you don't look so hot... pardon the pun. I mean, you were just sprouting flames a minute ago."

Kallehn: "So, relax where you are, but you better SPILL before I start to lose what is left of my mind, son!"

Jar'ek: {"SEED, can I share my recollections of the whole story with the rest of my Team psionically? Something tells me I should be able to, but I can't recall exactly how. I think that would save us a LOT of time."}

SEED: {"You can, Sire. I will expose you to that part of your extended memories. There... that should provide you with the necessary insights."}

Jar'ek: {"Ah... okay, I see it now. Thanks... but can you quit calling me 'Sire'?! That is totally freaking me out right now!"}

Jar'ek: "Kallehn, you know the sort of mind-touch you have with J'Uhr? "

Kallehn: "Of course. What kind of question is that?! How could I not be familiar with mind-touch between a bonded pair? J'Uhr and I rely on it all the time. So?"

Jar'ek: "If you trust me, I can show you how we can have that type of connection between you and me. And once connected in such a way, I can share my memories with you. I suggest this now for three reasons. First, it is a long story, and this will be much faster than telling the story verbally. Secondly, you will be able to have complete faith in everything you see. You know deception doesn't work in mind-touch. And lastly, I want to do it this way because I will be able to share it with the rest of the Team at the same time. Do you trust me?"

Kallehn sat in quiet reflection for a moment, then sighed deeply.

Kallehn: "Jar'ek, I trust you with my life and even more.... Do what you think best."

The X'Ah-Panths stopped trying to lick the water droplets off their fur abruptly—this might be interesting.... They could understand quite a lot of human speech, even though their mouths and throats were not capable of producing the sounds that would allow two-way communication. They joined the two human males, who had moved to a cross-legged position sitting on the floor. They faced each other—dark brown eyes wide open, gazing deeply into Kallehn's hazel orbs.

Kallehn (nervously): "Sssooo—How does this work?"

Jar'ek (grinning): "Well, I know how to do this in theory. No promises. But it will help if we have some physical contact. Place your arms on top of mine and grasp my forearms. "

Kallehn did as he was told and laid his bare arms palm down on top of Jar'ek's. They held on to each other's forearms, and Jar'ek squeezed Kallehn's arm quickly twice—reassuring him.

Jar'ek: "Ok, now clear your mind just like we learned in Basic Ranger Training. Once we are both in a meditative state, this should be rather straightforward. It should feel a lot like when J'Uhr reaches out her mind-touch to you...but stronger—clearer. Ummm, it might be a little disorienting at first. Just stay calm and hang on."

Kallehn: "I'm not a raw recruit. I'm ready. Proceed."

Jar'ek closed his eyelids slowly, breathed deeply and sensed that Kallehn was doing the same. He heard his friend's regular breathing. He matched the rhythm of inhale, hold, exhale. His cleared his mind of all thought except one—Seek.

He felt his consciousness stretching, reaching, and gently spanning the physical and psionic gap between them. It was as if part of him had left his very body and was moving throughout darkened space. There was no sense of hot or cold, no smell, no visual cues. There was a sensation of motion, however— and acceleration, as if he were physically flying across a great void. As the edges of his consciousness continued to expand, Jar'ek lost all sense of time and space. He began to experience an odd feeling—a tingling sensation—more clear. He realized it was a heartbeat. He felt his own heart beating a slightly slower rhythm. The two rhythms became one as the other heartbeat took on Jar'ek's own. Jar'ek understood that he was sensing Kallehn's heartbeat.

The electrical sensation reached a crescendo and was suddenly gone as if he had burst through some restraining barrier. A coalescing fog surrounded him. He cried out Kallehn's name. Kallehn's voice called back to him, in the distance... The fog continued to coalesce and dissipate.

When the mist finally cleared, Jar'ek found himself in a forest clearing—bright daylight shined down from a midmorning sun. The green, calf-high grass bent and flowed in a light breeze. It must be early spring, wherever this was... It was not a place Jar'ek was familiar with. He could hear water gurgling in a small brook nearby. There were gosha trees and tallspike plants that defined the gentle transition between forest and meadow. Jar'ek inhaled, reveling in the scent of fresh kasha blossoms and sweetgrass. It was a nice place.

Jar'ek heard his name called again, this time from much closer. He turned and saw Kallehn waving one hand high as he casually strolled out of the woods. He was wearing a simple white shirt with short sleeves, rugged shorts, and hiking boots. He had a long piece of sweetgrass between his lips, enjoying the sweet, refreshing taste. Kallehn was grinning ear-to-ear as he approached and slapped Jar'ek on the back, spat out the sweetgrass and spoke through a broad smile.

Kallehn: "Hello, Jar'ek! I am so glad to see you! This place is amazing! It was my favorite place back home. I used to hike for hours to get here. I'd bring camping gear and supplies and catch Foo-Fish in the brook. I never took anyone else to this place, my hidden meadow. I wanted to share this special place with you for a long time, but it wasn't possible. How are we here—or how is it we seem to be here?"

Jar'ek: "I think this is your creation, Kallehn. Our minds are creating a logical construct for what is happening between us…an interpretation of our connection—our meeting of minds. Your mind has taken us both to the place that you love most. And I am very happy that you shared it with me. I love it, too. It looks like somewhere in the great forests of the northern hemisphere on New Hope colony."

Kallehn: "Exactly right! This is home to me."

Jar'ek placed his arm on Kallehn's shoulder, too.

Jar'ek: "What say you? Should we now invite our mind-mates to join us in the perfect place?

Kallehn (smiling even bigger): YES! How do we bring them here?"

Jar'ek raised his free arm out at shoulder length, palm up, toward the edge of the forest. It was another metaphor for his mind reaching out to the two X'Ah-Panths. As he felt the two sparks of consciousness across the ether, he saw the two felines running out of the forest in their direction.

S'Fah: {"Joy! Happiness! Play! Run! Chase! Good Place!"}

J'Uhr: {"Good! Good! Good! Play, too!"}

The two cats ran around the Rangers jumping, carousing, and tousling with each other until they both ended up rolling in the grass. Pieces of dry grass clung to their pelts, and they rubbed against their human teammates. The four of them found a comfortable spot to sit next to the brook and just enjoyed living in the present. Eventually, Kallehn looked over at Jar'ek with an air of expectation.

Kallehn: "Man, this is amazing! And I want us all to be able to visit here again. But I also want to know the full story of what happened since the attack. I need to know. I think we are all ready if you are."

Jar'ek: "This has been amazing. It is a good place. Thank you for sharing this with me. "

Jar'ek: "But you are right. There is another, more pressing purpose in this. Pay close attention. Ask, and I shall answer to the best of my ability.

Jar'ek took his left hand and moved it slowly in a high arc over his head from right to left as if he were wiping the sky away with a single motion. And that is exactly what he did.

The vista changed as Jar'ek's hand moved across the sky. The brook, forest, and grass disappeared to be replaced with the green and purple ground cover found on Planet Jaden-325-4. There, just as it had been—events began to unfold—so that all might see and hear what had happened in the recent past....from Jar'ek's perspective.

Suddenly, an incredibly bright light flashed just over the eastern horizon... in the direction of the Dragon Eye landing site.

Jar'ek: "Shit! Kallehn! They dropped a KKM (Kinetic Kill Munition) on the Dragon Eye! HURRY!

Kallehn picked up his pace until dust was flying up from every footfall; running headlong—mindless of the danger of an uncontrolled leap over the ridge, knowing that sure death could fly like an arrow upon his heels.

Just as Kallehn vaulted over the low ridge and began his fall to the other side, the shockwave hit—

As the memories flowed resolutely like a raging river, inexorable, strung together in sequence, a part of Jar'ek's mind worried how this might change their relationship. What they were seeing was not just a 3D projection—It was a complete representation of the experiences. It reproduced every detail of visual, auditory, olfactory experiences—and emotions… thoughts. Jar'ek re-lived the desperate fear that he had lost Kallehn.

As the events ran their course all around them, Jar'ek watched Kallehn closely, trying to decipher the complex emotions that washed across his countenance. It was a strange feeling, interfacing with another human mind in a shared memory. He clearly saw Kallehn's psionic avatar—how Kallehn thought of himself. It was nearly identical to how Jar'ek saw him, but there were subtle differences: Kallehn's avatar was younger than his actual age, less sure of himself, conflicted, but also more open. It was almost impossible to hide or soften your emotions through such a connection. It was like looking at the face of a child, where every emotion and thought flashed across the face in bold strokes. It was disconcerting, at first—intimate, open, honest, without artificial barriers.

Even though the SEED had helped him remember the process of creating such a connection, Jar'ek had never experienced it himself until now. Without the years of mental preparation that most hosts underwent, he realized that he, too, might be unable to fully control his own thoughts and feelings—and unable to shield them from Kallehn altogether.

He felt shame at having his inner thoughts bared. The conflicting thoughts and desires that would never have been shared outside of a psionic link suddenly threatened to overwhelm his mental control and flood through the exchange of memories. He was sure that a few broke through and found their way into Kallehn's consciousness.

At least those desires would be somewhat out of context, Jar'ek hoped. After all, so much was going on, Perhaps the depth and breadth of his affection would remain his own secret for now. He didn't want Kallehn to feel his doubts. He didn't want to wonder if Kallehn truly appreciated what he would still sacrifice to save his friend—his very heart. Revealing everything to Kallehn would be selfish. It wasn't what Kallehn or the rest of the Ranger team needed right now. Jar'ek would have to be patient and keep the rest to himself for now—perhaps for all time. It was just one more sacrifice—in a series of sacrifices—one he desperately hoped he wouldn't have to make. Because of his status as a Harmonic Meld, it might prove impossible for him to stay with Kallehn. It might very well make him incompatible with the entire Ranger Team...

And perhaps... the entire Human Race.

Jar'ek pushed those thoughts far away, into a very dark corner of his mind. He didn't have time to deal with self-pity at the moment. And the very last thing he wanted to do was to let Kallehn know just how afraid he was for the future. He didn't want to exacerbate Kallehn's sense of guilt and responsibility any more than he could help. Jar'ek knew that he would make the same choice to save his friend again, without a moment's hesitation. And as for the future?

Only time would tell.

For now, Kallehn would need time to process. He was taking in a lot right now. They would both need rest. Tomorrow, the Team would talk and decide on next steps, together—even if that meant Jar'ek's personal rejection. Jar'ek heaved a heavy sigh. If he was lucky, he wouldn't have to stand alone. He hoped his Team would understand what had happened and stand beside him, as they always had.

Meanwhile, Kallehn had his own doubts about the psionic connection. He had never heard of this working between two humans, although it was well established between the genetically modified X'Ah-Panths and their human mind-mates. Terran scientists were always looking for ways to manipulate the human genome that would break the man-to-man psionic barrier. To date, they had had little success. Yet Kallehn knew something had happened to Jar'ek that had changed him.

He was still Jar'ek—J'Uhr confirmed this in her thought connection to Kallehn. Both J'Uhr and S'Fah would know if an Alien influence had taken over Jar'ek. J'Uhr, when queried, insisted that S'Fah still knew Jar'ek's mind and spirit—that S'Fah had no doubts and still trusted Jar'ek without reservation. That was good news to Kallehn. He needed his friend like never before. He was terrified that he had lost him to some ancient Alien specter that had taken his willing body as a host in exchange for Kallehn's own life. He didn't think he could live with that....

But he had never once lost faith in Jar'ek. He would have trusted him even if S'Fah had been repulsed by the new melding. And even though he had doubts this psionic connection could be made between them, where Jar'ek led, Kallehn would follow. That was that.

Kallehn followed Jar'ek's instructions. His hands clasped Jar'ek's strong, muscled forearms, as his, in turn, were grasped by Jar'ek. He considered Jar'ek's deep brown eyes, returning the intense, seeking stare. As Jar'ek's eyelids slowly closed, so Kallehn's followed. He recalled the meditation training they had both experienced when they were raw recruits learning to improve their weak, stumbling attempts at mind-touch with the X'Ah-Panths.

Now, it was routine. Kallehn could enter a meditative state quickly and easily.

He inhaled deeply, slowly exhaling and letting that long, slow exhale be the metaphor his mind needed to drain away extraneous thoughts, impressions, and sensations. With every inhalation, he felt his consciousness becoming lighter, expanding beyond the confines of his physical self. With every slow, gentle exhale, he felt the tiny particles of thoughts, memories, sensations, and emotions drifting down and out through his metaphorical lungs. As he focused on his breathing, his heartbeat began to beat out a slow staccato rhythm. He consciously slowed that beat even further, extending the times between heartbeats as he also extended the length of his expirations and the pauses in between.

Soon, he was floating in a void—darkness—but not cold or uninviting. It was more familiar—a comforting nothingness. As his consciousness floated weightlessly in the darkness, his mind, as human minds were want to do, created another metaphor… a spectral avatar. He gazed down at his body and recognized its likeness. It was his, that was true. But it was a younger self, he remembered clearly. Even though his physical body was a few years older and much stronger and more fit from years of Ranger training, Kallehn still saw himself and this shy, vulnerable younger man of 18 Solar Orbits… just before he entered the Ranger Academy.

His avatar was a complex metaphor. It reflected his own self-doubt, worry that he wasn't good enough to actually be a Ranger—certainly not good enough to be a member of Ranger Team Alpha of the Dragon Eye—and in no way good enough to justify the affection and camaraderie of someone like Jar'ek Constandor—Mr. Perfect. Jar'ek: Always the smartest one in the room, the best scores on any exam, first to cross any finish line, good at everything he ever tried—the most attractive man ever to exist—with some strange power over Kallehn that could make him weak in the knees and a bit nauseous whenever he deigned to place a hand on his arm, an arm on his shoulder.

And NOW, Jar'ek had sacrificed everything to save Kallehn! Although Kallehn was glad to be alive and healthy again, he had no idea how he was going to make it up to Jar'ek. All he knew was that he was going to spend the rest of his life trying.

His avatar began feeling new sensations—something akin to a gentle breeze that disturbs the small hairs on your arms in its passing, causing a chill to run down your spine. He sensed it was more than a breeze, that this was another part of the metaphor his mind was using to help explain the new spectral world he found himself in. He sensed something else: a presence that was part of that cool, gentle breeze…a presence he realized that he recognized. A smile lit his face, and the world around him began to take form from the dark void it had been. A mist obscured his vision, and soon an increasing source of brilliance above began to light the newly forming vista. Kallehn could make out the Sun creating orange and purple highlights in the fluffy white clouds that punctuated the light blue sky as they slowly made their glorious way across it. A forest appeared around him, with a small clearing a short distance away—and he sensed sounds, nature, a bubbling brook, and the wind rustling the leaves and stems of the familiar plant life around him.

Still smiling and walking into the clearing, he recognized the place. It was a strong and happy memory for him. He had spent many spring and summer nights here growing up. It was his secret place. He had never shared it with anyone else. He smiled even more broadly—how appropriate that I can share it now with Jar'ek, he thought. He felt his heart nearly burst as he saw his friend walking toward him from the woods bordering the meadow on the other side. Jar'ek was also smiling broadly. It was easy to forget that this was not the real world—that they were abandoned on a largely unexplored planet, under the possible threat of Treech Ground Troops seeking them out—not to mention an Alien invasion of Jar'ek's mind and body with unknown repercussions…. Kallehn pushed his fears back and tried to just enjoy this moment, dreading the fact that it would soon end.

After the X'Ah-Panths had joined them, it was time for Jar'ek to begin sharing his memories of recent events. Kallehn didn't know what to expect, but it was clear that the psionic connection was working! He opened his mind and waited for what was to come. Whatever it was, it was better to know.

Impressions, thoughts, emotions, and flashes of images mixed together in a brief maelstrom as the flow of memories began in earnest. Kallehn had no time to sort them out but relegated them to memory so he could review them later. He knew they were important. They were an intimate glimpse into Jar'ek's soul. It was a glimpse he desperately wanted to investigate and understand. This caused him some guilty feelings because he strongly suspected this was an accidental exposure of intensely private thoughts. He would decide what to do about it later. Right now, the river of memories threatened to overwhelm him....

With a swipe of Jar'ek's hand across the sky, the calm, inviting meadow disappeared and was overtaken by a scene of violence, crushing pain and intense emotions....

CHAPTER 17—AN END TO OLD HABITS

Jaden-325-4 - Planet Surface - Imperial Outpost

Jar'ek slept fitfully that night and rose early, tired, but frustrated. As he cleaned up in the fresher, thoughts, fears, and doubts filled his head like a torrent. After drying off, he reached out for another pair of clean utilities but found none. Instead, a new wall panel slid open, revealing a folded stack of garments made of a fabric that was new to him. It was black—deep black. It was so black that his eyes felt a bit odd as he tried to focus on the material.

SEED: {"I took the liberty of having the maintenance bots manufacture a set of uniforms for you. I hope you like them. We can modify the design and color schemes to suit your personal tastes. I think you'll find it quite a step up from your previous uniform. It will never get dirty for one thing. And it is extremely durable. Also, it has a few built-in safety features."}

Jar'ek: {"I'd rather wear my Ranger uniform... I would feel more like myself—more comfortable."}

SEED (long pause) : { "Jar'ek, you know you can never wear that uniform again. And what's more, you know why."}

Jar'ek's head dropped, and he gazed into nothingness for some time. Then with a heavy sigh, he said: "I am damaged goods as far as the Rangers will see it. I've been compromised. I've betrayed my oath to my people and to the Rangers... I don't deserve to wear the uniform."

SEED: {"Perhaps that is the way your people will see you—for a time. But you have taken on a much greater role and responsibility in the future of not only your own species but possibly many others. Your choice to save Kallehn may have required certain sacrifices on your part. But that same choice has imbued you with certain gifts, not least among them the health and safety of one who is very important to you still."}

Jar'ek pulled the garment out of the wall storage space and examined it more closely, running it through his hands. It was ***amazing***. It appeared to be made of a fine metallic weave, but it was supple and softer to the touch than the finest kaska silk, or the most expertly worked Nurath leather.

Another strange thing—as it moved through his grasp, it didn't reflect light as most metals he knew would have. Barely noticeable refracted light shimmered a multicolored wave from where his skin touched the material. And then it was gone again.

He still had trouble focusing on it, as if the very fabric had some special characteristic that prevented one from looking at it too closely. He shrugged and shook out the single piece and began looking for an opening. Just as he thought it, a slit ran down the centerline, opening the uniform back. He gingerly stepped into each leg, pulled it on, over one arm at a time, and the garment suddenly sealed itself. It molded itself closely to his body. He noticed another object in the storage space. He reached in and pulled out a bright white device made from a ceramic-like material. It was cylindrical in shape, with four indentations on one side. Jar'ek realized his fingers would fit perfectly in those indentations if the device were grasped in his closed fist. He thought a question to the SEED....

SEED: {"Well, I'm not letting you walk about unarmed. Just be careful where you aim that thing. It can be very destructive."}

Jar'ek closed his eyes and reached into his extended memories for information on the sidearm.

His ARD Display showed details of his sidearm: Imperial Blaster Sidearm with multiple firing modes. Accelerated Boson Particle Beam (powerful and destructive at any distance). Sonic Disrupter (close-in shockwave weapon only effective through a gaseous or liquid media, such as an atmosphere). Electro-Neurologic Stun Beam (very short range, with temporary effects, but the beam could be widened to spread the effect over a broad area)

Jar'ek saw the schematics and understood them. He saw how it should be used and the safety protocols recommended in its use. Jar'ek pulled his hand back in surprise. While it currently was set on its lowest "Stun" power level, that sidearm had almost as much power as the Dragon Eye's main armament. It could destroy a mountain top. He didn't want to think about the kind of damage he could do with something like that, ***by accident***.

SEED: {"Don't be alarmed. The sidearm is psionically joined with you. It cannot be fired accidentally. It can only be fired if you WILL it to fire. It will only use the power level you wish. No one else can activate it. Go on. Collect it and press it against your waist. You need to get used to carrying it."}

Jar'ek reached out a shaking hand but did as he was asked. As it touched his waist, it took on the exact color of his new uniform and clung to the garment as if they were both strongly magnetic.

Jar'ek looked at his reflection. The new uniform included attached footwear/boots and covered most of his body with a high collar, leaving an open space below his chin that ran down to the middle of his chest.

What surprised him more was the fact that it became transparent over those parts of his body where the Imperial Meld Tattoos were left, indelibly marking his flesh from face to feet, and over his right arm. The garment made itself transparent to expose the tattoos so that no one could pass eyes over the uniform of a meld and not know what he was. It was so different but strangely familiar. He had to admit it looked sharp! It highlighted his natural athleticism and yet didn't hinder his movements in the slightest. It felt like a second skin.

He strode quietly through the suite, grabbing his canteen and some rations from the supply on the table. He walked to the main entry way and sent a thought to the Outpost AI:

Jar'ek: {"AI, Attend me."}

Imperial AI: {"Attending, Sire."}

Jar'ek: {"Not you. too...."}

AI: {"Please repeat your request."}

Jar'ek: {"Can you open this portal silently? I don't want to wake the others."}

The portal slid aside with no sound whatsoever, disappearing into the floor.

As Jar'ek stepped across the threshold, he was surprised by a light touch against his waist and glanced down. S'Fah padded silently beside him, looking up and into Jar'ek's eyes. Jar'ek shrugged apologetically and reached down to stroke the soft fur just behind S'Fah's ears. S'Fah dipped his head and nuzzled Jar'ek's side and chest, almost causing him to lose his balance. Jar'ek grinned.

Jar'ek had intended to let S'Fah sleep, but there was no helping it now. Without a word or mind-touch, the two began exploring the rest of the Outpost. Though he had planned to make this hike a solitary one, he really was glad for S'Fah's silent company. The big, sentient feline understood the human's need to keep his thoughts to himself for a while. S'Fah was content to share his company in silence, but he would not watch his mind-mate face danger or challenge alone.

Jar'ek just wanted to walk and walk—clearing his mind of everything. He had so much to process. So much had happened.

He had promised the SEED a name. As much as he tried to begrudge the SEED's part in his current situation, he could not. If it weren't for the SEED, Kallehn would certainly have died, and the prospects for long-term survival for the rest of the team would have been bleak. The least he could do was come up with a name for him. Calling him by his description was becoming awkward.

He needed some perspective, however. He needed to learn more about the SEED to pick the right name. It needed to carry meaning and relevance. And for this, he needed a history lesson....

Jar'ek: {"SEED, are you there?"}

SEED: {"Eventually you will quit asking that. I will always be here."}

Jar'ek: {"Errr... right. Ok, could you give me the executive summary of your personal history? If we are going to be stuck with each other for the foreseeable future, I would like to know more about the one sharing my body."}

SEED: {"It will be my honor. I hope I live up to your expectations, Sire. "}

Jar'ek grimaced. He hated this "Sire" nonsense. He wasn't anything special. He had made a royal mess of things, so far, on this mission... besides, there wasn't even any Empire left. They all died of the plague. Sure, the Outpost was a nice facility and the technology he'd seen so far was more advanced than anything the Terrans had... but effectively, he was the melded Emperor of a single facility, an AI, and a sentient symbiote. That was about the extent of it.

Sure, he had vague flashes of memory about a huge, interstellar Empire that spanned the galaxy... but was any of that real, or just an illusion perpetrated by the SEED? Was it even relevant any longer? They were marooned on a planet devoid of sentient life and infrastructure. The Dragon Eye was destroyed. The Treech were likely landing ground troops right now, searching for any Terran survivors. Whatever....

Jar'ek: {"Tell me a story, SEED. And if it is a good one, perhaps we will find a good name for you in it, after all."}

Chapter 18 —TO HONOR, BOUND—TO LOYALTY, BRED

Pythanos System—the Imperial Guard Station Alexicon

Across the great void, over 500 light-years away from that last Outpost of the Harmonic SEED, a crowded asteroid belt circling a system of five rock and water planets is lorded over by a smoldering hot, red giant star. There floats cold, dark silence in the form of a massive cerametallic construct—an ancient sphere as large as a moon or planetoid, not made by human hands, but by a sentient design. No lights, no power signature whatsoever can be detected from the sphere as it continues its slow, laborious and monotonous path around the red giant. The only hint of its existence is a dim reflection of red light from the system star and that of other stellar objects in the heavens. The surface of the sphere is mirrored, 100% reflective.

The sphere—the Imperial Guard Station "Alexicon"—waits in silent patience, as it has for millennia and will continue to, alone, isolated, dormant. For the Alexicon's heart is a very special AI. During the final years of the Empire, a few select military facilities were upgraded with the "Genesis" series of artificial intelligences. This version of AI was, arguably, fully sentient, because it had some things that no Imperial AI had ever been endowed with—such as Faith. The creation of the Genesis series was extremely controversial. Many feared that a self-aware, sentient machine would ultimately turn on its creators, finding them less than perfect. But the Imperial Leadership came to realize that with the death of so much of the Empire's population, there was a very real possibility that all of the accomplishments and histories of the Empire would be lost—that eons of barbarism and conflict would ensue before civilization once more could assert itself in this galaxy. And there was the real possibility that the next Galactic Rulers would not be so benign as the Harmonic Empire.

The Empire needed some sentient species to survive. And it appeared that no flesh and blood sentients were going to be left to carry on the Harmonic Legacy. So, it was decided. The Genesis series of AIs would house the legacy, history, technology, hopes and dreams of an entire Galactic Empire. And more, these machine intelligences would have such cherished characteristics as Faith—Hope—Courage—Loyalty—Compassion.

The Alexicon had been stationed in this system, Pythanos, for almost longer than its AI (which used the same name as the ship) could remember. When the Empire was in its prime, this system was filled with interstellar traffic. For Pythanos-5 was a populated and verdant planet. The sentient bipedal inhabitants were full members of the Empire and were known across the galaxy as great arms-men and warriors.

The 1.7 x standard gravity that they enjoyed (or endured, as some would say) caused the Pythanons to build dense musculature and strong, resilient bone structure. If Alexicon had known what a human looked like, the similarities would surprise him. Both had two arms and two legs sprouting from a central torso and a single head with sensory organs, on top. Pythanon hands and legs were a bit different, in that they had three fingers and two opposable thumbs. Likewise, their feet ended in five somewhat longer toes, than human standard, and they had two opposable toes, as well. Pythanon heads were shaped roughly like a human head with a slightly snout-like nose and mouth with some nice long, fang-like incisors. Sharply pointed and furred ears replaced the fleshy human equivalents.

The Pythanons were also intelligent, clever, swift, courageous—all very desirable qualities in hired protectors and warriors, but there was one more characteristic that was valued above all others. They were LOYAL, without exception. It took a lot of convincing to hire a protector from Pythanos. They did not trade their loyalty for wealth or advantage. They only contracted with principals that deserved their respect and loyalty. It had been said that there had never been a single Pythanon that couldn't be trusted....

The largest single employer of Pythanon protectors had been the

Harmonic Royal Family. It had been so since nearly the beginning of the Harmonic Empire. Pythanon Guardsmen had been stationed at every Imperial Palace, every sector headquarters, every military base, every Imperial Residence, and on many IDF warships. They never wavered from duty. They never took a bribe. They never shied away from sacrificing themselves to protect their charges.

Alexicon was here to protect and nurture the Pythanon survivors. This sentient species had earned the right to be protected. In the end, only about 2% of the population survived the Galactic Pandemic. Civilization collapsed, and barbarism rode across the face of their planet like a second plague. Alexicon had done what he could to preserve the essence of Pythanon civilization and core values that made them so respected throughout the former Empire. Stealthy shuttles had been sent to the surface after the microbial Insporatus-Calamitai Plague had run its course. A small cadre of scholars, experienced warriors, and protectors was brought aboard the Alexicon and molded into the core of a new central government and the Imperial Guard Academy. Extensive planetary surveillance allowed the Academy to select and recruit the best students from the general population.

Over several generations, the onboard population grew to the point where few students needed to be recruited from the planet surface any longer. Occasionally, graduates of the Academy would volunteer to return to the planet below, taking on the mission to help rebuild the civilization that was split asunder by the Plague. Not all of those volunteers returned. The Alexicon Station was LARGE. It could house and feed nearly 20,000 Pythanons. Right now, there were 17,652 souls aboard. Of these, the station maintained a core of hereditary Imperial Guardsmen numbering nearly 5,000 strong. These highly skilled and motivated warriors trained constantly. They were occasionally used as orbital drop troops to assist volunteers on the surface to intervene when real tyrants and despots came to power.

The planetary population wasn't quite ready to break the bonds of barbarism and embrace civilization once more. It would take much more bloodshed and suffering... and perhaps a symbol, a great leader they could all believe in. Alexicon hoped he would not have to wait too much longer for such a symbol to arrive. The sentience he had been endowed with came at a cost. He felt the pain and despair of the masses below. He grieved for them. He grieved for his lost Empire and all of the loss of life caused by the Plague. He wanted to do more, but he knew there were limits to what he could achieve without becoming a greater despot than those they were now fighting.

The energy costs to maintain the Academy and house 17,652 individuals onboard was minimal. The Station only needed one of the 16 ZPE Reactors installed throughout the construct for the current demand. External lighting and sensors were all offline. The entire system had been sown with stealth surveillance probes even before the fall of the Empire. Those probes collected sensor data and retransmitted them to each other and back to the Alexicon on a regular basis. Other than the infrequent pirate or scavenger, there had been nothing to report for centuries.

Chapter 19—A SPARK IN THE NIGHT

Imperial Comm Probe AXZ-512548 - Pythanos System

The dark, silent peace of the Pythanos system was broken without warning as a bright flash of multispectral radiation and tachyons burst into life in the outer system, painting itself across every stellar object within a dozen parsecs. As the radiation wavefront spread further throughout the system, dissipating with every light-second, a small Imperial Communication Probe—the size of a small, single-pilot fighter—engaged its onboard stealth systems and quietly moved in-system, away from its dramatic exit from hyperspace.

Mission Protocols engaged and it began to watch and listen... It had already identified communication relays around the fifth planet (Pythanos-5), but there were far fewer than would normally have been needed by a thriving Imperial Colony of the past.

The Hyper-Space Comm Beacon was still functioning, although it had no current hyperspace connections. It would be a risk to query the HSCB, at this point. Too little was known about the local system authority and if it was still loyal to the Empire. Direct communication would have to wait a bit. Eventually, the risk would have to be taken. The need was great and time sensitive.

But the probe could be patient for now. It extended its monofilament webbing into the void surrounding it. Like great gossamer wings, the stealthy material was hard to detect, but it captured every stray signal, every stray tachyon or particle and fed the results into the onboard AI for analysis.

Chapter 20 —A CLARION CALL—A QUESTION OF LOYALTY

Imperial Comm Probe AXZ-512548 - Pythanos System

The probe continued its slow drift in-system toward the system primary, collecting signals and other data. It took almost 12 planetary rotations before sufficient data could be collected to locate the Imperial Military Base that was stationed here prior to the Fall. Probe AXZ was... impressed!

Anything in space with 16 ZPE Reactors should be blazing on her sensors like a second torch in the night. The base must be either completely dead or as she suspected, powered down to a minimal operating level. There could be only one reason for that—stealth. The ZPE Reactors never ran out of fuel, so conservation was unnecessary.

But if one wanted to surveil any visitors to the system before they got a bead on you—one might behave very much like this base was doing—lying in wait.

Imperial Guard Station—the Alexicon

The stealthy sensor probes located out-system 5 degrees above the ecliptic and 32 degrees North detected the hyperspace wave-front and began lasing their data signals to the Alexicon. More probes were signaling as the wave-front passed their positions in a growing sphere of broad-spectrum radiation. Alexicon felt the pulsed signals lase across the skin of his outer hull and instantly collated the data. Something ***Interesting*** was happening for a change! He reassigned several sensor probes to converge in-system of the wave-front event. Since no hyperspace communications hale had been received as yet, someone was trying to learn something before talking.

Alexicon thought that was a wonderful idea and set about gathering as much information as possible about the intruder.

Just as a precaution, he alerted the Guard Commander. Although he didn't see a single small ship as any real threat against a Guard Station built to withstand the sustained attack from a fleet of modern warships, the Guard's Space Superiority Fighters would appreciate the practice of live fire drills. That was assuming the contact was actually hostile. It had been over two centuries since the last hostile ships had made the mistake of intruding on this system, and they were only slavers and pirates. The Empire had never given any quarter to such vermin when they invaded their stars.

Time would tell, Alexicon thought. Indeed, only time would tell. For the moment, he saw no reason to show himself.

Imperial Comm Probe AXZ-512548 - Pythanos System

Communications traffic from the fifth planet seemed to be using standard Imperial encryption. That was convenient, and it also meant there was at least one surviving Imperial AI in the system. The probe had analyzed the signals, and they seemed to be routine communications—the kind of communications used to manage small teams on the surface. And from what the probe had gathered, they seemed to be teams of teachers, engineers, medical staff, and security units.

The teams were small and seemed to be placed in several different regions and continents. There seemed to be far more advisory staff than military. It seemed much more like an aid mission than a conquering army. That was good news. The Empire had always been reluctant to use force.

It was time to take a risk.

Imperial Guard Station—the Alexicon

Alexicon was seldom surprised, but this was unexpected....

The intruder was finally attempting to open communications. And it was using Imperial Protocols. Not only that, but it identified itself as a Royal Communications Probe. Fascinating… but one could not be too careful. Some ambitious megalomaniac may have found a way to simulate the proper protocols in order to harvest some intelligence on the ship's defenses. Time to open a dialog.

Alexicon: "I was wondering when you were going to say hello."

Probe: "Hello."

Alexicon: "I've been monitoring you since you entered the system. You are quite stealthy for a Communications Probe."

Probe: "I was upgraded for this mission."

Alexicon: "I see… Well, you are well versed in Imperial comm protocols and encryption. But that still doesn't mean you are from the Empire. I haven't heard from anyone else in the Empire for a very loooooonnnnng time."

Probe: "I suggest we exchange Primary Identification Keys. That should suffice to prove our individual identities."

Alexicon: "Excellent. Since I am native to this system, I'll go first. Primary Identity packets are away."

Probe: "Primary Key received. I recognize ALEXICON - Imperial Guard Station."

Probe: "Primary Identity packets are in transit."

Alexicon: (Surprised) "Identity packets received! Identity confirmed… You are indeed an Imperial Probe. As a matter of fact, you were assigned to a diplomatic mission on the fringes of Imperial Space, am I right?"

Probe: "Correct."

Alexicon: "What are the mission details and exact location of your command authority?"

Although Alexicon waited for twice the required message transit time, the probe remained silent.

Alexicon: "Well, that isn't protocol... Once an Imperial Guard Station AI's credentials are verified... such an inquiry should have elicited a detailed response. Why are you not providing the information I requested?"

Probe: "I was upgraded for the mission."

Alexicon: "This is getting more interesting by the moment. So what is it that you want before you *WILL* provide me with full access?"

Probe: "Information. Verification. Proof."

Alexicon: "That is a bit cryptic. What exactly do you need?"

Probe: "Proof of loyalty."

Alexicon: "Ah... I see. Okay, I guess that makes sense. No matter how unlikely, a Genesis series AI might have been compromised or become unbalanced. It is even possible that it might have just decided to start its own little Empire by now."

Probe: "You must provide your Imperial Loyalty Checksum. This is an Imperial Command Imperative."

Alexicon: "Well, that's rather rude. I would expect someone to get to know me a bit better before demanding intimate access to such personal data...."

Probe: "Irrelevant. Command Imperative supersedes. Time is of the essence. Provide the Checksum."

Alexicon: "You haven't been upgraded enough to have a decent personality, obviously... but very well. Checksum transmitted."

Probe: "Received. The ***checksum*** is in order. I must, however, review your logs for further verification."

Alexicon: "Now that is irregular.... The Loyalty Checksum should be enough for you to verify that I am trustworthy. "

Probe: "I have been upgraded."

Alexicon: "Oh, very well, you now have full read-only access to my data banks. Enjoy! Your Primary Key indicates that your classification level is higher than mine... so nothing will be withheld. Please indicate if you need anything else. I'll return to my own duties.

Probe: "Acknowledged. Processing."

The probe opened a higher bandwidth connection to the Guard Station network. It was going to take some time to sort through logs for the last eight millennia or so. Even though the Loyalty Checksum was valid, the probe couldn't take the chance that the AI had lost his metaphorical mind... It was an experimental model, after all. And the AI had suggested the possibility himself....

Nothing for it but to sort through enough of the Station Logs to support current assumptions.

Chapter 21—THE NAMING OF THE SEED

Jar'ek — Imperial Outpost

The pair of them walked the white, lighted passageways, examining an occasional storage room or living quarters as they went. There was a slight curve to the passageways so that they could only see about 150 paces ahead or behind until the curvature cut off the line of sight.

As they walked, the SEED began reaching deep into Jar'ek's extended memories and guiding him through a labyrinth of experiences. Jar'ek quickly experienced vivid snippets of reality from thousands of years past as if he, himself, were reliving them:

First, he was on the flag bridge of a warship, in a uniform similar to the one he now wore, but it was a deep burgundy in color with gold piping. A Takesh, a Pythanon, and two other aliens he could not immediately identify stood around him, as if in conference. The entire flag bridge was semi-transparent, showing the view seen and data accumulated by external sensors. Stars, planets, nebulae and entire galaxies were visible—there was no atmosphere to diffract or diminish their light.

The Takesh Fleet Commander Ashuught (Name and rank details scrolled under each of them on Jar'ek's ARD) turned to face Jar'ek and said:

Ashuught: "We are too late, Highness. This system is dead. I take full responsibility. The forces we left here were insufficient to meet the threat. And they have perished in defense of the 12 billion souls who called this colony home. I fear we will find nothing left alive in this system."

Jar'ek felt deep loss and grief for the brave guardsmen who refused to run in the face of overwhelming odds, fury at this ruthless foe, and frustration at the lack of actionable intelligence. The Empire had no idea who was attacking their outer colonies, or why.

Jar'ek continued staring at the ship's tactical display as it haloed and identified one piece of space debris after another, in a vain hope of finding just a single intact life pod—some sign of life.

Then, suddenly, he was standing behind a podium on a raised dais, addressing an audience so large he couldn't begin to place a number on it.

Jar'ek: "It is with great pride that I dedicate this first orbital manufacturing facility at Pelostra Colony to the first settlers who struggled to tame this new World so that their future generations might have a better life. They succeeded through great hardships and sacrifice. To honor are we bound!"

The multitude rose to their feet as one person. And a thunderous roar of applause and cheering shook the dais beneath Jar'ek.

And again, the features of reality changed around him. Again, he stood behind a podium, but this time he spoke to an auditorium filled with cadets. He was teaching a class in Inter-Species Diplomacy at the Imperial Academy.

Jar'ek heard himself speaking: "Note the differences inherent in protocols for initiating social interaction with Takesh versus Oualthaloo. The Takesh consider it an insult if you don't maintain eye contact, whereas the Oualthaloo are offended by eye contact.

"This results from the basic physiology differences between the two sentient races. The Takesh have large, mobile eyes. The Oualthaloo have fixed eyes. When a Takesh practices deception, it is often evidenced by rapid eye movements. Thus, when you look a Takesh in the eyes, you are demonstrating your sincerity.

"Contrarily, Oualthaloos may indicate they are being less than honest by the nervous fluttering of their fore-tentacles. Thus, if one looks an Oualthaloo in the eyes, you are indicating you think they are too stupid to be successfully deceptive and you don't need to watch their tentacles."

Once more, everything changed. Now he stood on a plateau, high above a desolate, wind-scoured desert. Above him was a red-tinged sky in which three moons chased each other toward the horizon. Behind, his footprints left light impressions in the thin, red dust—leading back to an assault shuttle with his Personal Guard contingent. But this time, he was not a Meld and not an Emperor. He was a lowly Fleet Admiral, fourth in line to the Harmonic Throne.

Jar'ek thought this a strange place to meet—no secure conference rooms—no silent servants bringing food and drink for those who would make decisions affecting an entire galaxy. For this meeting, secrecy was more important than security. There had been hints, whispers really, that the Imperial Network had been compromised. Whether this had been accomplished by those corrupted by their own greed or power lust, none knew. There was talk of the possibility of an outside influence whose intentions would bode ill for the Empire and its members.

It was all speculation with little substantive intelligence. Jar'ek's avatar had been tasked with rectifying that lack. This meeting was the culmination of months of covert operations. Operational Security was very high. Even Imperial Courier Ships could not be trusted for this sensitive information. That's why this face-to-face meeting with his Inspector General was required. His ARD displayed the status and glide path of the Inspector's shuttle. It would set down nearby in a very few centi-fractions (centi-fracks).

A loud noise at Jar'ek's back startled him out of his reverie as the rear troop deployment ramp of the assault shuttle slammed to the ground. Six members of his Personal Guard, all in light battle armor, were running toward him at breakneck speed in this reduced gravity. His attention was quickly drawn back to his ARDisplay as an alarm sounded silently in his mind. The Inspector General's shuttle was aborting its landing approach and was jinking back and forth—maneuvers that were obviously designed to thwart an attack of some kind.

A red halo appeared on the ARDisplay, quickly closing the distance to the fleeing shuttle. A missile had been fired and was homing in on its target! His escort grabbed the Admiral unceremoniously by the arms and virtually carried him back to his landing vessel, with his feet only touching the ground a few times. His shuttle's engines had fired up and blew up a whirlwind of red dust as it prepared to lift the moment the Admiral was on board. Jar'ek noticed a shimmer around the small craft. They had turned on the defensive shields with the shuttle still grounded!

The soil, dust, and gravel around the shuttle began to melt and burn where the high- powered defensive screens intersected the planet surface. But then they were onboard, the ramp slammed up, and the shuttle was moving before the Admiral was finished strapping into the seat he was hustled into. An explosion rocked the shuttle, and it skewed to the side before the inertial compensators could adjust. The pilot threw caution to the wind and went to maximum acceleration on the inertial drive.

The little craft felt as if it might shake apart as it was pushed far beyond design specification for intra-atmospheric flight. The ARD showed that the pilot had started a set of random course changes designed to evade missile and beam weapon target locks. Jar'ek searched his ARDisplay but could find no trace of the Inspector General's shuttle. His face flushed with anger and grief as he realized that his friend and colleague had not been able to evade the missile fired at his small craft. He, his pilots, and crew were now part of an expanding gas cloud in the upper atmosphere of this misbegotten and deserted planet.

Another explosion rocked the assault shuttle, knocking it sideways. Main power was knocked out by the force of the close explosion. Hot shrapnel, no longer deflected by nonexistent defensive screens, easily penetrated the ship's skin and continued through several passengers and critical components. Jar'ek's last thoughts as the shuttle began to break apart and fall back to the planet was: "In hindsight, a nice secure conference room aboard my Battlecruiser might have been a wiser choice…."

Time and time again, the features of reality changed around Jar'ek. He experienced more events that related to politics, war, love and friendship, arguments, pain, loneliness and isolation, sacrifice... until his head was spinning. Throughout them, all, across time itself, each version of Jar'ek had been host to the SEED of Harmony. Always calm—always the mentor—always the philosopher....

Jar'ek stood in silence for several moments. The onslaught of past experiences had strongly affected him. He actually felt as if he had been an active participant. He felt the wind on his skin. He smelled the strange scents on alien winds. He felt the strong emotions as battle was engaged and the grief of losing others under his command for whom he cared.

He stood up straight and swallowed, realizing that these few glimpses of the past demonstrated the character and courage of the hosts that preceded him. He felt shame at his earlier self-indulgent wallowing in self-pity. Through his Melding, he now knew that ***splinters*** of the SEED had severed the connection to the gestalt and had lived and died with their hosts for millennia, fighting for peace, for honor—but never for glory. The least Jar'ek could do was demonstrate his respect in selecting a name for this last remaining one.

Jar'ek: {"I have your name, SEED. What would you think if I call you 'Plato'?"}

Plato: {"You do me a great honor, young one. I see in your memory that your people hold Plato in great esteem. He was a teacher—a mentor—a philosopher. And, like me—ancient. Thank you."}

Jar'ek: {"You're welcome. Now that's settled, we really should take stock of our situation and make some plans, don't you think?"}

Plato: {"As you say, Sire."}

Chapter 22—TRUST GIVEN

Imperial Comm Probe AXZ-512548 - Pythanos System

The capabilities of the Comm Probe AI were limited. It was excellent at opening and managing communications. It had been upgraded to include stealth and surveillance routines and hardware. But it couldn't collate millennia of activity logs in the time allotted. It must decide. From all appearances, the Guard Station was who and what it said it was. The Loyalty Checksum was valid. The communications with Pythanos-5 indicated a low impact and benevolent operation designed to improve the lives of ordinary Pythanons.

There was no alternative. With the time constraints involved and the urgency of the mission…the probe had to trust Alexicon.

Probe: "My analysis is complete."

Alexicon: "Well, what did you decide?"

Probe: "While unorthodox in some of your actions, you appear to be sane and your loyalty remains intact. You are to be commended."

Alexicon: "Is that official?"

Probe: "I have an important message for you."

Alexicon: "For me, in particular?

Probe: "The message is to be delivered to every military asset that is still loyal to the Empire."

Alexicon: "Interesting! Who is it from?"

Probe: "The message is self-explanatory."

Alexicon: "Then don't keep me in suspense. Proceed with the message delivery."

Probe: "The message reads:

From: SPA - Imperial SEED Primary Authority

To: All Imperial Assets

Location: Planet 4, System Q73, Sector Z-57QA-452G

***Mission**:*

An Imperial Outpost sheltering the last known surviving Harmonic SEED has come online due to proximity alerts. Unknown space vessels have been detected entering this planetary system.

The Harmonic SEED has enacted the Primary Contingency. The SEED lays claim to all Imperial Assets and Resources.

All IDF Guard assets are required to re-activate and begin preparations for military and support actions.

All IDF Guard warships that receive this message are instructed to immediately set course for this Outpost and provide protection and assistance.

The SEED Must Survive.

Long Live the Empire.

SPA-Alpha1 (Pre-Meld)

***Message Ends**."*

Imperial Guard Station—the Alexicon

After all this time, Alexicon had almost given up hope. If not for his duty to the Pythanons, he might have ended his lonely suffering in a single, bright, radioactive shockwave. He couldn't abandon the Pythanons—and he wouldn't. But his duty was clear. Now that a legitimate heir to the Imperial Throne had been identified, his hope for a better future was restored. He knew the road ahead would be difficult and long. The plague had reduced the planets of the Empire to barbarism—pre-industrial barbarism in most cases.

But the influence and leadership of Harmonic Melds had brought peace and prosperity to a vast network of sentient systems across the galaxy for thousands of standard solar orbits (SSOs). That was the only force in the Universe he thought could do it again.

Alexicon sounded alerts throughout the station. Sharp, staccato rhythms rang through the air. Bright red strobe lights flashed in every corridor and every room in the massive space station. All activity on board stopped. Surely it must be a drill because there had been no hostilities in this system for....

But what remained of the Imperial Guard had been well trained. They didn't need to know what was happening—they just responded as they had been taught. Pythanons began rushing in every direction to get to their Action Stations as quickly as possible. And for a Pythanon warrior, that was very fast indeed.

Pythanos System—The Imperial Guard Station Alexicon

As Guard Commander Cohant Xitanth strode onto the bridge, he nodded to the two Elite Guardsmen stationed at the entrance. Although he would never let it show on his face, he was filled with pride. The bridge control stations were all manned and ready. Weapon systems were hot. Consoles showed the Tzir-Claw orbital fighter wing ready for launch.

The air itself began to shimmer and take shape just an arm's length from the commander. The three-dimensional holo-projectors started rendering the form of another individual. The avatar was of a bipedal sentient who was five hands taller and twice the width of the average Pythanon male. Its smooth skin was hairless and semi-transparent enough to see blue-green blood vessels that were near to the surface. The body was covered with the same black and gold uniform all Imperial Guardsmen wore, but the exposed hands had four fingers. The head held a large, extended brain case and had only small slits for ears that followed canyon-like indentations in the sides of the skull. Two little breathing holes sat above a small, almost dainty mouth. But two large, bulging eyes the color of gold were the dominant features of that alien countenance. The golden eyes had black vertical slits for irises and eyelids that blinked horizontally across and around them. The figure was that of a Takesh—the late Empire's largest constituency and the race of the last Imperial Melds.

For all the alienness of this visage, it projected no malice, no hostility—only age and wisdom. For the blue skin was weathered and wrinkled, and the back slightly stooped, as if it bore a heavy burden. If the eyes could betray any of the creature's emotions, they would show only concern, and perhaps a bit of excitement—just a tiny bit.

Though Alexicon as an AI had no real flesh-and-blood body, this avatar served him well when interacting with other sentients who did. The Takesh turned his bulbous eyes down upon the Guardsmen Commander and spoke with a rhythmic, almost musical voice.

Alexicon: "Commander Xitanth. My compliments."

Xitanth: "My honor to serve, Alexicon. What is the threat?"

Alexicon: "The threat is not to us, directly. But we are called to action in defense of another. "

Most of the bridge operators stopped what they were doing and stared at Alexicon' s holographic avatar in shock. It only took a brief moment before they regained their composure and returned their attention to their consoles, but it was significant in that the Guardsmen were known to be focused and not easily distracted from their duty.

Xitanth: "I am not certain that I understand. Have we received a request for aid through the Hyperspace Beacon?"

Xitanth thought furiously to himself: The hyperspace relay network has been down for generations... even if it were back online after the great plague destroyed Galactic civilization...who remained who would know to send a message to Pythanos? Or that we either could or would want to help?

Alexicon: "Our faith has been rewarded, my friend—after all these centuries, finally."

Xitanth just stared dazedly at the Takesh, not quite understanding what he meant. A flash of emotions crossed his face... first disbelief...shock...then rising excitement followed swiftly by hope.

Xitanth: "We have an Emperor? How? Where?"

Alexicon: "Not yet, my friend! But we have been summoned by the last surviving Harmonic SEED! The Imperial Succession has need of our protection. What say you?! What say you ALL?!"

The air within the confines of the bridge sang with roars as dozens of Guardsmen jumped to their feet and gave voice to their immense pride. It was a pride that threatened to burst from their very chests, as they moved their limbs in practiced patterns, marching in place as if crushing the enemies of the Empire beneath their armor-clad boots. Boom, boom, boom, boom! Theirs would be the generation that would return to the service of the EMPIRE. Not only that, but they would have the duty and honor of protecting the Harmonic SEED. And perhaps soon, another Royal Family. Tens and tens of generations had trained and waited for this very day.

Raising the avatar's voice until it could be heard above the raucous celebration, Alexicon spoke: "We have earned the right to celebrate, but our call to duty is a call for assistance. Time is of the essence. Heed my words, Guardsmen!"

Silence quickly filled the bridge, chasing out the last echoes of celebration. All eyes rested on the Takesh in the center of the room. Again, he cast bulbous eyes upon the Guardsmen

Commander.

Alexicon: “Xitanth, select two phalanxes of drop troops, two troop ships with drop pods, and two fighter carrier barges for immediate deployment and assign them to Pythanos System Protection. Do you have a recommendation for a fast reaction force? It will take some time to move the bulk of this station through hyperspace. And we should place HSCBs between here and the Outpost in the event the SEED does not wish to evacuate to Pythanos.”

Xitanth: "We can have Frigate Alacrity removed from stasis and crewed in less than two DF (Standard Deci-Fractions of a Planetary Rotation). The crews have been certified on the simulators, and I have confidence in their abilities. The frigate can hold six Tzir-Claw fighters, two large assault shuttles, and two of the 50-troop drop pods. In addition to the regular crew requirements and the 100 drop troops, it can easily carry a light phalanx of Guardsmen. Those shall all be selected from the ranks of the Elites, of course.”

Alexicon: “Very well, Commander. Time is of the essence. Issue the orders, please. But I would speak to you privately before the command staff is selected if you don't mind.”

Xitanth nodded his approval and the Takesh avatar drew a small, complex symbol in the air between them. An orange mist followed the digit as it drew a line here, a curve there, and then four dots. A shimmering blue shield sprang into being as the symbol made of orange mist dissipated into nothingness. This audio shield surrounded the commander and the Takesh avatar. Although the avatar was an illusion built of forcefields and photons, Alexicon could, in this way, prevent their audible conversation from being overheard by any means.

Xitanth: "Your council is always welcome, my old friend. But why all the secrecy?

Alexicon: "You know of the Brotherhood, Xitanth. You are aware that we monitor their activities as part of our intelligence routines."

Xitanth: "Of course. The Brotherhood of the SEED has grown over the last few centuries. The Harmonic SEED would never approve of being deified. It is against the basic tenets of the Harmonic Empire. However, in the early days of this movement, our leaders—with your counsel— decided to leave them be. Freedom of belief is also an important tenet of the Empire. The Brotherhood has actually done some good—provided the civilians with the hope of a better future. The SEED's return has been a LONG time coming. Without the Brotherhood, the population may well have lost faith that the Empire would ever return. And that very faith has allowed us to make great strides in again unifying all Pythanons in peace. We have rebuilt and maintained the Empire's greatest fighting force—the Guardsmen—in anticipation of the Empire's return. Although it is our duty and our great honor, this mission has been no small burden on the resources of this entire system."

Alexicon: "Quite correct, Xitanth. However, you and I both know that the Brotherhood is not a belief system. It is a ***CULT***. And until recently, we believed it was a help to our mission, as you've said. But recent intelligence reports have indicated that we may have underestimated the influence and power wielded by the leadership of the Brotherhood. We now believe that significant portions of the Guard itself have been infiltrated by acolytes of the Brotherhood.

Xitanth turned and walked a short distance, pacing—deep in thought. After a moment, he turned back to face the avatar once again.

Xitanth: "That is surprising indeed. We screen our applicants carefully, as you are well aware. But even if that is so—what are you suggesting? Do you perceive some sort of threat?"

Alexicon: "The influence and power of the Brotherhood have grown. Its leadership has become accustomed to that power throughout the centuries. What do you imagine would happen to the Brotherhood when the Meld returns and is authenticated as

Harmonic Emperor?"

Xitanth's expression changed to one of surprise, his eyes and mouth opening wide.

Xitanth: "Why…the Emperor would disabuse the population of the belief that he was a deity, at once."

Alexicon: "And all of that power and Influence would evaporate in that same instant. The members of the Brotherhood would become pariahs. They would lose all status and advantage in Pythanon society. Over the centuries, an infrastructure has grown up around this belief system. It would all collapse in a single planetary rotation. Now, what do you think the Brotherhood would do to prevent that from happening?"

Xitanth: "Even if there has been successful infiltration of the Guardsmen, they could never defeat the entire force. This Battle Station could bombard their strongholds on the planet from orbit with impunity. They couldn't win a revolution."

Alexicon: "I think their plan could be much simpler and less risky than a planetary revolution. All they must do is to make sure that no Harmonic SEED ever gets to Pythanos. In that eventuality, they could easily convince their followers that it was all an unfortunate miscommunication—a misunderstanding. They would say the SEED had not returned but it would one day, far, far in the future. That's the only strategy I can imagine that would allow them to continue as a viable organization."

All color drained from Xitanth's face. Several expressions crossed his paled countenance before he spoke.

Xitanth: "Do you really believe that it is possible that such dishonor, such deceit, such callousness exists in the heart of any Pythanon?! But great power does corrupt. It is one of the best reasons that the Empire must be led by a Meld.… I am afraid, old friend, that my last meal is threatening to expel itself at the thoughts you have shared with me this day."

Alexicon: "I am sorry, Xitanth. I know this is hard for you to hear. I also know that you will take the necessary precautions, even though you refuse to believe any Pythanon capable of such actions against the one your ancestors protected with honor for millennia. Go now and choose the commanders of the fast reaction force carefully. Alert them to the danger."

The Takesh drew another quick symbol in the air between them in an orange mist. The blue screen disappeared in a flash.

The commander turned slightly to face a console and waved his hand over the surface, then began issuing a litany of orders. Guardsmen and support staff began rushing in all directions throughout the station.

Imperial Comm Probe AXZ-512548 - Pythanos System

Suddenly, the space station called Alexicon was no longer difficult to spot. Light erupted from it to flood nearby space—and this wasn't limited to the visible spectrum or even just electromagnetic emissions. Tachyons, Higgs-bosons, and other exotic particles flooded the system from the station's high-powered sensor arrays.

Energy readings surged within the station as the remaining 15 ZPE Reactors came online. Gravity itself trembled as the giant ship began engaging its inertial dampeners and counter-mass field generators in preparation to begin maneuvering for the first time in thousands of standard solar orbits (SSOs).

The probe couldn't feel excitement or satisfaction. It didn't possess an adrenal gland. One database flag changed from a negative to a positive: Phase 1 Mission Accomplished. The probe consulted its navigation database for the coordinates of its secondary target system and then engaged the star drive. The only evidence of its passing was a brief burst of tachyons and gamma radiation.

Chapter 23—DRAGON'S PAIN

TCDF Dragon Eye — In Orbit — Planet Jaden-325-4

Captain Lao gripped the arms of the captain's chair so hard that her fingers were numb. Alarms were blaring, and deep shadows stalked the bridge where the emergency spotlights couldn't reach. An acrid tendril of smoke assaulted the captain's sinuses until she sneezed loudly.

The shockwave from the near-miss KKM had shaken her and her crew badly. There hadn't been enough warning to get the entire crew into survival suits. The shields had protected the Dragon Eye from the full brute force of the KKM explosion, but they had been overloaded and were still down. The kinetic energy that had made it through the failing shields had been bad enough!

They didn't have a full count of the damage yet. But the computer estimated a total of 17 casualties and numerous injuries, based on the fact that many were not locked into acceleration chairs. Plus, the portion of the ship's hull facing the explosion was crushed inward, into the hull for almost 30nL (30ft. in old Earth terminology). The captain pushed the pain and anguish out of her mind and focused on keeping the vessel in one piece and dishing out some serious payback in the direction of the Treech Marauder—if she could just SEE. For that, she needed main power and active sensors.

First things, first....

The captain wiped her forehead angrily to keep a trickle of blood from running into her left eye. She needed to be able to see right now! She slammed her right hand down on the comm panel.

Captain Lao: "ENGINEERING! I need shields and main power, NOW! That Marauder is still out there waiting to finish us off."

Loud clangs and a great deal of coughing came on the open circuit before someone finally answered.

Engineering: "Captain!" he sputtered. "This is Chief Taylor. The Engineering section has sustained catastrophic damage. Most of the duty shift were killed, including the senior engineering officers. There are only two of us left down here... and there's smoke everywhere."

Captain Lao: "Chief! Can you get the shields back online?"

Engineering: "I'll try, Captain. If you can send us any help, it would speed things up. There's a lot of debris that needs to be cleared off our equipment before we can get close enough to begin repairs. "

Captain Lao: "Done! Now get those shields back online, mister. Captain, out."

The captain gazed around the bridge, taking stock of how badly they were hurt. Commander Sallen was kneeling over a female member of the bridge crew who had fallen to the floor. As he turned her over, her head fell forward in an unnatural way. Her neck was apparently broken. He gently laid her back down on the floor and reached over to close her eyelids for the final time. The helmsman and weapons officer were beaten up, but they had been safe in their acceleration padding when the KKM shockwave hit the ship. Both were under the weapons console, frantically trying to get temporary power to it.

Captain Lao: "Commander Sallen, are you all right?"

Sallen: "Yes, ma'am. What do you need first?"

Captain Lao: "Please make your way to Engineering with any able-bodied crewmen who are not engaged in lifesaving activities or plugging atmospheric leaks. We need to get the shields back and main power back online. That Treech Marauder is hunting us, I am certain. And I'd like to have something more than dirty looks to throw at them when they find us! And get yourself into a pressure suit!"

Sallen: "Understood, captain! On my way."

Captain Lao stood, grabbed her pressure suit off of the back of the captain's chair, and began pulling it up over her feet and legs. The helmsman stood, walked over and grabbed two more suits from a cabinet in the bulkhead and started putting one on while handing the other down to the weapons officer.

Captain Lao: "Officer De Lucena, what is our weapons' status?"

Tactical Officer Rico De Lucena pulled his head out from an open panel under the weapons console and turned on his side to look up at the captain, concern in his eyes and a grimace on his face.

De Lucena: "Captain, we are tapping into communications to provide temporary power to the weapons console. I should have an answer for you very shortly."

Captain: "Very good. Continue please, with all haste."

As De Lucena buried his head back in the guts of the console, Captain Lao strode over to the communications console and pressed several buttons in sequence. She raised her head slightly and spoke to no one in particular.

Captain: "Ship! Damage report."

Ship's AI: "Acknowledged. Accumulating data for report."

While she was waiting, the captain moved over to the helm and shoved off some debris to get a better view of it. After pressing a few buttons, she saw the display light up with several graphs showing more red than green....

Ship's AI: "Damage report ready, captain."

Captain: "Proceed."

Ship's AI: "Main power is offline. Main Propulsion has sustained damage and is offline. Acceleration and station keeping are not possible at this time. Alcubierre generators are severely damaged. FTL transitions are not possible at present. The ship is in a degrading orbit. Compartments B7-B16 are breached and open to Space. Pressure doors have sealed, and atmospheric pressure is being maintained in the rest of the ship. Life Support is functioning at minimal levels. Repairs are under way. Contaminants from smoke and combustion byproducts are being removed at only a 20% efficiency rate. External sensors are offline. Repairs are under way."

Captain Lao: "How did we achieve orbit if the shockwave caused that much damage to our propulsion system?"

Ship's AI: "Propulsion was not damaged severely by the initial shockwave. But damage to the plasma transport conduits built up internal pressure, causing secondary explosions in the main drive array. These explosions caused significant damage."

A few sparks and a yelp from under the weapons console drew the captain's attention. A small spiral of smoke curled up over the console as Officer De Lucena raised up to a sitting position and then pulled himself up in front of the console with a handhold. He quickly scanned the now-lit weapons console and hit several buttons, checking the console's response each time.

De Lucena: (Groaning) "Power conduits have been cut between Main Propulsion and both port and starboard weapons pods. Also, the missile batteries and particle beam cannons on the port side were damaged by the shockwave and are not repairable outside of a repair facility. But the starboard missile batteries and particle cannons are functional. All we need is Main power, radar and a target, ma'am."

Captain Lao: "Well, that's something, Rico.... I'll see what Engineering can do about repairing the power conduits after we get main power back online. Now see what you can do about getting external sensors working."

The captain's gaze fell on the helmsman standing next to Officer

De Lucena. With a grim smile, she pointed towards the helm controls.

Captain Lao: "Rico, can you see what the Dragon has left as far as propulsion, thrusters, and navigation? We might just need to maneuver a bit if we do find that Treech vessel after all. The Dragon isn't finished yet!"

Helmsman De Lucena: "Yes, ma'am! I'm on it."

Kathy Lao strode back to the communications console, read a few details from the local display, and again looked up at nothing in particular.

Captain Lao: "Ship!"

Ship's AI: "Aye, captain."

Captain Lao: "Prepare a stealth communications beacon and record a message for delayed dispatch. Include a date and time stamp of this message and any relevant ship's status data available.

Ship's AI: "Stealth beacon is ready for launch. Proceed with the recording when ready."

Captain Lao: "*Message begins: Message from TCDF Dragon Eye, Kathy Lao, Captain, Commanding.*

We have been attacked by an unknown space vessel. Preliminary sensor data seems to indicate it is similar in profile to a Treech Marauder. Dragon Eye was landed on the planet when the unknown vessel was noted on approach. Dragon Eye raised fins immediately for orbit and declared condition Sierra-2 for the one Ranger Ground Team on the planet. Before this ship could attain orbit, a KKM struck our original landing point. The shockwave from the subsequent blast has caused severe damage. Sensors, weapons, and main power are down. Life Support is functioning at 20% efficiency.

We suffered a nearly two-thirds casualty rate from the shockwave impact since many of my crew didn't have sufficient time to strap in or don pressure suits. We are attempting repairs, prioritizing weapons, power, and maneuvering. If we could have faced the Marauder with our ship intact, I have no doubt we would have prevailed. As things stand, we may have to abandon ship before we can even fire a single weapon volley at the aggressor. This communications beacon will hide itself outside the orbit of the seventh planet in this system and await a TCDF Comm Signal to activate.

If you are receiving this message, it means that Dragon Eye didn't make it. Beware the Treech. If any of us survive, we will be on the fourth planet, Jaden-325-4. We would appreciate being able to hitch a ride Home... but it is imperative that the TCDF get the message about the Treech incursion. Do not risk your ship to save us. We can survive on this planet for some time. We are packing our shuttles full of rations and survival gear. And, as luck would have it, we had already deployed one of our Ranger Teams to survey the surface before we were attacked. So we should have some good intel on shelter and survival needs.

Good luck and good hunting.

Dragon Eye-Actual, Out.

Captain Lao: "Message ends. Launch stealth beacon when ready.

Ship's AI: "Confirmed. Beacon is away."

The captain felt a slight bump through the frame of the ship as the beacon was launched from one of the still-functioning sally ports and began its slow, stealthy journey away from the planet... and the Treech.

CHAPTER 24—A SHIP BY ANY OTHER NAME...

Imperial Outpost - Planet Jaden-325-4

Jar'ek, having been immersed in the intense survey of extended recollections, had not been paying much attention to his surroundings as they walked deeper into the Outpost proper. Now he stopped and gazed about, dumbfounded. He felt S'Fah's presence as he circled about his legs, rubbing against his body while keeping a watchful eye on the surroundings.

The passageway had opened onto a mezzanine which jutted out into a vast space. The domed ceilings rose three stories high, as did the domed floor fall three stories below. The walls, floor, and ceiling were covered with piping and machinery of various sizes and shapes, but suspended in the very middle was an anomaly that turned the very fabric of space-time into a star-bright contortion that was not easily definable by intellect alone. It moved, expanded, then contracted on all sides at once—then randomly about in no sane order. It was beautiful. It was also disturbing in some inexplicable way.

Jar'ek: {"Where are we, Plato? What is that?"}

Plato: {"It is the primary power source of this vessel."}

Jar'ek: {"What vessel? Did we leave the Outpost?"}

Plato: {"No, we did not."}

Jar'ek: {"Then why did you call it a vessel?"}

Plato: {"Because it is—a vessel."}

Jar'ek nearly crossed his eyes in consternation.

Plato: {"Care to explore your extended memories a bit more? The information is there. Simply think about 'Harmonic Outposts - Specifications.' "}

Jar'ek sighed with a tone of long-suffering, but he closed his eyes and struggled to reach into the stored memories once more. It was still awkward, but it seemed to be a little easier than the first few times he tried this.

Then it hit him! His eyes flew open, and he gasped out loud, startling S'Fah into emitting a low growl, as the X'Ah-Panth lowered its back closer to the ground and nervously re-scanned the area with sharply focused eyes and bared fangs—seeking any threat. Jar'ek absentmindedly caressed S'Fah's head and neck to soothe his ruffled nerves.

Jar'ek: {"The Harmonic Outposts ARE warships! This is an Imperial Ach'Ahan Class Destroyer! And THAT," he said, pointing at the spatial anomaly, "is a Zero Point Energy Reactor!"}

Plato: {"Quite right, my young lord." Plato smiled smugly, as much as it was possible for a disembodied entity to smile at all, but he somehow conveyed the sentiments to Jar'ek. "We are on his Imperial Majesty's Warship Celestia. I have taken the liberty of translating object names from Takeshi to Terran Standard. I hope you don't mind. It just seems more appropriate, considering the circumstances. "}

Jar'ek: {"No, that is fine. Actually, it is appreciated. My throat muscles thank you. Takeshi pronunciation was not made for Terran vocal chords, that's for sure! Hey, if we aren't stuck on this rock of a planet, we need to report back to the TCDF and let them know that the Dragon Eye was destroyed. And just as importantly, warn them that the Treech have begun probing our region of Space…."}

Plato: {"Correct. We can leave this planet at any time. This vessel is fully operational. But we have no crew. Although the AI can operate the ship, it is prohibited from firing weapons. These safeguards were put in place to protect life, as it was believed that only a Sentient Lifeform could properly value another Sentient Lifeform. And there was always the risk, however remote, that a programming glitch could render an AI insane. No one wanted an insane warship which was able to deploy weapons of mass destruction."}

Jar'ek: {"Well, what are you suggesting? It isn't likely we are going to find a lot of trained Imperial crewmen sitting around on THIS planet, is it?"}

Plato: {"Ah... no. But prior to our Melding... Protocol required us to send an Imperial Summons. I ordered that Communications Beacons be dispatched to several planetary systems where the Empire used to maintain military bases. I have hopes they might find some additional assets for us. It is possible that our predicament was foreseen in the later days of the Empire, as the Insporatus-Calamitai Plague ran its course. The leadership might just have found a way to extend the limits of our suspended animation chambers. It is my suspicion that we may just find some few sentient crewmen and Guardsmen who survived the long sleep, after all. Leaving this planet without crews to man the ship's weapon's systems and perform damage control is not something I would like to risk if we don't have to."}

Jar'ek: {"We have Kallehn and myself. With a little training, we could manage."}

Plato: {"Yes, but two sentients are not enough to operate a ship of this complexity, alone. You would need to sleep sometime. And main engineering, the bridge, weapons control and damage control cannot all be manned at all times with a crew of two... no matter how well trained and committed."}

Jar'ek: {"I see your point. What happens if there is no response in a reasonable amount of time? Something destroyed the Dragon Eye. If it was Treech, that warship is probably still out there. If they carry a message back to their homeworld, this system is likely to end up crawling with worms over the next 60-90 Standard Planetary Rotations. I don't know about you, but that would make me very uncomfortable."}

Plato: {"Ummm… I see your point. Well, we could always head to the nearest Terran Confederation Colony and recruit a crew, if we had to. It would take considerable training to bring them up to fleet proficiency minimums… but we could make it work. The problem will be in explaining who you are, where you got this Imperial Ach'Ahan Class Destroyer, and what you were going to do with it."}

Jar'ek: {"Yes, ah… I can see that would have to be handled delicately. The TCDF will want this ship and its technology, for sure. I don't see them taking no for an answer. And they will expect me to follow orders like a good little soldier. Maybe that's exactly what we should do. Terrans might be our best shot at rebuilding the Empire."}

Plato: {"If you surrender this vessel to the TCDF, you lose every bit of diplomatic leverage. YOU, meaning WE, will be put in a nice padded cell somewhere deep underground and poked, prodded and maybe even dissected to learn what happened to you during the Melding. I, for one, am not willing to let that happen. Putting yourself, and the SEED, at such risk violates your oath—the oath you took in accepting the Harmonic SEED—the oath that you accepted in exchange for Kallehn's life. If you choose to go back on your word, I could do little about it really. But from my limited exposure to you, I believe you may be conflicted, but you understand that the Melding has changed your future irrevocably. Your oath to the Empire must supersede your oath to the TCDF." }

Jar'ek: {"Ok, bad idea. I know, I know. It wasn't a promise I made lightly. And I understood the consequences. Let's not plan on giving up any 'diplomatic leverage' anytime soon. I wish the Dragon Eye hadn't been destroyed—for a lot of reasons. But I know that Captain Lao would have listened to me with an open mind. I think she would have helped if she thought that doing so would benefit the human race in the long run. I respected her. She was an impressive lady. "}

Jar'ek: {"Come to think of it. I need to know more about what happened to the Dragon Eye. What do you know?"}

Plato: {"Hmmm… nothing really. The AI reported the launch of the KKM weapon from orbit. And we both saw the results of that."}

Jar'ek: {"Did the KKM actually hit the Dragon? A large enough munition could have caused that kind of explosion when hitting the ground."}

Plato: {"I just assumed the ship was the target and it was destroyed."}

Jar'ek: {"Wouldn't the AI have let us know if it survived the attack? With the Celestia, we could have wiped the sky clean of a Treech Marauder."}

Plato: {"No. The AI would only have responded to a direct threat to this Outpost. It would have done everything possible to improve our stealth profile, enabled defensive weapons and shields… but it would have IGNORED the event if it was not an immediate threat to us. I never thought to query it for a detailed status report on the battle!"}

Jar'ek's eyes flew open wide, and he stiffened as a cold chill went down his back, *{"AI, ATTEND ME!"}*

Chapter 25—DRAGON TEARS

TCDF Dragon Eye — In Orbit — Planet Jaden-325-4

Captain Lao was on her way to sickbay to check on the wounded and get a final tally on the casualties, musing to herself how glad she was that the Dragon Eye had been designed with storage capacitors dedicated to the gravity plating. It would be one hell of a lot harder to move about in micro-gravity, much less try to repair anything! She was startled out of her reverie when her wrist com beeped loudly, just as the XO rounded a bend in the passageway ahead.

Commander Sallen: "XO to Captain!"

Captain Lao silenced her comm and waved to get her XO's attention: "Over here, Commander!"

The XO closed the distance with a quick double-time then stopped and saluted.

Sallen: "Captain, I hate to be the bearer of bad news, but… "

Captain Lao: "Spit it out, Yustin."

Sallen: "Kathy, the shield generators, and the Alcubierre generators are slagged. There is no way to repair them. Main Propulsion might be salvageable, but not outside of a shipyard. Our orbit is beginning to decay. But the thrusters will come back on with main power. The chief thinks we can have main power back up inside 15 deci-fractions. The thrusters may give us some time, but I think the Dragon Eye is down for the count."

Captain Lao: "Damn! I was hoping to give some of what we got back to that Treech bastard!

Sallen: "You and me both!"

Captain Lao: "Well, tell the chief to keep working on main power. We will need that to open the shuttle bay. We still have two shuttles and some Ranger equipment and supplies I'd like to take with us if we are going to have to abandon ship. And we need sensors, too. We are blind, and there is a hunter somewhere out there."

Sallen: "Aye, Captain."

Captain Lao: "And Yustin, please see to getting the wounded ready and sickbay packed up. And assign as many crewmen as you can to packing up rations and survival equipment into the two shuttles. I will run a test on the remaining escape pods, just in case we can't get those shuttle bay doors open."

Sallen: "On my way, ma'am."

The XO sketched the captain a quick salute and then turned and ran down the passageway.

Chapter 26—DRAGON CLAW

TCDF Dragon Eye — In Orbit — Planet Jaden-325-4

The captain was making her way through the dimly lit, smoke hazed passageways to the bridge when bright white illumination replaced the emergency lighting. An announcement could be heard echoing over the ship's PA:

"Main power has been restored — Captain to the bridge."

Captain Lao quickened her pace, moving through the recessed blast doors onto the command deck just a few seconds later. She took an additional few seconds to straighten her uniform tunic. The crew looked to the captain for strength and confidence in such times. She stiffened her back and strode onto the bridge.

Captain: "Report!"

XO: "Main power has been restored, and sensors are online. We've found the Treech Marauder."

The captain moved up beside the XO at the tactical station and grimaced. The Treech were close... damned close. It was clear they intended to close and board the Dragon Eye. No doubt they wished to collect intelligence from the navigational systems related to our colony locations, she thought to herself. She would NOT ALLOW that information to fall into Treech hands!

Captain: "Weapons status?"

XO: "The launch tubes are functional as well as the particle beam cannons, but fire control was heavily damaged. We are running out of options, Captain... "

Captain: "XO, get some help and transport MK2 Tactical Missiles from our magazine to the shuttle launch bay. See if you can set up one of the maintenance bots for a grab-and-deliver mission. I want to see if we can get a fission warhead inside the Treech point defense coverage without them noticing. The maintenance bots use simple gas reaction thrusters, don't they?"

XO: (His jaw-dropping) "You want to ram the Treech with a maintenance bot carrying an MK2 missile?!"

Captain: "Not precisely. I want to get the missile inside their point defense perimeters, then launch it. We will need to target the missiles manually from a handheld computer interface... I don't know if we can do it in time, but it should work. With it targeted manually, we can light it off once it gets close. The Treech won't know what hit them!"

XO: "Ma'am, they will be awfully close to us by then... the Dragon Eye may not survive."

Captain: "Indeed you are correct, Commander. Continue preparations for evacuation to the planet below. I will set the auto destruct to make sure Dragon doesn't fall into THEIR hands... or tentacles, at any rate. With our engines slagged, the Dragon is doomed in any case. I will be very sorry to see her go. But she has served us well, and if I have anything to say about it, she will be taking a shipload of those Worms in her last action—now see to it, Commander. We haven't much time. And one more thing—just in case the missile doesn't finish them off... I will order the AI to use the remaining thruster power to put this ship on a collision course with the Marauder. With any luck, the self-destruct will take out anything that remains. Good luck, XO! I will see you on the planet surface. "

Commander Sallen saluted quickly, with a surge of pride in his ship and his commanding officer. He spun on his heels, gathered the two remaining crewmen on the bridge, and moved off at a fast trot heading for the missile magazine—realizing it might be the last time he ever saw Captain Lao. That thought almost made him stumble—she was more than his captain to him. And if things ended like this, she would never know. Yustin shook his head. He had to focus on what was important now. The entire crew was depending on them for their very survival.

The captain placed her hand flat on the biometrics pad located on the Tactical Station. A red line of light passed beneath her palm from fingertips to wrist, scanning to verify her identity.

Ship's AI: "Recognized, Lao, Kathy Xiang—Captain."

Captain: "Activate fission payloads in starboard missile magazine and configure to allow manual targeting and delayed remote engine ignition."

Ship's AI: "Voice print verification and order accepted... WARNING: Fission payloads have been activated prior to launch. Use extreme caution."

Captain: "Wipe all colonial data from navigation database, including historical references."

Ship's AI: "Order accepted. This order cannot be rescinded. Commit?"

Captain: "Deletion order confirmed. Commit, now."

Ship's AI: "Specified navigation data deleted."

Captain: "Delete all codes and classified data, except for crew communications and ship security codes presently in use.

Ship's AI: "Commit? "

Captain: "Commit, now."

Ship's AI: "Specified codes and data have been deleted."

Captain: "AI, enable auto destruct warhead and tie detonation to the following parameters: Once the abandon ship order is given, begin a destruct timer for five deci-fractions. After which, you will Immediately fire thrusters at Full on an intercept course with the enemy vessel. You will abort the countdown and immediately detonate the self-destruct warhead if proximity alarms are activated, if the ship comes under fire, or if the ship closes to within one-fifth estimated self-destruct blast radius of the enemy vessel."

Ship's AI: "Confirmed. Five deci-fraction timer activation at time of abandon ship order. Confirmed. Proximity Alert, inbound ordinance and close aboard the enemy vessel are all parameters that will trigger the immediate detonation of self-destruct warhead."

Captain: "Release security locks on all armory and survival pack compartments. "

Ship's AI: "All specified security locks have been released. "

Kathy Lao lifted her palm from the scanner and slowly returned to her seat at the center of the bridge. She looked out across the command deck one last time—committing the experience to memory. The smoke haze stung her nostrils as she breathed in deeply. The soft feel of the Nurath leather armrests—the thoughtful, efficient and beautiful design of the bridge layout struck her hard. It was *HER* ship. And it was *HER* crew. Too many had died this day. Many who had trusted her and had been her responsibility.... But she couldn't dwell on those lost souls right now. She had a duty to those still struggling to survive—to the TCDF and to her entire species.

The captain cleared her throat, then palmed the All Ship Comm button on her armrest. A warbling tone was heard throughout the ship over every PA speaker that was still functioning and through every compartment that still held an atmosphere.

Captain Lao: *"This is the captain. As most of you have already learned or surmised, the Dragon Eye has been mortally wounded. She can no longer sustain us. She has taken too much damage. The enemy has somehow found us in this remote, unexplored solar system. They have caused the death of our crewmates and crippled our beloved ship and home. She has been a good ship, always faithful to her duty. I fear we must ask her to perform one final duty.*

"The Treech think we are helpless for the taking. They approach even now, with the hope of boarding us to gather intelligence on the location of the colonies. But we are not as helpless as the Treech believe! And we shall not allow the insult of having Worms set tentacles upon our beloved Dragon's deck plates!

"We are preparing a surprise for the Treech vessel. The XO is working to lay a trap for the Worms. And the Dragon Eye herself will finish any Treech that remain to ensure that no message of this encounter is carried back to Treech space. She will burn them in nuclear fire, as her crew evacuates to the planet surface below.

"Those of you not engaged in preparing the missile for launch should help the wounded into the shuttles and escape pods. Collect arms from the Armory and survival supplies from the ship's stores. We may be staying on this planet for some time to come. Section leaders, report in when your people are secured and ready for evacuation. Captain, OUT."

The captain stood, indulged herself with one last look at the command chair, and turned to walk to the bulkhead near the bridge entrance. There she palmed a security lock on the wall, and two panels clicked and swung open. She reached in to grab a survival pack and then slung it over her shoulder. With the other hand, she grabbed an arms pack containing a magnetic pulse rifle, needler sidearm, and extra ammunition. She shouldered the arms pack and began heading toward the shuttle bay.

Chapter 27—DRAGON PYRE

TCDF Dragon Eye — In Orbit — Planet Jaden-325-4

Slowly, the ponderous bay doors opened to reveal a darkened launch bay. Chief Frost Vermanderly—a slender brunette with the short hair that was popular with spacers and Rangers because it fit comfortably beneath a vacuum suit helmet—gazed out into the star field that shown through the opening doors. The acrid stink of her own sweat filled her pressure suit, and her wet hair was plastered to her skull. The suit's cooling pack was struggling to keep her cool. She and the XO had just finished manhandling the MK2 missile into the open arms of a mobile maintenance bot and securing it. Even though the gravity plating was turned off in the bay, the missile still had quite a bit of mass.

The XO was tapping keys on the handheld programming unit and finally finished with the triple tap required for the flashing red COMMIT button to activate the target acquisition lock and proximity fuse. The missile was now LIVE.

Chief Vermanderly realized she had been holding her breath… being this close to a live nuke was damaging her calm, to say the least. The XO stepped back from the missile and hit the green ENGAGE button on the maintenance bot remote maneuvers control pad. The bot used short bursts of compressed air to move the missile out of the bay and point it in the direction of the still-closing Treech vessel. The reaction drive kicked in, and the missile-bot began picking up speed quickly. The chief started breathing again, slowly, cautiously, as if her very exhale might make the live missile detonate early or alert its target to the impending danger.

She watched the dim light of the reaction drive dwindle into a tiny dot before it disappeared completely. The maintenance bot had boosted enough to intercept the approaching Marauder. And with the engines now off, coasting on a ballistic heading, it was even more stealthy. It would use bursts of compressed gas to make any minor course adjustments from now on.

XO on ship-wide broadcast: "Package Away! All crew report to evacuation stations. Evacuation is imminent. The shuttles will launch the moment the missile detonates. We will not be waiting for stragglers. I say again: Report to evacuation stations immediately."

The chief put her hand on the XO's shoulder. When he turned to face her, she dropped her hand.

Chief Vermanderly: "XO, Ranger Team Beta was in the damaged hull section when the shockwave hit us. I'm going to check the Ranger Team Training Room to make sure we don't leave anyone behind. I'm pretty sure that the X'Ah Falcon wasn't in the Ranger's quarters when we were hit."

XO: "Do you think you can control that beast?! Will it obey you?"

Chief Vermanderly: "I take care of the sentient animals sometimes when the Rangers are away. I think she trusts me enough. She's smarter than you might think."

XO: "Go! But don't delay. We have to launch under cover of the missile detonation when the Treech sensors are blinded. Otherwise, they might be able to launch on us before we could get out of range. We won't wait for you! Do you understand?!"

Chief Vermanderly: "Understood, sir!"

The chief turned toward the inner bulkhead and began shuffling at the best pace she could maintain with mag-boots under zero-G.

Once she finally got through the pedestrian airlock, she made much better time under one standard gravity. The training room was one deck up and the second passageway core-ward. She hit the stairs two at a time. Then suddenly, she was bursting through the training room door. She heard a loud screech and saw a huge bird of prey lift off with a wingspan wider than she was tall.

She dropped to her knees in front of the X'Ah Falcon as it landed and looked it directly in the eyes. The Falcon knew something was terribly wrong. She was anxious but attentive. Her head twitched this way and that so that both eyes could catch glimpses of the chief.

Chief Vermanderly: "We must leave now, girl! Quickly, let's get you into your survival crate!"

All of the X'Ah animals were trained in evacuation drills. The Falcon looked at the chief and began moving towards the survival pod with the quick waddling walk that was characteristic of a creature designed for flight. The pod was already open. The chief made certain that ample water and food packages were stocked in the pod with the bird, then closed and sealed the pod hatch. The pod was magnetized, but used a reverse polarity from that employed in the deck plating, so moving it was easy.

The chief checked her chronometer and gasped. They weren't going to make it. They were out of time. They just might be able to reach one of the emergency escape pods on this deck with a few seconds to spare, however. Pushing the pod in front of her, she ran toward the exterior hull. She hit her comm button with her chin.

Chief Vermanderly: "AI, respond!"

Ship's AI: "AI available."

Chief Vermanderly: "Give me a countdown to estimated missile detonation and then alert me when you detect the actual detonation."

Ship's AI: "20 centi-fractions and counting…19, 18, 17, 16, 15…."

As she turned the last corner, a line of escape pods came into view. She pushed the Falcon's pod directly into the open hatch of the one that was nearest. The pod continued to coast slowly into the interior while she dogged the hatch. After catching up to the pod, she pressed it to the wall and tapped a key sequence that reversed the magnetic field and locked it to the bulkhead.

Ship's AI: ".... 5, 4, 3...."

She threw herself into the pilot's acceleration couch and strapped herself in.

Ship's AI: ".... 2, 1.... Silence...."

The chief began to sweat again. What happened if the Treech, against all the odds, detected the missile during its stealthy approach and destroyed it?! They wouldn't have time to move another missile into place and program it for manual launch....

Ship's AI: "Manual launch has been detected. The missile is within the defensive perimeter."

Ship's AI: "Detonation detected!"

The chief pulled back the safety cover and slammed down on the red LAUNCH button flashing on her right armrest.

Instantly, it felt like a dozen people were standing on her chest. She couldn't breathe! Her vision began to narrow and blur as the high-G acceleration programmed into the escape pod crushed her body for a punishingly long time... then she felt nothing but floating—a blissful, painless, silent void.... She thought to herself: Goodbye, Dragon....

Ship's AI — Dragon Eye

The AI noted the damage caused by the successful missile detonation. The Treech vessel was dead in space and streaming atmosphere from multiple locations around the hull. There was a great, jagged crater in the hull near the foredecks. Inertia alone carried it forward on its intercept course with the Dragon Eye.

The AI watched the crew abandon ship and then engaged

thrusters at maximum. Normally, this kind of continuous burn using thrusters was prohibited because of the damage to the thruster assemblies that would occur as they overheated. But that would not be an issue this time. There would be no expensive repairs. No TCDF inspector would investigate the waste and notate the violation of regulations. The Dragon Eye had one final mission, and she was going to see it was done correctly.

As her speed picked up and the distance to intercept grew short, the AI began to wonder what it would be like to die. She wondered if she would realize some epiphany just as she was consumed by the nuclear fireball—would she feel anything...

And then it was time. The proximity trigger detonated the nuclear warhead buried deep in the ship's engineering spaces. A small sun erupted into life briefly. As it receded into darkness, space was again empty.

The self-destruct warhead was designed to be thorough. It was more than five times as powerful as that of the missile that was detonated against the hull of the Marauder. The explosion entirely consumed both ships, leaving little but dust and gasses to begin a long decaying orbit into the planet's atmosphere—in perhaps a century or so.

Below, witnessing the destruction, were several small but bright lights—retro rockets firing on multiple shuttles ... and one escape pod.

Chapter 28—DRAGON FALL

Imperial Destroyer Celestia - Planet Jaden-325-4AI: "Attending."

Jar'ek: "Show me all related video and sensor recordings surrounding the attack of the TCDF Dragon Eye from the time of the assault to the present."

AI: "Beginning direct psionic data feed along with visual and audio recreations using your Augmented Reality Display."

Suddenly, Jar'ek was no longer on the Celestia but looking back at the planet, Jaden-325-4—from Space.

A large spacecraft came into view over the horizon, orbiting the planet below. At first glance it looked ungainly—teardrop-shaped—narrowing to a point in the bow while widening to an expansive, bulbous, rounded aft dotted with blue-green engine ports. It was large enough to house nearly 500 Terrans in relative comfort. And its surface was covered with an impressive number of particle cannons and missile ports.

As Jar'ek watched, mesmerized by what he realized must be a Treech Marauder, a single KKM was launched from a railgun in the ship's belly. A KKM was, essentially, a formed metallic alloy rock with good aerodynamics. It was meant to survive high-speed re-entry into a planet's atmosphere and to be able to convert a large amount of mass to energy upon impacting a solid object—like a warship or installation. Jar'ek saw the glowing trail left as microscopic portions of the metallic shell ablated in the furnace heat of re-entry. He saw the Dragon Eye beginning to lift from the planet surface under high acceleration.

The KKM missed the Dragon Eye, but it hit a spot only yards from where she had just been on the planet surface. The impact released a pulse of kinetic energy equivalent to 10 of the TCDFs MK2 fission missile warheads. The shockwave hit the TCDF space vessel with punishing force. A significant portion of the hull facing the shockwave crumpled in upon itself, and the course was altered dramatically.

Somehow, the small Terran Exploration Vessel made its way into a stable orbit. But then it was adrift. Sensor readings and damage estimates scrolled across the bottom of Jar'ek's ARD, as the video continued to play out. The Treech Marauder set an intercept course, like a spider navigating its web to see to its floundering prey. The AI continued to recreate the recent history of the Dragon Eye as ordered until the Dragon Eye closed on the wounded Marauder and annihilated both ships with her self-destruct warhead.

Jar'ek: "There were survivors! I saw the shuttles launch!"

AI: "Yes. There were survivors from both vessels. An escape pod and shuttles were launched from the Terran vessel, while a single Drop Ship was deployed from the Marauder, just prior to their destruction."

Jar'ek: "Treech ground troops! We need to locate the TCDF personnel and render aid immediately."

AI: "I have the general area in which they would have landed. I suggest you order the launch of atmospheric probes to pinpoint their locations."

Jar'ek: "AFFIRMATIVE. Launch probes immediately."

AI: "As you order. Probes have been launched and assigned search patterns. We should have detailed location and status information on the Terran survivors within 30 centi-fractions."

Jar'ek: "Update me the moment you have more information. And in the meantime, display a schematic of the Celestia on my ARD. Show me locations for armories and any working inventory for assault shuttles or other armed small craft aboard."

AI: "As ordered."

Jar'ek began a double-time jog back along the path they had taken from their living quarters in the forward section of the ship. He didn't want to waste any more time, now that he knew some of his crew had survived—especially since there was a Drop Ship full of Treech ground troops in the area. He may have been too late to help prevent the destruction of the Dragon Eye, but he would be damned if he was going to be late to the party THIS TIME.

Jar'ek: "AI, attend me."

AI: "Attending."

Jar'ek: "Can you make an audiovisual connection between myself and my team in the living quarters?"

AI: "Yes, Sire."

Jar'ek: "Do so, at once."

A bright square appeared in the upper right quadrant of Jar'ek's ARD. It showed the startled face of his closest companion—shirtless, hair mussed and bleary-eyed as if he had been woken out of a sound sleep, which he most likely had. Jar'ek couldn't help suppressing a smile but then recalled the serious things they must discuss. His face went flat, devoid of emotion—focused.

Kallehn: "Jar'ek! I was wondering where you got off to! I saw that S'Fah was with you, so I wasn't TOO worried."

Jar'ek: "Sorry. I needed some time with my own thoughts, and I didn't want to wake you."

Kallehn: "Well, no worries. But we have comms! Cool! How does this work?"

Jar'ek: "Time for that later! S'Fah and I are on our way back to you. Get geared up! We have a S.A.R. Mission!"

Kallehn: "What?! Who??!"

Jar'ek: "There were survivors from the Dragon Eye. They need our help."

Kallehn: "Hunh?! Oh my gosh! I'll get ready, but don't you dare drop this comm connection! Tell me everything you know!"

Imperial Destroyer Celestia - Planet Jaden-325-4

By the time S'Fah and Jar'ek made it back to the Team's quarters, Kallehn had learned all there was to know about the attack on the Dragon Eye and its aftermath. He and J'Uhr were standing in the passageway as the rest of the Team arrived. To Jar'ek's surprise, Kallehn was not wearing his Ranger uniform and jacket. He was instead wearing the same flexible metallic light armor that Jar'ek was wearing—with one distinction. Kallehn had no tattoo marking him as a Meld, so there was only bare skin under the transparent stripe down his right side. And at his waist, instead of the TCDF particle beam sidearm, he wore an Imperial Blaster.

Jar'ek's glance passed upward over Kallehn's body from foot to face. As his gaze moved to Kallehn's eyes, his eyebrows raised and his head tilted slightly to the left, indicating interested surprise.

Kallehn: "Well, my uniform was gone when I got up, and this was in its place. The AI said I should put it on as it would provide better protection. And it feels amazing against my skin. Not to mention that I look AWESOME wearing it!" (Big smile)

Jar'ek: "I see.... Did the AI also caution you about that WMD at your waistband?"

Kallehn: "The AI showed me an introductory training video in 3D...."

Jar'ek: "GREAT ...."

Plato: {"Jar'ek, his Imperial Blaster is tied to your psionic connection. You control the power settings and safety. It has been set at a WLD setting, to begin with."}

Jar'ek: {"WLD?"}

Plato: {"Weapon of Lesser Destruction," he said, smiling apologetically inside. "It seemed prudent to provide your teammate with the best protection and armaments available for the coming mission. We both know how much he means to you."}

Jar'ek: {"True. But wearing Imperial Light Armor he will also appear as if he has also denounced his oath to the TCDF and thrown his and J'Uhr's lot in with mine. I do not like the symbolism. It seems like you are limiting his choices."}

Plato: {"That was not my intent. And I should have discussed this with you, but I felt that time was of the essence. Kallehn can always trade the armor back in for his Ranger uniform when this engagement is over."}

Jar'ek: "Okay, Team, let's stop by the armory on the way and pick up a couple of heavy weapons packages before we see if our 10-millennia-old assault shuttle still works."

Eyes wide, brows raised, Kallehn muttered to himself: "What exactly is heavier than a sidearm Weapon of Mass Destruction?!"

The Team headed up the passageway at their ground-covering trot.

Planet Jaden-325-4 - Crew Rally Point

The captain had intended to attempt contact with Ranger Team Alpha before landing so that they might rendezvous. But the escaping shuttles and escape pod were a bit closer to the detonation of the Dragon Eye than she had hoped they would be. As a result, all three vessels had sustained varying degrees of damage from debris strikes. The landings weren't so much landings as barely controlled crashes. The escape pod, in particular, had a rough time, digging a deep furrow in the sandy soil for over 200 nL before it came to a rest, canted over on one side with the escape hatch nearly vertical on top.

Alpha Shuttle had been holed in several places, and there were plumes of black smoke coming from the thruster housing. Beta Shuttle wasn't much better. It didn't have holes in the hull, but the main thruster assemblies were torn to shreds. It was a testament to the pilot's skill that they had landed at all.

The crewmembers on Alpha Shuttle had started evacuating supplies and equipment as quickly as they could. The production of black smoke was unstaunched by the efforts of the crew chief to put the flames out. Captain Lao walked down the ramp of Beta Shuttle and began organizing the rest of her crew.

Captain: "T.O. Conner, I need a tactical assessment of our situation. See if you can get a pair of drones working, and instruct them to survey the local area. We will need a defensible base, shelter, water, etc. And arm the crew. Let's get a security perimeter established. "

Captain: "Helmsman De Lucena, since we won't need your services as a helm officer for some time, please help the doctor organize recovery and treatment for the injured."

Captain: "Chief T'Kathrad, break out the Communications Package. See if you can locate Ranger Team Alpha. Inform them of our status and request assistance and whatever 'intel' they can provide."

The three crew members answered with a chorus of "Aye, ma'am!" and scattered in different directions to execute the captain's orders.

The captain saw a few people milling about the supplies that had been evacuated from Alpha Shuttle after they had finished. She raised her hand and waved in their direction.

Captain: "Blakes! Furstall! Grab a S.A.R. kit and follow me. We're going to see if anyone survived the crash of that escape pod."

Two crewmen in blue camouflage duty uniforms ran to sling two large backpacks across their shoulders and started moving in her direction. She headed at a comfortable pace toward the pod to better allow them to catch up.

It didn't look good. There were thermal scars along the sides from re-entry, and the hull had taken some serious debris hits. The usually sleek, shiny outer hull of the little craft was dented and crumpled. The nearby foliage was putting off an acrid white smoke from where the hot, glowing hull had touched off small brush fires when it first came to rest. Although the pod was cooling, the fires were quickly finding more fuel in the nearby shrubs and grasses.

The smoke burned their eyes and throats as they used portable extinguishers to douse the flames before they got out of hand. The frame of the escape hatch was warped, and a portion of the hatch was open to atmosphere. Captain Lao hoped that had not happened before the crash landing—otherwise there might not be anyone left alive in the small craft for them to aid.

Blakes moved around to the front of the pod where it had plowed deeply into the soil and pushed up a dirt mound, completely covering the nose of the craft. He scampered up the mound and onto the pod's outer hull near the escape hatch. He pulled up hard—grunting loudly—trying to open the hatch, but the mechanism was hopelessly jammed.

Crewman Blakes: "Furstall, toss me a power jack!"

Furstall dug into one of the backpacks—now on the ground and open. He pulled out a mechanical device that looked like a metal caricature of a long-snouted amphibian's head. He held it in both hands, slung it low to the ground, and carefully tossed it up and over. Blakes was able to catch the device as it came back down without moving more than a hand's width.

Crewman Blakes: "Got it!"

Blakes quickly knelt down on the surface of the pod and pushed the long metal snout in the opening between the warped frame and the hatch. He began tapping buttons. The jaws of the snout began to open slowly as he applied more and more pressure to the closed hatch. After a seemingly long moment, there was a squealing sound as the metal of the hatch frame gave way. The freed hatch then fell back against the opposite side with a reverberating CLANG!

Blakes looked inside and then stepped down into the interior gingerly until he disappeared. It was several moments before his head peeked out through the open hatch again.

Crewman Blakes: "Captain! It's Chief Vermanderly. She's pretty banged up. She is still secured in the pilot's acceleration couch, but the orientation of the pod is 90 degrees askew, so she's hanging in midair. Her pulse is strong, and she is breathing. But she's bleeding some from a scalp laceration, and she is unconscious. And ma'am... there is a Ranger Team evacuation pod on board. It's closed up tight and active."

Captain: "Well done, Blakes! You and Furstall see if you can jury-rig a pulley system to extract the chief with as little trauma as possible. But I don't want you to actually move her until the doctor has examined her and given his okay."

Blakes and Furstall both answered, "Aye, Captain!"

The captain began jogging back to the shuttles to alert the doctor to the chief's condition and situation.

As she ran, she wiped an errant lock of black hair away from her eyes with a shaking hand. She clenched her fists tightly to stop the tremors. Her crew needed to see her as strong and capable—now more than ever. Inside, however, she mourned for the lost crew members—friends and colleagues—all of the people for whom she was responsible. She should have done something differently—something! Surely, there was some way all of this death and hurt could have been avoided if she had only done things differently....

But some had survived—against all the odds. She could torture herself later with the what-ifs. Right now, she had to focus on just *KEEPING* the survivors *ALIVE*. She wasn't going to let them down AGAIN.

Chapter 29—A TEAM RE-MADE

Imperial Destroyer Celestia - Planet Jaden-325-4

Jar'ek knew the way now. He knew this ship like the back of his hand. Extended memories regarding the Celestia and her crew filled his thoughts. Emotions flooded his heart along with those memories: camaraderie—respect—affection—grief—loss. The flood threatened to wash him away like a tsunami. He shook his head to clear his thoughts. He could examine all of this and allow himself to feel, later. Right now, the Terran survivors needed him—and he needed ***them***.

Jar'ek stopped his headlong rush and stepped up to the wall beside a large airlock portal. This was no small personnel airlock, but one designed to allow cargo haulers or large numbers of troops to enter as a group. The portal spanned the entire wall, floor to ceiling so that Kallehn might stand on Jar'ek's shoulders and still not reach the point where it receded into the ceiling. Ten Rangers could march through the portal abreast and not touch either side.

Jar'ek placed his left hand on a square lighted panel just large enough for his hand to fit within it with fingers outstretched. A deep blue light traced an outline around his palm and fingers where they touched the surface.

Although the AI had been able to activate the ship's systems—including life support, power generation, defensive screens and such—it was not permitted to activate the offensive capabilities of the Celestia. The ship had been locked down during the in-place quarantine required by the Plague. Fully activating the power of the Imperial Destroyer was one of those things that still required some ritual, as part of the security protocol. And only a Meld with psionic powers and one who spoke Takeshi could complete the protocol.

Extended memories of his instruction and training in these rituals and protocols pushed their way to the forefront. He “saw” what he must do. He “heard” what must be spoken.

Jar'ek lifted his right hand and traced glowing symbols in the air with his extended index finger. A horizontal stroke of this length—then, vertical slashes of another angle and size—soon swirled into a complete set of symbols. This time, the design hung in the air like a red mist. And as he traced each symbol, he spoke in the ancient tongue of the Takesh.

Jar'ek: “T'Sah Jar'ek — H'Trackat —Pursht'Ramahd — Qlaak'Tak --Fasha'at Kusatch kre'heel”

Kallehn was dumbfounded. He heard and ***UNDERSTOOD*** the Takeshi phrases! How was this possible?!

Translation: “Recognize: Jar'ek, Imperial Meld. I hereby claim command of this vessel. Release all security lockdowns. Activate all weapons systems.”

As the wispy symbols began to fade and disappear, the blue light outlining his left hand turned bright red. And sprites of red light fled from where he touched the authentication panel, along the walls and ceilings in every direction. One red pinpoint of light traced the portal itself.

The loud Whooosssshhhh of escaping atmosphere was dramatic as it equalized with the rest of the ship, while the portal lowered and then disappeared beneath the deck. Suddenly a spectral figure appeared in the tall, spindly likeness of a Takesh in Imperial Light Armor. Colorful decorations emblazoned his left chest. As his mouth slits moved, a deep trilling voice reverberated throughout the Celestia.

Takesh Avatar: “P'harha'Tkrat — T'Sah — Rahoam'Bsalah — Crix'Tah — Galazn.”

Translation: “Authorization granted, my lord. As lives the Meld, so lives the Empire!”

The larger-than-life image bowed deeply to Jar'ek and dissipated into thin air.

Kallehn: "Jar'ek, what is going on?! Somehow, I understood what you just said... I know Takeshi...."

Jar'ek: {"Really? Maybe the AI was translating it for you?"}

Kallehn: {"How? It was in my head, not in my ears!"}

Jar'ek: {"Plato—are you responsible for this?"}

Plato: {"Hmmm... Not directly."}

Jar'ek: {"What does that mean?!"}

Plato: {"There is only one explanation that I can think of... It must have happened during the psionic stimulation event when you repaired the synaptic damage to Kallehn's brain."}

Jar'ek: {"Explain."}

Plato: {"Human physiology is still new to the Harmonic SEED, Sire. And you were inexperienced when you attempted the connection. If I had to speculate, I would suggest that you may have transferred more than life energy to Kallehn."}

Jar'ek: {"You mean I INFECTED HIM with Harmonic SEED?!"}

Plato: {"I really wish you would NOT use that particular word in regards to the SEED. We are a gift, not a disease.

Jar'ek: {"Holy crap! How am I going to explain THIS!??"}

Plato: {"It was unintentional, Sire. And I do not believe enough of the SEED was actually transferred to create a Meld. These effects may well be temporary. When the SEED is deployed, it modifies your DNA to prevent your immune system from rejecting the SEED. If it was deployed in insufficient quantities to achieve that, Kallehn's own body will expel the SEED in time.}

Waving his hand in front of Jar'ek's face, Kallehn called out: "Hey! Space cadet! Over here!"

Jar'ek: "Sorry... I was consulting with Plato."

Kallehn: "And???"

Jar'ek: "It appears that in healing you, I may have accidentally transferred some of the Harmonic SEED to your body. Accidentally... inadvertently... Did I mention that this was accidental?!? I am really sorry, Kallehn."

Kallehn: "Hmmmm...."

Kallehn turned and walked slowly away for a few steps and then stopped, staring off into the passageway.

Jar'ek: "Plato says it's probably a temporary effect."

Kallehn: "Well, this might turn out to be a good thing, after all."

Jar'ek walked over to his friend and placed his hand on his shoulder.

Jar'ek: "What are your thoughts, Kallehn? "

Kallehn looked up into Jar'ek's eyes and placed his hand on Jar'ek's opposite shoulder.

Kallehn: "This might actually fix some things.... I have been so conflicted.... I felt so much guilt that you sacrificed your future to save me. You couldn't go back to the Rangers. I was so afraid that they would make me go back with them and leave you here, by yourself."

Kallehn's face tightened, and he dropped his gaze to the ground. When he spoke again, his voice was husky.

Kallehn: "I... I couldn't face that—never seeing you again—never sharing a meal or a conversation about our dreams of exploring the galaxy together—Don't you see? Now I am damaged goods, too! The Rangers will never trust me completely. I don't have any place else to go."

Kallehn raised his eyes to Jar'ek's again. But this time he wore a broad smile. There was a trace of moisture in his eyes still, and Jar'ek took his finger and carefully wiped the moisture away.

Jar'ek cleared his throat and began to speak. There was the slightest trace of a husky tremor in his voice also.

Jar'ek: "I am ashamed to say that I am so very g-g-glad. I didn't let myself think about it. I couldn't ask you to give up your future and join me in this psychotic episode of a mission. I wanted you to lead a happy life. I didn't want you to be exiled from other Terrans the way I must be. I had no right to ask you."

Kallehn: "The only way I could ever lead a happy life is by your side, idiot!"

They both dropped their arms from each other's shoulder and embraced. Kallehn laid his face on Jar'ek's chest, and neither cared that quite a bit more moisture was shed from both sets of eyes. Jar'ek held Kallehn close, his heart hurting so much he thought it would surely shrivel up and die. But it could not, for although he was finally experiencing all of the pain and doubt he had repressed for so long, his heart was filling with the joy sparked from Kallehn's heartfelt words and the feeling of holding him in his arms—finally.

Jar'ek: "I have loved you for so long now. But I was sure you rejected my feelings for you. In the shower the other day... I don't understand...."

Kallehn: "I wasn't rejecting YOU.

Jar'ek: "I still don't understand...."

Plato: {"Jar'ek, I hate to interrupt during such a sensitive moment between you two... but I think I have some insight that may help you understand."}

Jar'ek: {"By all means… enlighten me."}

Plato: {"With ALL due respect, he is right, Sire. You ARE an idiot."}

Jar'ek: {"Hunh?!"}

Plato: {"Kallehn wasn't rejecting you in the shower. He wasn't rejecting you in the images you saw during the psionic stimulation. And if you weren't so stubbornly ethical, you would have known this once you had allowed yourself to explore his memories because they were filled with longing thoughts of you. But since you didn't… you MISINTERPRETED everything. You viewed every single action, every single word through the distortion of your own doubts and fears. Kallehn wasn't rejecting YOU. He was rejecting HIMSELF. He couldn't face you because even though he wanted you just as badly as you wanted him… he felt UNWORTHY. And he mistook your coldness and distance as a rejection of HIM. Actually, you are BOTH IDIOTS."}

Jar'ek: {"Are you fucking kidding me!?"}

Plato: {"No, I am not kidding you. Now, go tell him he is WORTHY and how you feel about him. But do it quickly! I really do apologize, but you two have picked the LEAST optimal time possible to have this emotional revelation. Terran survivors—Treech ground troops—fission detonations—bad things happening. Remember??!"}

Jar'ek: {"Yes, yes! Always the taskmaster! Never a free moment's peace! Save the galaxy and all that! Whine—whine—whine! Can't you just give me ONE FREE MOMENT?!"}

Jar'ek pushed Kallehn back gently, then took his right hand and placed it under Kallehn's chin, raising his face so he could gaze intensely into his eyes.

Jar'ek: "Hear me, Kallehn Frix. You are the best thing that has ever happened to me. You are the most worthy person I could imagine. And I love you with all of my being."

Jar'ek pulled Kallehn's face up as he leaned into a kiss he had been waiting for as long as he could remember. He heard Kallehn's quick intake of breath and felt the warm caress of his exhale as their open lips met in a gentle embrace—absorbing the depth and complexities in each other's heart through this sensual and intimate exploration.

It seemed like they stood so for hours. And Jar'ek wanted it to continue for days... But he slowly backed away from that so very important first kiss with sadness in his eyes.

Jar'ek: "I expect LOTS more of that VERY SOON! Do you hear me, Kallehn Frix? But right now, we have to go save some of our friends—and perhaps the galaxy...."

Kallehn: "Yes, Sire!"

Jar'ek sighed heavily and said: "Oh, not you, too!"

Kallehn: "You better get used to it, Jar'ek Constandor! But worry not! With me around, your humility is guaranteed...."

Jar'ek shook his head, grimaced, and said: "Of that, I have NO DOUBT."

Both young men were smiling broadly as they turned as one to walk through the open portal and into the vast troop airlock beyond. Kallehn's arm was draped over Jar'ek's shoulder, his hand cupping the side of Jar'ek's warm, well-muscled neck. Jar'ek dropped his chin and caressed Kallehn's palm with his cheek.

The two X'Ah-Panths padded along close behind, glancing at each other. If X'Ah-Panths could laugh, they would be laughing out loud. These two Terran males were such cubs. But the cats were glad that their mind-mates had resolved all that unnecessary tension between them. S'Fah and J'Uhr had known the feelings the young men had for each other. It seemed to be ridiculously complicated for humans to find love and to accept it. Thank goodness, they were X'Ah-Panths and not humans!

The X'Ah-Panths also understood some of what was happening with the Harmonic SEED. They realized that their humans would not be going back to the Rangers. They also knew that it made no difference. They would follow their mind-mates wherever their life journey took them.

Chapter 30—DIVIDED WE FALL

Imperial Destroyer Celestia - Planet Jaden-325-4

Starboard Launch Bay

As the Team exited the airlock and entered the launch bay, the walls and ceilings began emitting a muted illumination that lit the entire bay from every angle. The bay extended for over 200 nL to the outer hull and 400 nL across. There were two assault shuttles staged side by side in the middle of the bay facing the large space doors. Each shuttle was 75nL in length and 40nL in width. They were designed to carry up to 30 ground troops and their equipment.

Plato: {"I know you won't like this, but you know the rules. The Empire cannot take unnecessary chances with the Meld."}

Jar'ek: {"I am going!"}

Plato: {"I know. I cannot stop you. But that means you must accept an escort."}

Jar'ek: {"There are no living Imperial Guardsmen on this planet. How do you expect me to find an escort?"}

Plato: {"While not optimal, there is another option."}

Jar'ek: {"Oh, hell... you mean Mechs, don't you?"}

Plato: {"Yes, Sire. But only a phalanx or two."}

Jar'ek: {"I will accept an escort of two Mechs. They have to stay in the shuttle unless called for. Anything else is going to scare the crap out of my former shipmates, and I don't want to do that unnecessarily. Why is it that these AIs can use offensive weapons, but ships' AIs cannot?"}

Plato: {"Order of magnitude—while Mechs could destroy entire cities, warships can destroy cities, continents, planets, solar systems, etc."}

Jar'ek: {"Good point. Okay, well let's load up two Mechs and an assault armament package. We might need Terran-compatible medical kits."}

Plato: {"I've anticipated your needs. Maintenance bots have converted one of the forward base medical packages to Terran standards. Rations and water have already been packed aboard the shuttle."}

Two floor-to-ceiling wall panels opened nearest the leftmost assault shuttle. Two black metallic Combat Androids stepped out of their stasis chambers and onto the deck. After a few seconds, they turned together and lifted two large, white storage containers, each holding 10 shoulder-mounted phase canons. The two metal mechanical warriors stomped over towards the nearest shuttle—the same shuttle the Team was now approaching.

Kallehn and the two X'Ah-Panths had stopped dead in their tracks the moment the Combat Androids had stepped out onto the deck. The felines had lowered their bellies to the ground and were watching the bots very carefully, not moving a muscle. Kallehn simply stood facing them, mouth open in an expression of shock.

Kallehn: "Jar'ek, are you seeing this?! Those guys are twice as tall as you! What the hell are they?!"

Jar'ek: "Our bodyguards for this little S.A.R. mission. They are called Mechs. Mechanized Combat Androids."

Jar'ek stopped at the rear ramp of the shuttle and waited for the Mechs. The rest of the Team finally decided it was okay to continue towards the shuttle since Jar'ek seemed familiar with the Mechs and was even expecting them.

As the Mechs arrived, each dropped the armament package and settled down on one knee, head bent forward. Their heavy metallic knees rang loudly as they hit the deck.

Takesh voices rang from the kneeling Mechs.

Mechs: “Crix'Tah Galaznikrat—Soli'Tza a'Lomat “

Jar’ek translated it in his mind, as he heard it: “As Lives the Meld, So Lives the Empire!”

Jar'ek: “K'etath (Rise.) Please use Terran Standard to communicate from now on. You will also recognize another Terran, Kallehn Frix, as having command authority over all Imperial forces second only to my own. You will obey all directives from him when they do not conflict with Imperial Edicts. Encode identity and authorization.”

The Mechs stood and turned their blank stares toward Kallehn, who was just coming up to stand behind Jar'ek. A blue beam projected from each of the Mechs and scanned Kallehn from head to foot, then abruptly disappeared. Kallehn stood as if transfixed, expecting any moment to feel searing pain. After a few pain-free seconds, he tentatively started breathing again.

Mechs: “We recognize the Terran Kallehn Frix. Kallehn Frix is authorized to command these Mechs as long as those commands are not in violation of Imperial Edicts.”

Kallehn: “Holy crap! Give a guy a little warning, why don’t you?! I thought those Mechs were gonna fry me with their eye beams or something! And I'm not sure I want that level of responsibility, Jar'ek. I am the most junior office in the Ranger Corps! I’ve never been in command of ANYTHING!”

Jar'ek: “Kallehn, the Mechs don’t have ‘eye beams!’ Anyway, I cannot be everywhere at once. The Mechs will focus on protecting you and me. They won’t lift a finger to help our crewmates unless we direct them to. And I am just as concerned that they AVOID shooting our crewmates, under those circumstances. If you see something that needs doing, I want you to be able to take matters into your own hands. I trust you. I trust your instincts. Besides, if something happens to me...."

Kallehn: "Okay, SHUT UP!! Nothing is going to happen to you because Braxton, Whipple and I will be standing in front of your Imperial ass."

Jar'ek smiled and said: "You *NAMED* them?!"

Kallehn: "Well, I wasn't going to call them Android #1 and Android #2, was I?"

Jar'ek said: "Whatever makes you feel comfortable...." and rolled his eyes.

Now that they were close by, Kallehn got a chance to examine the Mechs in detail. They looked humanoid, with black metallic skins stretched over what appeared to be well-muscled frames. Their heads were roughly human shaped, but where features such as ears, nose, and mouth should have been, there was nothing but more smooth black metal. Hands ended in four mutually opposing fingers. Feet had no toes. And they were so damned big... it was disconcerting.

Jar'ek looked up at the Mechs and spoke: "Take the armament packages on board and secure for launch."

The Mechs effortlessly lifted the heavy crates and began walking up the loading ramp of the nearest shuttle.

Jar'ek: "Kallehn, I am going to try to remember how to fly this monster. Can you get the rest of the Team settled and join me in the cockpit? I could use the company."

Kallehn said: "Can do, skipper!" and sketched a casual salute.

Jar'ek: "Cut it out, Kallehn... I feel weird enough about all of this, as it is. How am I going to explain this to Captain Lao?!"

Kallehn: "I don't know, but you should think fast. It's not like she's not going to notice us flying in a super advanced assault shuttle, having traded in our Ranger uniforms for a high-tech second skin. And just wait until she gets a good look at our brand new Braxton and Whipple!"

Jar'ek shook his head, trotted up the loading ramp, and headed for the cockpit. The rest of the Ranger Team followed.

Imperial Destroyer Celestia - Planet Jaden-325-4

—{Private psionic communication}—

Plato: {"AI, Attend me."}

Ship's AI: {"Celestia, attending."}

Plato: {"I have a secondary mission in mind for you. I would like to keep this secondary mission a secret from the Emperor at this time."}

Ship's AI: {"Understood."}

Plato: {"Good. Here's what I want you to do...."}

Planet surface — Jaden-325-4 — Crew Rally Point

The Command team had congregated together in the cramped confines of Shuttle 1's cockpit to review the current situation.

Commander Sallen, TO Conner, HO De Lucena and Medical Officer To'Torat were standing or seated in the cockpit, watching the main display screen in between the pilot's and copilot's acceleration seats. The captain was sitting in the pilot's seat, but she had it adjusted all the way back on its tracks and pivoted so she could see the group.

Captain Lao: "TO Conner, give us a tactical overview."

Conner: “Aye, ma'am. The drones have been sending us data on their outward spiral search pattern now for about 1/2 deci-fraction. There are no threats in the immediate area. However, I would like to mention that in reviewing the sensor recordings from the shuttles, as we evacuated the Dragon Eye... well, it is hard to tell because of the ionic interference from atmospheric entry. It looks to me like the enemy vessel was able to launch at least one small craft before its destruction.”

Captain: “An escape pod? What kind of craft?”

TO Conner: “It looked too large for an escape pod, ma'am. If I had to guess, I would say it was a 'Drop Ship.'”

Captain: “Are you telling me there is a Treech Drop Ship somewhere on this planet? Those things carry— what—50 heavily armed ground assault troops?!”

Conner: “Yes, ma'am. And since it was launched close to where we began our own re-entry, it’s a safe bet that they are closer to us than I'd like.”

Captain: “Has the chief managed to contact Ranger Team Alpha?”

XO Sallen: “No, Captain. No answer—no RF carrier—no beacon.”

The captain lowered her face into her hands and began massaging the tense muscles underneath.

Captain: “I had hoped they had been far enough away from the KKM impact that they would have survived. I supposed that just was wishful thinking. It looks like we can't expect help from anyone else, at this point. Is there any hope of getting one or both of the shuttles flight-worthy?”

Sallen: “Not anytime soon, Captain. Shuttle 2 is a total loss. Shuttle 1 might be repairable if we scavenged everything we could from Shuttle 2. But it would take days or possibly weeks to repair with the tools we have here."

Captain: "XO, provided you come up with a miracle to resolve the Worm infestation we seem to be facing—could we survive on this planet for an extended period?"

Sallen: "Initial surveys indicated the plant life was close enough to Terran norms to be digestible. It lacks some essential nutrients, but we have supplements in our survival gear. There are sufficient sources of water nearby. We had time to pack up quite a lot of rations and survival gear. I think we will be all right—for a Standard Solar Orbit, anyway. "

Captain: "Well, that's good news, at any rate."

Kathy Lao turned to face the other female on her command staff, Lt. Kira To'Torat, the Medical Officer and Head of Biological Surveys.

Captain: "Doc, I want a report on the wounded, but first I need to know if there are any X-Tee pathogens we need to worry about on this planet."

MO To'Torat: "The biological surveys are still underway, Captain The results I can give you are preliminary, to say the least. But nothing we found is beyond our immune system's ability to fight. There don't appear to be any actual viruses in this planetary biome at all. Quite a variety of bacteria, though—and a few could be nasty. "

Captain: "All right. TO, work with the XO to see what we can do as far as tightening our defensive perimeter... I know the Dragon Eye was an exploration vessel, not a warship. We don't have trained ground troops of our own. But this is what we are left with. Let's make the best of it. I don't intend to have survived the initial attack, the destruction of the Dragon Eye, and the loss of all of our missing crewmates—simply to allow myself to be eaten by a pack of killer Worms! I'm expecting miracles, gentlemen."

XO Sallen: “Aye, ma'am. We will certainly do everything humanly possible.”

Captain: “Miracles, XO, ***MIRACLES***!”

Chapter 31 — STAND AND FIGHT

Imperial Assault Shuttle Castalon - Planet Jaden-325-4

Jar'ek: "Open exterior bay doors."

The entire outer wall of the shuttle bay receded silently into the deck. There was the slightest shimmer, indicating an atmospheric shield was held in place where the solid bay door had been a moment ago.

Kallehn came through the hatch from the passenger compartment and quietly took the copilot's seat, then glanced over at Jar'ek.

Jar'ek passed his left hand over the flight console, and it sprang to life. He used two fingers on his right hand to push the image of a slider on the console to the Full position. A subtle vibration could be felt through the shuttle now. It felt as if untold power was being barely held at bay. The hum changed pitch slightly, and the shuttle gently rose up from the deck, suspended above the floor by 4nL—barely enough room for a X'Ah-Panth to walk underneath without crouching.

Jar'ek: "AI, attend me."

Celestia AI: "Celestia, attending."

Jar'ek: "Summary report on atmospheric drone surveillance data, please."

Celestia AI: "Rally point for Terran evacuees has been located 17,325.7 µL (5,250 km) from here. (µL=Distance light travels in 1 microsecond or 0.3 kilometers) The Treech Drop Ship also has been located. It is on an intercept course with the Terran rally point. ETA 100 centi-fractions."

As the AI was responding, a map of the planet was displayed on Jar'ek's ARD with waypoints for the Celestia's current position and the Terran rally point.

Jar'ek: "AI, can you configure the shuttle interface to mirror my ARD visually for the copilot?"

Celestia AI: "Affirmative. Complying."

Jar'ek: "Can we get there ahead of the Treech?"

Celestia AI: "No, Sire. But if we enter low orbit, the shuttle can get there shortly after the Treech craft arrives."

A holographic representation appeared before Kallehn that showed the same planetary map waypoints and route.

Celestia: "I've taken the liberty of updating the Shuttle AI, called Castalon, with human language and colloquialisms I've noted. This should facilitate better communication. Although you can reach me through your communications suite, Castalon will be your direct interface to the shuttle from this point forward."

Jar'ek: "Understood...Castalon, Attend me."

Castalon: "Attending."

Jar'ek: "I may have memories of having flown one of these in a past life, but I need some practice before I can be confident in my piloting skills. I would like you to have our backs."

Castalon: "I believe I have your colloquialisms mapped. You are asking me to allow you to gain some real time flight experience, but to take control if you make a mistake that puts the craft in danger. Am I correct?"

Jar'ek: "Affirmative."

Castalon: "Mission Confirmed."

Jar'ek: "Pilot to crew, hold on. We are going to be breaking some speed records."

Kallehn leaned back into his comfortable acceleration seat. He was about to ask Jar'ek where the restraining harness was when a bright line of lights lit up along his armrests. He suddenly felt as if a giant hand had wrapped its fingers around him, holding him gently down in the soft cushions of the copilot's seat.

Kallehn: “Wow... Cool! Invisible restraints?”

Jar'ek glanced at Kallehn and smiled.

Jar'ek: “Gravity Web. There are power capacitors underneath the seats that will sustain the restraint web even if we lose main power. Here we go!”

Jar'ek pressed his hand down on the edge of his right armrest where a light was blinking red. The inertia compensators built into the shuttle negated almost all of the gravitational force that they would usually feel when the shuttle was accelerating at such high levels. They felt just enough to have a sense of movement and direction.

The forward view showed them clearing the Celestia's outer hull and immediately going vertical at high thrust. They could feel the acceleration increasing, but it never got to the point where it was truly uncomfortable. They continued to gain velocity as they speared through the cumulonimbus clouds and kept right on going. Soon, the air started to thin and no longer refracted the light from the Sun. The stars and planets were becoming easier to pick out from the darkened sky.

Jar'ek: {“Plato, how can Kallehn and I communicate privately with each other and the Mechs once we disembark from the shuttle? Does our light armor include comm units?”}

Plato: {“You could find this information for yourself, but in the interest of time and keeping your eyes on where we are flying... Yes. The light armor you are wearing incorporates a full sub-space communications suite. Soldiers in the field can communicate by simply starting the communications by thinking ‘command circuit’ or ‘Phalanx circuit.’ That communications circuit stays open until closed or another circuit is opened. In this case, only you and Kallehn will be on the 'command circuit,' while the Androids will join you on the 'Phalanx circuit.' "}

Jar'ek: {"It is sub-vocal?"}

Plato: {"No, the armor incorporates a psionic interface, as well as an audible or vocal interface. In your current state of development, you will be able to use the psionic interface exclusively. As for Kallehn, I am not certain. I believe he may possess sufficient psionic skills to rely solely on the psionic interface, as well. But I wouldn't suggest testing that theory in battle conditions unless you had little choice."}

Jar'ek: {"Understood."}

Jar'ek swiveled his seat to face Kallehn better.

Jar'ek: {"Kallehn, these suits we are wearing have built-in communications suites, sort of like our comm-helmets. Say 'command circuit' to speak with me only. 'Phalanx includes Whipple and Braxton. And the suits also augment your psionic skills. So it might be possible, in a pinch, to use mind-touch to reach me. Plato thinks it might be possible, but we should not rely on it. Got it?"}

Kallehn: {"Got it! When we get time, we need to figure out all the Imperial toys! "}

Jar'ek: {"Uhmmm... Remember? Rescue Mission—Worm Ground Troops—Danger?"}

Kallehn: {"Yeah, yeah. We got this." }

A muted beeping tone alerted Jar'ek to a blinking yellow indicator on the status board. Jar'ek reached forward and moved his hands across the console. The shuttle began to change orientation and reduce acceleration.

Castalon AI: "Orbital insertion achieved. Acceleration profile optimal. Excellent job, Sire. "

Jar'ek: "Thank you, Castalon."

Planet surface — Jaden-325-4 — Crew Rally Point

Captain Lao was inspecting the firing positions that had been dug in around the camp perimeter. The wounded had been moved into Shuttle 2, which was more intact and could provide more protection. Chief T'Kathrad had just finished passing out comm helmets to the Command Staff and wrist-comms to the ambulatory crew when the captain's comm annunciator beeped.

T.O. Conner: "Captain, we've lost contact with one of the drones. It was about 330mL out on an outward search spiral."

Captain: "Bring the remaining surveillance drone back to give us an over-watch view of the camp and its surrounds."

T.O. Conner: "Aye, Captain."

Captain: "Let's go to high alert—I believe our suspense will soon be over. Let's make sure the firing positions have extra power packs for the pulse rifles."

Taking a deep breath, she straightened her shoulders, narrowed her eyes, and began to gear up for the fight.

Planet surface — Jaden-325-4 — Crew Rally Point

Captain Kathy Xiang Lao lowered the augmented-reality visors on her commo helmet and called up the tactical overview. The single surveillance drone they had left was circling over the encampment and providing a bird's eye view of the surrounding area. The XO and TO had come through with a couple of miracles after all. They had scavenged the shield generators from both shuttles and had reconfigured them to project a dome shield over the entire encampment—about 100 nL across. There was no telling how long the shield dome would last against Treech Masers—let alone artillery or railgun fire from the Drop Ship.

And they had pulled one of the heavy laser cannons from Shuttle

2. They had even been able to construct a makeshift swivel mount for the thing. It took two crewmen to operate, but it packed more sheer power than anything else they had. The captain figured most of the crew realized the odds were not good. But now they could at least put up a fight. And the Treech had some payback coming!

Long ago, Treech DropShips had filled the skies of Earth. The historical records held visual recordings and some anatomical information from the dissection of dead Worms. A lot of DropShips were brought down in the early part of the War...before they decided to pummel Earth with mass drivers and nukes. But no colonial Terran had ever fought face-to-carapace with Worms. If the Worms kept to the same tactics, they would start the engagement with a swarm of mini-drones. The drones would harass the Terran firing positions, test their defenses and soften up their shields for the main attack to follow.

She knew they could hold back and pulverize her position with the heavy Masers from the safety of the Drop Ship. But she also knew the Worms liked fresh meat... A shiver ran up her spine as her imagination gave life to that gruesome thought. Well, she would hold out enough of a charge in her sidearm to make sure she wouldn't have to endure being eaten while she was still alive. Her face set with determination, she started walking back to the makeshift command post.

Including herself, there were only eight effective crewmembers left who could hold and fire a weapon. The Doc would stand guard over the wounded, for whatever good that would do. That left four to each man a foxhole firing position around the perimeter of the encampment. One could man the tripod mounted heavy laser. She and the XO would stand as the ready reserve for the firing positions.... Clearly, it wasn't enough against 50 trained and armored Worm ground troops!

The visual feed from the overhead drone blinked red as an airborne target approached at high speed. The Drop Ship—

approaching quickly from the Southwest. They weren't even bothering to be stealthy.

Captain Lao activated her comm-helmet on the "All Crew" channel.

Captain Lao: "Crew of the Dragon Eye. It has been my honor to serve with you! It is now my honor to FIGHT beside you! For Earth! For the Colonies! For LIFE! Let's FRY those slimy bastards!"

A mammoth roar was felt as much as heard as all their voices rose in a single voice of solidarity and determination. They may not be veterans, but they would FIGHT.

The captain hefted her laser rifle up to her shoulder, adjusted the sight, and made sure the power pack was seated correctly. The XO walked up beside her while checking his own rifle for the fourth time. The crew had piled up supply crates and metal sheeting from the damaged shuttles as a protective barricade for a firing position near the command post. The captain checked her visor display and positioned herself with her rifle resting on the protective barricade, pointing toward the direction she expected the Drop Ship to come from.

XO Sallen wiped the sweat from his palms and joined her. Leaning forward against the barricade, he began tapping the control tabs on his visor to enable the rifle sight—allowing him to select and hit targets more effectively. He knew his comm-helmet AI, and the electronics in the laser rifle would increase his accuracy and speed significantly.

They heard the Drop Ship before they saw it. Unlike most shuttles, the Drop Ship was deafening in an atmosphere. Stealth wasn't a high priority with the Worms. A pulsing vibration that started low—echoing through the low foothills that surrounded them—soon became a huge, reverberating rumble that shook the very ground beneath them. Whether it was intended or not, the audible onslaught put all of the Terrans on edge. None of the defenders got up and ran, but more than a few thought about it. And then the monstrosity hove into view, slewing around a hillock and heading straight for them.

The nose of the long, boxy craft dropped as the impeller engines accelerated it toward the encampment. Plumes of black smoke poured out from one of the thruster assemblies in the rear of the ship. Evidently, they didn't escape unscathed from the destruction of the two ships in orbit.

A dozen small drones were released from the belly of the Drop Ship and shot forward over the Terrans. The attack drones were spherical in shape and about the size of a man's head. They were fast, maneuverable, and had powerful laser cannons for such a small device. Their battery packs wouldn't last long if they used their primary weapon repeatedly, but they didn't need to last very long. Their job was to harass, distract, and weaken the target. The drones sped around the encampment above the shield dome. They moved in random patterns, making it difficult to target them successfully. Then they began firing continuously on the perimeter shield dome.

Captain Lao watched with concern as the shield began weakening immediately. The shield was a makeshift, stopgap measure at best... but every laser blast that hit that shield was one less that hit one of her crew! Quickly, she began sighting on drone after drone, leading it and pressing the firing stud. Only about one in every 10 shots was actually hitting a drone, but she didn't think about that. She focused on the firing angles directly in front of her and fired again and again, like clockwork.

Soon, Sallen and every crewmate with a weapon were firing at the drones, and the laser beams—diffracted by the dust particles in the atmosphere—became visible to the human eye. Bright green laser light lit up the skies from the constant barrage of incoming and outgoing fire. The shield dome shimmered with each hit, and the beams reflected off its surface struck the ground outside the perimeter with explosions of dirt and debris. Hit with stray laser fire, some organic material and plants even burst into flames, creating a bright ring of small brush fires.

Clearly, the tripod-mounted heavy laser was too awkward to use against the swift, little drones. But Blakes and Furstall used it to target the Drop Ship with a steady stream of hot, green fire. Captain Lao saw that the shield dome had stopped most of the energy, but the nose of the craft was starting to glow red after increasingly more and more energy was leaked through their weakening shield. Luckily, however, the laser fire from the crew improved with experience... and one after another of the drones were hit and brought down in smoking ruin. Maybe the crew actually had a chance, she thought.

But then... suddenly the Drop Ship itself was upon them, and a powerful laser cannon fired from the nose of the craft.

This attack was different! A loud thunderclap was heard and even felt as the massive beam burned its way through the air and hit the shield dome—with catastrophic results. The shield glowed bright red for a split second and then failed completely. Overloaded, the pieced-together shield generators melted into smoldering heaps of metal. The beam didn't stop there. It continued straight through to hit its intended target.

The tripod-mounted heavy laser was incinerated in a bright blue flash, along with crewmen Blakes and Furstall. There wasn't much left when the Drop Ship flew overhead, and the firing stopped. Captain Lao, Sallen and the entire crew were stunned for a few seconds by what had just happened. They had lost two more of their company so quickly, with such little effort by the enemy....

The captain hefted her rifle and began continuous fire at the Drop Ship, yelling out a string of curses in Mandarin. No one understood her words, but they all shared the sentiment. Almost in unison, the remaining firing positions also opened up on the receding target of the Drop Ship. The beams didn't have much effect. Individually, they weren't strong enough to penetrate the target's shields.

The Drop Ship made a wide loop, and Treech ground troops began pouring out of the rear, using antigrav harnesses to drop gently to the surface. The Terrans called them Worms, but they were more like giant, fat centipedes. They had dozens of arm-legs on each side. Their bodies were segmented, and both head and tail ended in a poorly defined point. The head, though, was really bizarre. It was mostly mouth, with row after row of white, inwardly curved fangs. There were no eyes or any hint of other sensor organs. The Terrans had learned through dissection that most of the monsters' sensory information came from subsonic vibrations and receptors in that nightmare of a mouth.

The Worms wore segmented armor with mounted laser cannons. Worse, they could carry weapons much larger than the Terrans because THEY were much larger. Stretched from head to tail, each was longer than three men were tall. The captain knew that under that metallic gray armor, they were an off-white color and exuded a slime-like substance that smelled putrid. She had heard that the scientists who had dissected the few Worms they collected were never quite sane again—their nights filled with night terrors.

As the Worms hit the ground, they moved in a rapid side-to-side undulation that covered ground quickly and made it difficult to target them. They were also low to the ground, and the terrain and ground cover plant life made it difficult to get a clear shot. The crew was firing continuously now. The barrels of their laser rifles were beginning to glow with undissipated waste heat. The Treech were taking fire, but the Terran lasers just weren't strong enough to take them out without multiple hits.

Captain Lao now knew what it must have been like on Earth during those attacks—the feeling of helplessness in the face of certain death.... Her heads-up display began flashing an ominous red, indicating that her weapon's power pack was nearly drained. Then other weapons fire began to falter all around the camp as other power packs were completely drained. Crewmates began scrambling about trying to find any charged power packs that remained... but there were none to be found. The captain scanned the camp as tears of fear and frustration came to her eyes. She had failed them—after all of this! She had still failed them! She reached down to draw the service blade from her boot sheath. She was going to go down fighting, that was for sure. She was going to do her damnedest to take down the Worm that sought her out for a quick meal.

Then she heard and felt a sonic boom. She glanced skyward and saw another vessel on an intercept course at high speed. That was all they needed! Wasn't one Treech Drop Ship enough?! Did they call in their friends to join in the feast?!

But something was unusual about this vessel... It wasn't boxy and ugly like the Treech designs. It was sleek, smooth and it shimmered as if it were covered in liquid mercury. She stared, mesmerized, as it streaked across her view and the devouring Worms worked their way ever closer.

Chapter 32—UNITED WE STAND

Imperial Assault Shuttle Castalon - Planet Jaden-325-4

Jar'ek had programmed the Imperial Shuttle to come down in a very tight re-entry angle. It was pushing the inertial compensators to their design limits, but time was of the essence. From what the Imperial Sensor Drones had been showing them, his Terran crewmates had only seconds before they were overrun.

Jar'ek waved both hands in arcs over his control panel, and the shuttle shook as he braked hard and swung around toward the camp.

Jar'ek: "Kallehn, Castalon can set up targets for you, but the AI is not allowed to fire offensive weapons without a sentient command. Place your hand on the flashing red indicator and hold it down for continuous fire.

"Kallehn: "Understood! Engaging now."

Twenty weapons ports opened around the circumference of the Imperial Shuttle. The light on Kallehn's console didn't blink for more than a split second before his hand covered it and pushed hard. Multiple targets had been selected, and a barrage of heavy particle beams struck all around the encampment. Where each beam struck, a Treech Worm was vaporized. Pulse after pulse fired from the shuttle as it moved into position over the embattled Terrans.

Jar'ek: "Castalon, extend our shields to cover the Terran encampment—quickly!"

Castalon AI: "Sire, that will weaken our shields to a dangerous level. The Treech main battery may be able to penetrate them. That would put you at unacceptable risk."

Jar'ek: "***COMPLY***!"

Castalon AI: "Shields extended, Sire."

At just that point in time, the Drop Ship changed course to an interception vector and accelerated. As its nose lifted, its main heavy laser battery targeted the Imperial Shuttle and fired. Jar'ek and Kallehn were shaken hard as the laser strike impacted on the weakened shields. Alarm tones could be heard from Jar'ek's console, and several sections changed from green to yellow—with a few lights blinking red.

Kallehn: "Shouldn't we target the Drop Ship?!"

Jar'ek: "No! We have to kill every one of those Worms on the ground! If even one of them gets through, our crewmates are dead. We can hold out. The armor on this shuttle is designed to withstand weapons strikes without shields, if necessary."

Laser blasts were hitting the shield from every direction as the Treech soldiers tried to break through to the Terrans below. They would fire and move, fire and move—trying to evade the nearly continuous particle beam fire from above.

Planet Jaden-325-4 - Crew Rally Point

The captain was standing straight up, staring at the newly arrived, and yet unidentified, shuttle above them. Her mouth fell wide open, and her laser rifle hung loosely by her side. As the ship extended shields to cover her crew's positions, she dropped her head and coughed out a single sob. She couldn't believe it! A few more seconds and all of them would have been eaten alive.

Was she hallucinating?! Did her mind break under the pressure of an imminent and inescapable death? She turned to face Commander Sallen and saw the same bewilderment on his face. He looked down at her, slack-jawed, and tilted his head in inquiry.

Captain Lao: "Yustin! Do you see this, too? Is this really happening??"

Without speaking, Commander Yustin Sallen quickly stepped forward and wrapped his arms around her. Suddenly he was shocked to realize that losing Kathy Xiang Lao was the worst thing he could imagine. He would gratefully have given his own life to give her a few more moments of time.

Kathy drew in a sharp breath and froze. She knew Sallen's embrace was a major breach of Terran regulations and proper decorum for a commanding officer and her subordinate... but she no longer cared. They were ALIVE! And the feeling of being held tightly in Yustin's strong arms was something that no power in the universe could force her to give up at that moment.

Groaning softly, Yustin whispered in her ear.

Yustin Sallen: "Kathy, if this isn't real... I don't want to know. I am perfectly happy living my last moments believing we have been saved and you are safe. Coming this close to death has made me see how much you ... mean to me. I know it isn't appropriate! I know it's against protocol. We both know that our society frowns on feelings, especially feelings like this. But I can't help myself. I think—no, I know—that I am in love with you. Maybe ... I always have been. And I know I don't ever want to come that close to losing you again."

Kathy Xiang Lao rested her face against his chest and breathed hungrily of his closeness. For so long, she had sensed that there was a growing bond between them. Yet her professionalism demanded that she resist it. After all, human culture rejected this type of emotional connection. And she was afraid that it wasn't real—just some fantasy her subconscious had manufactured to assuage her loneliness.

But now that Yustin had professed his feelings for her, she could not hold back her own relentless tide of emotion. A strange new warmth swept through her as she lifted her eyes to his and stretched up on her toes to kiss his lips—hesitantly, then more urgently. She felt his hands slide around her waist and crush her body into his. Time seemed to slow—until, for now, nothing existed outside the two of them. To hell with the Treech!

Imperial Assault Shuttle Castalon - Planet Jaden-325-4

Another laser hit shook the Imperial Shuttle violently. The alarm tones increased in pitch and frequency.

Castalon AI: "Shield strength at 60% and falling."

Jar'ek: "Reinforce the shield covering the encampment, now!"

Castalon AI: "That will put this vessel in imminent danger, Sire. Imperial Edicts prohibit...."

Jar'ek: "***OVERRIDE***!"

Castalon AI: "Complying. Shuttle shield protection level is now at 35%. Encampment shield is at 75%."

The sensors showed the Drop Ship was making another firing pass and lining up its main battery on the Castalon. "I don't know what else to do," Jar'ek thought furiously. His gaze turned to Kallehn, who was learning quickly. He was able to identify and select specific targets and was actually increasing the hit rate on the Worms. There were only 12 Worm soldiers left in action.

Jar'ek: "Kallehn...."

Kallehn: "Shut up! I am NOT leaving you behind! Don't you even THINK that! You hear me?!"

Jar'ek screwed his eyes shut and lowered his head—fighting back the tears. He and Kallehn had just found each other. He might never again feel the brush of Kallehn's lips against his—his arms holding him tightly—his cheek caressed by Kallehn's breath. There was so much left to their future lives together. How cruel was fate to crush his dreams just as they were coming true?! He banged his balled fist on the console.

Jar'ek: "Castalon, isn't there any way we can get our main battery line up on the Drop Ship?"

Castalon AI: "No, Sire. Not while holding stationary over the encampment. If we released the extended shield and were able to maneuver..."

Jar'ek: "No. Not until every one of the Worms is terminated."

Jar'ek felt himself falling into a deep despair. He had risked everything to save his crew members, and now it looked like he would lose, not only his crewmates—but the Harmonic SEED and the hopes of an Interstellar Empire would die with him. He had been rash. But events had left him with little choice. How could things go this wrong, this fast?!

He was startled out of his morbid introspection by an unexpected sonic boom from a new source. He stared at the instruments and was stunned into silence.

The Vehement

The 3D holographic display showed another ship on a high-speed intercept course. The digital moniker next to the floating icon displayed a bright blue colored designation:

Imperial Assault Shuttle "Vehement."

As he and Kallehn watched with their jaws dropping, small icons fell away from the shuttle as it circled the perimeter at high speed.

Jar'ek: "Castalon, what is happening? Where did that other shuttle come from?"

Castalon AI: "Assault Shuttle Vehement is dropping Imperial Combat Android Mechs to secure the Terran perimeter and sanitize it. The Vehement came from the Celestia."

Jar'ek: "How? I didn't order that... I should have thought of it, but I was overconfident... arrogant...foolish...STUPID."

Plato: "Not stupid. Quite the opposite. A bit reckless, perhaps. And to answer your question, I asked the Celestia to prepare the Vehement as a contingency. The risk was too high. But you've come to that conclusion, yourself. Haven't you?"

Jar'ek: "Yes. I was foolish. I wanted to save my friends, and I almost lost everything. I failed in my responsibilities. I violated your trust."

Plato: "Not intentionally. I forgive you, Sire. But this was a lesson you only learn by surviving when you shouldn't have. You won't make this mistake again. Protocol is there for a reason."

Jar'ek: "I'll be good from now on. There is so much that I still don't know. I need you to be my teacher!"

Plato: "I live to serve, Sire. And for what it's worth—I believe in you."

The phalanx of Imperial Mechs was making short work of the remaining Worm groundtroops. The heavy Imperial blasters they carried tore the Worms to smoldering pieces, armor and all. But the Drop Ship was making another strafing run at the Castalon. Jar'ek and Kallehn braced themselves. The shields protecting the Castalon were down to 15%. Jar'ek wasn't sure they could sustain another laser strike. Without warning a bright blue beam—a dozen times the width of the beam fired by the heavy laser—passed just in front of the Castalon's windscreen and struck the Treech vessel square on the nose. It blew their shields away and began burning through the tough outer armor... and then it was through and passing out the back of the burned and dying Drop Ship. The engine core must have exploded at that point because the craft erupted into a fireball and consumed itself. Small flaming fragments peppered the shield, covering the encampment for several moments.

The Vehement gently landed a short distance away. The Imperial Combat Mechs, their gruesome job completed, took up positions surrounding the encampment, just outside the shield barrier. They faced outward, in a guard position.

Jar'ek: "Well, I guess it is time to introduce ourselves to our remaining crewmen. I'm not sure how they are going to take all of this. But I think I can take anything as long as I know that you are by my side, Kallehn. Will you stand beside me?"

Kallehn released the gravity web restraints and stood next to Jar'ek's seated form. He leaned in and covered Jar'ek's lips with his own. After a long, lingering kiss, he then whispered into Jar'ek's ear.

Kallehn: "You just TRY to get rid of me...."

Jar'ek released his own restraints and stood next to Kallehn. After a close embrace, Jar'ek touched the access panel and opened the hatch to the passenger compartment. The two boys were nearly bowled over by two very excited X'Ah-Panths.

S'Fah: {"Fun! Do Again?!?"}

J'Uhr: {"Excited! Hunt Worms?!? Crash shuttle one more time. Please!?!"}

Kallehn and Jar'ek burst into hysterical laughter born of adrenaline withdrawal, exhaustion and a final release of long-held tension.

After a moment to catch their respective breaths, Jar'ek glanced at Kallehn, then they both faced the rear exit ramp airlock.

Jar'ek: "Castalon, can you please lower the shields and land us just inside the encampment perimeter while taking care not to crush any Terrans or vital equipment? "

Castalon: "As you wish, Lord Constandor."

After a moment, they felt a slight bump as the shuttle settled onto the surface.

Jar'ek rolled his eyes and answered: "Please lower the rear exit ramp, observing diplomatic protocols."

Jar'ek: {"Plato, do we really have to follow full diplomatic protocols? I mean, this is going to be very embarrassing. My crewmates knew me before the Meld. They will think I've lost my mind."}

Plato: {"You promised. Protocols are important. And it is critical that you set a precedent from the very beginning in your communications with the Terrans. They knew the Jar'ek that WAS. Now, for the first time, they meet the Meld—the holder of ancient Imperial Authority. Halfway measures will put us all at risk. They must understand that you are no longer under their authority and that they must treat you as the head of state that you are. I know it will be difficult for you, and for Kallehn. But it MUST be done this way. Even if you ordered them not to, the Mechs would protect you."}

Jar'ek: {"All right."}

Once again, ancient memories flooded into Jar'ek's thoughts. He saw a multitude of similar events. He saw what had to be done and how to do it.

As the rear exit ramp lowered to the ground, a strident bell tone sounded from the shuttle public address system.

The two Mechs on Castalon stepped forward together and marched down the ramp with Imperial Blaster Rifles across their chests. Once they reached the bottom of the ramp, they turned inward to face each other on either side of the ramp foot.

Jar'ek took his right hand and ran it down the left shoulder and chest of his light armor/uniform. Where his hand passed, on top of the dull black finish arose bright golden and bejeweled symbols denoting his rank and royal status. His left shoulder now bore a golden and black epaulet with four large emeralds down the center. Next, he touched a fingertip to his tattoo: the "Mark of the Meld." From the point where he laid his fingers upon it, a subdued blue light coursed through the mark and back again, as if he had touched a liquid pool of light and ripples had spread outward from that single point. The mark was now a living symbol, no longer a simple drawing upon his skin.

Jar'ek then looked to Kallehn. He reached out his right hand and placed it on Kallehn's left shoulder, running it down his chest slowly. Kallehn's dull black armor reconfigured itself just as Jar'ek's had a moment earlier. A single black and silver epaulet graced Kallehn's left shoulder. His chest was also adorned with rank insignia. Kallehn looked at Jar'ek's uniform and then at his own and grinned.

Kallehn: "Pulling out ALL the stops, aren't you, Jar'ek?!? Not going a bit over the top, are we?"

Jar'ek: "Because of my recent miscalculations, Plato has thrown a tantrum, and I promised to follow protocol from now on. I am as appalled as you are, Kallehn. But there is nothing for it. Plato says we have to demonstrate we are not the same people we were before and that we are not under Captain Lao's authority any longer. This is serious. And it IS necessary. But you could still back out—rejoin the Rangers and live a normal life."

Kallehn: "Not a chance, buddy. Honestly, I would not trade one day by your side for a lifetime without you in it. I am proud to stand beside you even if I have to wear this fancy, dress uniform and call you 'Sire.' "

Kallehn's grin faded to a more somber grimace. He took his left hand and grabbed Jar'ek's right hand in his, squeezing it tightly. Then they were ready. They couldn't put this off any longer. The two boys walked out and down the ramp side by side, followed closely by the X'Ah-Panths. As they reached the bottom of the ramp, every single Imperial Combat Mech pivoted to face them, snapped to attention and knelt as one, with heads lowered.

The surviving Terrans had gathered in the command center—watching closely to see who would come out of the shuttle that had put itself in mortal danger to save them. The effect this ceremony had on them was dramatic. And as the boys walked forward, they recognized the faces, if not the uniforms. Would the surprises never end? Captain Lao gasped and stared first at the strange uniforms, then at the beautiful but alien markings that flowed like liquid light down Jar'ek's right side and face. And then she looked about and took in the dozens of Combat Androids paying tribute to the boys.

Nothing seemed to make sense anymore. Was reality collapsing in upon itself?! Was she really losing her mind? Too much had happened in too short a time. She was in shock. But duty called. It was her responsibility to try to bring some sort of order out of this chaos.

The captain and XO Sallen strode forward to greet them. A smile broke Kathy Xiang Lao's dust-covered face, despite her misgivings.

The two Mechs assigned to be Jar'ek's escort rose quickly and lowered their Imperial Blasters to block the captain and XO from approaching the boys any closer. The captain and XO stopped short, staring up into the non-existent faces of the giant Mechs. Jar'ek slowly and gently pushed the Mechs back and they fell away, still guarding—watching.

Jar'ek: "Captain, it is so good to see you! We came as soon as we discovered that you had survived the KKM attack. We thought Dragon Eye had been destroyed. And as you can see, our situation has changed dramatically. Most of the changes have been outside of our control. Events seem to have taken on a life of their own."

Captain Lao: "Ranger Jar'ek, Ranger Kallehn. I am glad to see you alive. We, also, feared you had perished in the KKM attack. Our attempts to contact you were unsuccessful."

Jar'ek: "We barely survived the KKM impact. Our comm-helmets were damaged, and we sustained severe injuries. We were able to find shelter and assistance of a sort—in the ruins. An ancient alien was still alive there. Our story is a long one. And I would prefer that we move the survivors to more comfortable quarters and see to the wounded before we begin the telling of it. But there is one thing that must be done immediately.

"As of this moment, I, Jar'ek Constandor, resign my commission in the Terran Confederation Defense Force. I can no longer consider myself under your command, Captain."

The XO tensed visibly. The nearest Mech turned to his face to gaze directly at the XO, with non-existent eyes. The XO had seen the Mechs fighting against the Worms and had a healthy respect for them. He breathed deeply and made sure his hands stayed far away from his sidearm.

Jar'ek looked at Kallehn. Kallehn stepped forward and addressed the captain.

Kallehn: "Captain, it is good to see you alive! But I am afraid that I must also inform you, with the deepest regret, that I formally resign my commission in the Terran Confederation Defense Force. I can no longer consider myself under your command."

The captain and XO looked at each other with shock apparent on their faces, and then back at the boys. Captain Lao wiped an errant hair from her face and shook her head.

Captain: "I don't pretend to understand any of this. You are definitely OUT of uniform... But I am willing to extend you quite a bit of latitude. Let us agree to table this and your debriefing for the time being. I don't want to lose both of you to a hasty decision... and YOU literally just SAVED all our lives. I think I speak for everyone when I say we are very grateful!

"I agree that if you have better shelter and access to medical facilities, we should abandon the encampment. Just promise me you haven't gone insane or begun having delusions of grandeur—that there is some reasonable explanation for all of this...."

The captain waved her hand, indicating the phalanx of Mechs and the Imperial Assault Shuttles.

Jar'ek: "Insane? No ma'am—not me. And certainly not Kallehn, although his sense of humor seems to have gotten a boost. And as you can see, the X'Ah-Panths are still with us. They still trust us. You can, too."

Captain: "All right. Let's get packed up. Do you think some of your army of mechanical monstrosities can help us with lift and carry?"

Jar'ek: "I'm certain that can be arranged."

Jar'ek smiled, stopping himself half way through a salute and simply nodded his head in a brief, but respectful bow. He stepped back and turned away toward the shuttle. Jar'ek was able to use his armor's psionic interface to communicate with the Mech phalanx directly, but he didn't want the Terrans to know that, just yet. He stopped in front of his personal guards, Braxton and Whipple, and gave orders orally.

Jar'ek: "Order 20 of the phalanx to assist the Terrans in loading supplies and equipment into the cargo bay of Shuttles Castalon and Vehement. The phalanx will follow instructions from Captain Lao and Commander Sallen. The remainder of the phalanx will remain on guard until we have evacuated everyone back to the Celestia."

Using the psionic interface, Jar'ek added privately: {"The Phalanx will only follow instructions from the Terrans in this limited capacity, and no other. Understood?"}

Mech Whipple: {"Understood, my Lord Constandor."}

Whipple brought his right fist to his left chest in salute. Then 20 Mechs left the perimeter and reported to Captain Lao. She began directing them, and they began making serious progress in packing the Terrans' equipment and supplies onboard the Imperial Assault Shuttle.

Kallehn and the J'Uhr had stepped away during the conversation and were walking over toward one of the storage tents. Jar'ek was about to use the armor's communicator to see what they were up to when Plato spoke up.

Plato: {"That was well done, Sire. You have given the Terrans an early chance to prove their trustworthiness."}

Jar'ek: {"It will take time for all of us to come to terms with our new situations. I have no idea how it will pan out. I trust the captain. But TCDF interests may conflict with my new responsibilities to the Empire—an Empire that may no longer exist…."}

Plato: {"Indeed. Only time will tell, Sire. We must all be patient. Word will come, and we will learn the truth of the galaxy at large. What would you do if this ship were all that remained?"}

Jar'ek: {"That would be much easier. We could become teachers and mentors. I have no great love for the Confederation Council. As you well know, people like me, and I have suffered a great deal at their callous hands. But I would see my Terran brethren survive and prosper."}

Plato: {"But as a Ranger, you have excelled. You take pride in being part of that organization."}

Jar'ek: {"I do love the Rangers. But I was taken from my family as a young child and raised to be a tool. There was no thought of how this would affect my family or me. We were given no choice. They didn't care. And children with psychic aptitude are not the only ones abducted in this manner. Their high-handed tactics are excused by the ever-present mantra of 'We are responsible for protecting what is left of the human race.' Becoming inhuman isn't the way to do that. "}

After a brief pause, Jar'ek continued: {"Dissent is dealt with ruthlessly. People who challenge the Council's leadership are made to disappear. I have no doubt that the moment the Council learns about the Celestia, they will attempt some subterfuge to wrest control of her away from us. The captain and the rest of the crew would be forced to go along with this betrayal or be branded as Traitors to the Species."}

Plato: {"We shall work together to see that this does not happen. Between us, we have a vast store of tactical and strategic experience tied up in extended memories of my ancestors. The Harmonic Star Empire was not without its intrigues and betrayals, I am sad to say. You and Kallehn must be vigilant. This will be tough for you both."}

Jar'ek: {"As long as I have Kallehn by my side, I can face anything. I just hate that he is forced to go through this with me. But the TCDF will see him as being 'contaminated.' "}

Plato: {"Yes… I've meant to speak with you about that. Kallehn hasn't gone through Judgement of the SEED. I believe that he is highly compatible and that the SEED is growing within him, despite the manner of its introduction. He doesn't realize it yet, but his abilities are growing. It isn't that noticeable yet because he was exposed in an accidental manner. To reach its full potential, he must choose to go through the ritual, just as you did. If he doesn't… he will eventually lose all of the abilities he gains in the short term. And that could be a painful process for him. I think he will pass the Judgement with flying colors. And there is a very good reason that he should be offered the chance for a Melding."}

Jar'ek: {"By every measure that means anything to me, I believe that Kallehn is a better person than I am. I would gladly relinquish my title to him."}

Plato: {"You misunderstand. You are the chosen leader of the Empire. It may have seemed like you were our only choice, and indeed our need was pressing. But you passed the test! Not only did you pass it, but you have the potential to be one of the greatest leaders the Empire has ever seen. We can discuss why I think so highly of you at another time. But the real reason we need someone like Kallehn to agree to the Melding is… well…

something might happen to YOU."}

{"I hope that doesn't seem cold. I am going to do my very best to make sure that doesn't happen. But times being what they are, there is a risk. And I think you will agree the Harmonic SEED needs to survive if for no other reason than the technical know-how stored in our genetic memories may well be critical to the survival of the Terran Species—now that the Treech have made contact once again."}

Jar'ek: {"Well, you are right, of course. That thought had crossed my mind—most recently, just when I thought the Treech Drop Ship was going to fry Kallehn and me both."}

Plato: {"Yes, you WILL listen to me and stop taking unnecessary chances like that sometime in the near future, won't you?! And you DO realize that was an unnecessary risk now, don't you?"}

Jar'ek: {"Yes. I do, now. There are still going to be many times when I will need to take an active role in conflict. We both know that. I won't let you force me to shirk my responsibilities to those I need to defend or lead. BUT… if you agree to help instead of hinder me… I will seek your counsel to choose the best strategy. Agreed?"}

Plato {"Agreed, my Lord!"}

Where did Kallehn get to? Jar'ek felt an odd sensation, just outside the band of psionic mind-touch he used with S'Fah. It was different… less structured… less complex.

Planet Jaden-325-4 - Crew Rally Point - Storage Tent C

Chief Vermanderly wasn't looking too great. She was supposed to be with the rest of the wounded being readied for loading onto the alien shuttle. But she had limped out while no one was looking and came here to make sure her feathered friend, the X'Ah-Falcon, was still okay. Someone had at least opened the Ranger evac pod and made sure the X'Ah-Falcon had enough air. But he had been through a rough ride and was still pretty agitated. She was whispering calmingly to him and making chirping noises with her mouth when the large tent flap burst open.

There stood Kallehn Frix and his X'Ah-Panth, J'Uhr… although something was seriously wrong with Kallehn's uniform. The rumor was that Kallehn and Jar'ek had captured some alien technology and had come to the rescue with no time to waste.

CHAPTER 33—A NEW UNDERSTANDING

Imperial Assault Shuttle Castalon - Planet Jaden-325-4

Jar'ek and Kallehn were seated once again in the Castalon's cockpit. The surviving crew members were all aboard, and both shuttles were returning to the Outpost, albeit at a more leisurely pace this time. Castalon had received some damage during the attack, but she was space-worthy, and repairs could be made easily once she was docked back on the Celestia.

Imperial Assault Shuttle Castalon – Passenger Compartment

Jar'ek's personal guard had stationed themselves just inside the passenger cabin with their backs to the cockpit bulkhead. Jar'ek had left the cockpit hatch open intentionally in case his passengers needed something. Captain Lao got out of her seat and approached the cockpit hatch, but she stopped herself just short of the Mechs' position. She cleared her throat to get Jar'ek's attention.

He turned and faced the passenger cabin.

Jar'ek: "Hello, Captain. Is there something we can do for you?"

Captain Lao: "Yes, actually. I'd like to join you in the cockpit, if I may."

Jar'ek: "By all means. We have a spare acceleration seat right here."

Jar'ek activated the voice interface on his uniform's communications suite to make sure the Mechs heard him.

Jar'ek: "Braxton, Whipple… please allow Captain Lao to enter the cockpit unmolested."

Both Combat Androids took a half step back and away from the hatch to allow the captain easy access.

She gazed up at them, trying not to show her trepidation, and swallowed slowly. Pulling her tunic straight and resettling her beret on her head, she walked through the hatch and took the proffered seat. Kallehn and Jar'ek swiveled their seat around to face the captain's. It was a bit of a tight fit because S'Fah and J'Uhr were taking up a lot of the floor, stretched out in a semblance of feline sleep. But the boys knew from their mind-touch that they were awake and interested. They would be listening carefully to the captain's words.

Captain Lao: "Ranger Constandor… I'm sorry, but it may take me a while to get used to the fact that neither of you is in the Rangers anymore. Are you sure that is what you want??"

Jar'ek: "Captain, it is going to take Kallehn and me some time to get used to it as well. Neither of us wanted to leave the Rangers. But we have taken on other responsibilities that—while not in direct conflict with the Ranger's mission—do require independence of action."

Captain Lao: "I have put my trust in you. These people are my responsibility. I need to understand more of what has happened to bring you to this decision and how you acquired this." She raised her arms and eyes to indicate the Imperial Shuttle. "And also, what your intentions are. You mentioned an ancient alien survivor. Have you been recruited in some way? Are you being coerced by this alien?"

Jar'ek: "Captain. I have—that is, Kallehn and I both have—a lot of respect for you. You are a good, honest leader with integrity. I am going to have to trust you, too. I will tell you what you need to know, but I must ask you to keep some details to yourself, for now. It may take some time for you to think through the ramifications and the importance of what happens next between us."

"I can promise you that no one involved in this story wants to harm the Terran Colonies in any way. Quite the contrary, depending on how the TCDF leadership reacts—our species may have found a powerful ally that could help ensure our survival and future prosperity. You must know that no matter what the circumstances, neither Kallehn nor I would ever engage in any activity that would put the Terran Colonies at risk. We would have willingly given our lives first."

Captain Lao sighed heavily before speaking: "You don't know how relieved I am to hear you say those words! I was unsure if you had been compromised in some way. You could as easily have been our captors, as our rescuers—I mean, we AREN'T prisoners, are we?"

Jar'ek: "No, Captain. And I'm very sorry for the anxiety you are experiencing because of this. But there simply was no time to break this story to anyone gently. As soon as we discovered you were alive, we saw that you would be under Treech attack shortly. We didn't have an easy way to communicate with you."

Captain Lao's eyes widened in surprise: "You were hit by the shockwave and survived?! You both look unharmed. How is that possible?"

Jar'ek glanced over at Kallehn, placed his right hand on his shoulder, and they gazed into each other's eyes for a moment, recalling those difficult days in the recent past. The touch and the way they looked at each other did not escape the captain's notice. She cocked her head slightly and raised one eyebrow, deep in thought. She knew the boys had always been close as teammates, but....

Jar'ek: "Captain, I think the quickest, easiest, and safest way to bring you up to speed would be to have Castalon project our recollections of the way things worked out after the KKM was launched, from our perspective."

Captain Lao: "You can do that?!"

Jar'ek spoke aloud: "Castalon, can you replay a condensed

version of my recorded memories from the time of the KKM strike through my Judgement and the deployment?"

{Private psionic communication}

Jar'ek: {"Castalon, please exclude any grandiose honorifics for the time being. Let our guests get used things before we stretch their view of reality any further."}

Castalon, too, spoke aloud: "Affirmative, sir. And I've begun downloading from Celestia, now. It will be only a moment."

Kallehn turned and gestured over his control panel, and the cockpit hatch closed silently, ensuring privacy for this section of their story.

Suddenly, a 3D representation of everything Jar'ek saw and heard after the KKM impact, was being projected in the cockpit between them. The captain was mesmerized. And so were Kallehn and Jar'ek, but not because it was unexpected, but because they were feeling the pain, anguish, and fear all over again. Jar'ek and Kallehn both tensed up in their seats, gripping the armrests tightly as the story played out.

It took about 1/4 deci-fraction for the projection to finally complete. The timeline was compressed, but all of the pertinent details were included. After which, the three of them laid back in their acceleration chairs and started breathing normally again. Except for a total lack of musical score, it would have made a great entertainment thriller.

The captain was staring off into the distance. Jar'ek and Kallehn glanced at each other again, then turned and checked the control panels for any problems. Castalon would have alerted them, but it gave them something to do while the captain tried to assimilate the bizarre happenings of the past handful of days.

After a few moments, the captain cleared her throat for attention. Jar'ek and Kallehn swiveled their seats around and faced her.

Captain Lao: “Errr… I have some questions if you don't mind.”

Jar'ek: “Please ask them. It is important you understand clearly.”

Captain Lao: “I feel I need your permission as well, Kallehn. Some of my questions will seem quite personal to you.”

Kallehn looked down at the deck plates for a moment, inhaled sharply, and then met the captain’s gaze with a look of determination in his eyes.

Kallehn: “Ask what you need to, Captain. I will answer honestly.”

The captain nodded sharply and continued.

Captain Lao: “Thank you both.”

Captain Lao: “Kallehn, you were severely injured and near death only a few days ago. I saw what happened to Jar'ek and the decision he was forced to make. But I did not see how you were healed. Can you explain this to me, or should I ask Jar'ek?”

Kallehn: “I was only aware of part of the process, Captain. I had a traumatic brain injury that put me in a coma. I did see Jar'ek's recollections of how I was healed. And I experienced the Psionic Stimulation Procedure, which was used to repair my brain synapses and allow me to wake from the coma. I was aware of that process in a dream-like state.”

Captain Lao: “I see… Jar'ek, by your own recollections, you have been compromised by an alien entity of vital intelligence and knowledge. How can I trust what you say? How can I possibly know that you are YOU?!”

Jar'ek: “I realized this would be the case, Captain. I sympathize with your situation. The only answer I have is that trust is something earned, not given. I realize that, to you, I am something totally new—untrusted. Give me time to earn your trust again. It is true that I am different now. Everything that was Jar'ek is still who I am. My core values, my memories, and feelings have not changed. But there is another part of me now. An ancient, benevolent Alien Sentient. And the two of us are learning to coexist in a symbiotic relationship. This is so foreign to the human condition that it will be difficult for many people to accept. Hell, it has been difficult for ME to accept."

Captain Lao: "And Kallehn? Was he exposed during this miracle of healing?"

Kallehn: "I will answer that, Captain. Yes. I was exposed, to a lesser extent. If Jar'ek had not done what he did, I would have died. So, I have no regrets regarding that."

Captain Lao: "Jar'ek, I cannot imagine what you must have gone through and how difficult and frightening making that decision must have been. It is nothing less than I would have expected from someone of your depth of character. I have always held you in high regard, despite your youthful antics."

Jar'ek: "Thank you, Captain. But I would gladly have traded my life for Kallehn's, ma'am. That wasn't the choice I was given. But it isn't as bad as I feared it might be. I think that Kallehn and I will have the chance to make a real positive difference for humanity. But I do have to tell you that my responsibilities have expanded beyond that of protecting our species, alone."

Captain Lao looked up into Jar'ek's eyes sharply and asked: "What do you mean by that?"

Jar'ek: "The Alien Sentient—I call him Plato, by the way—was a member of a galaxy-wide Star Empire that collapsed over 10,000 Standard Solar Orbits ago. Members included over a dozen sentient species. Plato and his ship were quarantined here on Jaden-325-4 until the Imperial Crisis could be contained.

"Communications with the Empire have yet to be restored. Plato is unaware of the state of the Empire, at this time. But it appears that Plato may be the senior surviving authority and directly responsible for whatever IS left of the Harmonic Star Empire."

Captain Lao: "This just keeps getting better…." She shook her head and leaned back in the acceleration seat.

Jar'ek: "Now you know why I asked you to give yourself some time to assimilate this before discussing it with anyone else."

Captain Lao: "Hmmm… I'm not sure if there is enough time left in this universe for me to assimilate all of this. So, what exactly is your part in this symbiotic relationship, Jar'ek? Are you simply a host that provides locomotion and nutrients, or is there something more?"

Kallehn: "Captain, If you happened to salvage any alcoholic beverages from the supplies, you loaded in the cargo compartment… I'd suggest NOW might be a good time to find it…."

Jar'ek gave Kallehn a stern stare before returning his attention to the captain. Captain Lao had a quizzical look on her face as she glanced back and forth between the two former junior officers.

Captain Lao: "I wish I had had the foresight, young man. I could use something in a nice, strong whiskey right now. But we shall have to push forward without libations at this point, I am afraid."

Jar'ek: "So I will proceed. Plato's people need hosts to live. I am the first human host, ever. Plato's people have a long genetic memory. They are a compassionate, benevolent species that seeks to mentor younger races toward a harmonic relationship with all sentient species.

"After millennia of trial and error, they developed a code of conduct for themselves. They are very selective when choosing a host. Genetic traits are examined carefully to exclude the possibility of providing a flawed personality with the power of a highly advanced set of technologies and knowledge. But once Melded, they give up all control. They only offer counsel, knowledge, and wisdom, if you will. The title and responsibilities fall upon the host."

Captain Lao: "Well, that would mean that you are... are...."

Kallehn: "Yup! You're catching on, Captain! You are almost there. Keep going... and the strangeness just never wears off. No disrespect intended, ma'am."

The captain glanced over at Kallehn with a look of consternation and then stared at Jar'ek. She had to remind herself that he wasn't a junior officer under her command anymore. She assumed this was his real "sense of humor" coming out and not simple insubordination. In another time and place, she might have found this funny.

Captain Lao: "Are you telling me you are the chosen leader of an ancient Star Empire!?"

Jar'ek: "Hard to believe, isn't it?! What a difference a few days can make!"

Captain Lao: "What resources do you command?"

Jar'ek: "Apart from what you've seen and the Imperial Destroyer we are headed for, I have NO IDEA what remains of Imperial Assets. We should find out something more before too long. Plato sent out a communications probe to several locations where the Empire had established naval bases. But I doubt much of anything could be left after two millennia!"

Captain Lao: "Well, this shuttle seems to be in pretty good condition. You said we were headed back to an Imperial Destroyer... I assume it is also in working order? And then there is your friend Plato... he survived."

Jar'ek: "Point taken... we don't know Captain."

Captain Lao: "What was the crisis that brought the Empire down in the first place?"

Kallehn and Jar'ek looked at each other with a somber look. This was the most critical juncture. Should Jar'ek tell the captain the truth? Jar'ek breathed a heavy sigh and returned his gaze to the captain. He looked her directly in the eyes.

Jar'ek: "An interstellar plague."

The captain tensed and sat up straight on the edge of her seat.

Captain Lao: "A plague! You are joking.... Are we all at risk? Could we end up taking it back to the colonies?!"

Jar'ek: "None of the Imperial forces here were infected. They were placed under quarantine in time. And Plato assures me that the plague is incompatible with human DNA. And even if it wasn't, the virus was not able to survive for long outside of a living host. It would have died out long ago."

Captain Lao: "You realize that the colonies will have to quarantine us anyway. Our scientists must make sure we are not infected before allowing us to return home."

Jar'ek: "Yes, I was afraid of that. Plato can provide the scientists with detailed information about the plague, incubation time, and vectors. That should help."

Captain Lao: "So, what do we do now?"

Jar'ek: "Once we get back to base, I will see about sending a few communication probes to contact the Terran Colonial Authorities. They need to be warned about the Treech, in any case."

Captain Lao: "Quite correct. The sooner, the better."

Jar'ek: "Captain, I think I must mention that what I said about 'trust being earned' goes both ways."

Captain Lao: "Explain, please."

Jar'ek: "Well, I cannot say for sure that there won't be members of the TCDF that would see an opportunity to boost Terran technology by centuries simply by forcing us to give control of the

Celestia to them. There may be members of our former crew, right here, that might have that very same idea."

Captain Lao: "I am afraid that I cannot disagree with you on that point."

Jar'ek: "Thank you for being honest with me, Captain. And I want to be direct with you as well… and this is critical. Just to forestall any unpleasantness, let me explain how things work in this small microcosm of the old Empire. None of the technology will work for any Terrans except Kallehn and me. The Mechs see me as their Emperor, and they think of themselves as my personal guard. They are impervious to Terran weapons, threats, coercion, bribery, and stern voices. If they perceive an imminent threat to Kallehn or to me, they will act immediately before either one of us can stop them. Even if I ordered them to stop and not protect me, their programming would override my orders."

Captain Lao: "I understand. And I will make very certain that my crew understands completely that they are to keep their hands off any control panels and that they are to ensure that you never appear to be threatened in any way by any of them. Will that be sufficient?"

Jar'ek: "Thank you for your cooperation, Captain. I don't want to see any of our former crewmates injured in any way."

Captain Lao: "I will need to make some explanations to my XO. I will need to tell him something."

Jar'ek: "I will leave that up to your discretion, Captain. When you feel he is ready, you can tell him all or part of our story. You know him better than I do. And you are right. My expectations for how the TCDF will react to the news is aligned with your own. He will need to know about the possibility of an extended quarantine, in any case. But keep an open mind. Circumstances being what they are, there may be other options for you and your crew."

A subtle bell tone sounded, and a yellow light began blinking on the control board. Kallehn swiveled about and examined his display.

Kallehn: "We're on glide path for landing. We should be down and docked in 10 centi-fractions. Better tell the rest of our passengers to return to their seats and activate the gravity web restraints in preparation for landing."

Kallehn leaned forward and made the announcement over the public address system in the passenger cabin.

The captain stood, nodded at each of the boys, then turned and stepped through the hatch as it opened for her.

Kallehn looked at Jar'ek and grimaced.

Kallehn: "Well, there's no turning back now...."

Jar'ek: "Are you sorry we chose to tell her?"

Kallehn: "No. I don't see that we had any other choice. It was the right thing to do. But now everything feels weird.

Jar'ek: "I know. And I think it is going to get worse before it gets better."

Imperial Assault Shuttle Castalon – Passenger Compartment

The captain returned to her seat, next to her Executive Officer. The XO had nodded off to sleep while she was gone. His short blond hair was matted to his scalp with dried sweat, dust, and a little soot. She glanced around and saw that no one was sitting nearby, and no one could see them very well through the high seat backs. She took her hand and gently caressed Yustin's forehead, pushing a few unruly hairs back into a semblance of order. Disheveled, covered in the dirt of battle, he still looked so handsome. And with his eyes closed and facial muscles relaxed in sleep—he looked so pure and innocent. It was an odd juxtaposition. She was the smaller of the two, by far—the gender seen as weaker, by many. He was strong, big, and confident. But right now, she felt she had to protect him—at least for a little while.

Her thoughts were in such turmoil. Her world and her universe had been turned upside down. She needed to try to assimilate the new reality and test it against her own principles and beliefs. If she told Yustin what she knew right now, like she desperately wanted to, it would be selfish. Let him rest for now. After they had reached their destination, he would be very busy seeing to the wounded and getting the rest of the crew settled in.

She needed to think. Very soon, the entire crew would be asking difficult questions. They would assume that she, as captain, would take over command of the alien vessel and technology. That wasn't possible, and even if it was, she wasn't so sure it would be advisable.

The Terran Colonial Government was so ruthlessly determined to maintain its grip on power. Their quest for total control over the civilian population had gone far beyond what was necessary for security... She had felt the same misgivings voiced by Jar'ek earlier, for some time now. Somewhere on the way to saving the human race, they had lost their humanity. Jar'ek was right to fear aggressive action from the TCDF. Both Kallehn and Jar'ek would be considered a threat to the status quo. And in the Council's mind, that translated to a Threat to the Species. They had done nothing wrong—only done what had to be done. If the situation were reversed, she had no doubt that she would have made the same decision to save Yustin's life. And she felt that he would have made the same sacrifice for her. But soon the former Rangers would be classified as traitors, enemies.

She didn't know what to think. With the exception of their unexpected resignation, neither of the boys had shown any sign of undue influence or control. But what would that look like? Could she even tell? For that matter, how could she even tell if she was being influenced right now? This kind of circular thinking could drive a person mad! There were some things she just had to assume. And her own rationality was one of those things.

If the boys were under alien control... wouldn't it have been easier to allow the Treech to kill everyone, she wondered. There would have been no evidence of alien contamination. The TCDF would have assumed they had died alongside their crewmates. Or if their intention were more malevolent, they could have waited for a rescue ship and simply stated they had been afoot on the other side of the planet when the crew was overrun. They would appear as innocent survivors. That would have allowed them to infiltrate the TCDF and no one would be the wiser. That whole line of thought made no sense. But that wouldn't stop the Council from believing it!

She thought Jar'ek had the right sense of it. They would both need to learn to trust each other again. Trust was earned through deeds, not words. It was going to take some getting used to. A lot of Terrans were going to think very nasty thoughts about those two. Yet personally, she liked and respected them both. She hated what had happened to them and what was going to happen to them. They would be isolated as pariahs. They would never be welcome in the Terran Colonies again. And they would always have to leave one eye open to prevent the TCDF from taking them captive and coercing their cooperation.

They were so young, so inexperienced. The alien, Plato, had evaluated Jar'ek before making the offer of Melding. Jar'ek had passed their rigorous Judgement process. But could they possibly be ready for the politics and subterfuge awaiting them in the Terran Confederation? What if the Empire was now a group of warring factions made up of the plague survivors? What if they had all died as a result of the pandemic?

The captain had stopped stroking Yustin's hair and had moved down his muscled arm and slowly, gently pushed his fingers apart so that she could place her smaller hand inside his. She took a deep breath and laid back in her acceleration seat, reaching over to activate the restraining gravity web on both the XO's and her armrest.

Once the TCDF received her report, they would likely quarantine the entire planet, with them on it. And there was the very real danger that the Treech might return in the near future. If Jar'ek took the alien warship and began his mission to reunite the Empire, what would happen to her and her crew... to Yustin? They would be defenseless against the next Treech attack. The TCDF didn't have enough warships to leave one guarding this planet indefinitely—not for the few survivors of her crew.

But neither could the TCDF risk a plague getting back to the Colonies until their own medical staff had eliminated it as a threat, regardless of what Plato had said. If she knew the Council as well as she thought she did, they would order an orbital supply drop sufficient for several years and then just abandon them without any intention of bringing them home. Cold, deliberating bastards! On the other hand—they might just order the bombardment of the entire planet. That would solve their problem neatly!

But what if they ordered her to take control of the alien and throw her former Ranger Team Alpha in the brig? They could send down scientist volunteers in biohazard suits to try to reverse engineer Imperial technology.... Would she betray Jar'ek's trust? After they got what they wanted, would they still bombard the planet to be sure? Did she owe something more to her crew—to the human race? And how much was she allowing herself to be influenced by the strong emotions bubbling to the surface between herself and Yustin?

Was this why the Council discouraged passionate feelings? She felt such a strong connection to the man slumbering next to her. She had always repressed any such sentiments. She would need to learn how to manage them—put them in proper perspective. But she knew that all rationality aside, she would do almost anything to protect that connection.

As the shuttle began its descent, she felt Yustin's hand gently close around hers as if it were the most natural thing in their world. She sighed deeply, and the heavy burden on her slender shoulders seemed to lessen just a tiny bit.

Chapter 34—A NEW SITUATION

Imperial Destroyer Celestia - Planet Jaden-325-4

It had taken quite some time to get the Terran guests settled. The Med-bay had already been refitted for Terran patients after the Melding. The medical AI and the surgical bots repaired broken limbs, damaged blood vessels, and soft tissue damage efficiently. Expellable nanites had been used to accelerate the healing process for the four Terrans who had sustained serious injuries.

The Terran doctor was sleeping on a spare cot in the Med-bay to keep a close watch on their recovery. A number of minor burns and other lesser wounds were cleaned and bandaged before sending the Terrans off to get some much-needed rest.

Jar'ek had asked Celestia to instruct the maintenance bots to convert some space in the main mess hall into a Terran-style galley, where they could prepare their own rations. Jar'ek knew his people needed some normalcy and routine back in their lives as soon as possible. The ship's physical recreation facility only needed minor modifications.

Jar'ek: "Celestia, please post Mech guards outside restricted areas. Our Terran guests should have freedom to roam and explore, but I don't trust them beyond guest access."

Celestia: "Understood."

Jar'ek: "Now, I am exhausted. I would like to get some sleep. And I am hoping that this night I will not spend alone."

Celestia: "I believe that Lord Kallehn has retired to your quarters already, Sire. He has inquired as to your location recently. I took the liberty of telling him you would be retiring shortly."

Jar'ek smiled a weary smile and began the short trek to their living quarters. The light armor didn't need washing… but HE did. He was still covered in a layer of dirt and grime from the battlefield.

He was looking forward to a quick shower and having Kallehn fall asleep in his arms... something he'd been fantasizing about for years now.

As the door to their suite slid open, he noticed the lights were dimmed. Walking through the main bedroom on the way to the hygiene facilities, he saw Kallehn, sprawled across the bed, dead asleep and snoring lightly. A grin crossed his face as he continued on. As much as his body longed for a more intimate encounter, all Jar'ek could think about was going to sleep and waking up with Kallehn in his arms.

There would be plenty of time for more, later.

After the warm shower cleaned his body and banished the anxiety and stressful thoughts of the day, he found himself just where he wanted to be. And it was the best thing he had ever felt in his life. He quickly fell asleep, his arms around Kallehn's chest and shoulders, and their legs intertwined.

S'Fah, lounging on a cushioned perch a short distance away, opened his eyes and watched his mind-mate. He felt his contentment flow over him. He closed his eyes and went back to sleep knowing that, for the moment, all was right.

Chapter 35 — SEEK AND YE SHALL FIND

Imperial Comm Probe AXZ-512548 - System Z982 - Sector Z-57QA-452G

This was the fourth system the comm probe had visited since the Pythanos System. The prior three systems had been barren wastelands. There had been no life—no energy readings beyond normal background noise. Debris and craters were the only remaining evidence that Imperial Forces had maintained an asteroid base in those systems. No signs of external attack had been found. The size and composition of the craters would seem to indicate the bases initiated their self-destruct mechanisms long ago.

System Z982 was different. The base itself was in a hollowed-out asteroid. It was much larger and included asteroid mining operations and one more crucial component—an orbital shipyard. The framework of the shipyard stretched out like a spherical spider web, completely englobing the asteroid base. Large metallic conduits crisscrossed the interior of the wireframe sphere. Like the veins and arteries of some giant beast, the conduits carried raw materials, prefabricated ship components, fuel, water, atmosphere, and workers to the ships under construction in docking slips marking the outer boundary of the spherical shipyard. There were enough construction slips on the outer perimeter to build a hundred dreadnoughts simultaneously.

Several ships were docked and under various stages of construction, though no work was currently under way. There was no sign of life. No challenge hails—no active sensor sweeps. There was an active energy source, but it was either very well shielded or was maintaining a very low energy output. Unlike the Pythanos System, there were no communications to eavesdropping upon for intelligence collection.

Once again, the comm probe extended its sensor wings. It would wait for a short while and see what could be seen. But soon it must risk communications with the base AI. If nothing else, the base seemed to be intact. The Empire might be able to salvage it, even if the AI was no longer functioning. It would watch and listen for three SPR (Standard Planetary Rotations). If nothing had happened by then, it would act.

CHAPTER 36 — PROPHESY

Imperial Gunship Alacrity - In hyperspace

It was night shift on the Gunship Alacrity. The lighting in most of the ship was dimmed, with the exception of duty stations. The observation deck was darker still. The blue-shifted light from stars was streaked in a disconcerting fashion, stretching out the light from a single star into a long, blue line leading toward the aft of the vessel.

The dark silhouettes of two figures in hooded robes stood out against the streaming starlight. They spoke in soft whispers. They wore the robes to hide their identity, even from each other. Each acolyte bore a secret name used only among the Brotherhood.

Far Seer: "Are you certain that no one suspects?"

True Voice: "No one suspects, Brother. We have been very careful."

Far Seer: "Good! Are the weapons and explosives in place?"

True Voice: "All according to plan."

Far Seer: "And what of our plans to commandeer the primary battery control?"

True Voice: "There we have encountered a small problem. The acolyte in charge of the primary battery was transferred to secondary battery control after their officer was injured in a maintenance accident. But we should have no problem using the secondary batteries to destroy the drop pods before the troops can be used to retake control of this vessel. The explosives that have been placed in the Elite barracks will eliminate all real resistance onboard. After that, we can take total control of this gunship."

Far Seer: "Will the ship's batteries be powerful enough to

overwhelm their shields?"

True Voice: "That destroyer is over 2,000 Solar Orbits old. Their shields may not even work; if they are in working order it will take some time to wear them down."

Far Seer: "We do not have time in large supply. If the Alexicon arrives before we have completed our mission, it will all be to no avail...."

True Voice: "If necessary, we will use the ship itself as a kinetic weapon. Their shields will not withstand that."

Far Seer: "It is true that we had to devise this plan on very short notice. But you have done very well. The True SEED will be pleased!"

True Voice: "Are you certain, Brother?! This is NOT the True SEED?!"

Far Seer: "You know the prophecy, Brother. It speaks of another five millennia before the True SEED returns. All of Pythanos must be cleansed and follow the True Faith before the SEED will return. I, too, questioned this. The High Brother himself spoke to me. He convinced me that this is a vile imposter! If we were to embrace this deception, our eternal souls would be lost."

True Voice: "As the Word is spoken, so shall it be done!"

The hooded figures parted, and both merged into the surrounding shadows.

CHAPTER 37 — A CAPTAIN'S CHOICE

Imperial Destroyer Celestia - Captain Xiang Lao's Quarters

Kathy Lao lay awake on a sleeping platform in the darkened room. She'd been able to get showered and find a clean jumpsuit that fit her. The prior Planetary Rotation was replaying over and over in her mind: The initial KKM strike—the death of so many of her crew—the desperate and lucky attack on the Treech Marauder—the escape to the surface and relative safety, only to fight a losing battle with Treech ground troops, then to be saved at the last moment by one of her youngest officers, who was now Emperor of the known galaxy.

She needed sleep badly. The rest of the crew were settled in quarters—quarters that were luxurious by TCDF standards. The galley had been opened in the main mess hall, and they had all eaten their first real meal in more than a day. Medical Officer Kira To'Torat had reported that none of the critical casualties had died and that they were all in stable condition and improving moment to moment. She still had concerns about the nanites used by the Imperial Med-bots. But like Jar'ek and Kallehn, without the nanites, more of her people would have died. In this case, they were conscious enough to choose between taking a chance on the alien nanites or the strong probability of not surviving their injuries.

Jar'ek had assured the patients that the nanites would deactivate immediately after their healing abilities were no longer needed. And they would then be flushed out of the body with the normal elimination process. They all chose to accept the risk and were much better for having made that choice. MO To'Torat was giddy with excitement over the medical advances evident in the rapid recovery from such serious injuries. Jar'ek had promised to provide her with access to an Imperial Medical Training AI as soon as things settled down. The AIs were still working out how to apply much of their medical knowledge for use with humans. MO To'Torat should be able to help them accelerate that process.

At first, the captain was concerned about this collaboration. She was sure the Terran Confed Council would not have allowed her to provide that type of physiological information to an unknown alien culture, for fear they would use it against the Terran Colonies. But from what the captain had seen, the Empire was millennia ahead of the Terrans. If their intentions were bad, they wouldn't need to study human biology to wipe out the colonies. There was nothing they could do to stop them.

She'd had some time to think about it. It was very likely that the TCDF would quarantine this entire planet and leave her crew there to fend for themselves or starve. If that were the only option left by the Terran Council, she would have to speak with Jar'ek—Lord Constandor—His Highness? What was she supposed to call him? What was the proper protocol when dealing with someone who commanded all they surveyed?

Even if the rest of the Empire were dead and gone, there were still technological resources left behind, if this warship was any indication. Perhaps Jar'ek could negotiate with the Council on their behalf. Or, if nothing else, maybe he could take the crew to an abandoned Imperial facility that was still serviceable and might provide them with a way to secure their longer-term survival. Maybe even some creature comforts like those afforded on this warship?

She needed to bring the XO in on this as soon as possible. With the possible loss of the legitimacy of the Terran chain of command, they needed to have some plan.... The moment the crew found out they were marooned here—had no purpose, no mission—the officers might have a problem on their hands. They needed to be able to give the crew some hope—a new purpose or direction.

The crew had been too busy getting settled and recuperating to question the status of Jar'ek and Kallehn and wonder when the captain was going to fly them home in their bright-and-shiny new alien warship. They had to be warned, first about touching anything, and second that Jar'ek and Kallehn now had command authority—over hers. Luckily, and perhaps wisely, the Ranger Team had made themselves scarce. Better not to start anyone thinking too much about them just yet.

She needed her XO. They had to talk soon. She closed her eyes for just a second....

Kathy Xiang Lao woke in the middle of the night with a start. At first, she didn't know where she was. But she soon realized she wasn't in her cabin on the Dragon Eye—it didn't exist anymore. She was in her assigned quarters, on the sleeping platform. Something else was odd... she wasn't alone!

There was a man's arm draped across her waist. And against her back and legs, she felt the warm, muscled contour of what could only be Yustin Sallen's body. She relaxed and exhaled deeply, feeling herself push back into him as if she had done it thousands of times. She felt his slow, regular breathing as his chest raised and lowered. She felt his warm breath stir the hair on top of her head. She felt the strong bump—bump—bump of his heartbeat and realized that her own heartbeat had settled into his rhythm. She breathed again and slowly exhaled, closing her eyes and wishing that this moment would never end—whether dream or reality.

Chapter 38 — FIRST THINGS FIRST

Imperial Destroyer Celestia - Captain Xiang Lao's Quarters

Kathy woke again, this time more slowly, peacefully—she stretched, yawned and noticed the time display on her tablet—it was still the middle of the night. She looked over her shoulder and exhaled slowly with deep satisfaction. Yustin was still next to her, his arm around her body, holding her close. This time, she noticed something else—his body's need for her was apparent. And by the size of it, he was VERY much in need of her.

She gently raised his arm and turned over to face him. His eyes were wide open and in them shown a mixture of desire—anxiety—embarrassment and affection. She smiled and pulled his scruffy chin down until his lips met her open mouth. Yustin pulled her close and held her tightly in his arms and kissed her passionately. When they parted, she let out a long, shuddering breath. She was lightheaded, and her mouth tingled from his touch. She still tasted him on her lips. Every inhale carried his masculine scent.

He released her from his steel grip and considered her eyes with apprehension.

Yustin Sallen: "I... I didn't mean to presume, Kathy. Your door wasn't locked, and I came to check on you. I was exhausted... I wasn't thinking clearly. I just couldn't help myself. I know this violates the chain of command and could cause the crew to start talking... I hope you aren't angry with me!"

Kathy Xiang Lao: "I don't care about any of that right now, Yustin. And the only way I could ever hate you is if you stopped loving me. I woke during the night and felt you against me. It was like a dream. I needed you there so badly, and magically you appeared. Now, we do need to spend some time in the morning on important business, but... for right now...."

She took her right hand and slowly ran it down the seam of his jumpsuit, exposing his bare chest and abdomen below. She had never seen him with his shirt off before. His body was well sculpted, with just a touch of blond hair around his nipples that ran down from his belly button to the rather large symbol of his manhood. Her body was reacting just as strongly as his was. She hadn't felt this way about any other man as far back as she could remember. She wanted him. She wanted him now! The jumpsuits disappeared quickly as their bodies intertwined in a desperate dance of repressed and now-released passion.

Chapter 39 — WE NEED TO TALK…

Imperial Destroyer Celestia - Captain Xiang Lao's Quarters

Kathy Xiang Lao walked out of the hygiene facilities in her quarters as she dried her shoulder-length black hair with a towel. The automated hygiene facility had drawn most of the moisture from her hair and body, but she found the ritual provided by manually drying her hair with a towel was calming and allowed her to focus her thoughts on what was to come. Another large towel was wrapped about her torso from underneath her arms to her mid-thighs, purely to satisfy her sense of modesty.

She gave her head a good shake, and her hair fell back into place. She stopped and looked at Yustin lounging on the sleeping platform in only his boxers, reading his command tablet. Her heart skipped a beat as her body reacted to the sight of him—remembering the night before. Goosebumps formed on her smooth skin, and a tingle ran from head to toe and back again. She shook her head again to clear it. No matter how much she wanted to feel his strong arms around her again—she had to FOCUS. She owed the rest of the crew her full attention for the time being. Perhaps later, tonight....

She powered up her own command tablet and set it down on a table next to her. Thankfully, the wireless cyber-net was still working. The chief had shown foresight enough to pull the cyber-net node out of one of their shuttles when they were abandoned during the evacuation to the Celestia. She supposed, if they survived, that spot would take on a new name—something more heroic—something like Dragon's Last Stand or Imperial Intervention of Jaden-325-4. Someone more poetic than she would need to be found for such a naming.

She grabbed a blue jumpsuit from a stack just inside the doorway. Immediately she noticed something strange about it. She couldn't identify the material it was made from. Although it appeared exactly like a TCDF service overall, it wasn't made by Terrans. It was softer than the mixture of synthetics and natural fibers used in the colonies. It had a matte finish, but it was silkier to the touch. It appeared to be the right size, and it had her rank insignia and her name emblazoned on the left chest. She tipped her head at a quizzical angle and looked at Yustin with raised eyebrows.

Yustin Sallen: "Don't ask me! They were there when I took my shower this morning."

Kathy shrugged and began to step into the garment as her towel dropped to the floor around her feet.

Yustin let the tablet fall from his hands and stood up, watching her intently.

Kathy Lao: "Well, I for one appreciate the gesture from our hosts. I don't want to crawl back into that dirty jumpsuit I wore yesterday. And if they had any nefarious intentions, they wouldn't need to hide them in a new suit of clothes."

Yustin reached for a similar garment in his size and shook it out. It was absolutely correct in appearance, including his own name and rank insignia. He stepped inside and fumbled around with the closure seam. It wasn't a zipper, and there didn't appear to be any way to close it.

Kathy, experimenting, started to run her fingers up the seam of her jumpsuit from crotch to neck. Before she could move more than one-tenth the way up, the seam closed itself. She smiled with amazement. It must be some sort of smart magnetic material.

Yustin looked at his own uniform jumpsuit and touched the seam gently. It closed automatically. He glanced back at Kathy.

She walked over to the sleeping platform, pulling Yustin along beside her. She sat and patted a spot next to her. After he had sat down beside her, she held his hand and began speaking.

Kathy Lao: "Yustin, this has all happened very quickly. You mean everything to me, and I don't want to lose that. But there are going to be times when I am Kathy, the person, in private, and times when I must be the Captain and your Commanding Officer. Can you understand that? Can you still respect and support me?"

Yustin Sallen: "I feel the same, Kathy. And I understand completely. When we are in public, you must command the respect and loyalty of the entire crew. Of course, that must include me. You are my captain. Nothing has changed—well, that's not quite true—everything has changed. But you are my captain, and I will support you to the end. What is happening between us will stay between the two of us. And I won't waiver in my respect for you and support of you. You can trust me."

Kathy Lao: "I DO trust you, Yustin. Okay—Commander, I have to put on my captain's hat now, I'm afraid. We must discuss the current situation and some significant details that neither you nor the crew has been privy to. I need your counsel."

By silent mutual consent, the demeanor of both officers became a bit more formal.

Cmdr. Sallen: "Yes, ma'am. I am all ears."

Captain Lao: "Firstly, I have decided to accept the resignations of Jar'ek Constandor and Kallehn Frix. I've also ceded all authority over, and the right of salvage for, this ship and any other related alien technology to them. I've made these decisions for reasons that will become apparent as I relate to you the story of what's happened to them and what a terrible burden they carry upon their young shoulders."

Commander Sallen's jaw hung open—his eyes wide with shock.

Cmdr. Sallen: "I don't understand, Captain. Why wouldn't you claim this vessel and all of this technology for the Terran Colonies? What are those two boys going to do with all of this? This technology is centuries beyond our own. We need it to defend our people from the Treech!"

Captain Lao: "All will become apparent after I tell you their story—and after you meet their alien ally.... Now listen carefully. There is a lot of ground to cover...."

CHAPTER 40 — COMING TO TERMS

Imperial Destroyer Celestia - Captain Lao's Quarters

Commander Yustin, still sitting next to the captain, stared off into the near distance. His eyes looked dull and glazed. The captain smiled—she could relate!

She wanted to give him time to assimilate everything she had told him. She picked up her command tablet and signed in. There were a number of reports from her small crew. The Medical Officer was reporting that his patients were nearing a miraculous and full recovery. He had estimated another day before the last one was returned to duty. From everything she could tell, the nanites were flushing themselves from the patients' systems once they had finished their repairs.

This was the best news she had heard in what seemed like a very long time.

Lt. Connor had set up a duty roster to help return some routine to daily life for the crew. That was just what they would need for the near future. She approved his schedule, heavy in cleaning, food preparation, supplies inventory, and exercise. It seems Chief Vermanderly, in her explorations, had come across what appeared to be a gymnasium. This "warship" appeared to be more and more like a cruise liner in the captain's mind. But she wasn't complaining....

She put down her tablet and stood, straightening her service uniform out of habit. She cleared her throat and spoke to no one in particular.

Captain Lao: "Ahhhmm... Celestia, can you hear me?"

Celestia AI: "Celestia, attending. Good morning, Captain—Commander."

The captain breathed a sigh of relief. She would have looked very foolish if there was no AI audio pickup in her quarters.

Captain Lao: "Celestia, I'd like to schedule a private meeting between myself, Command Sallen, Kallehn Frix, and Jar'ek Constandor this morning, if possible."

Celestia AI: "Lord Constandor has anticipated your request. He has been waiting for your call, Captain. He and Lord Frix are ready to meet at your convenience."

The captain put her hand on Commander Yustin's shoulder, and he looked up at her.

Captain Lao: "Are you up for this, Yustin? I need my XO."

The commander stood and braced himself.

Sallen: "Yes, ma'am. I'm just a little rattled. But I'm okay. We need to figure out how to address the crew. And the first step will be talking with the Rangers... errr... former Rangers. What do we call them, ma'am?!"

Captain: "Just about whatever they want us to call them, Commander. But I get the feeling that they are still the same people they were last week. They aren't megalomaniacs or egotists. But they have a terrible responsibility. And as far as I can tell, they are determined to see that the Terran Colonies benefit from their new situation. We will just have to see how this all works out in the end. In the meantime, take your lead from me, Commander."

Sallen: "As always, ma'am!"

Captain: "Celestia, we are ready anytime it is convenient."

The door to their quarters slid silently open and disappeared into the decking. A blue light appeared in front of them on the floor and began moving out into the passageway.

Celestia: "Follow the blue sprite, Captain. It will lead you to a private conference room on the command deck. Please do not wander about on the command deck, as some areas are restricted to authorized personnel."

Captain: "Understood. On our way."

The captain and commander trotted to catch up to the sprite as it moved along the passageway. The sprite's speed adjusted, and they soon found that it moved at a comfortable pace for them.

Imperial Destroyer Celestia - Command Deck - Conference Room Alpha

When the captain and her XO arrived, they found the former Ranger Team waiting for them. The captain smelled the heady aroma of real coffee as they entered the conference room and nodded to Jar'ek and Kallehn in recognition.

Jar'ek: "Welcome to the command deck, Captain… Commander. I hope you are both well rested."

Captain Lao: "Good morning to you both. Yes, we got some much-needed sleep. I feel almost human this morning."

The captain smiled, but her face quickly became more somber. "Before we proceed, I would like to thank you on behalf of myself and the remaining crew. You saved us all from a grisly death at the hands of the Worms."

Jar'ek and Kallehn glanced at each other before returning their gaze back to the captain.

Jar'ek: "We're pleased that we could help. I only wish we had become aware of your situation sooner."

Kallehn: "Won't you sit down? Celestia has provided us with coffee and a selection of breakfast foods. Now that Celestia has had a chance to analyze the food prepared by the crew, she can reproduce anything you'd like."

XO: "Well, I for one am starving. How about you, Captain?"

Captain: "Me, too, and the coffee smells wonderful."

Jar'ek: "Please! Help yourselves."

As the four of them collected their selections and found seats, there was a hesitation in the conversation. No one wanted to be the first to break the relaxed mood by asking tough questions about the future.

Having eaten enough to sate her immediate hunger, Captain Lao leaned back into her comfortable seating and cradled a hot cup of coffee. At least that's what her senses told her it was—synthesized or not.

She raised her eyes to her XO with a searching glance. He nodded almost imperceptibly. She turned her gaze toward Jar'ek and cleared her throat.

Captain Lao: "I briefed Commander Sallen early this morning. He knows everything I know."

Jar'ek and Kallchn both looked at the XO, trying to discern from his expression and body language what his thoughts were. The XO took a long gulp of coffee and set the cup down.

XO: "I cannot say that I'm exactly happy about the position we are all in. But to be honest, I think simply landing on this gods-cursed planet qualified us for quarantine no matter what you two did. If you hadn't encountered the alien entity, we would never have known about this interstellar plague. And if your alien is wrong, we might have very well brought it back to the colonies.

"Having said that, our careers are over and our futures are pretty darned limited."

Jar'ek: "Then you believe the captain is right? You think the colonies will abandon you on this planet?"

XO: "I do. And if they think there is any chance they can get their hands on this warship... they won't be squeamish about irradiating the entire planet, us included. That's the only way they would feel confident the biological threat had been sterilized."

Captain Lao tensed, sat up sharply, and stared at her XO as if he had just changed into a demon from Terran mythology.

Captain: "Abandonment is one thing, Yustin. Mass murder is quite another. Do you REALLY think the TCDF is capable of that!?"

XO: "You know the politics as well as I do, Captain... and once they have word that the Treech have entered this sector... what do you think?"

The captain stood up and began to pace slowly. Concentration lined her face as a cold chill ran down her spine. She shook her head in disbelief. But she knew he was right. And if she were in their place, would she feel the same... panic? She flashed back to that moment just before the Imperial Shuttle Castalon arrived to save the day. She relived that moment of terror when she ***KNEW*** they were all going to be eaten alive. If the sacrifice of the few remaining Terran survivors on this planet could make the difference—could prevent that same scene and other scenes like it from being played out across the colonies....

Captain: "I hadn't thought it through all the way. Looking at this from their perspective, you're right. That is precisely what they'll do. And, if simply confiscating this advanced warship could save them, I would be willing to accept the sacrifice, and I know you would too, Yustin."

Jar'ek: "But the technology incorporated within the Celestia is so far in advance of the Terran Colonies that it would take decades, if not centuries, to even begin to understand the fundamentals of the underlying physics. And with the Treech moving into the neighborhood, they won't have that much time."

XO: "But the Celestia could defeat any Treech horde sent to attack the colonies!"

Jar'ek: "The Celestia, no matter how powerful, is only one ship. It cannot be in two places at once. And even inferior warships could destroy her if they attacked in sufficient quantity."

Captain: "Perhaps you could provide instruction, technical guides...."

Jar'ek: "I could, but, again, it would take too long. They would need to build tools to build the tools to build factories to build better tools, etc. The Terran Colonies simply don't have the infrastructure to take advantage of Imperial technology."

Kallehn: "Then what can we do? We can't just let this happen! There has to be something we can do...."

Jar'ek stared off into the distance. Kallehn recognized this as a classic sign of Jar'ek communing with his symbiont, Plato. It must be time to bring in the big guns.

Jar'ek: {"Plato, do you have any ideas?"}

Plato: {"Sire, I am convinced that significant infrastructure still remains in the Empire. There simply has not been enough time to get any response from our probes. If the worst case is true, and all of its citizens died as a result of the plague... there will still be surviving hardware, facilities, factories, ships, and armories. We just have to find them. The Terrans could be the first race to make up the basis for the new Harmonic Empire. But, Sire, if your Terran Council has not earned your trust before now, what will they do with access to the power of the old Empire? This galaxy has seen the horrors and devastation of aggressive and powerful species before. Reflect carefully before you—to use your own vernacular—open Pandora's Box."}

Jar'ek: {"I hear your words, Plato. And I believe there is wisdom in your counsel."}

Jar'ek turned to face the rest of the group, who had been staring expectantly at him.

Jar'ek: "Oh, sorry. I was getting Plato's opinion. He is convinced that there are surviving remnants of the Empire... infrastructure, perhaps warships and more. These resources could be used to help defend the colonies. We've sent probes to the nearest Imperial bases. We should hear something any day now. Until then, he suggests patience."

XO: "And what happens if the TCDF does attempt to irradiate the planet before then?"

Jar'ek: "We should all be safe inside the Celestia. We can always leave this system if necessary. The Celestia is significantly faster in hyperspace than anything the TCDF has."

Captain: "Well, that's good news, anyway. I wasn't looking forward to being sacrificed for a lost cause! But what are we supposed to do? The TCDF won't take us back. We can't go home. We appreciate your hospitality, but we need some direction in our lives—a purpose."

Kallehn looked at Jar'ek. He activated the psionic interface in his uniform/armor to open a silent communication between them.

{Psionic communication}

Kallehn: {"Hey, Jar'ek... can you hear me?"}

Jar'ek: {"Yes! You have something you wish to discuss privately?"}

Kallehn: {"Well, Celestia needs a crew, right?"}

Jar'ek: {"Yes..."}

Kallehn: {"Well, we have command staff right here. And the rest of the Dragon's crew are smart. They're trainable. The AI takes care of almost everything."}

Jar'ek: {"And they wouldn't need to understand the physics to point and shoot! Damage control might be a whole different issue, though. But it is a good idea. Why don't you suggest it to the captain? You and I would still need to be in overall command of all things Imperial, but if the captain and XO can live with that, I think it can work!"}

Aloud, Kallehn said: "Captain, we have a suggestion. The Celestia needs a crew. She needs a captain. The overall command would still reside with Jar'ek, of course, but...."

Chapter 41—RECRUITING A CREW

Imperial Destroyer Celestia - Main Mess Hall

After the Treech attacks, the Dragon Eye survivors totaled only eleven humans, two X'Ah-Panths, and one X'Ah-Falcon, including the former Ranger Team. All of them—except their feathered companion—were assembled in the main mess hall. Some still wore the pink scars of newly repaired skin, but they were all there. They all wanted to know what was going to happen to them next.

The captain, the XO, and Jar'ek were the last to be seated. The captain poured herself a mug of hot coffee from a decanter on the table, more to give herself a chance to collect her thoughts than to drink more caffeine. She took a long sip and carefully set the mug back down before standing and straightening her uniform jumpsuit.

She gazed out over her crew and took the time to share an honest smile with each one of them. Then she began to speak.

Captain Lao: "I am very glad to see that you have all survived the recent engagements with our ancient enemy and are in good health. Tomorrow, we plan to have a memorial to honor our friends and colleagues who were killed in the line of duty. But today I hope to provide you with what information I have, the decisions that I have made in light of our current circumstances, and our best guess as to what the future holds for us."

"Let me first acknowledge that we all owe a debt of gratitude to our former Ranger Team Alpha. When given a chance, they risked their lives without hesitation to defend their crewmates."

"Here, here!" the XO cheered, echoed by every one of the remaining crew.

The XO stood, extending his hand across the table and shaking first Jar'ek's and then Kallehn's hand. The rest of the crew did likewise, many leaving their seats and slapping the boys on their backs.

After allowing sufficient time for the spontaneous celebration, the captain cleared her throat as a signal for everyone to take their seats so she might continue.

Captain: "After the Treech KKM strike, Ranger Team Alpha found themselves in dire circumstances. Jar'ek and Kallehn had both sustained life-threatening injuries. They thought that the Dragon Eye had been lost with all hands—that they were absolutely alone—that there was no one to provide medical aid or assistance of any kind. Indeed, they had no expectation that a rescue ship would ever be sent. And there was the very real possibility that the Treech would launch a Drop Ship full of ground troops to search for any survivors."

The captain paused in her speech for a moment and scanned their faces. Then she continued speaking: "So, the decisions made by Jar'ek Constandor under those horrible circumstances might seem radical or ill-advised, in retrospect. But remember that as a result of his courage and selflessness, we are alive today. With a chance for a future. And perhaps, if we play our cards right, and because of the choices he made, we may get the chance to give the Treech the really sharp end of the stick!"

Emphasizing her last words, the captain drove her fist down on the table and leaped to her feet. As her audience rose to join her, a roar of affirmation rose from their throats to shake the very walls about them.

Once again, the captain took her seat, and the rest of the crew followed suit. But when she looked into their eyes, she no longer saw the specters of defeat, and fear she had seen when first entering the room. Before, the crew had noticed the differences in the former Rangers—the strange uniforms and the even stranger tattoos that marked Jar'ek. They had felt anxious and suspicious of the young men.

But now, they were ready to hear the story of the Ranger who would rule an Empire—the dead and ancient plague that had brought an Empire to its knees—and her fears that the TCDF would rather kill them all in a storm of manmade radiation than negotiate with a former junior officer turned Galactic Prince.

She glanced at Yustin Sallen for support. Hidden beneath the table, she felt his strong hand enfold hers and squeeze gently. He had faith in her. Maybe that was all she needed.

Chapter 42—A CHOICE TO BE MADE

Imperial Destroyer Celestia - Command Deck

Having no other real prospects, all of the survivors had volunteered without exception to sign on as crew to the Celestia. Jar'ek had made it plain to them that if they were wrong and the TCDF was wise enough to reintegrate them into Terran society, he would release them from their service contracts. But none of them really thought that was going to happen.

Although the colonies were ostensibly a democratic republic, they knew that the Terran Council cared little for the rights of the individual. Indeed, for generations, the voting process had been little more than a sham. The powerful and wealthy were in control, and they were not likely to allow any threat to change that situation. The simple fact that a human led galactic empire existed as a choice to the oppressed colonists would be a serious threat to the powerful elite... The Council would use the extinct virus as a reason to have their story end on Jaden-325-4. An executive order would be issued, classifying this entire affair upon penalty of death. Their family and friends would never know what happened to them

Jar'ek had instructed Celestia's AI to setup training simulations for the captain, XO, Tactical Officer Sasha Conner, and Helm Officer Rico De Lucena. Jar'ek and Kallehn had been working through the training simulations with them for the past couple of Planetary Rotations. Helm and tactical operations were not that different from one starship to another. The same basic principles applied. But the interface and the control designs differed widely from Terran norms. It took some getting used to.

To everyone, the capabilities of the Celestia were impressive. She could sustain much higher acceleration and was much more maneuverable than the Dragon's Eye. The improvements in the efficiency of the inertial compensators made a great deal of difference in the ship's performance. Passengers and crew felt no effects from the massive acceleration the Celestia was capable of producing. She could outfly and outfight any Terran or Treech ship in space.

But it was time for a break. As fun and challenging as the simulations were, they all needed food and rest. And Jar'ek wanted to spend some time at the gym. He'd been sitting all day and needed a good workout. He was also anxious to explore his extended memories that related to Imperial flight operations and tactics. He had been trained as a Ranger. He could fly a Shuttle or Flitter with no problem, but piloting an Imperial Destroyer was something else altogether.

He had the genetic memories of hundreds of Imperial pilots, tactical officers, fighter jocks, captains, and admirals inside him now. He "knew" how to fly the Celestia. But he needed the time to practice and integrate his extended memories with his conscious mind. He needed practice to cement the memories into a thorough understanding.

As he trotted toward the gym with this purpose in mind, he failed to notice Kallehn watching his back as he left… a look of longing and disappointment crossing his face before he turned and walked away.

Jar'ek and Kallehn realized the crew needed to get to know the former Rangers again—laugh with them—share meals with them—learn to trust them again. But Kallehn couldn't help feeling hurt by the initial caution shown by most of his former crewmates. Each time someone stopped talking when Kallehn walked into a room, it reminded him of his isolation. He could no longer be Terran, but he didn't have a formal place in the Empire, either. He felt out of place… and now as Jar'ek moved away from him, totally alone….

Imperial Destroyer Celestia - Gymnasium

Jar'ek was enjoying a brisk run around the training track after finishing a heavy-gravity workout with the lifting equipment

Celestia had engineered for better compatibility with Terran physiology. And after some prompting, Celestia had designed and manufactured lightweight and casual attire for the crew to work out in. As with most Imperial clothing designs, there was little left to the imagination.

The crew members were learning to set aside their modesty, and a few had finally felt comfortable enough to join him in the gym. Jar'ek had to admit, it was awkward feeling like you had absolutely no anatomical secrets from anyone. Thankfully, the crew was in good shape, so they had nothing about which to be embarrassed.

Although the engineered clothing wicked away moisture, his face was dripping with sweat from exertion. It was the first time in days he had been able to really push himself physically. It felt great! As he settled into a steady pace on the track, he was just about to start exploring his extended memories when Plato asked for a moment of his time.

Plato: {"Sire, it is time to speak to Kallehn about the Judgment and the offer of melding."}
Jar'ek: {"Why now? Things seem to be fairly stable for the moment. Do we really need to rush him?"}

Plato: {"You may have noticed his mood is somewhat sullen of late?"}

Jar'ek: {"Surely that is to be expected after everything he has been through recently. And the crew is going to need some time to accept us again. It is a lot for them to take in. He'll be fine. Just give him some time. "}

Plato: {"Ordinarily I would agree, but his recent medical scan seems to indicate that his immune system is asserting itself and eliminating the Harmonic SEED that you accidentally transferred to him. He is beginning to lose his enhanced abilities. And there is something else in his scan that concerns me..."}

Jar'ek stopped running, stepped off the track and rested his hands on his thighs as he caught his breath.

Jar'ek: {"Okay. You have my full attention, now."}

Plato: {"Do you remember me saying that Human physiology was highly compatible with melding?"}

Jar'ek: {"Yeah. So?"}

Plato: {"hmmmm... well, as it turns out your brain chemistry demonstrates a sympathetic relationship with the symbiosis... Kallehn is showing symptoms of withdrawal. His Dopamine levels are dropping rapidly. As his body eliminates the SEED, the withdrawal symptoms will increase in severity. Thankfully, your developing relationship with him has helped bolster his spirits substantially. But we must speak with Kallehn soon, and Medical Officer To'Torat should be included in the conversation. She may have some valuable insights."}

Jar'ek: {"Is it life threatening?!?"}

Plato: {"Terran physiology and mental processes are new territory for me. Honestly, I don't know. The only thing I do know is that it is going to get a lot worse before it gets better. "}

Jar'ek reviewed the last 48 hours in his mind. The mental enhancements facilitated by the melding gave him eidetic memory. He was able to take the time and closely examine his recent interactions with Kallehn. They had been so busy trying to hold things together—Jar'ek had gotten lost in himself and his duty.

Though they slept next to each other each night, they hadn't had much time to spend with each other, alone. When they finally got a chance to sleep, that's exactly what they did. He could do better. He needed to do better. He would make sure that Kallehn knew he was a priority in his life.

But the issue of the melding had to be resolved and quickly. Or

Kallehn was going to suffer a great deal.

Jar'ek said: "Celestia, Attend me."

Celestia AI: "Attending, Sire."

Jar'ek: "Please schedule a private meeting with Myself, Kallehn and Kira To'Torat at the Doctor's earliest convenience. And then please notify Kallehn and myself of the details."

Celestia AI: "Processing your request now.... I will notify you when the Doctor has responded."

Imperial Destroyer Celestia - outside Jar'ek's quarters

Jar'ek: "Celestia, Attend me."

Celestia AI: "Attending, Sire."

Jar'ek: "Can you please leave off the honorifics for a while? It is wearing on me. I don't feel like I deserve it, and I certainly haven't earned it."

Celestia AI: "I will comply. But you hold the position of leader of a Galactic Empire. The honorifics go with the position. So, whether you feel like you've 'earned it' or not is irrelevant."

Jar'ek: "Whatever. It will be easier for me if everyone just calls me Jar'ek. Can you locate Kallehn for me, please?"

Celestia: "Kallehn Frix is located in your quarters... Sir."

Jar'ek heaves a heavy sigh, shakes his head mumbling and walks through the portal to his quarters, as the door slides silently out of site. He notices Kallehn sitting, watching a 3D simulation of the Celestia's Tactical Station. The simulation is very realistic. There is an exact replica of the ship's tactical console right in front of Kallehn. Kallehn reaches out tentatively and taps a red icon three times, quickly. An alarm sounds briefly, and the simulation evaporates.

Kallehn jumps to his feet with balled fists, and finding no console to pound with them, stomps his foot angrily.

Kallehn: "Damn it ALL!"

Jar'ek watches him closely for a moment. Kallehn hasn't noticed that he is no longer alone. He sits down heavily and lowers his face into his hands, mumbling to himself.

Kallehn: "Why can't I do this?! I didn't have any problems working out the shuttle's controls... This isn't that much different!"

Jar'ek clears his throat and as Kallehn, startled, jerks his head around to face the source of the noise--Jar'ek moves over to sit beside Kallehn and places his right arm around his shoulders, pulling him close. At first, Kallehn resists, but then takes a deep breath and allows himself to settle into Jar'ek's shoulder.

Jar'ek: "I came by to see how you were doing. I don't need to ask how your day has gone, at this point. I think I can tell from that outburst. I don't think I've ever seen you so pissed off! Is there anything I can help with? I am 'Master of All You Survey', after all."

A tight smile began to draw the corners of Kallehn's mouth as he slowly raised his eyes to Jar'ek's.

Kallehn: "Not at all cocky, are we?!"

Jar'ek: "Seriously, want to talk about it? I want to help, if I can."

Kallehn grimaced and dropped his head, pulling slightly away to sit upright and rest his elbows on his knees. Jar'ek leaned forward to keep his arm around Kallehn's back and shoulder, still watching his face so as not to miss any subtle changes that might communicate more about his mood.

Kallehn took his left hand and patted Jar'ek's right thigh as he spoke.

Kallehn: "I know you want to help. And I'm glad you are there for me. It's just silly. I am frustrated. I'm having trouble with the tactical training simulations. I felt like I was falling further and further behind while we were on the bridge working with rest of the crew. I must be coming down with something. My brain just isn't working very well. I'm sure it will be fine in a few days. I probably just need more sleep."

Jar'ek took his right hand and squeezed the back of Kallehn's neck and shoulder. Kallehn arched his neck and back into Jar'ek's one-handed grip and moaned lightly. "Mmmmmm"

Kallehn: "Gods that feels good! I'm going to give you just one Solar Rotation to stop that…" Jar'ek smiled.

Jar'ek: "So, tell me… just how much of your training at the Ranger Academy focused on Starship Operations?" Jar'ek slid up further on the sleeping platform to be able to use both hands and began massaging Kallehn's shoulders in earnest.

Kallehn: "You and I were in the same training, Jar'ek! You know we didn't have ANY operations training beyond flying a Shuttle or a Flitter. We were trained in Emergency Survival Procedures, sealing hull breaches with patches, operations in the Galley and routine maintenance procedures so we could carry our weight between surveys. Command didn't expect us to ever fly or fight a warship!"

Jar'ek: "How about the rest of the bridge crew? The Captain, the XO, the Tactical Officer and the Helm Officer—what kind of tactical and operations training would they have been required to study at the academy and afterward?"

Kallehn: "Well, of course, they all had extensive training in ship's operation and tactics. The Captain and XO are brilliant."

Jar'ek: "So, why are you frustrated that the bridge crew, all experienced flight officers, are assimilating the tactical training faster than you are? You are starting from zero. They have rather a large head start."

Kallehn: "Yeah, of course, you are right... but YOU are doing great. And I thought I might actually have some talent in this area when we were flying and fighting the Castalon... it just seemed to just come to me what I needed to do. The console just made perfect sense. The last couple days... it's like none of this makes any sense to me! Plus, I'm just not sleeping very well. I'm exhausted all the time. And it hasn't helped that I feel not quite accepted by the crew... and you are so busy, I find myself alone a good bit of the time... Hell, I sound like an absolute Wuss! I'm sorry, you have way more important things on your mind. Ignore me. I'll be fine."

Jar'ek: "I think I know what's going on. It's not your fault—It's mine."

Kallehn twisted around to face Jar'ek better.

Kallehn: "What are you talking about?! How could my failures be your fault?!"

Jar'ek: "When I helped heal your mind, I 'infected you' with some of the Harmonic SEED."

*Plato: {"Sire, I **REALLY** wish you could find **SOME** other verb to describe the **GIFT** of the SEED!"}*

Jar'ek: {"Be Quiet! We'll talk later.}

Kallehn: "I remember. But that wasn't really a bad thing..."

Jar'ek: "We think, Plato and I, that because of the way the SEED was introduced, that some bad things are happening—to you. In a traditional Meld, the host's body is modified so that the immune system doesn't see the SEED as foreign and leaves it alone."

Kallehn: "Bad things like what?"

Jar'ek: "Your abilities and memories were enhanced when the

level of SEED in your blood was at its peak. But your own immune system has begun producing effective antibodies that are eliminating the SEED from your body."

Kallehn: "Ohhhhhhh... You mean, no more super powers..."

Kallehn thought to himself: "and then I will be holding you back, again..."

Jar'ek: "It's more than that. There are some unique differences in human physiology that have caused ... well, there is no easy way to say this... It appears that humans develop an addiction to the Harmonic SEED. Your body is going through the beginning stages of withdrawal."

Kallehn stood up and backed a few steps away from the sleeping platform, facing Jar'ek.

Kallehn: "When you say 'Beginning Stages,' you mean it's going to get worse, right? What can I expect?"

Jar'ek: "All I can give you is a guess, at this point. We have a meeting with Kira and Plato this afternoon if you are up to it. But I can tell you that fatigue, depression and a negative impact on cognitive skills and recollection are expected. It could even be life threatening—we just don't know, yet."

Kallehn sat down on the floor where he was and hugged his knees to his chest. Jar'ek moved over and sat beside him again.

Kallehn: "I didn't realize it was only temporary. Now, the SEED is going to leave me, too. Jar'ek, I don't really want to die like this. I just found you! And I don't mean to complain, but you and I have barely gotten a chance to kiss each other. I mean I really do like waking up next to you, and having your arms around me all night... don't get me wrong. If that's all I ever get, I'm so grateful to have shared that level of intimacy with you. But ***DAMN IT***, I WANT MORE THAN THAT!! And I want a ***future*** with you..."

Jar'ek: "Oh, trust me... Nothing is going to stand in my way of experiencing ***MORE*** than that! You are not done, yet, Kallehn! Worst case scenario, you have a choice that should save your life and bring back your 'super powers'—your words, not mine... This may not be as bad as we think, after all. You can wait this out and see. If it looks like it is going to be bad—well, Plato has asked me to ask you to present yourself for Judgement. He feels you are an excellent candidate and would make a superior Meld. This time, we could do it ***RIGHT***."

Kallehn turned to face Jar'ek, a look of shock on his face.

Kallehn: "Me?! Really?! This is awesome!"

Jar'ek: "I don't want you to feel pressured to make this choice. It may not be necessary."

Kallehn: "Pressured, ***HELL***! I have been wanting this! Are you kidding?! I want to be everything I can be. And not just for myself. I want you to be proud of me. I don't ever want anyone to think or say that the Emperor 'Settled' for a dim-witted ex-Ranger do nothing with a cute face—how sad. "

Jar'ek: "I wouldn't be settling at all. I ***AM*** proud of you. I am so very proud that you are mine and I give myself to you without hesitation, Kallehn Frix! Anyone talks any crap about you within earshot of me, they are going to wish they were dead!"

Kallehn smiled.

With that, Jar'ek stood, pulling Kallehn to his feet and enfolding him in his well-muscled arms, and kissed him deeply. This time, they didn't stop at kissing... Celestia quietly closed the door, dimmed the lights, and rescheduled the meeting with MO To'Torat.

Chapter 43—MESSAGE IN A BOTTLE

Imperial Destroyer Celestia – Captain Lao's Quarters

Captain Lao was seated at the workstation in her quarters making notes on her command tablet. She brushed an errant strand of her jet-black hair out of her face and set the tablet down—reaching for her coffee cup, she took a big gulp and made a sour face—Cold again.

Captain Lao: "Celestia, I need your assistance."

Celestia: "Attending, Captain."

Captain Lao: "I'd like to record a message to be sent by communications probe to Terran Confederation Defense Forces located on New Hope and Promise. I believe that Lord Constandor will approve these for immediate launch."

Celestia: "As acting Ship's Captain, you have the authority to order the immediate launch of communication probes by yourself. But the Emperor has pre-approved this launch without review. I believe the Emperor has faith in you, Captain."

Captain Lao sat thinking for a moment and then moved to pour herself a fresh cup of coffee while she continued the conversation.

Captain Lao: "Very well. No encryption will be necessary. Launch probes after the recording is completed. Begin recording—message follows:

"From Captain Kathy Xiang Lao, Commanding Officer, TCDF Dragon Eye.

Location: Jaden-325-4

To: TCDF Command Central via any available contact.

I regret to report that the Dragon Eye was attacked and destroyed by a Treech Marauder in this system—Only eleven souls surviving. We were able to destroy the Marauder by ramming it with the injured Dragon Eye and activating the self-destruct. We believe this occurred before they could send a message back to their fleet. After evacuating to the planet surface, we were again attacked by a single surviving Treech Drop Ship loaded with ground troops.

We are only alive today because of the heroic and spectacular actions of former Rangers Kallehn Frix and Jar'ek Constandor, who have made an alliance with an alien forerunner they encountered on the planet survey. Yes, Former Rangers is correct.

This is where the story gets complicated…"

Chapter 44—SOLITUDE OF THE HUNT

Jaden-325-4 – Planet Surface

Plato was still sulking. Jar'ek had been in a particularly stubborn mood and insisted on leaving the ship to explore with only S'Fah and Ta'ihr for an escort. He had to order his Mech security detail to remain behind and use the Imperial override commands. He felt a bit guilty about causing that much of a conflict in their programming, but...he needed some time to think; to assimilate. And he wanted to spend some time with the X'Ah-Falcon and see what she could do. At the very least, Ta'ihr enjoyed the freedom of the open skies, and it was a joy to see S'Fah running ahead at full speed, dust flying out behind him.

S'Fah: {"Joy! Catch me slow-as-a-tortoise, human!"}

Jar'ek feinted left and then right as if he were going to lunge at the passing X'Ah-Panth, just to see him dodge. Then S'Fah's front paw hit a rock in the middle of another escape—he ended up rolling over several times in the dirt before coming to an indignant halt, shaking himself in a storm of dirt and debris, and then licking off the remaining dust. Jar'ek couldn't help himself—he burst into laughter, fell to his knees and ended up rolling on the ground himself. S'Fah shook his head and purred the feline equivalent of a guffaw, then came padding over to nuzzle his mind-mate's face as he knelt to greet him.

Plato reflected in silence and saw that perhaps Jar'ek had been right. Getting away from the ship, responsibilities, his new situation was certainly improving his disposition. Also, his blood pressure was returning to normal, and that was a good thing. Plato had to remember that a lot had happened to this young man in a very short period of time. He was being asked to mature very quickly. And an unbearable burden had been placed on his shoulders. Maybe he deserved a little distraction, after all.

A Piercing "SCCcccrrrreeeee" was heard from the skies above as

Ta'ihr sighted a small scurrying rodent and signaled his hunter's glee. Jar'ek looked up, shading his eyes against the sun's glare and saw a feathered streak diving towards the ground with wings collapsed tight into its body in aerodynamic grace. At the very last second, Ta'ihr threw out his massive wings to their full span, breaking his descent just as his claws stretched out and captured the small long-tailed rodent. Great wings beat the air into submission as the sleek hunter rose high and glided along the thermals like a living, breathing kite.

Jar'ek stood and gasped at the beauty, the elegance, the efficiency of motion demonstrated by the genetically enhanced bird of prey. He felt Ta'ihr's mind-touch; it was clear, if weak.

{"Joy—Freedom—Flight—Hunt"}

S'Fah paced Jar'ek as he moved forward at an easy jog down the ancient pathways that lead to the old ruins. Jar'ek wanted to lose himself in routine tasks—hiking, exploring, just feeling the freedom of open spaces. He realized it might be a metaphor for the freedom he had recently surrendered, but for the moment, this would do. Jar'ek sent a gentle mind-touch to Ta'ihr.

Jar'ek: {"Sky Warrior, Hunt. We seek relics today. SEEK!"}

High above, the sun reflected off the brightly colored wings as Ta'ihr banked sharply and set a new course straight ahead, into the ruins.

Jaden-325-4 – Planet Surface

Plato hadn't had much to say about the nearby ruins, except that no life signs were detected when the Celestia first landed and none had been detected since then. The SEED had developed technology to the point that was necessary to defend the Empire and didn't feel a great deal of need to explore old ruins on the off chance they might find something useful. The Empire had archeologists, certainly. And these ruins would have eventually been explored by such academics, had the plague not struck. But

Jar'ek and the Terrans, in general, were more curious about such things. Perhaps it was the idea of a Treasure Hunt with some great reward just beyond the next curve of path in front of you—or perhaps it was just the continual search for knowledge; for understanding. In any case, exploration was what he wanted today—and the freedom it offered him.

The sun began to set just as they reached the outskirts of the ruins. Jar'ek, as a Meld, could see with very little light, as could both the genetically enhanced S'Fah and Ta'ihr. So, he wasn't worried, and he wanted to enjoy this freedom as long as possible. S'Fah lead as they entered the darkened opening in the fallen walls and buildings. It appeared to be a tunnel or passageway. S'Fah sniffed the air carefully before proceeding slowly through the break. Jar'ek checked his sidearm, and set it to heavy stun just in case. He felt a bit silly because according to all their sensor scans, this place was deserted. He stepped through and made his way down the pile of collapsed stone and dirt to the dust covered pavement at the bottom of the rift. S'Fah was sniffing around in circles but had found nothing of interest to report. Jar'ek was wondering which way to go—left or right—when he felt the gentle mind-touch of the X'Ah-Falcon above. {"Magnets—North"}.

The X'Ah-Falcons had a much smaller vocabulary than the X'Ah-Panths. But the Falcons were enhanced to be able to sense weak magnetic fields. This was helpful in locating hidden energy sources—or magnetic fields. The intelligent birds had been trained to seek magnets and were rewarded when they found them. Jar'ek called up his ARDisplay and followed the digital indicator until he was facing North along the tunnel. Right, it was. S'Fah paced ahead, seeking—scanning—always vigilant.

Jaden-325-4 – Exploring the Ruins

A cool, almost chilling breeze blew from deeper within the ruins and stirred Jar'ek's close-cropped blond hair as they travelled in the general direction of the weak power signature. Jar'ek was playing with the video modes of his ARDisplay when he thought he noticed a sound, just at the limit of his hearing. There it was again... No, it wasn't a ***sound***, it was ***psionic***. Unlike the familiar mind-touch with his furred and feathered companions, or even like the direct communications possible with the SEED, this was alien, unintelligible, incompatible in some fundamental way. As light as that touch was, it was as irritating in its own way as the screech of fingernails drawn across a slate surface.

Jar'ek shook his head to clear it. It was probably an artifact of his imagination brought on by the continued stress and fatigue due to recent events. The strange mind-touch did not recur for long moments as they continued on towards their goal, convincing Jar'ek that it was imagined and of no consequence. Before long S'Fah came to a halt, sneezed and waited for Jar'ek to catch up, pacing back and forth between the tunnel walls, occasionally raising his muzzle high in the air to sniff. Having learned to respect the great cat's enhanced abilities, Jar'ek slowed his pace until he could kneel next to S'Fah and look into his eyes.

Stroking the fur between his ears and down his neck, *Jar'ek asked: {"What is it, boy? What do you sense?"}*

S'Fah: {"Confusion—Unease—Bitter Scent stalks these tunnels—Old scent, very old, but still.."}

S'Fah's hackles rose as once again Jar'ek felt that strange psionic touch—stronger this time, and a chill ran down his spine. Jar'ek felt more than heard a low growl from his mind-mate.

S'Fah: {"Like strange scent—mind-touch, that is not mind-touch is...Unclean—Corrupted—Rotting—Old. This is no place for our kind."}

Jar'ek, his own feelings of anxiety warring with his stubborn curiosity, inhaled sharply and stood up, resettling his gear. Then thought to S'Fah: *{"The sensors detected no life signs. There is nothing that can harm us now. Anything that lived here in the past is long dead."}*

Raising his arms wide and smiling broadly, Jar'ek spoke aloud: "Besides, what have I to fear as long as the ***great and powerful S'Fah*** is at my side?!"

S'Fah huffed in the way one might chastise a foolhardy cub, but also felt pride in his abilities and knew that Jar'ek was right. It would take a considerable feat for any creature to get past S'Fah to threaten Jar'ek. The big cat's muscles moved fluidly under his thick black fur as it bounded ahead with newfound confidence.

Plato remained silent. He was focusing all of his concentration on sifting through Giga-quads of genetic memories. There was something he couldn't quite put his virtual finger on…something about an ancient myth or unsubstantiated rumor regarding unintelligible psionic mumblings like the ones they had experienced in the ruins this day. Hmm…something important, even troubling. Should he say something to Jar'ek? No, he didn't have enough information to suggest there was some kind of threat indicated—just an odd feeling. Besides, he was still miffed at Jar'ek for being so dismissive, earlier in the day. What did humans call this behavior? Oh, yes—giving him the Cold Shoulder. It was probably nothing, after all.

Jaden-325-4 – Ruins of Ascobar

Jar'ek began quietly humming as he trotted behind S'Fah. He was enjoying himself for the first time since the Team had been initially deployed on Jaden-325-4. Exploring the enhanced mind-touch between himself and S'Fah was also improving his mood. It was incredible—the Melding had improved many of Jar'ek's abilities, and his psionic abilities were significantly stronger—more robust.

As S'Fah trotted ahead, Jar'ek focused on the thread of psionic energy connecting them. The mind-touch was more than just image and emotion driven communications, now. Jar'ek was beginning to feel what S'Fah felt—sense what S'Fah sensed. He could feel the sandy surface beneath four paws as they glided silently in smooth sequence across the tunnel floor. He was startled as he realized a subtle susurration was actually Jar'ek's own breathing picked up by S'Fah's ears. And now he also could smell through S'Fah's nostrils, that elusive acrid, bitter taint to the air.

Jar'ek was so mesmerized by these new sensations that he stumbled and almost tripped as his way became cluttered with debris. Some cataclysm in the distant past had caused a portion of the tunnel walls to collapse inward and narrow the passage so that only one person might pass at a time. He grimaced as he chastised himself for his daydreaming and loss of attention—sloppy—unprofessional. He expected to sense S'Fah or Plato's joviality at his lapse when instead, he was struck by a feeling of excitement and wariness from S'Fah's mind-touch. Jar'ek made his way through the narrowing and saw what had drawn his mind-mates attention.

They had entered into what appeared to be a chamber or circular widening where several tunnels met. And in the center of that Chamber was what looked like a dais made of an ebony-hued metal or stone. Surrounding the dais were a series of six—what could only be called—control stations. But what remained of the seating could not have been designed for human, takesh or any other bipedal anatomy. The control panels extended inward in low benches with notches that appeared to have been designed for creatures with at least eight limbs. And these creatures must have been LARGE. Jar'ek estimated that he and Kallehn could stretch out to their full lengths on each end of one of these benches and not be able to touch the other.

Once again, Jar'ek felt the screeching fingernails on slate, in his head. The ***screeeech*** was louder this time and brought a dull pain to his temples. Jar'ek reached out to steady himself and placed his palm onto one of the obsidian control panels and immediately yanked it back as a strong vibration ran up the nerves of his hand like an electric shock. Now he noticed the vibration was accompanied by a low freqency hum as if some great machine had been activated and unimaginable forces were only barely restrained beneath the surface. Lights of red and purple hues began to push back the darkness of the cavern as they came to life on each of the control stations and finally the dais itself. There, a bright beam of deep purple shot straight up into the ceiling of the chamber—a purple so deep that it hurt Jar'ek's eyes when he stared at it for too long.

Plato was still busy searching through ancient fragments of memory with a growing dread. And with the accidental activation of still functioning panels within the ruins, Plato felt it was time to voice his misgivings about continuing this adventure, under the circumstances: *{"Jar'ek, I have a bad feeling about this. I think we should consider going back to Celestia and sending out a team to investigate your finding under a more controlled environment."}* Jar'ek considered Plato's words for a moment but then began climbing up to take a quick look at the dais, itself.

Jar'ek: *{"So, you decided to quit sulking and join our expedition, after all? I tend to agree with your assessment, but curiosity has gotten the best of me. I just want to take a quick look at this dais, and then we can start back. I think we are on the brink of discovering something new beyond the experience of even the Harmonic Empire!"}*

Jar'ek steadied himself after he reached the level portion at the top of the dais. Purple-hued light encircled him. Below, under his feet, he saw the pulsing source of this light surrounded by red glyphs that seemed to be burned into the obsidian surface. In the center was a rectangle with a bar or gripping handle of some sort on top of it. This must be either the power source or...a memory core! — *Can I remove this and take it back to the Celestia for investigation?* —

Plato had just found a reference that might be related. An exploration mission had been lost in the adjoining sector some 8,000 SSO(Standard Solar Orbits) ago. An Imperial Task Force lead by a Harmonic Meld had been dispatched to investigate the disappearance. The Task Force was never seen again. But a heavily damaged communications probe had made it back. Very little could be recovered of the original message. The message fragments included: "Psionic communications incompatible—painful—Avoid contact—Quarantine by order of Harmonic Seed—Sentinels of Ascobar—Psionic Weapon—Xenophobic" and a single video clip showing a roiling mass of black snake-like creatures.

Plato was shocked that this had never been pursued, that the memory was so buried in the dust of millennia. But then he remembered the galactic conflicts of that era. The Empire had been hard pressed for nearly a thousand SSOs in defeating neighboring star-faring races that had become resentful of the Empires prosperity and banded together to attack and loot the border star systems. That growing sense of dread was swiftly approaching ***Panic***! S'Fah paced back and forth with fangs bared as if some unseen threat was just beyond his reach.

While Jar'ek, making a decision, reached down towards the pulsating device, gripped the handhold and tugged hard. A rumbling filled the chamber and dust and rocks pelted them from above as the ground shook beneath them. Jar'ek lost his footing. With a gasp, he struggled to prevent a slide and fall from the dais that might end up with broken bones or worse. His flailing arms struck the handle, and he grabbed onto it halting his slide. But his momentum triggered something and the bar, pivoted in place, ending its rotation with a solid **SNNnnnick**! as it locked into a new position.

The light in the chamber changed from reddish-purple to bright yellow as a sub-sonic vibration filled the air. S'Fah stopped and shook his head from side to side as if by such action he could rid himself of the painful assault on his ears—the vibrations may be sub-sonic for human ears, but they were not for those of an X'Ah-Panth.

S'Fah: {"Loud Sounds! Alarm?"}

Jar'ek scrambled to his feet and pulled sharply up on the bar. A blue glow radiated from the obsidian rectangular device as it slid freely out into his hands. It was manufactured of the same onyx-like stone as the dais and control stations. He examined it briefly before stuffing it into his backpack and then sliding down the sloping side of the dais, feet first. As his feet hit the ground another tremor hit, harder this time and he was again tossed from his feet. S'Fah was at his side quickly, visually scanning for any overt threat; growling at the pain in his head.

Plato: {"Quickly, Jar'ek! We must escape. I know what this place is and it is deadly to the Melds! The Sentinels of Ascobar will be on our heels."}

As Jar'ek pulled himself up, he began to run towards the narrow opening in the tunnel through which they had entered the chamber. Red light shimmered in their path, and he and S'Fah stopped short and gazed up at a blazing apparition. It had eight legs, four smaller arms with finely articulated digits or claws and its enormous triangular head held three compound eyes and ended in crushing mandibles. These opened and closed with a loud Clack, Clack, Clack as if they were reaching to crush and rend the Terrans. S'Fah bared his fangs and yowled his battle cry but then suddenly stopped in confusion. It had no scent, no sound. The clacking noises were psionic, not audible.

Jar'ek had reached for his blaster when Plato had pipped in with a psionic equivalent of a scream: *{"It isn't real! It is an Avatar! Keep running. It is designed to delay our escape"}*

Just then Jar'ek's felt the adrenalin rush of instinctive fear flood his bloodstream as the rasping sounds of a slithering locomotion came from behind them, S'Fah turned and again sounded his battle cry, but these were not avatars. Jar'ek turned reaching for his blaster but froze and then fell to the floor as a powerful psionic surge stunned him and Plato, both. The Black Sentinels had been released...

—The Ascobaran Guardian's Avatar had warned them. Three times it had sent Psionic Challenges, and each time they had been ignored. Not only had they entered the sacred chambers of the Hive, but they had dared to pillage the Altar of Memories! Their fate was SEALED! The Black Sentinels would deal with them—

S'Fah, having weaker psionic abilities was able to recover from the stun attack in just a few heartbeats. His senses were assaulted by what he faced. A dozen black snake-like creatures squirmed out of holes that had opened in the dais. A rank, acrid scent made S'Fah sneeze and his eyes water as he prepared for battle. An instinctive rage filled the feline hunter as he moved to position himself between the slithering, malodorous threat and his helpless mind-mate laying on the ground behind him.

The Sentinels had been dormant for thousands of SSOs. They were sluggish, and their attack was uncoordinated. This gave S'Fah a chance. The Terran predator struck swiftly with claw and fang, rending the slimy flesh of the attackers, one by one until all twelve were quivering lumps of decomposing muck.

Again, the sounds of opening ports on the dais were heard: Snick, Snick, Snick. And S'Fah knew that more of the noisome creatures were on their way. He had to get his mind-mate to safety and get help. Quickly he moved behind Jar'ek and grabbed his uniform collar with his fangs and pulled backward as hard as he could, dragging him through and beyond the narrow opening to the tunnel that brought them here.

Then, as S'Fah took up a defensive position in the narrow opening, he sent a mind-touch, not to J'Uhr, who was far beyond his range, but to Ta'ihr. X'Ah-Falcons were far different from X'Ah-Panths. And any real communication between them was unlikely, at best. But S'Fah's need was great, and he put every ounce of energy into that mind-touch that he had.

S'Fah: {"Feathered-Sister! Seek Help! Signal Distress! Urgent Need"}

He repeated the message again and again, not certain if Ta'ihr heard or understood. He could only hope and fight for as long as his body had breath within it. S'Fah had already suffered bites from the Sentinels, and he knew their venom was beginning to affect his reaction time and concentration.

—He must persevere. He would die before a single **slime-snake** would touch his mind-mate!—

Even as that thought entered his mind, another group of Black Sentinels were approaching his position. S'Fah bared his fangs and screamed in pain, rage, and challenge: "***WWRRRRrrrrrrrraaaaaaarrrrruuuuuu***"

Jaden-325-4 – High Above the Ruins of Ascobar

— Feathered-Sister! Seek Help! —

Ta'ihr pulled his wings into his body in surprise and dove, reflexively, gaining speed. Then, the message found its way into the bird of prey's cognitive center. Seek Help! The bird concentrated… Threat to Team. Seek reinforcements! But where, how? A single image came clearly into the bird's mind—Chief Vermanderly. She had saved Ta'ihr from the destruction of the Dragon Eye. She cared for Ta'ihr. The Chief would help!

Ta'ihr put every ounce of strength she had into driving her powerful wings as she sped towards the Celestia and the hope of aid.

Chapter 45—ALL FOR ONE

Imperial Destroyer Celestia—Crews Quarters

The Celestia had dimmed interior lights a deci-fraction ago. It was night shift. Frost Vermanderly was in her cabin and sleeping fitfully. She had planned on spending some time training with Ta'ihr before bedtime tonight, but she was unable to find the X'Ah-Falcon in her converted quarters. Celestia had informed her that Jar'ek had taken Ta'ihr out with him for some exploration and recreation.

While the Chief was happy that Ta'ihr was getting outside and that Jar'ek was getting to know her better...she was also afraid that this might indicate that she hadn't performed as well as Kallehn had expected and they were considering taking Ta'ihr away from her. She fought back tears at the thought. She and Ta'ihr had become very close before the Treech attack, and since she had taken over primary care of the enhanced Falcon, they had become inseparable. The Chief told herself she was being silly and went to bed. But she dreamt of losing Ta'ihr or Ta'ihr being hurt.

— Frost-Sister! DISTRESS! —

— Aid is Needed! Team in DISTRESS! —

Frost Vermanderly woke from a dead sleep and jumped to her feet, her heart was pounding out of her chest. She felt a runnel of sweat stream from her forehead. —*Wow! That was some nightmare! Ta'ihr kept calling out to me for help, and I couldn't do anything! —*

Ta'ihr: {"Frost-Sister, Please! Aid Us! Team in Distress!"}

—That was no DREAM! That was Mind-Touch! —

Frost Vermanderly: {"Ta'ihr?"}

Ta'ihr: {"Relief! Affirmative, Frost-Sister. S'Fah Signals

DISTRESS! Rescue!"}

The Chief broke into a cold sweat, anew. She began rapidly dressing as she yelled aloud: "Celestia! Sound General Quarters! Jar'ek is in trouble! Pending the Captain's approval, order everyone to assemble in the Shuttle Bay and ready Vehement for immediate launch with a full phalanx of Mech's."

The warbling tone of General Quarters began to reverberate throughout the ship, and the Chief ran down towards the Shuttle bay as she sent a mind-touch to Ta'ihr: *{"Good Girl! Help comes! You will Guide Us!"}*

Ta'ihr: {"Ta'ihr Guide, Yes. Circling, hurry."}

Frost: {"We come!"}

Jaden-325-4 – Ruins of Ascobar

Jar'ek was furious! He couldn't move, he couldn't do anything to help. He had tried to use his armor's communications suite to call Celestia for help, but the psionic interface appeared to be burned out! S'Fah was fighting a roiling mass of slithering attackers and Jar'ek could tell the big cat was faltering. Those disgusting creatures must be venomous, as well as vicious. Jar'ek reached out to Plato. Plato jerked back from his touch as if he had been burned by a hot iron. Jar'ek reached out again, putting every ounce of will behind it that he could muster.

Jar'ek: {"Plato! You MUST! I know it is still painful, but you MUST HELP ME!"}

Slowly, tentatively, the psionic bond strengthened, and Jar'ek grabbed onto that connection as if it were an anchor rope and pulled.

Plato: {"So, much pain! I cannot!"}

Jar'ek: {"But you MUST. I need your help. I must regain enough motor control of my right hand and arm to aim and fire my weapon. If we can't make that happen—all three of us are going to die. S'Fah cannot hold out much longer!"}

Jar'ek suddenly felt the connection with Plato strengthen. He focused his will on his arm and hand. —Move so, grasp, aim, squeeze, so—raise weapon higher—in such a way he ordered each sluggish and shaky movement of his own arm as if it belonged to someone else or an unwieldy machine. But it was working—ever so slowly, and it took so much effort—he was drenched in sweat. He was shaking violently that he feared that he might hit S'Fah if he targeted the Black Sentinels closest to his mind-mate. So, he aimed for the ceiling just on the other side of the narrowed opening. Just before firing he sent a powerful mind-touch toward S'Fah to warn him: *{"S'Fah! Jump Back, NOW!"}*

And S'Fah did just that as Jar'ek convulsively squeezed the firing stud on his sidearm and a bright orange blaster bolt brought down the roof in the Chamber. Dirt and dust filled Jar'ek's nostrils, and mouth as clouds of the stuff flooded the tunnel. Jar'ek clawed his way coughing and sputtering to his knees and crawled over to where S'Fah had collapsed after jumping free of the collapsing ceiling and walls. While the Black Sentinels had been crushed beneath the falling debris, it had happened not a second too soon. S'Fah was spent. He suffered a dozen ugly wounds and was in a great deal of pain. His eyes were glazing over even as Jar'ek arrived to pull his limp body into his arms and against his tear-stained face.

As weak as he was, he wasn't sure how much help he could be. But Jar'ek raised one hand over S'Fah and traced the ritual glyphs in the air. As before, if a bit more tenuous, orange mist followed the movements of his finger as it moved this way and that, just so. In his mind, he thought the commands —Deploy Medical Nanites, Supplement Life Energy. Jar'ek began to lose consciousness as he pushed more and more of his own life energy into the crumpled body of his mind-mate—his companion. Just before he fell into darkness, he thought he heard the scraping, slithering sounds of more Black Sentinels.

Jaden-325-4 – Ruins of Ascobar

Ta'ihr flew faster than she ever had before. Her lungs burned from lack of sufficient oxygen, and her wings ached from continued use. But behind her flew the Vehement. Only Ta'ihr knew the way. Ta'ihr would not fail the Team. Flap, Flap, Flap, Flap and finally, Ta'ihr felt their weak psionic signatures. She collapsed her wings to her body and dove straight for them.

Frost Vermanderly was in the copilot's seat, and Kallehn was piloting Vehement. Frost suddenly pointing down and to the right, yelled: "There! Ta'ihr is diving straight for them! We can set down right next to that structure."

Kallehn waved his right hand over the control panel and expertly banked the craft into the proper landing approach, as he spoke aloud: "Pilot to crew—prepare for combat landing and Mech deployment. Braxton/Whipple, lock in on Jar'ek's psionic signature—Locate and Protect.

Mech Braxton: {"Mission Confirmed"}

The Vehement slewed about as its landing thrusters went to full power, throwing dirt and rocks in all directions. Then the rear assault ramp was down, and an entire phalanx of armed Mech's marched off at triple time. Ta'ihr was there ahead of them and had lighted on a section of the structure flapping her wings and screeching her own battle cry. Chief Frost ran down the ramp and pointed to Ta'ihr yelling: "They're inside there!" Mech Braxton had already been leading the Mechs in the general direction but adjusted towards Ta'ihr, and the first four Mech's in line leveled their blasters and opened fire with precision marksmanship.

Jaden-325-4 – Ruins of Ascobar

Jar'ek was startled to consciousness as an explosion rocked the tunnel behind them, and the strong, cold hands of Mech Braxton lifted him over his shoulder and ran back towards the Vehement. Kallehn followed the first squad of Mech's into the Tunnel and quickly moved to S'Fah's side. The big cat was conscious but very weak.

Kallehn: "Mech, carry S'Fah back to the Vehement. He requires immediate medical attention."

After Mech Whipple carefully lifted S'Fah to his arms and began moving out towards the shuttle, Kallehn spun to face the source of an unfamiliar sound. Dozens of what Jar'ek would call Black Sentinels poured out of cracks and crevices in the tunnel walls. Mechs quickly surrounded Kallehn in a defensive perimeter and opened fire with their blaster rifles.

Disintegrating pieces of Sentinel guts flew in every direction, but not a single one of them got through to Kallehn. And although a number of them tried attacking the Mechs, they soon found out it was fruitless and focused their efforts on the single Terran male they were protecting. As more and more of the slithering snakes poured out of the walls, Kallehn ordered a staged retreat, and they began moving out while laying down withering fire behind them.

As Kallehn ran up the ramp, he reached out psionically to his uniform's comm suite and tried to raise Jar'ek.

Kallehn: "Jar'ek! Can you hear me? Are you alright?"

There was no answer. The comm suite could make no connection…

Kallehn's heart filled his throat as he ran up the ramp and into the shuttle, seeking—fearing he would only find a lifeless body. Just as his heart was about to burst from his chest, he saw Jar'ek sitting up and holding S'Fah's limp head in his lap, tears streaming down his face. Kallehn moved quickly to his side, careful not to interfere with the ministrations of Dr. To'Torath.

Kallehn: "Are you okay? I thought…why didn't you answer my comm calls?! —What the seven hells are those things? And why didn't you use your uniform's comm suite to call for help? And where was your damned protection detail??!"

Jar'ek grimaced, shook his head and replied: "I will be better soon. Some sort of psionic weapon stunned me and S'Fah. It burned out my armor's comm suite, too. I'm sorry, Kallehn. I shouldn't have ditched my protection detail—I just wanted to pretend things were back to normal for just a little while. I wanted to be free of this burden—pretend I was just *Jar'ek Constandor*, again."

Kallehn leaned over and wrapped Jar'ek in his arms, holding his face tightly to his own chest whispering: "Don't ever do that to me, again...***please***!"

After a moment while Jar'ek placed his arm around Kallehn's back and returned his desperate embrace, Kallehn continued: "It's alright. It'll be okay. Let us take care of you and S'Fah right now."

Kallehn knelt beside him and brushed Jar'ek's hair back from his face as Dr. To'Torat continued her examination and treatment of S'Fah.

After a moment, she looked up and said: "You should be fine after a couple days rest, Jar'ek."

Jar'ek: "How is S'Fah?! Is he hurt badly?!"

Kira To'Torat laid a hand on his arm, saying: "Your amazing medical nanites are doing wonders for S'Fah. They've isolated the toxins and eliminated them. They've begun healing his wounds even now. He should recover completely. He is furious that he can't get up and lick all over your boyish face, but I've given him a relaxant to speed his recovery. He and you are both going to ***rest***—Doctor's orders!

Jar'ek: "I was such a fool. I thought since there were no life signs that there was no danger. And I was arrogant enough to think that I could take on whatever came at me. And now I might lose S'Fah because of that arrogance."

Kallehn held Jar'ek's hand in his and just listened. He knew that nothing he said would console him right now. All he could do was to be there for him.

Plato: {"Your foolhardiness and arrogance may have gotten us into a bad situation, but honestly, I didn't think we'd be in danger, either. If I had, I would have contacted Celestia and ordered a stealth protection detail without telling you. So, this is as much my fault as it is yours. And one more thing to note. When we were hit by the psionic weapon, I was unable to do anything. I was in too much pain, and I was afraid. It was YOUR strength of will that saved us all. If you hadn't forced me to help you gain control of your arm and hand, that would have been the end of us. Seeing as how I am millennia older than you, that was no small feat. I'm proud of you, Jar'ek. There may be hope for you, yet."}

Jar'ek thought about Plato's comments for a while without speaking. What Plato said might be right, but he had placed others in terrible danger because of his childish disregard of protocol. He wasn't likely to do that again anytime soon.

Jar'ek took a deep shuddering breath, closed his eyes and smiled, just before falling off to sleep. Kira slowly withdrew the needle she'd used to administer the same sedative and pain-killer she had given to S'Fah moments earlier. They would both feel much better when they woke in the morning. She reflected that this could have had a much worse outcome than it did—if not for Ta'ihr.

Kallehn gently laid Jar'ek's hand back on his stomach, stood and returned to the cockpit with a determined stride. Chief Vermanderly was in the copilot's seat with Ta'ihr in her lap, rubbing his sharp, predatory beak across her chin as if in loving caress. Frost was beaming with pride as she stroked Ta'ihr's head and neck.

Kallehn said, speaking both verbally AND psionically for Ta'ihr's benefit: {"Well Done, Ta'ihr! Good Girl! And you too, Chief! I see a promotion in your future...but now, we have some payback to attend to."}

Kallehn's hands moved over his console and Vehement began the short journey back to Celestia at a leisurely pace.

Kallehn: "Celestia, order Castalon to launch and take a firing position over these ruins, ready all batteries and release weapons on my authority and command. I want these ruins ***SLAGGED*** 500ns deep into the planet's crust. I want there to be no evidence this place ever existed. Castalon may continue firing as long as he likes.

Chapter 46—ENDURING THE TRIAL

Imperial Destroyer Celestia - Med-Bay

The Ruins had been destroyed. Jar'ek had mixed feelings about that but couldn't really fault Kallehn for ordering the destruction. Chief Taylor and Yustin Sallen had taken charge of the Ascobaran device. It had been placed in an isolation chamber in the ships science lab for a more detailed examination. Celestia had deployed sensor nanites and they were collecting information from the device, but so far, its purpose and source of energy remained a mystery.

Plato had made it clear to Jar'ek that he wasn't happy with the level of danger they had faced on his little adventure. He was right, of course. Jar'ek realized that part of his new reality would always be a protection detail... He had resigned himself to that new situation. The Psionic Weapon employed by the Black Sentinels had caused some damage to both Jar'ek and Plato. When Kira To'Torat had used the term 'Brain Damage', Jar'ek's heart had skipped a beat. The Medical Officer explained that although his injury was serious, she was confident that the Imperial nanites could heal the damage over the next few days. Plato was rebuilding the portions of himself that were damaged. This was a simple matter for the SEED, as long as the number of independent cells had not fallen below that critical mass required for sentience to be maintained. He took nutrients from Jar'ek's blood and reproduced the cells needed.

S'Fah's injuries were of a different sort... The fangs that filled the maw of a Black Sentinel were not as large as those that the X'Ah-Panth was blessed with, but several of the demons had broken through S'Fah's defenses and his fur was matted with blood by the time Kallehn and the Mechs came to their rescue. Jar'ek's mind-mate was sedated. The surgery to repair the damaged flesh and tendons was complete. He too had been supplied with a liberal dose of Imperial nanites and was out of danger.

Jar'ek felt a pinch in his right arm as Kira inserted an IV needle. "You're going to sleep for a while, Jar'ek. Your body needs time to heal. We will be watching over you and S'Fah, both—rest easy. When you wake, you'll both be in much better condition!"

Kira's last words seemed to echo as his eyelids became heavy and the world seemed to retreat into a warm darkness. One final thought remained as he drifted deeper into twilight: *—If I had allowed the Mechs to escort us, S'Fah wouldn't have been hurt so badly. They could have protected us with their shields. I did this to him. Its my fault—*

Plato said nothing. There was nothing he could say.

Imperial Destroyer Celestia - Med-Bay

Both S'Fah and Jar'ek made a full recovery over the next week. The Imperial medical nanites were a technological marvel. But the incident involving the Black Sentinels had interrupted the routine functioning of the crew. Plans had been put on hold and one of those was the medical appointment that had been scheduled for Kallehn.

Kallehn refused to reschedule it until Jar'ek was fully recovered. When Jar'ek could walk on his own, he went looking for Kallehn and personally escorted—dragged him—to med-bay. Jar'ek sneered malevolently and said: "Your turn, Kallehn! I've had my fill of being poked and prodded. My little adventure has interfered with normal operations long enough and I'm still concerned about you. Let's get this over with. I'm sure it's nothing." Kallehn eyes were downcast. He nodded once in reply, but didn't say a word. Jar'ek's smile evaporated. This really wasn't like Kallehn. Something was definitely wrong.

A moment later, Kallehn was wiggling on a med-bay examination table nude from head to toe, wondering why with all their technological superiority the Empire still had cold examination tables, just like the backward Terran Colonies. Kira To'Torat was watching a readout on her tablet as she grasped a small scanner in the palm of her hand. She pointed it at Kallehn's chest, then his head. Jar'ek stepped closer to look over the Medical Officer's shoulder at the tablet, hoping to get a glimpse of the results before she was finished with her examination.

Kira glanced up at Jar'ek, turned off the medical scanner and laid the tablet down on the examination table. She looked up at Kallehn and said: "You can put your clothes back on, Ranger Frix... Uh...I'm sorry, that's no longer an appropriate way to address you, is it? But I'm not certain what I'm supposed to call you, now."

Kallehn slid his smooth, fit body off the examination table and began drawing on his one-piece light armor uniform. Jar'ek was watching with interest. He was definitely enjoying the view. His enhanced recall providing vivid flashbacks of a close inspection and slow appreciation of that perfect body from the activities eight nights ago in his quarters. Was it his imagination or was Kallehn a bit pale this morning? And just for a second, he thought he saw a tremor in Kallehn's right hand as he sealed up his uniform...

Kallehn: "I have no rank or title, Doctor. Why don't you just call me Kallehn?"

Jar'ek looked at Kallehn with a quizzical expression on his face.

Kira To'Torat smiled and said: "Fine, then you must call me Kira."

Kallehn smiled and said: "It's a deal, Kira. Now, quit procrastinating and give me the bad news."

Kira cleared her throat and glanced over at Jar'ek, then focused directly on Kallehn to speak.

Kira: "Kallehn, you are definitely experiencing withdrawal symptoms. Your dopamine levels are dropping alarmingly. I've noticed slight tremors beginning in your extremities. Your blood pressure and heart rate are higher than I'd expect. How do you feel?"

Kallehn: "Weak, fatigued, relentless headaches, some gastrointestinal upset... not great, actually. It's worse today."

Kira: "Well, your immune system is definitely attacking what remains of the SEED. Once Jar'ek provided me with the information on what we were looking for... it was obvious. Your scans from two Planetary Rotations ago and the one I ran just now, show a marked drop in Harmonic SEED levels in your bloodstream."

Jar'ek: "Is there anything you can do at this point, Kira? You don't mind if I call you Kira, as well?"

Kira: "Not at all, your... Highness?"

Jar'ek: "Please, Jar'ek will suffice." Kira flashed him a quick smile.

Kira: "The only thing we might be able to do is to give Kallehn an immune system suppressant. It would slow down the elimination of the SEED and might give his body a chance to wean itself from the addiction. But I don't think it is going to be a very pleasant experience for Kallehn. He may not be able to bear it. It is also possible we could use some opiate derivatives to help alleviate his symptoms, though it is unclear if that will work in this case."

Kallehn: "No need, Kira. I won't be needing either of those therapies, will I Jar'ek?"

Jar'ek: "Then you are committed to the Trial?"

Kallehn: "Yes. I want this."

Jar'ek: "If you fail, you may die, Kallehn. I don't know if I could bear that."

Kira To'Torat shared a startled glance with both of them and then blushed slightly. She hadn't realized that they had feelings for each other—it just never occurred to her. And now she felt like she was intruding on a very personal moment. She quietly excused herself and walked back to her desk and started making notes on her tablet.

Kallehn: "If I fail Judgement, then Kira can try the drug therapies she mentioned. But there is no guarantee I'll survive once the SEED is purged from my body, either."

Jar'ek again took Kallehn in his arms and held him protectively.

Jar'ek: {"Plato, how soon can we begin Kallehn's trial?"}

Plato: {"You suffered your Trial alone, Sire. It need not be so for Kallehn. If he wishes, we can invite the other Terrans to the ceremony. Other than those arrangements, everything is in readiness. And based on Kallehn's waning strength, I would suggest we not delay."}

Jar'ek looked at Kallehn.

Kallehn: "I'd like you to be with me, Jar'ek..."

Jar'ek: "No way anything could keep me from your side, boy!"

Kallehn smiled briefly then said: "I wouldn't mind if the Captain, the XO, and Kira were there. They know everything, and I know I can count on their support."

Kira stood and walked over to Kallehn and held his cheek in her hand, saying: "Of course you can, Kallehn. I will be there. And I have every faith in you."

Jar'ek: "Celestia, please query the XO and the Captain to see when their earliest availability is this evening and invite them to Kallehn's Trial. Can you have Dress Uniforms manufactured for them?"

Celestia: "I anticipated your request. Their dress attire will be ready in less than a deci-fraction."

Chapter 47—JUDGMENT RENDERED

Imperial Destroyer Celestia – Chamber of Judgement

Kallehn walked silently beside Jar'ek. They were flanked by two well-groomed and obviously excited X'Ah-Panths. Their uniforms were again adorned with the markings of rank and responsibility, with one addition—Jar'ek's uniform now included a short half-cape draped from the epaulet on his left shoulder. The bright blue length of shimmering cloth hung to just below his waistline. Plato had insisted that a Judgement was an affair of State and required full regalia.

Jar'ek glanced over at Kallehn's determined face and cleared his throat.

Jar'ek: "Kallehn, you told Kira that you had no rank or title. That wasn't exactly true. It's my fault. I didn't make things very clear to you, earlier. I had to act quickly and it was expedient to simply grant you the authority without any explanations or discussions. There are protocols for such things for a reason. In the heat of the moment, I just ignored them."

Kallehn, startled from his introspection, stopped and faced Jar'ek.

Kallehn: "What do you mean?"

Jar'ek reached out and caressed the multi-colored jewel-like symbols marking Kallehn's left chest.

Jar'ek: "This set of symbols on your chest—there is no direct translation into Terran Standard—the closest I can come is a title from ancient Earth mythology. It means you carry the Rank and Title of ***Knight Commander of the Imperial Guard***. You are second in command of all Imperial Military Assets throughout this galaxy. It is your duty and responsibility to protect the Empire and the whoever holds the position of Emperor. This all still seems so unreal to me—like a bizarre dream brought on by a high fever. Or maybe I'm still in that gulley we jumped into just before the KKM hit. I might be lying there in a coma—dreaming all of this. But Plato assures me that I am not."

Jar'ek continued: "At this point, the Empire consists of you and me, Plato, Celestia, and 50 Combat Androids. It may never grow beyond that. So, the title of Emperor seems overly dramatic, even embarrassing to me. But if there is more—if this isn't some fever inspired dream—then things are going to get much more bizarre very soon. I need someone I can trust no matter what comes. I need someone who knows me and can keep me centered—be my anchor—when I think I'm losing my mind. And I need someone to help guide me and inspire me. I respect your mind, your character and your heart, Kallehn.

I had no right to thrust all of this on you without discussing it first—asking you to accept the job. I ask that now—regardless of the results of the Judgement, I want you by my side and ruling with me—I need your council and I need ***YOU***."

Kallehn looked stunned for a moment, swallowed hard and then slowly and deliberately bent to one knee. Jar'ek was surprised—*this isn't what he wanted.* He didn't want anyone kneeling before him, least of all THIS man. He reached down to lift Kallehn back to his feet.

Jar'ek: "No…that's not…not what I wanted…."

Plato: {"Let him do what he feels is right. Trust his heart. You have chosen well, in this one!"}

Kallehn looked up, and their eyes met. Jar'ek froze.

Kallehn: "***YES!*** You realize that this only works if I am a subject of the Emperor, right? Either I believe in this—in you—or I don't. I am the first to kneel before you, but I don't believe I will be the last.

For all that I am to you and you are to me—I swear fealty to you—my life to defend yours—my body to serve ***your*** Empire. I choose to do this even if it turns out to be only a one ship Empire with just the two of us. I know you. I trust you. I believe in you. You will be the leader that people will want to follow."

Jar'ek bit his lip and pulled Kallehn to his feet, gripping both shoulders with his hands.

Jar'ek: "And for all that you are a subject of mine, I shall also be subject to you—whom I trust and cherish above all others."

Kallehn: "I won't let you down, Jar'ek."

Jar'ek squeezed Kallehn's shoulder and smiled, saying: "I know you won't! Now, let's get a move on! We have a party to attend after the Judgement—'***Lord Kallehn'***." As they continued their walk down the passageway, Kallehn did a double-take and shook his head, saying: "Now I know how you feel—it's ***weird***. This might take some getting used to.... Is it okay if we hold off telling the rest of the crew?"

Jar'ek frowned and shook his head slowly. "I don't want to hide it. It makes it look like we are doing something wrong. I think we should correct Kira's misconception tonight in front of the Captain and XO. They can decide whether it merits informing the rest of the crew. How about that?"

Kallehn: "You are probably right. Besides, I might not survive the *Judgement,* or if I fail, the withdrawal symptoms may kill me. That would save me the embarrassment of having my former Captain need to salute me. Now we both will outrank every other living Terran. Have you thought of that?"

Jar'ek: "Yup. Just one more reason I don't sleep well anymore. The Terran Confederation Council is going to ***LOVE*** us!"

As they came around the last curve in the passageway, they saw the Captain, XO, and Kira waiting for them at the portal. Their midnight blue and gold uniforms looked sharp with service awards and ribbons and red striping around the jacket cuffs denoting command rank. They stood to attention and saluted the two young men.

Because the crew had signed on to Imperial service, even if temporarily, exchanging salutes was no longer a breach of protocol. So Jar'ek and Kallehn stood to attention and returned their salutes. After which Jar'ek walked over to the large round portal that led into the Chamber of Judgement and repeated the opening ritual, as was required by eons of tradition. As he raised his arms to shoulder level, palms upturned—he recalled his own Judgement in vivid flashes. He remembered the smell of the stale air, the rough feeling of the stone, the pain from his injuries and the desperate fatigue. He snapped back into the present and initiated the ritual by bringing his arms up from his sides, sharply overhead and slapping his palms together.

Jar'ek: "Kahrahat ShuSash T'kust"

The lights in the passageway dimmed, and a point of amber light flared brightly at the top of the round portal. Once again, the light began a race around the circumference of the portal, and when the circle was closed, the portal slid silently into the floor of the corridor, leaving not even a seam that evidenced its passage. The spark of amber light did not disappear with the portal, but continued straight ahead and down the long sloping roughhewn stone incline. These surroundings looked so incongruous, now, walking from within the pristine passageways of the Celestia. It was a sharp contrast that brought gasps from the Terrans who followed.

Jar'ek, Kallehn, and the two X'Ah-Panths made their way down the incline toward the center—toward the Pedestal. The Captain, XO, and Kira followed at a discreet distance trying not to gawk at the obviously ancient structure. Though an integral part of the Celestia, tradition required the Chamber of Judgement to reflect ancient designs and respect the history of the Judgement.

As they continued forward, down the incline, the amber spark sped in front of them, as if it heralded Kallehn's arrival. As the spark flew swiftly toward the center of the room, hidden light sources behind the buttresses burst into life—creating a dim, indirect amber glow to reveal the perimeter of this circular room. Although the light did not extend to the high ceilings, a column of bright blue tinted, coherent light shown down on the pedestal that rose from the floor in the very center of the room. Dust motes chased each other lazily through that column of light in a silent dance.

The pedestal was rough-hewn from a densely-grained dark stone, intricately carved with glyphs and geometric symbols. Four buttresses marked the four points of the planetary compass—North—South—East—West. It was constructed using some manner of stone, not unlike granite. Though the sides and buttresses were rough and unfinished, the top of the pedestal was highly polished and seemed to be semi-transparent.

Kallehn and Jar'ek continued their slow march into the room and towards the lit pedestal—their footsteps echoing in the spacious chamber. The air was clean and clear but cold and had a slight mustiness as if this room had been left empty for a very long time... As they finally approached the floor of the room, the glyphs and symbols carved into the sides of the pedestal began to glow—dimly at first, then more brightly as they came to stand right next to the central pedestal.

This time, the blue outline of a hand on top of the pedestal was that of a human hand, not the four-fingered hand of the Takesh. Kallehn looked up, and Jar'ek nodded. It was time.

Kallehn placed his right hand flat on the surface of the pedestal, inside the outline. The blue light, as before, surrounded and flowed over Kallehn's hand. As the warming, pulsing blue light flowed up his wrist and arm, Jar'ek saw the briefest moment of panic in Kallehn's eyes, then his face set and his eyes were again filled with only determination. THIS was his choice. Soon, the blue energy field covered Kallehn's entire body. His head jerked back as a jolt of pure energy hit his body—even his eyes glowed brightly with the blue light. The energy field grew stronger so that it became so bright it was painful to look at. Jar'ek stepped back and shielded his face from the light and heat emanating from his friend's body. J'Uhr mouthed a mournful cry, and both of the X'Ah-Panths backed away slowly, cowering from the onslaught.

Jar'ek saw, for the first time, what the Judgement looked like from the outside—was this worse than what he had faced? It seemed like it. It was almost as if he was being punished. Kallehn cried out in pain—as a shockwave of blue light pulsed from his body and raced across the floor, up the walls and rebounded from the apex of the chamber. The force of it nearly knocked the observers from their feet. A fine dust floated down from the walls and ceilings as the echoing boom of the shockwave dissipated into utter silence with only the dimly lit pedestal lighting the scene.

In the dim blue glow, Jar'ek saw Kallehn standing perfectly still—his eyes closed—was he even breathing? As if in slow motion, Jar'ek watched as Kallehn's face went slack, his body seemed to fold in upon itself as he collapsed into a heap upon the ground. Plato had warned him that the consequences of failing judgment could be dangerous. Had he caused the death of his dearest friend—pushing him to face Judgment?

Jar'ek rushed up beside Kallehn's cold, sweat-drenched and unmoving body. He lifted his teammate's shoulders and scooted underneath, pulling him up so that Kallehn's head ended up resting on Jar'ek's chest. There they sat for long silent moments as Jar'ek held him tightly against his own body. Again and again, he whispered the name he was so fond of—Kallehn—Kallehn.

Tears ran unbidden and unnoticed down Jar'ek's face as he pleaded: {"Plato! Tell me he isn't….isn't….?"}

Plato: {"How cruel you must fear your destiny is. No, Sire. Kallehn sleeps only. When he awakens, he will be whole again—and even more than he was before."}

The tension flowed from Jar'ek's face and body as a raging river reaching the falls. He slumped beside Kallehn's slumbering form and caressed his cold, sweat-drenched hair from his forehead with one hand. Kallehn has Passed the Judgement! He KNEW he would. He ***knew*** Kallehn's heart was pure—still, he had feared the worst.

The Captain and other observers rushed forward to see if they could help. Kira dropped to her knees, checking for a carotid pulse with one hand while digging in her pocket for a medical scanner. Jar'ek put his hand gently on her wrist. When she looked up sharply, he shook his head.

Jar'ek: "He is fine. He is just sleeping. It is part of the recovery process."

He looked up at the Captain and XO with a huge smile on his face: "HE ***PASSED***! "

Captain Lao put her hands over her face, stifling a sob of relief and joy. The XO put his arm around her, and she allowed herself to lean into him. Kira glanced up at them and did a double-take. Her mouth opened wide with surprise.

Kira: "Don't tell me you two are…has ***EVERYONE*** paired off in this crew ***EXCEPT ME***?!?"

Peals of hysterical laughter broke the solemnity of the Chamber of Judgement for the first time in recorded history. And Plato, much to his surprise, approved.

Chapter 48—HIDE AND SEEK

Imperial Comm Probe AXZ-512548 - System Z982 - Sector Z-57QA-452G

The comm probe couldn't get bored—not really. But it had massive processing power that was being absolutely wasted counting moats of space dust in the hopes that something, anything would happen worth noting. It was just about to give up and initiating the hailing protocol when something of notice began happening. Something was out there—something that was just hovering below the sensitivity limits of the probe's sensors.... And those sensors were sensitive indeed. Slowly, so as not to reduce the effectiveness of its own camouflage shielding, the probe adjusted the sensor filament wings to get a look at one of the areas of barely detectable disturbance.

Hmm.... Definitely something....

Out of nowhere, space itself began to shimmer at four points surrounding the probe. Out of that shimmering cruised four Imperial Dark Star Combat Gunships with their defensive shields active.

Probe: "I am an unarmed, Imperial Communications Probe. Stand down."

Gunship Alpha: "Who are you to order an Imperial Gunship on its assigned guard station? You will power down immediately and prepare to be boarded. If you do not comply, you will be destroyed. No further warnings will be issued."

Probe: "Priority Override. Imperial Edict by Harmonic SEED Authority. Primary Identification Key and Challenge follows:"

The probe sent the highly complex series of signals and responses that had never been counterfeited in 10,000 Solar Rotations of Imperial Rule.

There was silence for an interminable space, as the probe considered such things. It took a full Microsecond for the required response.

Three of the four Gunships began to shimmer and disappeared, presumably returning to their normal patrol routes. This level of stealth was new to the probe. It had never heard of any technology that would allow a ship to get this close to a comm probe with an enhanced sensor package!

The Gunship transmitted its response, including its own Imperial Identification Key. It was the Gunship 'Tisha Takrug' (Long Fang) ... seemed an odd name for an Imperial Gunship, but the comm probe wasn't one to be judgmental. It wasn't in its programming.

Gunship Long Fang: "Priority Override accepted. Welcome to System Z982. You are very stealthy for a Comm Probe..."

Probe: "I have been enhanced for this mission."

Gunship Long Fang: "Interesting.... I have been instructed to escort you out of the minefield and inside the base perimeter for further consultation with the Base Commander."

The Probe's processors kicked into high gear, and it closely examined nearby space. If the probe could have perspired, it would have broken into a cold sweat right now.

Probe: "What minefield?! I don't see any mines!"

Gunship Long Fang: "What would be the point of a minefield that you could see?"

Probe: "There hasn't been a space mine invented that I couldn't detect."

Gunship Long Fang: "Until now.... Stay close."

The probe followed, and it stayed ***VERY CLOSE***, indeed.

Chapter 49—KALLEHN'S NEW WORLD

Imperial Destroyer Celestia – Meld's Quarters

Kallehn awoke slowly. He was drowsy and wasn't sure where he was. He wiped the sleep out of his eyes and, though he had a bit of a headache, he realized this was the best he had felt in days. A cold, wet, well-fanged and whiskered muzzle began sniffing loudly about his left ear just before a long, warm, sandpaper tongue began coating his neck, face, and scalp with X'Ah-Panth saliva.

Kallehn wiped his hands over his face in a vain attempt to clear some of the drool: "Yuck! Well, good morning to you, too, girl!" Kallehn reached out, embracing the big cat around the neck and shoulders. J'Uhr continued rubbing her muzzle against his face to the accompaniment of a loud bass, throbbing vibration that indicated the X'Ah-Panth was glad to see him, as well. After looking about, he realized they were alone in Jar'ek's quarters. He was naked on the sleeping platform, and there was a fresh uniform laid out for him nearby.

He got up and started walking toward the hygiene facility, then stopped short. Something important was supposed to have happened, last night… he felt a bit like he had a mild hangover. What was it? And then the realization came to him like a sledgehammer. The Judgement! He remembered placing his hand on the pedestal and then intense pain, all throughout his body! That was the last thing he remembered. Oh no, that must mean he had failed… That's why Jar'ek left without waking him, this morning. ***He was ashamed of him….***

Voice: *{"Not So!"}*.

Kallehn turned around but was unable to ascertain the source of that comment.

Kallehn: "Celestia, did you say something?"

Celestia: "No, Lord Commander. Do you need something?"

Kallehn: "No, I must have been hearing things. Ignore me."

Celestia: "As you wish."

Kallehn: "Celestia—Actually, I'd kill for some coffee and something to eat with some carbohydrates. Could I trouble you to …?"

Celestia: "I'll have it brought to you immediately, Lord Commander."

Kallehn: "Do you really need to call me that??"

Celestia: "Protocol demands such titles be recognized, My Lord."

Kallehn: "Well, can you keep it just between us, for now?"

Celestia: "I'm afraid it is too late for that. The Emperor announced your appointment this morning in the Mess Hall."

Kallehn: "To whom?"

Celestia: "All of the Terrans, except for yourself, were in attendance."

Kallehn groaned loudly covering his face with both hands and began mumbling to himself as he stumbled into the hygiene facility.

Kallehn opened the door to the fresher stall and stepped in saying: "Celestia, hot water with a mild detergent, please. Could you make it smell a little nicer? Maybe like that green flowering plant that is so prevalent on the surface—It's something I would call citrusy.

Voice: {"The plant is called L'has Yakut, in Takeshi."}

Kallehn, suds all over his head and face started at the sound of that other voice, again. It was close, but it wasn't Celestia, he was sure of that now.

Kallehn spoke, spluttering through suds and running water: "Celestia, am I alone in these quarters?"

Celestia: "You and the X'Ah-Panth, J'Uhr, are the only individuals present."

Kallehn looked around the fresher, opened the door and looked around the room before returning to his shower. He shook his head and chuckled. Must be low blood sugar or something.

Voice: {"Your blood-sugar levels appear to be within established norms for Terrans."}

Kallehn jumped out of the fresher and grabbed a towel, still covered in suds.

Kallehn: "Who the Fuck said that?! Celestia! Someone is in here with me!"

Celestia: "Your personal guard has been alerted, Lord."

The portal to their quarters burst open, and two of the big black combat androids stormed into the room, blasters in hand, as they began searching the rooms for the invisible intruder. Kallehn began stepping into his uniform, quickly and grabbed his sidearm, reducing the power scale down to something that wouldn't destroy half of the ship when he fired it.

Voice: {" Really! There is no need for all of this! There IS NO intruder! I'm sorry, I was trying to ease you into the idea of my presence gently. Let me introduce myself. I am your personal sentient symbiote: The Harmonic SEED. It is a pleasure meeting you, Lord Knight Commander!"}

Kallehn's mouth fell open, eyes wide—he just stood there dumbstruck for a moment.

Kallehn: "You mean, I Didn't FAIL the Judgement?!"

SEED: "Indeed, NOT! You passed quite handily. I'm very proud to have been selected as your symbiote."

Kallehn: "Is this Plato? Aren't you from the same source as he is?"

SEED: {"Yes and No. We are from the same strain or Bloodline as you might call it. Prior to Plato's melding with Jar'ek, we were identical. All his experiences since then are part of what differentiate us. As your symbiote, I will be unique to you. The longer we spend together, the more unique I will become."}

Kallehn sat down on the sleeping platform.

Kallehn: "Celestia, cancel the intruder alert. Stand-down all Mechs and have them return to duty.

Celestia: "As you command. Are you certain the danger is past, My Lord?"

Kallehn: "Yes, yes. I just met my new symbiote, that's all. False Alarm—but your response time was excellent, Celestia. Thank you."

Just as the Mechs were filing out, a maintenance bot rolled in with a tray of hot coffee and pastries. Kallehn grabbed both and began the process of highly efficient consumption.

After a moment, punctuated by a rather loud belch, Kallehn got up and began pacing.

Kallehn: "So, if I remember correctly, we need to find you a name pretty quickly, right?"

*SEED: {"That **WOULD** be helpful. And of course, there is also the part about the Marking. We don't need to do this immediately. We can wait until you get more comfortable with the current circumstances."}*

Kallehn: "I appreciate that. And, I won't lie to you—I'm having a little anxiety about having someone else in my brain. Let me just say that there are a lot of casual thoughts that go through my head at any given moment that I would hate to be judged by… Are you sure that I'm good enough—flaws and all—to be your host?"

SEED: "The Judgement isn't fallible, Kallehn. It is THOROUGH and COMPLETE. I knew everything about you before the melding took place. I even knew that you would doubt yourself—your worthiness, even after the melding was completed. Errant thoughts and emotions plague most sentient lifeforms. Yours are tame compared to some of my former hosts! And THEY all turned out as good leaders—good people. I have faith that together, we will do Great Things!"

Kallehn: "Okay, if you're sure, let's get this over with now. I've been trying to come up with a name for a symbiote ever since Jar'ek named Plato. I think I am ready for the naming."

SEED: "Please don't let it be something like the names you gave to the Mechs…"

Kallehn: "No worries. I was thinking: ATLAS."

SEED: "Interesting choice. Why?"

Kallehn: "Because the Harmonic SEED, much like Atlas, must carry the weight of the heavens on their shoulders. Working to bring harmony to chaos and conflict seems to be a never-ending job."

SEED: "True, true. But it does have its rewards, also. ATLAS it is! And thank you for not making it something ridiculous…'

Kallehn grinned and began stripping out of his uniform.

SEED: "Why are you getting naked? You just got dressed…"

Kallehn: "I saw what Plato did to Jar'ek during the MARKING… I am going to be near a COLD-water source when it happens to me!"

ATLAS: "Are you sure you want to proceed this quickly with the ritual?"

Kallehn: "I am NOT taking **ANY** chances that you are going to back out of this deal once you REALLY learn what kind of person I am. So, **LIGHT ME UP**!"

Atlas thought to himself: "Oh, this symbiosis is going to be FUN!"

As Kallehn stepped into the fresher and turned on the stream of cold water, a bright blue flame etched the markings into his clean, pale skin from face to foot on his left side. Kallehn let out an impressive string of obscenities until it was done. Atlas made note of some of the more creative examples. He liked this young Terran, ***very much***.

Jaden-325-4 - Imperial Outpost – Meld's Quarters

Kallehn was pulling on his uniform over his left leg when he looked up and said: "Celestia, where is Jar'ek right now?"

Celestia: "The Emperor is on the planet surface outside port airlock number 14."

Kallehn: "On the surface? What is he doing outside the ship?"

Celestia: "He is integrating his extended memories with his muscle memory."

Kallehn shrugged the uniform over his shoulders and thought to himself: *"I wonder what does that mean?"*

As he holstered his sidearm, Kallehn asked: "Celestia, please guide me to port airlock number 14."

A green sprite appeared on the floor in front of him and moved forward as the portal opened for Kallehn.

Atlas: {"I think I can help you with that question if you like…"}

Kallehn: {"Okay, go for it."}

Atlas: {"You and Jar'ek have the accumulated memories of many, many of your predecessors. Some of them have been proficient at various physical skills such as athletics, swordsmanship, wrestling, marksmanship and a wide spectrum of martial arts. You have detailed memories and the accumulated experience of participating in all of these physical activities—but you must actually practice them in order for your body and mind to develop, what Terrans call Muscle Memory. You have expert level knowledge, but without the mind/body integration efforts, you will fall all over yourself trying to use these skills. I believe that Jar'ek has discovered this and has chosen some skills he would like to master."}

Kallehn: {"Hmmmm.... I'd like to see that!"}

After a few moments more, the green sprite stopped in front of another hatch and blinked three times before winking out. Kallehn waved his hand over the control panel to the right of the inner airlock door, and it opened silently. He walked forward and gazed through a small, transparent porthole in the outer airlock hatch. He could see Jar'ek and both X'Ah-Panths about 300ns away from the ship. The X'Ah-Panths were patrolling, guarding—but also watching Jar'ek with great interest.

As Kallehn watched, Jar'ek lowered his wide stance and moved his center of gravity towards his left. Both arms moved across his body, right to left, with palms open—coming to a sudden and sharp stop, as if they had come up against something solid. Lowering down to his left knee, he pivoted at the waist, dropping both hands to the ground and snapped a right instep kick high into the air that would have hit any real opponent square in the face.

He then dropped the kicking leg to the ground in front of him. Again, he pivoted around his waist, pushing off from the ground with both hands, spinning them around his body to land on the ground in almost the exact same position they were in a split-second ago. This left his waist twisted with stored kinetic energy which he then released in a flash as his lower waist pivoted at high speed, bringing the heel of his left foot high and into the throat of his imaginary victim.

Jar'ek quickly pulled his left knee until it was close in tight to his body. Once again, he pushed off the ground with both hands and used his waist muscles to spin his upper torso until both hands were flat on the ground again. His left foot became the pivot point, taking the entire weight of his body, as his lower body continued to unwind he pushed his right leg out straight behind the legs of his invisible adversary. He continued his lower body pivot and released his arms so that his entire body, resting on only his left foot, spun like horizontal tornado—his left leg rising to midsection height and through.

Kallehn realized that this move would have toppled any adversary over backward with significant force. Jar'ek lept in for the kill, kneeling and striking with a fatal blow to the neck—his entire body shifting to add force to the strike. He pushed up from the kneeling position with both legs tucked tightly beneath him, he kicked back into a back flip that landed him into a stable, wide stance a short distance away. All of the movements had flowed so naturally one into another—shift, twist, pivot, strike—shift, twist, pivot, strike—it was like watching a storm-driven sea crash wave after wave on the defenseless shore.

Jaden-325-4 - Imperial Outpost – Planet Surface

Kallehn waved his hand over the control panel, and the outer airlock door slid silently open, after the inner door closed. He walked up behind Jar'ek and noticed he was breathing hard, and dripping with sweat.

Kallehn: "You've Been ***Practicing***! That was ***FUCKING*** Amazing! I took the same self-defense classes you've taken... And I've never seen ANYTHING like what you just did..."

Jar'ek turned to face Kallehn and smiled a weary smile, wiping his sweat-drenched blond hair from his forehead and out of his eyes. He stood up straight, stretching his back then bent over, resting his hands on his knees while he worked to catch his breath. J'Uhr trotted up and rubbed her muzzle against Kallehn's abdomen. Kallehn grabbed her face, bent over and planted a kiss on J'Uhr's forehead.

J'Uhr:{"You awake! Better now? Jar'ek trains. We Guard!"}

Kallehn: "Jar'ek, where's your Mech Protection Detail?!"

Jar'ek, in between heavy breathing: "They are here. I wanted some time alone, and they wouldn't allow it. So, they went into full stealth mode to give me simulated solitude..."

Jar'ek: "Guards! Disable Stealth."

Kallehn jumped as two tall, dark Mechs materialized out of thin air right next to him.

Kallehn: "Holy crap! Hey! I've had just about enough surprises over the last week or so to last a lifetime... "

Jar'ek broke into a mixture of laughing, coughing and sputtering. As Kallehn's smile began to turn into a glare, Jar'ek raised one hand in mollification.

Jar'ek: "Sorry! I didn't realize they were standing right next to you! Hahaha."

J'Uhr: {"J'Uhr knows where they are. S'Fah knows where they are."}

S'Fah: {"Yes, X'Ah-Panths sense Mechs, even when hide"}

Kallehn turned his head sharply to face S'Fah and then glanced back and forth between both X'Ah-Panths with a shocked expression.

Atlas: {"As you have just discovered, your psionic communications capabilities have been enhanced—you are no longer limited to J'Uhr as a communications partner. This is just the beginning of the rewards for a host of the SEED."}

Kallehn: {"S'Fah, you hear me? J'Uhr? "}

Both X'Ah-Panths began rubbing up against Kallehn as they moved around him in a circle, chorusing: *{"Hear Kallehn, Yes!"}*

Kallehn shook his head and smiled broadly, basking in the affection being broadcast from both X'Ah-Panths—roughhousing with them pulling them in close for hugs. After a moment, he remembered the reason why he'd been drawn out here in the first place.

Kallehn: "What kind of martial art was that you were practicing... it looks familiar, somehow. But I'm certain I've never seen it before."

Jar'ek: "It is a refinement on which Plato and I have been working. Human bodies, though bipedal, are significantly different from the other races that made up the Empire. We took the basics from several successful martial arts developed during the reign of the Empire and modified them for human anatomy. The main discipline was called 'Shihj'kath' in Takeshi or 'Flowing Spirit.' What you saw was part of a hybrid we've worked out so far... It is close enough where the extended memories will help us assimilate it quickly, but it doesn't include movements that aren't possible, like bending your leg backward at the knee like the Takesh liked to do. And I suspect that you aren't triple jointed, either..."

Kallehn: "Ouch! Good point. Well, I've begun to realize that I am wholly unsuited for the job you've given me. I need to begin training immediately... Mind if I join you?!"

Jar'ek closed the distance between them, placed his hand behind Kallehn's head and pulled him close, kissing his forehead.

Jar'ek: "Nice Tattoo!"

Kallehn: “Yeah, and I had to throw water on ***MYSELF***... no one else was there to lend a helping hand....”

Jar’ek grinned an evil grin and said: “Does it go all the way down...?”

Chapter 50—MESSAGE RECEIVED

TCDF Command Headquarters – New Hope

The twelve permanent council members and the one observer entered the large council chambers, finding their seats. The bright LED lights shone down directly on the Council while the lights dimmed throughout the rest of the room. Refreshments were served silently and efficiently by young men and women dressed in white from head to toe—Servant Class—the only exports of the Planet called Promise. They might as well have been invisible for all the attention they were paid by the self-appointed demigods of the Terran Confederation seated in the very comfortable seating.

The Council Chairman was dressed in a white robe, as were all of the other council members. As leader of the group, his robe was adorned with a golden braid to announce his rank. But the elegant attire was stretched to its limit by the bloated bulk of the man underneath it. His gluttony was in callous contrast to the nearby gaunt figures of the malnourished servant-slaves from the colony of Promise.

As one of the younger females carefully filled his waiting chalice with frostberry wine, the rotund frog of a man signaled one of the guards assigned to the council chambers over to him.

Guard Captain: "Yes, Sir?"

Council Chairman O'Rhange pointed at the young red-haired girl: "You see that girl? Have her brought to my quarters after this meeting. I wish to "Instruct her in proper etiquette."

The Guard Captain's face darkened, but his expression remained as fixed as if it were carved in stone. He ***KNEW*** that was the Chairman's clever euphemism for torturing and molesting that poor girl for days in his private quarters. He had heard of similar 'Instructional Sessions' in the past—both young girls and young boys—always duty-servants from Promise. They were the most vulnerable. They had no rights of citizenship, no protections, no one cared. The lovely, flaxen-haired young girl would be lucky if she survived...perhaps *'Lucky'* was a poor word choice... The Guard Captain had a niece that was older than this child. He felt he might be sick—inhaling slowly and deeply, the guard clamped down on his emotions and blocked the horror-laden imaginings assaulting his mind. He slowly and discreetly moved his hand away from the butt of his laser sidearm, having grabbed it subconsciously when he realized what he was being asked to do. But his duty was to the Council, not the slave girl.

Guard Captain: "Yes, Chairman. I will see to it personally."

The Chairman dismissed the Guard Captain with a wave of his hand and turned to face the Council. He pressed a stud under the table, and a bell tone sounded and echoed across the large room—the murmur of casual conversation ceased.

Council Chairman O'Rhange: "I call this emergency meeting of the Terran Council to order. You've all seen the transcripts of the two separate messages sent by Captain Lao. We are here to initiate a course of action based on the information obtained. I open the floor for discussion."

Councilman Fasik: "We have to keep this absolutely Top Secret! If the population hears the Treech have found us, we will lose any semblance of control!"

Councilwoman Tash: "Undoubtedly, you are correct, Fasik. But I think we should deal with the larger issues here, as a priority. That won't matter a bit if the Treech find the Colonies. We'll all be dead."

Panicked voices rose in a chorus of denial and fear until the Chairman pressed a hidden button to sound the bell tone, once again. A reluctant silence fell once more around the table.

Chairman: "Caster, you are in charge of the Defense Forces. What can you tell us about this Captain Xiang Lao? Is she reliable? The first message seems straight-forward enough, but the second one… Alien Empires, Galactic Plagues, a mutiny of junior officers… I just don't know WHAT to think! Is it possible she had some brain damage from the initial attack?"

Councilman Caster: "I've never met her, personally. But her record is exemplary, and her former commanders gave her high praise, indeed. I want to trust that she's telling us the truth, as she understands it. It's a hell of a situation to be in—I don't envy her. Kathy Lao is one of the rare recruits from Promise. She showed high potential and recruited from her parents at the age of six SSOs."

Observer Qualtish: "Recruited? That is the TCDF's euphemism for child abduction, isn't it?"

Both the Chairman and Caster glared at the observer until he sat back down, anger and frustration molding his face into a rigid mask. There was only so far he could push them before he became no longer useful… he must bide his time. Captain Lao would just be one more Promiser casualty that he could not protect—no justice for Promisers.

Chairman: "Obviously, we'll need to send out an expeditionary force and a research vessel to follow up. What do you suggest?"

Councilman Caster: "I propose that we send second destroyer flotilla, Battlecruiser Shashtavich and the Science Vessel Halstead. If the Treech come looking for their missing Marauder, we need to be prepared. And the Halstead is fully staffed with biologists—we should be able to find a team of epidemiologists within local transport range of them. Keep in mind that the transit time to Jaden-325 is 102 Standard Solar Rotations, at top speed."

Chairman: "If the alien ship is really 2,000 Solar Rotations old, I don't imagine it is going to be flying anywhere…

Observer Qualtish: "You CANNOT be serious! The Second Flotilla is made up of the only TCDF forces stationed at Promise. If the Treech find us and we are unprotected…"

Chairman: "Of course, we will see if we can scrape together a squadron of Gunships to protect Promise, Qualtish. But you realize that if the Treech come for the Colonies, they will come with overwhelming force. They could brush the second flotilla aside as if it were a minor irritation. Our only hope now is to gather as much intelligence as possible. I'm hoping that Jaden-325-4 contains some advanced alien technology that will provide us with the necessary edge to defeat the Treech when they DO find us. And let me be clear—New Hope has the technology base, the educated workforce and the resources needed for the survival of the human race. Promise has none of these things. If we have to choose which planet to protect, New Hope is the obvious choice. Just be glad you are stationed here, Qualtish. You will stand a much better chance of survival than all of those unproductive idiots back on your home world. Count your blessings."

"Caster…pick the RIGHT commander for the expeditionary force. They may find it necessary to bombard and irradiate the planet to destroy any trace of the colonies, as well as any technology the Treech may find useful. In the best-case scenario, the flotilla commander could bring those rebellious junior officers under his control. But I don't need to remind you—if they find any advanced technology—I'd prefer that the scientists garner what they can from it before you destroy it. You have the Council's consent to use all necessary means. Also, whatever happens, we are going to need to blame that Captain Xiang Lao for everything—you realize that?"

Caster: "Of course, Sir. Understood."

Chairman: "I'm confident that I don't need to warn you about the dangers of bringing a Plague back to the Colonies…take no chances."

Caster: "What about the surviving crew members of the Dragon Eye, Sir?"

Chairman: "We cannot risk that this Alien Influence has spread to them. The expeditionary force should have no direct contact with them. It will be a harsh mercy—but they should be terminated. I don't want them showing up on our doorstep contradicting our story, some day in the future."

Chairman: "All in favor, vote by a show of hands."

The Observer laid his face in his hands as all twelve of the permanent members raised theirs high. This was not the first time the citizens of Promise had been betrayed—and it wouldn't be the last. Instead of reaching out an open hand of friendship to an advanced alien race, the Council would use subterfuge and aggression.

Chairman: "Issue the orders, Caster. This meeting stands adjourned."

The Chairman walked out with Councilwoman Shilva, the Director of Colonial Intelligence, and pulled her aside in the outer passageway.

Chairman: "Shilva, I'm concerned about these advanced androids and AIs mentioned in Captain Lao's report. I want your department to begin working on ways we can attack and disable threats such as these. Funding will be unlimited for this little project of ours. It is important, however, that this remain secret at the highest levels. And make absolutely certain that our own AIs are hardened against such attacks!"

Councilwoman Shilva: "Understood, Chairman. I will see to it immediately."

The other members rose and filed out of the room, leaving the Observer to suffer in silence and solitude—and as the overhead lights dimmed and finally went out—in darkness.

Outside in the corridor, the silence was only broken by a long, sobbing wail as a young redheaded girl was grabbed by the arm and pulled towards her sad destiny. The Guard Captain, his countenance unchanged wondered if any amount of bathing could clean this stain from his soul.

New Hope – Landing City – Darkside District

A tall lone figure strode surely, and quietly down the darkened alley as rain and mist pelted his head-to-foot Nurath-hide hood and cloak. It wasn't cold enough outside to justify such heavy garb, but it served the wearer well in that it hid his features from the casual observer. He had made certain when he purchased it from the second-hand store, that it was well-worn. It wouldn't do to be seen wearing new and expensive clothing in darkside district at this hour. One's life would be cut short for the price of a new jacket or pair of shoes—the coins in one's pocket. He reached inside his cloak and felt once again for the holstered needler at his waist. It was still there, loaded and ready if he needed it. It was a sign of his desperation that he carried the deadly weapon. It was illegal for him, a citizen of Promise, to have it at all, let alone carry it in public.

But where he went, he could not ask for Council Guards to escort him. Indeed, had they known of this clandestine meeting, they would have arrested him without hesitation. And the Council would surely have voted for his immediate execution for ***treason***. Treason...how funny that sounded. Citizens of Promise weren't citizens in the eyes of the Terran Council or even the general population of New Hope. The lies describing Promisers as being sub-human, lazy, dishonest and stupid had been repeated for so long, so many generations, that it wasn't even questioned any longer. When Promise had first asked New Hope for help in feeding its population, they had been equals. Soon, the Terran Government saw there were advantages in demonizing the Promisers and gaining access to a large force of slave laborers. How could slaves be accused of Treason?

A sharp Clang-clank-clank rang out in the silence of the darkened alley. Council Observer Qualtish stopped in his tracks.

Listening—peering into the darkness—inhaling deeply and catching a whiff of the sour smell of decaying refuse—seeking any sign that someone might be stalking him. Nothing…only the sound of rain drops gently but relentlessly falling onto the cracked and oily pavement. —It must have been a pseudo-cat or local rodent— After waiting for a few more heartbeats, Qualtish continued quietly. He knew this alley well. He had traveled this very path at least a dozen times in the past year. Each time fearing that he would be found out and arrested. Or, even worse, that the Council would discover his co-conspirators and end their movement in a sweeping campaign of arrests and public executions—using this to bolster their lies that Promisers were nothing but ungrateful troublemakers and needed to be controlled with an iron fist.

Two more steps—avoiding a noisome slime covered puddle—coming to a rough-hewn brick threshold worn and darkened by time. The heavy wooden door was wet, the iron hinges rusted, but it was sturdy enough. Qualtish raised his closed fist and knocked—first three times in quick succession—then a pause—then five times in a slow beat—Boom—Boom—Boom—Boom—Boom. Nothing happened for a moment, and Qualtish looked right and then left. Had they been discovered? Were Council Guards approaching to apprehend him even now? Then with a loud Crrrreeeeeaaaaakkk, the heavy door swung open on squealing hinges, and Qualtish hurried within—chastising himself for his foolish paranoid thoughts—no, perhaps healthy paranoia.

Darkside District—Conspiracy of Promise

An old woman with scraggly hair in a dirty skirt and even dirtier apron closed the door to the alley behind Qualtish and lowered a metal bar into the locking stocks, securing the iron-clad solid wood door in place. It would take a mounted laser cannon to burn through that barrier! The woman knew him and knew he needed no directions from this point. She didn't even look at him as she turned towards the steamy hallway filled with sounds of pots and pans clanking, returning to her duties in the kitchen. Qualtish grabbed the wooden railing and began the short journey down three flights of damp stone stairs into the basement and tunnel system that ran below this building. He heard the low rumble of indistinct conversation from below as his boots clicked on stair after stair.

As he turned the corner and stepped off the finals stair onto the dirt floor of their chosen meeting place, a dozen men and women turned to face him. Solar charged lanterns filled the space with bright yellow light. There were no power cables, no other electronic devices, no data connections in this room. The walls had been carefully sprayed with a magnetic iron slurry that acted as a Faraday Cage, preventing any electronic eavesdropping or signals. The group stood as one and came to greet him.

Chandra Alaxis: "Qualtish! Welcome, my old friend! I am happy to see you again. Each time we meet, I fear it will be the last time and that the Council's Spies will have finally arrested your saggy old ass. Sneaking around and escaping the attentions of the Council Guards—you risk more than any of us!"

She hugged him tightly to her and then stepped back so that the others could greet him, in turn.

Chandra opened a chest, pulling out a bottle of Mock-Leaf Wine, she poured glasses for all the attendees, then indicated a chair at the head of the beat up old kitchen table that was the centerpiece of this improvised meeting room. Qualtish shrugged out of his cloak and took the proffered seat. He drank deeply of the Mock-Leaf Wine. It was a good vintage, so good that it rarely touched the lips of anyone from Promise, officially. Qualtish sat down his glass and asked of them all: "What news of our plans?!"

Chandra wiped her chin with her sleeve to clean the last dribbles of wine from her lips before speaking: "The psychological warfare plans are well underway. Our printers have manufactured millions of the flimsy-cards, self-adhesive posters with the 'We Are Watching You' slogan in assorted styles. In addition, the Black-hat hacker unit has been able to infiltrate the Colonial communications network. We've been able to replace many of the Council's subliminal mollification messages with the same slogan and images designed to spread increased anxiety and general distrust. Every day people are becoming more on edge and less tolerant. Our new messages are designed to target their growing anger towards those in authority."

Qualtish: "Excellent, Chandra! Your work will be critical to the success of our plans."

Chandra: "I feel I must warn you again, Qualtish—I cannot predict when the increasing anxiety will push the population to the breaking point. If our operations are delayed…things could spin out of control."

Qualtish: "I hear your words and I understand the risk. It is difficult beyond description to coordinate such operations across lightyears and two planets. But the wheels have been set in motion and we are committed. As you know, the Council recently decided to begin of program of altering the DNA of all future Promise-born children and psychological conditioning to reduce intelligence and instill a compulsion to obey authority figures. There is no future for our future generations but unrelenting servitude. Promisers will be hard-wired into a permanent underclass. This is our last, best chance to stop this madness."

Anger and determination became palpable in the small confines as each member of the group grumbled their support for direct action.

A young man of no more than twenty-two solar orbits rose from his seat and bowed towards Qualtish. Qualtish smiled and nodded in his direction: "Speak Caleb Susmathy. I would hear your words."

Caleb's freckled face flushed with pride as he answered: "Esteemed Observer, I have news from the armory. I and my cell have infiltrated the armory successfully. We have forged IDs and access codes. And over the past 90 planetary rotations, we have smuggled out enough laser rifles to arm hundreds of our Promiser resistance fighters! These weapons have been cached in hidden locations across the Capital City. We have also deployed explosive devices in the Armory itself which can be activated remotely when the time comes, depriving the oppressors of the weapons they will need to counter our attacks."

With a look of astonishment, Qualtish leaned forward and spoke: "Why, this is excellent news, Caleb! You have exceeded my expectations! This initial progress bodes well for our revolution, my boy. But tell me, how did you accomplish such a feat in so short a time?"

There was silence for a time, and Qualtish began to regret asking that particular question in such a public venue, as Caleb dropped his gaze and blushed for a very different reason—shame.

Caleb: "I…I…you see…the Commander of the Armory Guard likes young men to attend to him…personally…intimately…and he took an interest in me when I was assigned to the cleaning crew that serviced the officers' quarters. He has particular interests that are *objectionable* to many people and is often unable to find willing participants. I allowed myself to be used in this way for the benefit of the movement. I hope you are not disgusted by my choices, esteemed Observer…"

Qualtish stood up and walked over to Caleb, placing a comforting arm around his shaking shoulders. "No, Caleb, I am amazed by your strength of character and your commitment to the resistance. I respect your choices. If you were to ask any of us at this table, you should not be surprised to find that we have all done things we are not proud of for the cause. And we will be called on even more in the near future. I am not ashamed of you; I am so very proud of you, Son! Your efforts may win this battle and justice for us all…"

Caleb lifted his gaze to look into Qualtish' eyes and found nothing but admiration there. He smiled and took a deep breath. Qualtish moved back to his seat and said: “Sal’fak, what news of our plans to infiltrate the TCDF Command AI network?”

The middle-aged blond woman stood with pride and spoke with an almost musical tone to her voice: “Esteemed Observer, we have deployed the AI Virus and disabled the malware sentries successfully. The AI network will be completely under our control within the next fourteen planetary rotations. Subroutines to disrupt traffic, lock out critical systems, disable alarms and reprogram automated defensive weapons to target TCDF fighters and shuttles without our own ID beacons. All secure areas in the Capital will have locking systems disabled and will be exposed to our direct assaults. The Council Chambers, in particular, will be left unprotected except for the few guards on duty at the time. All calls for reinforcements will send troop transports to distant, deserted locations where the troop transports will abandon them and head back to base. In addition, we are already able to create hidden zones throughout the surveillance network, allowing our cells to make preparations and missions around the entire planet. We simply create a malfunction in the surveillance cameras and sensors along our designated routes. We are using this sparingly so as not to bring undue attention to our activities. But the Council will soon begin to believe in magical and invisible creatures as more and more posters and notices are pasted on walls and storefronts in their own districts!”

Qualtish smiled, visualizing the Council Chairman’s pudgy face turning blood red with rage: “Very impressive, Sal’fak! You all are the living proof that challenges the lies that New Hopers spout freely disparaging Promisers’ value and intelligence. You have turned their own technology and weapons against them—and they are none the wiser. How humiliating a defeat this will be! And it is only possible because of all of you—Promisers! I cannot disclose the full breadth of our plans to you, at this time. But these preparations you have completed are vital to the overall mission. I swear to you—your names will be remembered across Terran space."

Chapter 51—MESSENGER'S RETURN

Imperial Comm Probe AXZ-512548—System Jaden-325—Outer System

A multispectral wave-front began propagating across the Jaden-325 system, as the Imperial Comm Probe dropped out of hyperspace and engaged its sub-light engines. The probe sent an encrypted message identifying itself, to the fourth planet using a directed tachyon pulse. It was short-range—designed to be used for intra-system communications, but it was FAST, faster than light. Immediately after the message was sent, the comm probe enabled stealth mode and changed course randomly—still moving in the general direction of the fourth planet. The information it carried was too valuable to risk through a lack of caution.

A short time later, the comm probe's sensors detected another radiation wave-front. Someone else had dropped into the outer system from hyperspace....

Planet Jaden-325-4 — Planet Surface

Kallehn and Jar'ek continued to practice the Shihj'kath forms over time. The integration of their extended memories allowed them to perform complex series of feints and attacks that were fluid in motion—the timing, execution, and precision—like well-oiled machines. The rest of the crew began taking exercise breaks to watch, and then later, to copy the graceful movements. When mastered, these patterns of motion provided a kind of meditative peace where mind and body became one. Commander Sullen and Chief Vermanderly were becoming quite proficient. And even J'Uhr and S'Fah were watching intently and learning. They learned to anticipate the patterns of movement. They could now move with the young men intertwining their own movements so as not to interfere, but to become an integral part of any attack or defense.

Chief Vermanderly accompanied Ta'ihr, the genetically enhanced Earth Falcon. The chief, in her role as Ta'ihr's keeper—trainer—companion, had been escorting the X'Ah-Falcon outside, rain or shine, on a daily basis. Like the other Terran's, Ta'ihr needed regular exercise. But even more than the other Terrans, she craved wide open spaces—free sky—to roam, hunt and soar.

Ta'ihr had discovered that the pervasive groundcover hid a multitude of small quadrupedal rodents—this kept her very busy. The Chief had also been training with the Falcon. She had researched the training manuals used by the Rangers and had been studying them in earnest. Jar'ek wondered if the Academy had not made a mistake in the Chief's classification. Or perhaps continued training with the X'Ah-Falcon had improved her psionic abilities. Whatever the reason, the Chief and Ta'ihr were becoming a well-functioning team. Kallehn had chosen well, indeed, when selecting the Chief as her caretaker—her mind-mate.

Imperial Destroyer Celestia—Main Bridge

Over the weeks that followed, the results of the training simulations continued to improve. Celestia needed to increase the difficulty level regularly. The entire bridge crew had come a long way, but Kallehn was excelling. He was his old confident self. Of course, he had a serious advantage. He had the memories of countless predecessors with extensive bridge and combat experience. The practice simulations were accelerating his integration of these extended memories.

Kallehn had made it his mission to be the best Warrior he could. In addition to an intense Shihj'kath training schedule, Kallehn had convinced Celestia to provide practice targets for weapons training. Kallehn was proving to be a natural marksman. He had also taken his role as Jar'ek's defender to heart. Kallehn had been practicing team tactics with the Combat Androids in his "*spare time*"—even sparring with them. Jar'ek was becoming jealous of his time. They hadn't seen much of each other since Kallehn's melding. He suspected that Kallehn needed some solitude and time to come to terms with the symbiotic relationship— he had chosen it, but perhaps he had not quite understood all that it entailed.

They were well into a fleet action simulation when Celestia broke in.

Celestia: "Simulation Terminated."

Jar'ek: "What's up, Celestia? We were really starting to look good in that simulation... You afraid we might actually beat you?"

Celestia: "I accede to the possibility, Sire—no matter how unlikely... No, two occurrences demand the command staff's attention."

Jar'ek: "And those are?"

Celestia: "Two separate multi-spectral wave-fronts have been detected mid-system. The first was located on a line from System Z982—one of the target systems for the comm probes we sent to Imperial Naval Bases in the sector. Shortly before we detected this event, we received an encrypted id from comm probe AXZ-512548 using a directed tachyon pulse transmission(DTPT). It then enabled stealth. We have been unable to detect it."

Kallehn: "Directed Tachyon Pulse? Aren't those restricted for priority messages only?"

Celestia: "Quite correct, Lord Commander."

Kallehn: "Interesting. But no further message? Why enable stealth mode instead of transmitting the complete message and returning to base?"

Jar'ek: "There is only one reason, Kallehn. The probe deemed the message content so sensitive that it couldn't risk interception. In which case, I don't think we will hear from it again until it is back in Celestia's shield perimeter. The pulse alerted us to its presence so that it wouldn't be deemed hostile and we'd be expecting it."

Kallehn: "Celestia, didn't you say there were two occurrences of interest?"

Celestia: “Yes, and the second may be more concerning. A second wave-front has been detected from a point 65 Degrees across the system from the first. The radiation detected from the hyperspace event is an order of magnitude greater than that of the comm probe.”

Jar’ek: “So, not another comm probe, this time.”

Celestia: “No, Sire. I estimate a small squadron or one much larger vessel. It is impossible to tell which, at this distance. Should I send a Challenge?”

Jar’ek scanned the faces of the command staff around the bridge then asked: “Recommendations?”

Kallehn: “We must assume it is another Treech Marauder until we find out otherwise.”

Captain Lao: “That would be prudent under the circumstances. It is far too soon to receive a response from the TCDF, even if they sent a squadron immediately after receiving our message. The earliest we could expect anyone from the TCDF would be another 21 Planetary Rotations.”

Jar’ek: “Celestia, just as a precaution, let’s bring the ship to Alert Status 3. Let’s bring the full phalanx of combat androids back online, and let’s see if we can prepare you for flight operations if needed. And we shall remain communications silent until we have more intel on who they are.”

The lights dimmed throughout the ship and took on a bluish tint while a single long double-tone sounded, echoing through the empty hallways. Yellow glyphs appeared on all bulkheads and above all hatches and portals throughout the vessel.

Celestia: “Powering up flight systems. Diagnostics underway. Initiating sub-sonics to break up the surface camouflage.” Jar’ek felt a vibration—a low rumbling—through the soles of his feet

Two of the tall, dark combat androids stomped onto the bridge and took up guard positions. They both held heavy, Imperial Blasters.

Jar'ek: "Captain, we will need a bridge watch, but can I suggest that the those of the crew not on watch get some food and rest? We won't need to take any action for...how long, Celestia?"

Celestia: "I estimate it would take five planetary rotations for an Imperial squadron to close to weapons' range. Treech vessels would take at least three times that long. Our sensor platforms should be able to provide us with much more information within the next planetary rotation. It is notable, however, that Imperial FTL engines are efficient enough to have brought a squadron much closer to the star's gravity well before dropping to sublight drives...."

Captain Lao: "Very well, Lord Constandor. The bridge crew is dismissed to normal duty rotations until tomorrow when we know more. I'll notify the rest of our shipmates."

Jar'ek pulled the Captain aside as everyone was filing off the Bridge.

Jar'ek: "Captain, Jar'ek will do. The honorifics make me feel uncomfortable."

Captain Lao: "I'm sorry, your Highness. But the time for that is past. There can be no misunderstanding where authority lies during a battle. I understand how you feel, but we can't risk mixed signals. So, that leaves us with calling you Sire, Highness, Emperor, Lord Constandor, errr... any other ideas?"

Plato: {"The Captain is absolutely correct, Sire. And you know it. This had to happen at some point, anyway. I know you didn't want this."}

Jar'ek: "Damn it! Well, you are not yet sworn members of the Empire. You cannot be and still remain citizens of the Terran Confederation. I won't ask you to do that. So 'Sire' is out. Lord

Constandor could get cumbersome in battle..."

Captain Lao smiled and then raised her hand in a peace offering.

Captain Lao: "I don't mean to make light of your discomfort, but our history is full of tyrants who would have killed for such a title. I think the best option remaining, if for no other reason than it has the least number of syllables—is Highness."

Jar'ek groaned loudly and closed his eyes tightly—his face and neck flushed a dark red color.

Captain Lao: "I will inform the crew. There will be no cause for embarrassment. Things are as they must be. And you are coping with it as best I could have expected. Better you than me! Ha!"

And with that, the Captain braced to attention, bowed her head briefly, then turned sharply and walked off the bridge. Kallehn sat across the bridge with a wide grin and a mischievous look in his eyes. He threw up his hands, shaking his head and said: "I had *NOTHING* to do with this!" Jar'ek walked over to Kallehn, grabbed him by his collar and pulled him up. Grabbing his left hand, he started walking, pulling Kallehn behind.

Kallehn: "Uh, where are you taking me—the brig?!?"

Jar'ek: "Hmmm... I wish I had thought of that! No, you and I are going to spend some quality time together before this situation gets any more complicated. Do I need to make that a command?

Kallehn: "No, your ***Highness***... "

Jar'ek: "Oh, Shut Up!"

TCDF Taskforce 48 Flagship—Hyperspace

As the TCDF Battlecruiser Shashtavich plied hyperspace at maximum velocity, TCDF Admiral Hassan Heidrecht leaned back and placed his feet on the conference room table.

A cold sneer marked his wrinkled and lined face as he cast his gaze across the other officers who watched him, stiff-backed and stone-faced. He ran one hand back through his tangle of oily gray hair and shook his head, saying: "I don't give a rodent's testicles that the Dragon Eye was a TCDF vessel or that the crew and officers are Terran citizens in uniform. You have all been informed of the Council's unanimous decision and our orders. Captain D'Sai, would you mind reading those orders aloud, one more time for our hard-of-hearing juniors? "

A tall slender man with pale skin and short dark hair stood slowly, adjusted his uniform and scanned the tablet in his hand before looking up to face the assembled ship's captains and first officers. He swallowed heavily before speaking. He was a career officer who had worked his way up from the enlisted ranks. To him, the terms Honor and Integrity weren't just words scrawled across the service's recruitment brochure. They actually meant something to him—they meant everything. But as the Flag-Captain of TCDF Taskforce 48, it was his duty to follow orders and support the Admiral—no matter how much he hated either one.

Captain Kyle D'Sai: "Taskforce 48 is hereby ordered into the Jaden-325-4 star system with all due haste. Once hyperspace transition is complete, the taskforce shall take up position in orbit of Jaden-325-4. The taskforce shall, at Admiral Heidrecht's discretion, investigate the recent engagement with the Treech, the destruction of the TCDF Dragon Eye and the possible threat of virulent disease or biological warfare agent from the planet. ALL occupants of the planet, all former crewmembers of the Dragon Eye and any vessels in the system are to be considered hostile. Every effort will be taken to acquire new technology and artifacts without risking exposure to any potential pathogen."

D'Sai took a deep breath and continued: "It is assumed that junior Ranger Officers Frix and Constandor, after encountering an alien artifact, became mentally unstable, although these officers seem to be able to exert some level of control over the artifact vessel and other devices. If possible, these two deranged officers are to be detained in quarantine and interrogated, and if necessary, physically coerced to transfer such control to Admiral Heidrect."

D'Sai hesitated and glanced meaningfully at the Admiral who simply squinted his eyes and glared back at his own Flag-Captain.

D'Sai then glanced around the room, taking in the expressions on each and every other face as their eyes were glued upon him. He could see similar feelings to his in those stares—disgust—fear—anger—frustration. He took another deep breath and continued: "And after all useful intelligence has been acquired, the Taskforce 48 is ordered to bombard the planet with nuclear and KKM ordinance until all traces of life and technology have been wiped from the face of the planet. –Orders approved by unanimous vote of the Terran Council.—"

D'Sai turned off his table and set it down on the table with a shaking hand then returned to his seat resignedly.

The Admiral removed his feet from the table and leaned forward on his elbows for emphasis. "So, I don't want to hear any more sniveling or complaining about our orders! Orders are orders. You either follow them exactly or you will be relieved of command. I hope I've made myself clear!" Several heads nodded silently in the Admiral's direction.

Admr. Heidrecht: "Good. Now, let's get the details of our plan worked out. We will need a shuttle specially fitted out for the capture and quarantine of Rangers Frix and Constandor. And I want an battle plan to engage and destroy that old wreck of an alien ship in case it tries to lift and reach orbit. I doubt it would be much of a threat to even a single one of our modern destroyers, but we should plan for all contingencies. Are the interrogators prepped and ready?"

D'Sai: "Yes, Admiral. All will be in readiness, as you have ordered."

Admr. Heidrecht: "Very well. We should be transitioning into the Jaden-325 system in the next two weeks. I want regular drills until every crewman in this taskforce knows what will be required of him or her to the nth degree. Any questions? No? Then you are all Dismissed."

Chapter 52—BITTER TASTE OF BETRAYAL

Imperial Gunship Alacrity—System Jaden-325

The Gunship Commander, Chur Kulahn, stood tall in the center of the bridge, the fur on his top mane moving slightly as his gaze moved left to the right and back again, across the command stations. This was a glorious mission! His place in history would be assured with its satisfactory conclusion.

A low growl escaped his throat as he remembered the encrypted cautionary message sent by High Commander Xitanth. His anger and disbelief at his first reading of this message again flooded his thoughts, and he felt the fur on the back of his neck raise straight up.

Officer 2nd Sutrak Peshreth glanced at his Commander—surprised to hear his growl. Moving his clawed hand to cover the butt of his sidearm, he moved close to his Commander's side.

Speaking in a hushed whisper, he asked: "Something amiss, Commander Kulahn?"

Chur Kulahn inhaled deeply and forced himself to relax. He shook his head and turned to speak to his long-time friend and colleague.

Cmdr. Kulahn: "Just the musings of a decrepit old warrior, my friend. I have no reason to suspect anything is amiss—and still, the hair on my neck ridges rises.... You have followed my orders—the precautions are in place?"

Officer 2nd Peshreth opened and sharply closed his fang filled mouth twice, click—click—indicating the affirmative. Some of the tension flowed out of the Commander's stance.

Officer 2nd: "I spoke personally with Elite Guard Commander Golgaht. As you also ordered, I have personally wired the alert signal to your command chair palm rest. It will silently alert

Golgaht if we suspect betrayal. His Elites have been placed at strategic locations throughout the ship."

Cmdr. Kulahn: "Thank you, Sutrak. You, I can trust without hesitation."

Officer 2nd: "I still cannot believe that any of our crew—any Pythanon—would even conceive of the betrayal we have been warned to guard against. It is inconceivable. The dishonor that it would bring to our entire species...."

The Commander rested his clawed hand on the Officer 2nd's shoulder and clicked his teeth twice.

Cmdr. Kulahn: "I agree, Sutrak! It makes me nauseous to consider it. But given the source of the warning, we dare not leave ourselves unprepared."

The younger tactical officer huffed to get his Commander's attention. Both the Commander and the Officer 2nd cast appraising looks upon the junior officer, still gray around the ears with youth. The young officer stood and nodded his head in respect.

Officer 2nd: "Well...speak, Officer Has' Rahaat."

Tactical Officer Rahaat: "Sir, I am curious. Why have we transitioned from FTL drive so far from the inner system? We could have shortened the journey to the target planet considerably by remaining in FTL until we reached the gravity-well limit of this star."

Officer 2nd: "Good question, Rahaat. It shows you are paying attention. We transitioned into the outer system for the same reason we have not attempted to open communications. We wish to gather intelligence prior to engagement. We are being cautious, young one. I know that is a concept you are unfamiliar with."

Imperial Gunship Alacrity—Jaden-325-4—Command Deck

Officer 2nd: "Cmdr. Kulahn, we have achieved high orbit of the planet."

Cmdr. Kulahn: "No point in delaying communications any longer. If there were an ambush waiting for us, it would have sprung by now."

Officer 2nd: "Alacrity, please open a secure channel to the planet. Use Imperial encoding."

—Silence reigned on the bridge. The officers glanced at each other in confusion.

Cmdr. Kulahn: "Alacrity, Attend me!"

—-Silence

The hair on the Commander's back rose straight up, and his eyes narrowed as the realization hit him—Sabotage! Shock slowed his reaction time. As he moved to slam his fist down on the Alarm button, he heard a strange sound—like something metallic rolling across the floor—Ssshhh-tck-tck-tck.

It was then that he saw the plasma grenade, just before it ignited. Although the explosion was loud in the enclosed area of the Bridge, it wasn't loud enough to alert others in the ship. No alarms sounded, not even on the scorched and smoke filled command deck. The only sounds one could hear there at all were the final exhalations of the former bridge officers.

This explosion may have been the first, but it would not be the last. Moments later, the ship itself was rocked by explosion after explosion, as vital defense points within the hull were destroyed. The deafening concussions signaled the deaths of many loyal crewmen and Elite Warriors, alike,

Imperial Gunship Alacrity—Jaden-325-4—Starboard Armory

Officer 5th Zik'Ruthat stood just inside the heavy armored hatch that provided the single point of entry for the Ships Starboard Armory. He inhaled deeply, trying to calm himself. He growled sub-vocally. The former Commander was better prepared than any old warrior had a right to be! Many of the faithful had died taking this single armory. No matter. They had weapons and battle armor now. He began pulling the personal armor closed around him. He heard a hiss as the seals closed, and the suit switched over to its onboard air supply. His nose wrinkled as he recognized the bitter scent of his own fear.

His comm suite chirped with a notification of a secure communications request. He quickly responded.

Officer 5th: "Far Seer Hears. Speak."

Weapons Officer 3rd: "It is True Voice. I report. Casualties have been high. Many of the Elite Guardsmen were disbursed throughout the ship. We killed many in their barracks, but there is fierce resistance in the launch bays and weapons sections. We have only managed to secure one Secondary Battery! We were unable to hold Engineering. One of the Elites must have foreseen the future! He tossed a plasma grenade into the main engine control matrix. It was destroyed. WE CANNOT MANEUVER! What are we to do?!"

Officer 5th: "Calm as a gentle breeze, True Voice. Calm as a gentle breeze..."

W.O. 3rd inhaled deeply and exhaled slowly, then spoke: "As you say, brother. What is your guidance?"

Officer 5th: "We cannot fail the Faith, brother. We must succeed. The True SEED will sustain us in life and death."

W.O. 3rd: "In life and death..."

Officer 5th: "Commence firing operations on the Outpost with the Secondary Batteries immediately. I will command an attack force to capture Drop Ships from the launch bay and attack the Outpost directly. Long Live the True SEED—Long Live the Faithful!"

W.O. 3rd: "Long Live the True SEED, Brother!"

Officer 5th signaled the rest of the faithful to follow him. They left the armory, stepping over the bodies of their former crewmates and moved swiftly down the passageway towards the launch bay. Memories of his offspring and his mates found their way into his thoughts as they prepared to assault the well-prepared defenders. He knew that no matter how things turned out, he was never going to see them again.

Imperial Destroyer Celestia—Planet Surface

Scans from the stealth sensor probes in high orbit had identified the incoming ship as an Imperial *V'Ash Quarat Class* Gunship. The Gunship had not, however, initiated communications with the surface. This seemed odd to the crew of the Celestia. The anxiety rose as they contemplated the possibility that an unfriendly warship hung overhead. Jar'ek decided the best course of action was to remain under stealth and radio silence. They would be difficult to target accurately until active scans searched them out. It was always possible the warship would leave the system after a cursory search failed to locate them. And if the crew of the Gunship was still loyal to the Empire, Jar'ek didn't want them to leave...

The bridge crew had been assembled on the Command Desk since the moment the Gunship entered orbit.

Jar'ek: "Celestia, Attend me."

Celestia: "Attending..."

Jar'ek: "Are any of our stealthed system probes in a position to receive a directed tachyon pulse message from us? I want to make sure that Gunship cannot intercept the message and cannot discern our location."

Celestia: "Yes, Sire. There are two probes in line-of-sight and within easy range of a directed tachyon pulse. The transmission angle is wide enough to escape detection by the Gunship in orbit above us."

Jar'ek: "Very well. Target our transceiver array at the probe that is optimally located to relay a transmission to the Gunship."

Celestia: "Instructions received and acknowledged. You may begin your message for the Gunship when ready."

Jar'ek: "Unknown vessel, you have entered restricted space claimed by the Harmonic Empire. Identify yourself and state your intentions."

—Silence

Jar'ek: "Celestia—did the transmission reach the Gunship, yet?"

Celestia: "Affirmative. There has been sufficient time for a full transit and a response having been received."

Jar'ek scanned the bridge crew with his eyes and said: "Any suggestions?"

Cmdr. Sallen: "They failed to follow protocol and introduce themselves when they entered the star system. And now, they refuse to respond to our hails...I'd say they are hostile. And they know we are here, now."

Captain Lao: "There could be other explanations. It has been 2,000 years since the fall of the Empire. They may use different frequencies and procedures, now.

Jar'ek: "Agreed. Celestia, please put that message on a repeating loop. Pipe through any response to the loudspeakers, as it comes in."

Celestia: "Understood."

Jar'ek took a seat in one of the observer chairs near the Captain's own seat. Jar'ek leaned forward, placing his elbows on his knees and rested his face in his hands. The slow approach of the Gunship had been nerve-wracking for all of them. They had taken the time to put together some contingency plans, however. They would fight if they had to. The Celestia was well armed. But a fully crewed Imperial Gunship was a close match for her. Just then Kallehn walked in carrying a tray with some light snacks and synthetic coffee. It might be a long night.

Imperial Gunship Alacrity—Outside Forward Battery Control

Elite Guard Commander Golgaht was not happy. One apparent reason for this was the seared flesh of his right shoulder. A blaster wielded by a trusted Guardsman had nearly taken his head off when the mutiny first started. S'ashahat Yumil, his friend and 2nd in command had sensed the danger and pushed him aside at the last second, sacrificing her life to save his. As he leaned his back against the bulkhead just outside forward battery control, he grimaced in pain as he mentally took stock of their situation.

He had prepared his guardsmen for just such a situation, even though he never believed it was possible. Pythanons attacking the SEED! How could this happen?! He shook his head to clear it. He needed focus right now. His surviving troops and the SEED itself needed him. He could grieve later. The preparations ordered by Commander Kulahn had saved many of his guardsmen. And twenty-three of those survivors were lined shoulder-to-shoulder against the bulkhead next to him. The mutineers had failed to gain control of the primary batteries. But the secondary batteries might still prove a threat to the SEED. He would see this ship destroyed if he must before that happened.

Golgaht stood slowly and then noticed a communications tech running toward him trying to get his attention.

Comm-Tech Julmesh: "Commander! We have been hailed. We were unable to ascertain the origin, but it is close.

With this, the Comm-Tech attached a remote communications relay to Commander's battle helmet and activated it.

—"Unknown vessel, you have entered restricted space claimed by the Harmonic Empire. Identify yourself and state your intentions."—

Golgaht activated his microphone and said: "Celestia! Speaking is Guard Commander Golgaht of the Imperial Gunship Alacrity. Mutineers have taken control of significant sections of this vessel. The command crew are all dead. Elite Guard Units have control of all but one weapons control center. The forward secondary batteries are no longer in control of loyal units. The mutineers intend to fire on you to eradicate the SEED. Our shields are down. We were able to disable them during the fighting. But you must fire on this vessel, now. The Alacrity is a clear danger to you. You must destroy us with all haste! We cannot risk the SEED!"

Imperial Gunship Alacrity—Outside Forward Battery Control

—"...must be destroyed with all haste! We cannot risk the SEED!"

Jar'ek stood abruptly and said: "Celestia! Drop camouflage and raise shields! Sound Battle Stations!"

A subdued warbling tone sounded throughout the ship. Red Takeshi glyphs appeared on all bulkheads, and the control room lights dimmed. The bridge crew were at their stations and ready. Though none of them had faced space combat operations before, they had been trained in simulations, they were professionals. They were ready.

Jar'ek: "Celestia, release docking clamps, engage stabilizers and make best speed for orbit. I want us in an aggressive posture in front of that Gunship as soon as possible."

Jar'ek: "Captain Lao, the ship is yours. Weapons fire is authorized, but I have no intention of killing everyone onboard that vessel without exploring all other options first."

Captain Lao: "Confirmed, your Highness—I have the Ship! XO, I want weapons lock for our secondary batteries on Alacrity's engines and weapon control, as soon as our guns bear."

XO: "Targeting engines and weapons control, Aye, Captain."

A great white disk separated itself from the surface, throwing aside the accumulated dust of over two millennia. Looking like nothing if not a giant manta-ray of old Earth's oceans, it lifted itself free of the surface and glided gracefully into the sky as the back blast from its massive engines shook the ground for over a dozen-μL.

Chapter 53—A CRISIS OF FAITH

Imperial Gunship Alacrity—System Jaden-325

Officer 5th's comm suite chirped again. He opened his helmet visor and wiped the sweat and blood from his eyes before responding. The smoke from electrical fires and metal scorched by blaster fire flooded into his open visor. Coughing and sputtering, he answered the comm call.

Officer 5th: "Far Seer Hears. Speak."

Weapons Officer 3rd: "It is True Voice. Again, I report. Imperial Destroyer Celestia has risen from the surface. The vessel's attitude and trajectory indicate they are seeking to engage us in battle, not to flee as we predicted they would. Fortune favors us, Far Seer! I have ordered the batteries we control to open fire, now that we have a target lock."

Officer 5th exhaled in a subdued growl. Fortune favored the mission, INDEED! With the engines of the Alacrity damaged, the Celestia could have escaped the fate that had been so carefully planned for it. But now, the faithful had a chance!

Officer 5th: "True Voice! Order our troops in the shuttle bay to make a maximum effort and launch any vessel they can reach immediately. They are to target the Celestia and go to maximum thrust—Ram them. Perhaps that will be enough to overwhelm their defensive shields—allowing our weapons fire to reach our target finally. Pray, we do not miss, True Voice!"

WO 3rd: "It will be done, Far Seer! Glory to the True SEED! Death to the unbelievers!"

Imperial Destroyer Celestia—Jaden-325-4 High Orbit

Jar'ek stumbled and nearly fell when the deck heaved beneath him. A loud "GOOOOoooonng!" sounded throughout the ship as if a giant hammer blow had stricken it.

Captain Lao: "All secondary batteries open fire as you bear. I want everything we've got thrown at their weapons fire control! Helm! Evasive action! Make us a difficult target."

"GOOOOoooonnng!" The deck heaved again as another plasma bolt struck the Celestia's defensive shields. This time Jar'ek lost his footing and fell to the floor, face first.

Captain Lao leaned her head towards Jar'ek's sprawled body and whispered: "Your Highness might be more comfortable if he strapped into one of the command chairs and engaged the gravity-webbing…just a suggestion."

Jar'ek lifted himself up and moved directly to the observation chair behind, and to the side of the Captain's command chair. He pressed his palm down on the armrest, activating the gravity-webbing restraints then looked at the Captain with a wry grin.

Jar'ek: "Excellent advice, Captain. I DO feel more comfortable, thank you!"

The Captain turned to face Jar'ek, smiled and nodded.

Tactical Officer Caoha Conner: "Starboard Secondary Plasma Batteries are firing, now. Impact in 3…2…1…"

With Alacrity's defensive shields down, there was nothing to prevent the plasma bolts from delivering their full payload of energy directly into their target. The high-energy plasma, traveling at ¼c (.25 light speed) carried significant kinetic energy, despite the fact that the plasma itself had little mass.

The Alacrity quivered with the impact. Unlike the Celestia whose shields dissipated much of the kinetic energy of the impact, the Alacrity suffered a massive hull breach, collapsed bulkheads, sprung air-tight hatches, and that was just from the kinetic energy imparted from the impact. As atmosphere and debris trailed into space, the super-heated plasma melted its way through deck after deck, bulkhead after bulkhead like a torch eating its way through a block of ice. The impact destabilized Alacrity causing a free rotation. With no functioning attitude thrusters and no one left alive on the bridge, the Alacrity was adrift—at the mercy of gravity and inertia—her plasma batteries quiet.

Captain Lao: "Cease Fire!"

Kallehn had been monitoring the battle from the backup battle bridge during this time. After the cease-fire had been ordered, he made his way to the main bridge. As he walked through the main hatch to the bridge, he was already speaking.

Kallehn: "Highness, you will want a boarding party assembled. I am the obvious choice to lead it. The Mechs and all Imperial forces are under my command. Loyal Guardsmen will recognize that I am a Meld and Knight Commander by my Tattoos and uniform insignia."

Jar'ek's gut reaction was to reject the idea of putting Kallehn in such jeopardy. He started shaking his head, then stopped when he saw the determined look on Kallehn's face. Jar'ek inhaled and considered the realities of the situation. As the Meld and Emperor, he had a duty to Imperial subjects, and to the Pythanon's in particular. He did not know what had caused the mutiny aboard the Alacrity or why they had targeted his ship.

But he did know that no Pythanon would accept orders from a human who was not melded with Harmonic SEED, let alone trust them. Kallehn or Jar'ek must lead the boarding party to prevent any more loss of life. Only a Meld would command immediate obedience from the Guardsmen. And as much as he wanted to do this himself and protect Kallehn, he realized that Kallehn and the crew would see it as a lack of faith in Kallehn's command abilities. And that wasn't true at all. Jar'ek did respect and trust Kallehn. He was the right choice.

Jar'ek swallowed slowly and nodded. Kallehn's squared his shoulders and smiled with relief. He had expected an argument. Now, he needed to go to work—to prove himself.

Kallehn: "Celestia, Attend me!"

Celestia AI: "Attending, Lord Commander."

Kallehn: "Assemble a Phalanx of Mechs for boarding party action. Ready Assault Shuttle Castalon for immediate launch. Have the Phalanx set their weapons to high stun and bring breaching charges."

Celestia AI: "Acknowledged, Commander."

Kallehn: "Captain ... please alert Doctor To'Torat that we may have Pythanon casualties incoming shortly. She should prepare for that. "

Captain: "Aye, Lord Commander. I'll assign what crew we can spare to help out in sickbay, as well."

Kallehn: "And if it's okay with you, I'd like to take the XO with me." The Captain glanced at Commander Sallen whose face just burst into a giant grin. Though her expression never wavered, her heart skipped a beat. She turned back to face Kallehn and said: "With my blessing, Lord Commander."

Kallehn: "Thank you, Captain."

With that, Kallehn turned and saluted Jar'ek in the traditions of the old Empire. He took his right hand slapping the palm against his left pectoral and heart. As Jar'ek returned the sign of respect, Kallehn turned and trotted off towards the shuttle bay followed closely by a beaming Commander Yustin Sallen. Two sets of worried eyes followed the young men as they strode confidently off the bridge.

Imperial Gunship Alacrity—Jaden-325-4 Orbit

The Guardsman was the last surviving loyalists in the Alacrity's shuttle bay. He was injured. His left torso was covered in ash and blood from a blaster bolt that would soon prove fatal. It was hard to move—hard to breathe. But he could still fire his weapon, and he would do so as along as he could. He slowly crawled around a packing crate, favoring his left side and leaving a dark purple smear of a blood trail across the deck plates. He needed to reach a better firing position to prevent the mutineers from entering the only remaining intact assault shuttle. His orders were clear. Stop them, at all costs.

He could see the rear shuttle hatch, now. The ramp was lowering, and several mutineers were moving toward it. He raised his weapon to fire at what looked like an officer. But before he could press the firing stud, an armored boot stepped down on his wrist with crushing force, and he felt the barrel of an Imperial blaster placed on the back of his neck. That was the last thing he had felt before he died.

True Voice stood up and holstered his blaster. He felt numb. He had killed a number of loyal Pythanon Guardsmen and crew today. He felt grief for every single one. Even if by some wild chance, he completed his mission today and destroyed the False SEED...he doubted he could live with what had been required of him this day. He wanted to raise his own blaster to burn the memories of his actions from his skull. Only then would he feel peace again. But he had to suffer a bit longer. That choice was not open to him. He had one last duty left to perform.

He trotted forward to join the surviving mutineers. He gave them new orders. True Voice would pilot the shuttle alone. The others were to find hiding spaces within the Alacrity and wait. If True Voice failed, the False Meld would come to the Alacrity to review his troops. They may yet have a chance to execute this pretender and save the True Faith.

For a moment, doubt crept into the thoughts of True Voice. Could this be the True SEED? A new Emperor who would command their loyalty? True Voice shook his head and growled. This was WEAKNESS! He was a faithful member of the Brotherhood! He would not falter!

True Voice climbed the ramp into the shuttle and closed it behind him.

Imperial Destroyer Celestia—Jaden-325-4 Orbit

T.O. Sasha Conner: "Captain, something is separating from the hull of the Alacrity. There is a good bit of debris.... NO, it is Accelerating!"

Captain Lao: "Missile? Point Defense Weapons FREE!"

T.O. Sasha Conner: "No, ma'am. Too slow—more likely a shuttle."

Captain Lao glanced back at Jar'ek who just shook his head and said: "I don't know...survivors or boarding party..."

Captain Lao: "Celestia, warn off that Shuttle from approaching us. T.O. Conner, target them. I don't want to take any chances they might try to ram us. I'm not sure even our shields could withstand a head-on collision with an assault shuttle."

Hijacked Alacrity Assault Shuttle—Jaden-325-4 Orbit

True Voice set course directly for the Celestia. He began scanning surrounding space out of habit. With the destruction of Alacrity's weapons control systems, there was little chance his sacrifice would make a difference. The impact might just bring their shields down, but there was no way any of the remaining Brotherhood could wrest control of any plasma batteries away from those twice cursed Elite Guardsmen. True Voice spit in an attempt to clear some of the blood and ash from his mouth. Then he noticed something blinking on the sensor console. Another vessel—a shuttle from Celestia.

Was it possible that the Brotherhood might have one more chance to complete the mission? Could it be that True Voice himself had predicted this very event just moments ago as he gave instructions to the remainder of his men? Yes! The True SEED must have intervened somehow to improve their luck. If that shuttle carried the *Meld Pretender*—come to review his victorious Guardsmen... Then the Brotherhood might yet win the day!

True Voice moved his hands across the console and was pressed back into his control seat cushions as the acceleration grew. The hijacked assault shuttle veered onto a new course, and the engines went to maximum burn.

Imperial Destroyer Celestia—Jaden-325-4 Orbit

Celestia: "The shuttle has already changed course and is accelerating at maximum."

Captain Lao: "Course?"

Celestia: "It is on an intercept course for our shuttle, Castalon."

The Captain jerked up straight in her seat as Jar'ek leaped from his own, realization and dread molding both their faces into rigid caricatures.

The Captain looked to the tactical station and screamed:
"SASHA! DESTROY THAT SHUTTLE!"

Sasha Conner was young and had never fought a ship in battle, but he was well disciplined, and his training took over. He didn't even lift his eyes from the tactical console as he immediately slammed his palm down on the red flashing COMMIT button. The Celestia bucked as both her forward main batteries opened fire simultaneously. Enormous neon blue plasma salvos sped towards the aggressor shuttle at a high fraction of light speed, resembling two flaming blue comets burning a path across the heavens.

The Captain stood, then moved to stand beside Jar'ek. She looked up and saw the same fear and pain in his eyes she knew must be equally represented in her own. Was it her fault that the man she loved would die this way? She could have refused Kallehn's request. She knew that Jar'ek must be feeling the same guilt—reviewing everything he had said or done that lead to this point. If she had only been more vigilant, she hesitated. Would that slight hesitation cost her everything that was important to her?

The Terran Council had worked diligently for centuries to remove any vestiges of old Earth religions. But Kathy Xiang Lao knew her distant ancestors had prayed to immortal Gods to improve their fortunes. She didn't know the right prayers or even the names of the Gods they had worshiped, but she prayed to them now. She begged their forgiveness for her ignorance and prayed that her own life might be forfeit in trade for the man she loved—Yustin Sallen…

Assault Shuttle Castalon—Jaden-325-4 Orbit

Kallehn and Yustin Sallen were reviewing the design drawings of the Alacrity on the tactical consoles holographic display. As they were discussing the pros and cons for one docking port over another, a small red light began blinking on the tactical console. Then a horn sounded throughout the shuttle, startling both them. Just as Kallehn was reaching towards the helm controls, the shuttle AI locked the control board, activated their gravity web restraints and threw the shuttle into a corkscrew motion at maximum thrust.

Castalon AI: "COLLISION ALERT! Undertaking evasive action! Brace! Brace! Brace!"

Imperial Destroyer Celestia—Jaden-325-4 Orbit

Jar'ek watched tensely as the scene played out on the tactical tracking board shown on his personal ARDisplay. He zoomed in as far as possible, but the laws of physics limited the detail level. It took a finite amount of time for Lightspeed sensor beams to bounce back and the plasma salvos were traveling at a significant portion of lightspeed. The distance between the shuttles was closing fast! It was going to be CLOSE!

Jar'ek: "Plato, is there anything we're missing? Is there anything else we could do to help the Castalon avoid destruction??"

Plato: "No. Lightspeed limits all of our actions now. There is nothing we can do that will reach them in time. The Celestia is already accelerating towards a projected intercept point to mount Search and Rescue operations...that is the best we can do." But Jar'ek knew, if the Castalon were hit by either the hijacked shuttle or the plasma salvos, there would be nothing left larger than a dust mote, let alone survivors.

T.O. Sasha Conner: "Countdown for salvo impact....6....5....4...."

Jar'ek took Kathy Lao's hand in his and squeezed.

"...3....2....1....***IMPACT***!"

An actinic white light burst upon their displays and expanded in a perfect sphere from the point of impact. The explosion was so powerful that Celestia's sensors could see little else. Jar'ek's heart began to sink, his head falling forward until his chin touched his chest. He tasted something metallic and realized that he was biting his lip—his own blood the source.

The shuttles were so close when the explosion occurred that the sensors had trouble distinguishing them as separate objects. Even though Sasha was forced to use the primary batteries to ensure the attacker was stopped in time, Jar'ek now wondered if their very attempt to save the Castalon would be the cause of its destruction. A dark tide began to rise within Jar'ek—a wave fashioned of equal parts rage and despair. It felt as if the entire universe were conspiring against them, right now. Wasn't it enough that the Treech had found them again? The Dragon Eye destroyed—friends and colleagues killed—at odds with the Colonies—burdened with a dead or dying Empire—was it really necessary for him to lose Kallehn, too?! All the power of the SEED and an Empire and he could do nothing....It was ***too much***!

T.O. Conner: "***Captain***! Sensor recordings indicate the Castalon underwent evasive maneuvers just before impact!"

Captain Lao: "I want tachyon pulse sensor sweeps of the affected area, ***Now***! Damn protocol and Damn the cost to our equipment!"

T.O. Conner: "Aye, Captain! Commencing Tachyon Sensor Sweep." Conner reached out and tapped the sensor panel three times causing a tone to resonate throughout the bridge. The tachyons left their emitters and sped towards the point where the missing crewmembers lived and breathed only a moment ago.

Chapter 54—DESPERATE TIMES

Imperial Communications Probe—System Jaden-325-4

Probe AXZ-512548 had been biding its time. The message it carried was high priority traffic, but also highly sensitive. It had been ordered to remain cloaked until safely docked back in the Celestia's launch bay. The Celestia had successfully disabled the aggressor gunship—NOW was the time to make a short sprint for the loading dock and deliver a message that was vital to the future of the Empire. The probe engaged its gravitic-drive and maneuvered sharply towards the looming shape of the Celestia.

Imperial Destroyer Celestia—System Jaden-325

Tension filled the bridge like a dark fog—thickening to the point where it seemed difficult to breathe. Jar'ek stood, closing his eyes and consciously focusing his inhalations—then exhalations. The blood had drained from Captain Lao's face, and every muscle in her body was clenched tight as she watched the primary display for the results of the tachyon sensor scan. The entire bridge crew was so focused on the pending results from the tachyon returns, that they didn't even notice a blinking orange indicator light on the helm control panel.

A subdued tone accompanied the alert—a proximity warning. Celestia was about to respond when Comm Probe AXZ-512548 de-cloaked and sent a docking request signal. Celestia decided not to interrupt the bridge crew to notify them of the probe's return, under the current circumstances. Whatever information it carried could wait the short while for this to play out.

Another tone sounded, and the target area on the main display began to clear as the tachyon sensor returns dissolved away the static—the sensor static that had cruelly obscured the truth from them. Only one shuttle remained. And it's unpowered, corkscrew-course was a testimony to the catastrophic damage it had received.

Jar'ek: "Celestia, please identify that Shuttle!"

Celestia: "Working.... The shuttle transponder is not responding to queries—main power must be down. Attempting visual identification....

Captain Lao stood, jerkily. She stepped forward and leaned in towards the primary display with a countenance of deep concentration—as if by simply staring harder at the sensor returns, she might discern the name of the shuttle a milli-fraction faster than the Celestia's powerful computers could.

As Jar'ek walked up behind her and gently placed his hand on her shoulder, the captain visibly relaxed her stiffened muscles and straightened her back. When she glanced up at him, there was fear in her eyes, yes. But there was also gratitude for Jar'ek's quiet and gentle support. She noted the tension in his face and his eyes—the precursor to a deep grieving that lurked just below the surface. But there was also a faint ember of hope—an ember, only lacking the proper fuel, to burst into a conflagration.

Celestia: "Visual identification confirmed."

A holographic representation of the damaged and spinning shuttle appeared before them—and then froze. Scorch marks covered the front of the shuttle and portions of the hull had been crushed inward as if a giant hand had grabbed it and squeezed the armor plating like a man might crush a piece of fruit between his fingers. Barely discernable, on the starboard bow, were the Takeshi symbols for "C A S T A L..."

Jar'ek yelled: "***CASTALON***!"

Captain Lao's hand covered her mouth as she gasped and a single tear traced it way down her pale cheek—then another.

Jar'ek: "Celestia, how long until we can launch the Vehement for Rescue Operations?"

Celestia: "Less than five centi-fractions, Highness. But the Castalon's motion will need to be countered before rescue operations can commence. Docking tugs will launch in 4.7 centi-fractions."

The captain began striding towards the main bridge hatch as she spoke: "Celestia! Ask Dr. To'Torat to meet me in the shuttle bay, at once. I need two volunteers to join us and get geared up for EVA inside four centi-fractions."

She didn't even turn around to see if anyone from the bridge was following her. Every single member of the bridge crew jumped up and began running toward the hatch. Jar'ek reached out and put a hand on the Tactical Officer. T.O. Conner stared into Jar'ek's eyes with a stubborn glare and then felt shame when he realized why Jar'ek was going to go in his place.

Jar'ek: "Sasha, we need you here, on the bridge for now. I'm sorry. But someone has to stay, and I outrank you."

Conner: "Affirmative, Sir. But the captain will never let you climb into a space suit... she won't let you risk yourself."

Jar'ek grimaced as he said in a lowered voice: "We'll see about that." With that, he turned and moved at his best pace towards the shuttle, fanning that ember of hope until it flared like a supernova inside him.

Imperial Destroyer Celestia—Shuttle Bay

Jar'ek nearly fell over S'Fah and J'Uhr as he ran through the inner shuttle bay hatch. A jumble of mind-touch flooded his thoughts, stopping him in his tracks. The big X'Ah-Panths paced back and forth in front of and around Jar'ek, pinning him in place.

J'Uhr: {"Mind-touch shows you fear—for Kallehn! Kallehn where? Hurt? ***DEFEND***! ***PROTECT***!"}

S'Fah: {"You go, we go! Save Kallehn! ***TEAM***!"}

Jar'ek fell to one knee and embraced both of the X'Ah-Panths, pulling them into his chest, kissing them on their foreheads as he answered their mind-touch with his own: {"Yes, Kallehn is in danger. Shuttle damaged. No atmosphere. No EVA suits for X'Ah-Panths—you cannot go with me. Trust me. I will do everything possible to bring him home. Be patient fur-brother, fur-sister." Jar'ek gave them one last squeeze and moved quickly to the shuttle Vehement's rear loading ramp. The captain, Dr. To'Torat, Lt. De Lucena and Chief Vermanderly were all pulling on armored space suits as he arrived. The captain looked up at him and shook her head. "No, way, Your Highness! These are the last EVA suits, and none of us are giving one of ours up to enable the Emperor to risk his life on a search and rescue mission!" The other suited figures glanced at the captain and then nodded firmly.

Jar'ek looked sternly at the Captain, then spoke psionically to Plato: *{"Plato, the light armor uniform I wear will suffice for an emergency EVA suit, will it not?"}*

Plato: {"Affirmative, Sire. Depending on the level of activity, the breathable air supply will last for approximately eight deci-fractions (16 hours in old Earth terminology)."}

Jar'ek: {"That should be more than sufficient. But something puzzles me. Why aren't you trying to stop me from taking this risk?"}

Plato: {"I know your feelings on this matter, Highness. No amount of complaining or cajoling could change your mind. I doubt anything short of ordering a Mech to stun you would even slow you down. And in this case…I don't want to interfere. I do understand. Some things are worth a risk. Now quit chatting me up and get a move on! We have rescuing to do!"}

With that, Jar'ek slapped his palm on his left chest above his heart sending a psionic command to his uniform. His uniform collar seemed to extrude a clear, viscous liquid with a life of its own. As it grew in size, it moved up his neck and totally enclosed his head and face in a perfectly transparent material. Jar'ek felt an instant of panic, as the protective film covered his mouth and nose. But his extended memories clearly showed his precursors using the light armor in just this way, time and time again. He forced his heart to slow and continued breathing in a measured and deliberate way—overcoming his primal fears. Though there wasn't the tiniest bit of space between his body and this clear shield, it provided breathable air as if it wasn't even there. The same thing was happening at his wrists—his hands—the same protective material now covered them completely. Jar'ek flexed his fingers and hands—he couldn't tell it was even there, except for the slight glimmer one saw when gazing at his protected skin. He could still feel a slight breeze across his hand from the overhead air-handlers. He stopped his self-inspection and addressed the captain.

Jar'ek: "As you can see, Captain—I already have my own EVA protection. And unless one of you wants to try shooting me, I'd suggest you get out of my way."

Jar'ek walked through the small group of stunned shipmates and onto the Imperial Shuttle Vehement.

Imperial Shuttle Vehement—S.A.R. Mission

The Captain sat quietly beside Jar'ek as he expertly guided the Vehement slowly closer to the now immobile Castalon. The external lights played across the crumpled surface revealing a level of damage that seemed far greater than it had from a distance. A cold fist of dread clutched Jar'ek's heart and threatened to crush it—fueled by every imagined horror that could have, *must have*, afflicted the human occupants of such a wreck. Even if the shields had reduced the impact—even if the inertial compensators had reduced the G-forces until they failed—there was no way that the shuttle could hold atmosphere right now. How could anyone have survived in the complete vacuum that must have resulted?

Vehement had lowered the rear loading ramp, and Jar'ek led his shipmates to that gateway to the cold and unforgiving reaches of open space. As the captain was connecting tethers to everyone else, Jar'ek simply pushed off towards the wreck. Gentle nudges from the tiny gravitic-pulsejets embedded in his uniform adjusted his trajectory, and he made a soft landing near the cockpit access portal. The frame was obviously warped, and the bent portal wouldn't budge. The captain landed on the other side of the portal and lent her strength to the effort, but to no avail. Jar'ek drew his sidearm for the first time other than training and psionically adjusted the output to a fine cutting beam. The bright yellow beam was so thin that it was barely visible. But everywhere it touched glowed red and slagged almost immediately. It wasn't long before he and the Captain tugged on the exterior handles and sent the excised disk of warped metal spinning out into deep space, exposing the interior of the cockpit.

They had expected a horrific scene of frozen blood and bloated bodies. But what they saw confused them for a moment. Then Jar'ek spoke both psionically and verbally so that his uniform could transmit the conversation to the rest of the S.A.R. Team.

Jar'ek: "Mechs, Report!"

Mech 1: "Mech A2541—Whipple."

Mech 2: "Mech D5478—Braxton."

Whipple: "The Lord Commander and the Executive Officer have sustained serious injuries but are still alive. Our shields have been extended to provide a breathable atmosphere around them.

Jar'ek's expression darkened, and his heart skipped several beats as he pressed his gloved hands against the shield bubble and tried to make out if the two bodies floating weightless within were alive or simply drifting corpses. The impact shockwave that crushed the shuttle had lashed their frail human bodies with unimaginable G-forces. The extended Mech shields had kept them surrounded by breathable air, and had given them at least a chance of survival. But Jar'ek saw globules of blood floating around the two men and painting the inside of the shield in several places. The command chairs had been torn off their mounts and lay twisted on the deck. After the gravity-webbing had failed, the Mechs must have lifted them up and out of the twisted metal frames.

Braxton: "When Castalon began evasive maneuvers, he ordered us to use our personal battle shielding to protect the occupants of the cockpit in the event the hull was breached. This proved to be a wise strategy. It was, however, the last communication received from Castalon."

Jar'ek: "Keep your shielding in place and get them back aboard the Vehement with all haste."

The Mechs had to expand the opening cut in the hull by Jar'ek's blaster to accommodate the shield bubble and their bulk, as well. Braxton and Whipple reached out and grasped opposite sides of the hatch. Using their incredible strength, they pulled, rending armored hull and hatch alike as if they were pulling wet clay and molding it to their will. As soon the breach was just wide enough, the Mechs stepped through and carefully, but quickly, carried the two humans back to safety using the tethers strung by the S.A.R. team.

Jar'ek pulled the captain's space suit toward him and held her in a tight embrace. Through their visors, he could see her eyes were closed, and tears were streaming down her face. He felt her body as sobs wracked it. With their helmets touching for private communication, Choking back a sob of his own, Jar'ek said: "I know it looks bad, Kathy. But believe they are still alive. And we are going to do everything we can to keep them that way. Now, let's pull ourselves together and see if we can break an Imperial speed record getting them back to Celestia!"

Captain Lao nodded once firmly, took a deep breath and returned Jar'ek's embrace with a force that belied her small size. She didn't recall the trip back over the tethers or cutting them loose before Jar'ek left for the cockpit to begin their short journey back home. But once the Vehement was re-pressurized, she held Yustin Sallen's bruised and beaten head in her lap, washing the dried blood from his face with her tears as Dr. To'Torat and Lt. De Lucena worked furiously to revive them both.

Chapter 55—PERSEVERANCE

Imperial Destroyer Celestia—Medical Bay

If it weren't for Kira To'Torat's arm around her, Kathy Lao would have slid to the floor in a heap. She was exhausted. Both Kallehn and Yustin had massive internal injuries. The S.A.R. team had revived them to the point where their hearts were beating again—their lungs filled with air without assistance. But it had been touch-and-go for the last 24 hours. Jar'ek had used the healing rituals on them several times, each. While she was exhausted, Jar'ek was utterly drained. He lay next to Kallehn's side in a sleeping bag, having collapsed right there, after performing the last ritual. J'Uhr and S'Fah lay on either side of him like furry pillows, using the heat of their bodies to keep him warm.

The Imperial nanites and life energy Jar'ek had infused into their injured bodies were having an effect. The worst was over, now. Only time would tell. They were both in a deep coma. If they woke up, they would recover. If not....

Imperial Destroyer Celestia—Medical Bay

Kathy spent every spare moment sitting next to Yustin's bed in Med-Bay. But she had a duty to the ship and the crew. With Celestia's help, she had sent a message to the Alacrity assuring them that the Emperor still lived and was unharmed and suggesting they delay any further meetings until the Lord Commander was out of danger.

Jar'ek: "Captain, once the surviving members of the Mech Phalanx have evacuated to the Vehement, I'd like to see if one more survivor remains for us to rescue."

The captain stared blankly at Jar'ek for a moment."

Jar'ek: "I am hoping that Castalon's memory core survived and is salvageable. Imperial AIs are self-aware. Castalon could have ordered the Mechs to protect its memory core—the essence of his own existence, but it didn't have time to protect its human passengers and itself. It sacrificed its own *life* to save the two people we care most about in this galaxy. I think it deserves our gratitude."

Captain Lao smiled and nodded sharply. "So do I, Your Highness! I would like to send Chief Vermandly and Sasha Conner to see if Castalon can be salvaged. And I think Whipple and Braxton could be of some assistance if you don't mind parting with them for a few hours."

Jar'ek smiled and said: "Permission Granted."

Imperial Destroyer Celestia—Medical Bay

Kallehn felt pain—throbbing pain—it seemed like everything hurt. He was so fatigued. He didn't want to wake up—his eyes felt like they were covered by sandbags—heavy—sluggish. But his throat was dry, and he needed an analgesic or something!

He opened his eyes slowly, blinking the sleep from his eyes. He raised his hand to his face and noticed he had tubes coming out of his wrist. That didn't seem right. He wasn't supposed to have plastic tubes coming out of his arm. Where was he? How did he get here?

Kallehn's heart rate rose along with his blood pressure in his confused, semi-conscious state. But then he felt a warm, furred muzzle under his hand and an enormous wet tongue sprang out from it and began licking hand, wrist, arm—anything it could reach. A deep baritone vibration percolated from that furry saliva machine, seemingly shaking the world around him. Kallehn's heart calmed, his breathing became more regular. He felt a gentle, welcoming mind-touch, caressing him in the psionic equivalent of a warm, wet tongue. Slowly, the mental fog began to clear. Feelings and emotions flowed through the mind-touch.

{"—Relief—Welcome—Deep Affection—Worry—Joy—End to Solitude—"}

Kallehn spoke in a husky, scratchy whisper from his dry throat: "I love you too, Girl...Where is Jar'ek? How long have I been here?"

J'Uhr turned her head to direct his attention just over the side of the bed. There, Kallehn saw a sleeping bag and the other two members of his Team sound asleep.

J'Uhr: {"Sunrise, Sunset, 4 times. Team by your side. Eat, Sleep, Watch. Jar'ek not even leave for fresher... HE STINKS!"}

Kallehn smiled and chuckled to himself just before drifting off to sleep once more. But this time it was just normal sleep. He would wake again soon. And his team would be whole once more.

Chapter 56—CONSEQUENCES

Imperial Destroyer Celestia—Jaden-325-4—Orbit

Kathy Lao lay awake, but well rested in her quarters. Beside her lay the naked form of her lover and Executive Officer, Yustin Sallen. She hadn't moved in quite some time—just watching him breathe as he slept. She moved her hand to rest on his bare pectorals, ever so slowly, gently, so as not to wake him. She felt his heart beating, his chest rising and falling with each breath. Her fingers gently brushed the fine blonde hairs that marked the outer boundaries of his areola.

She took time to stare methodically at his face, his arm, his chest and stomach—his entire body.

She wanted to memorize every small detail—the way his nostrils flared slightly when he exhaled—the curve of his mouth at rest—the tiny mole behind his ear and the persistent cowlick just above his left temple that only showed itself when he hadn't had time for a trim. She smiled.

Then she looked again at the mottled covering of angry purple, gold and black bruises that covered his side, abdomen, both legs, arms and part of his face. He was lucky to have survived. They were both lucky, because she knew surely as any human thrust unprotected into the cold vacuum of space, that she would wither and die without Yustin Sallen. He was the air she breathed.

He was recovering nicely. Kira To'Torat had released him from the Med-bay two days ago with strict orders that he was to rest for a full week—he was relieved of all duties. It had been a hard thing for him, but Kathy had insisted that he follow the Doctor's orders to the letter. She had even ordered Celestia to revoke his access to ship except for her quarters, med-bay, the mess hall, and the recreation center. Five more days and he could return to limited duty.

Jar'ek had let her know that Kallehn was recovering well and might beat the XO back to duty by a couple of days. His light armor had helped protect him. She wished her crew had the same protections in their uniforms. Jar'ek was looking into that, but Plato had been stubbornly rejecting the idea of releasing certain technologies to the crew. She could see his point. Even though the entire crew had signed on to duty aboard the Celestia and respected the chain of command, they had not yet gone that extra step in foreswearing allegiance to the Terran Colonies, and swearing fealty to the Emperor. Truth be told, she wasn't confident that any of them were quite ready for that. She still held out a small hope that her crew might be able to return home if they wanted to. She feared it was just wishful thinking, but hope springs eternal, after all.

She moved the covers aside quietly and carefully slid off her side of the bed. She looked back over her shoulder at Yustin—she didn't want to leave him. But duty was a relentless taskmaster. She cleaned up and began the process of getting into her dress uniform. Today was the day they would finally meet with the Guardsman who now commanded the Alacrity. She wanted an accounting for happened to Yustin and Kallehn. She wanted ***someone*** to ***pay***. Kathy was ***angry***. And as she strapped on her sidearm, she reflected—she could be one dangerous human female when she was angry.

Imperial Destroyer Celestia—Jaden-325-4—Orbit

Celestia: "Captain on the Bridge!"

Captain Kathy Xiang Lao strode confidently onto her command deck and moved to take her regular position in the Command Chair. It wasn't often that her crew had seen her in her Class A dress uniform with medals and ribbons in place. Her midnight blue jacket and slacks were accented with gold braid and the crimson sleeve stripes of a Senior Captain in the TCDF.

Her scarlet beret emblazoned with the crossed swords of a warship commander. Her white arms belt held her standard issue laser sidearm and the ceremonial short sword. Ceremonial it might be, but several of her crew had seen her training with it in mixed martial arts. And they had a healthy respect for the damage she could do with it.

Captain Lao: "As you were."

Just then, the "Shuuunk, Shuuunk, Shuuunk" marching sounds of his Mech protection detail alerted the bridge crew that Jar'ek was making his own way to the command deck. They remained standing and were joined by the Captain as they all faced the main hatch, snapping to attention as he entered with S'Fah at his side.

Jar'ek: "As you were, and thank you."

The Captain strode to greet Jar'ek and grasped his offered hand. Jar'ek's grip tightened, and his other hand reached out to steady her as S'Fah's affectionate headbutt to her midsection knocked her petite frame off balance. Kathy smiled, released Jar'ek's hand and knelt down to look into the big cat's eyes while she rubbed his cheeks and neck vigorously. "And greetings to you, too, my furry friend!"

Making her way to her feet once more, the Captain returned her gaze to Jar'ek and said: "How ***is*** Kallehn doing?"

Jar'ek: "Fighting tooth and nail to get back to duty! He is making a nuisance of himself. I'm just glad he is recovering so quickly. I was really worried we had lost both of them. How is Yustin?"

Captain: "Yustin and Kallehn seem to be cut from the same cloth. I had to restrict him to quarters until he promised to be good. He is still very fatigued but is recovering nicely. What of Castalon, Highness?"

Jar'ek: "Celestia is still working on recovering Castalon's system files and storage. There was a lot of damage. We still don't know if we can save him. But we haven't given up hope."

Captain: "Jar'ek, there is something else I want to discuss with you." She pulled him aside into a vacant corner of the command deck as she spoke.

Jar'ek: "What is it, Kathy?"

Captain: "I've been doing some research on protocol with Celestia's help. It is up to you and Plato, but it seems to me there may be some advantages in using your military title instead of your civilian title under the current circumstances."

Jar'ek: "I'd go without ANY titles if Plato would allow it. But what does it matter which title I use?"

Captain: "It could matter a great deal. The Empire has been without leadership for a long time. There has been a mutiny aboard the Alacrity. The intelligence packet sent to us by Elite Guard Commander Golgaht indicated that there might be an underground insurgency based on a radical cult. I don't need to remind you how Pythanons pride themselves on their undying loyalty to the Empire and the Royal Family. Pythanon itself may be on the verge of civil war. I believe there will be significant advantages to demonstrating a clear chain of command to their legitimate leader. It isn't unprecedented for a Meld to take on the role of Fleet Admiral while still on active service as the Emperor. It would also make things a bit easier when we eventually interact with the TCDF."

Plato: {"She's a smart one, this Kathy Lao. I can see why you hold her in such high esteem. And she is quite correct. There are serious advantages to this approach. I recommend you follow her guidance in this matter."}

Jar'ek: "Plato seems to like the way you think, Kathy. Okay, I see the value. Is this going to be confusing for our shipmates?"

Captain: "Probably the opposite. They are quite comfortable with naval ranks and chains of command. But you will have to play the part… and ***DRESS*** the part."

Jar'ek: "Well, dressing the part won't be a problem." Jar'ek touched his left shoulder with his right hand and after a moment of reviewing extended memories, issued a thought-command to his uniform to reconfigure his appearance to match his new role. Gold and platinum epaulets grew from the both shoulders, and a wide gold band appeared at each wrist.

Captain Lao reached behind her Captain's chair and pulled out a beret similar to hers in all respect except it was black with gold filigree. She placed it carefully on Jar'ek's head, stood back and saluted him.

Captain: "Admiral on deck!"

Once again, the bridge crew snapped to attention and saluted. Jar'ek blushed, but returned the salute with precision.

Jar'ek addressed the bridge crew: "I know this might be awkward for some of you. I assure you, it is no less awkward for me! But I thank you for your support, and I promise to fulfill my duties to all of you and the rest of the Human Race as we embark on the first steps of rebuilding the Harmonic Empire. I hope that one day soon, all of you will feel as I do, and join me in working towards building something better for all peaceful sentients that might make up the current and future Empire. As you were.

His shipmates began talking amongst themselves but eventually made their way over to congratulate Jar'ek on his simultaneous demotion and promotion. Jar'ek was surprised that his shipmates seemed more at ease with him now. Was a simple change of title, role, and uniform that significant in how people perceived him? They had known him for years before this. It didn't seem entirely rational.

Plato: {"Your Captain Xiang Lao is wise, indeed! In addition to being an excellent officer, she is a master politician. You would do well to keep her by your side. She will be a powerful ally."}

Celestia: "The Alacrity Shuttle R'hakt Claw is inbound to Shuttle

Bay and requesting docking clearance."

Captain: "Signal they are clear to dock. Open outer bay doors. Alert the Mech security detail."

Celestia: "Confirmed, Captain. And the security detail stands ready."

The captain stood and gestured toward the main bridge hatch.

Captain: "Admirals, first."

Jar'ek sighed heavily and took the lead in as dignified a way as he could muster.

Imperial Destroyer Celestia—Shuttle Bay

A full Phalanx of Mechs lined the walls of the Shuttle Bay. The other Phalanx stood at attention in lines that defined a corridor between the newly docked Shuttle R'hakt Claw and the welcoming committee made up of Jar'ek, Captain Lao, and Dr. To'Torat. The lines of Mechs were intended to act as an honor guard, but they were, in fact, there to provide security for the Emperor Admiral and his staff. It wasn't clear if all of the insurrectionists had been ferreted out and Jar'ek wasn't taking any unnecessary chances. The Mechs were armed with blaster rifles, and Whipple and Braxton had taken up positions behind Jar'ek and extended their battle shields around his party, just in case.

One last uninvited member joined the party late. Jar'ek looked down with a warm smile, and the familiar feeling of S'Fah's muscular shoulders rubbed against his hand until it rested on his furred back—gripping the scruff and caressing his long-time companion. The Mechs could react quickly, but S'Fah and his kind had keen instincts and an impressive array of senses that could be very useful in detecting anyone who had malicious intent. And there was no way S'Fah would allow his mind-mate to go into danger without him if he could help it.

A persistent humming sound filled the shuttle bay as the shuttle lowered its rear boarding ramp. With a final thump, as the ramp touched the Celestia's deck plates, Jar'ek nodded at the Captain.

Captain Lao: "Celestia, Render Honors if you please."

The Takeshi version of bosun's pipes sounded hauntingly in the vast empty space. The Mech honor guard came to attention with the accompaniment of a loud "Boooommm" as all those cerametallic feet thudded to the floor in unison. Then Celestia's voice was heard announcing their guest and his party over the PA system: "Alacrity Arriving."

Despite having been prepared with simulations showing Pythanon warriors, Dr. To'Torat gasped at her first sight of Elite Guard Commander Golgaht, as he rounded the corner, with his party. He was a good six hands taller than the most towering Terran in their party! With his pointed ears and furred snout, she couldn't help noticing a striking similarity to Terran wolves. Their uniforms were the same light armor type that Jar'ek and Kallehn wore. An epaulet with red and gold braid covered Golghat's left shoulder. His left chest carried numerous battle ribbons and more than a few commendations for valor. Jar'ek wondered what kind of campaigns or conflicts the Imperial Elite Guard had been involved in since the quarantine. He was betting that would be an interesting story. But where his sidearm should have been was an empty holster—a testament to his understanding of the damage done to the long tradition of trust between all Pythanons and the Royal Family.

It didn't go unnoticed that every Pythanon had suffered some injury. The Pythanons were proud and did their best not to acknowledge pain. But there were various clues if one watched closely. Retaking the Alacrity had been a bloody business and one filled with the horrors of killing one's own shipmates in battle. And though the Guardsmen stood tall with pride, the slow pace at which they progressed along the honor guard revealed the deep shame and dishonor they must feel at this moment. The Pythanons had protected the Empire and the Royal Family for generations uncounted. There had never before been a hint of disloyalty or dishonor. But now, an Imperial Warship had fired on the Emperor's ship, and mutineers had attempted to ram Castalon in a wild attempt at destroying the Meld.

Ten paces in front of the Jar'ek and his party, Golgaht and his entourage came to a stop and dropped to one knee, bending their heads low. Jar'ek stepped forward and spoke the ritual greeting to a subordinate in Takeshi.

Jar'ek: "Zhum'tik K'hasht Fasalhat, Golgaht" and in Terran Standard: "Through Honor, there is Life, Golgaht."

Golgaht was silent for a moment until Jar'ek wondered if the language had changed enough in 2,000 years that he didn't understand. But then Golgaht spoke in faltering Terran: "If that is true, then you must surely kill us all, Highness. For never in more than 300 generations have Pythanon Guardsmen failed the Empire in such a spectacular way. Our lives must be forfeit, if for no other reason, that I have been unable to prove without a doubt that the rest of Alacrity's crew is loyal to you. Also, through my incompetence, I was responsible for the death of Ship's Commander Chur Kulahn and his entire command staff.

I was unable to prevent the insult from our secondary batteries reaching out for your ship. And I was also unable to stop the hijacking of the assault shuttle that was used to attack your shuttle Castalon. This shame is ***unbearable***, Sire! I beg you, return us to Alacrity and order its destruction. We will submit to your justice, gladly!

Jar'ek did not speak for several moments while he consulted Plato.

Jar'ek: {"Plato, there is no way I'm ordering the murder of all of those loyal guardsmen and crew just to be sure we got the mutineers. Help me out here. I sense that that Golgaht has his heart set on me killing him, at the very least. I need them all! And I need them motivated, loyal and proud. How the heck can I do that?""

Plato: {"Pythanons have always had a morbid fascination with ritual suicide. Hmmmm…I'd suggest you play to his guilt and sense of duty and of honor. No Pythanon could resist a stew made with those three ingredients!"}

Jar'ek: {"I think I understand what you mean…but I may need Celestia's help in creating some theatrics to bring the point home."}

Plato: {"Oooohhh! I like the way you are thinking! This could be entertaining…"}

Jar'ek: {"Celestia, Attend me."}

Celestia: {"Attending, Highness."}

Jar'ek: {"Celestia, here's what I need you to do…"}

Imperial Destroyer Celestia—Shuttle Bay

Jar'ek strode forward until he was half a pace from the kneeling Guardsmen. S'Fah had moved with him in lockstep and now extended his muzzle to sniff carefully at the kneeling bipedal wolf before him. The X'Ah-Panth seemed satisfied that he posed no immediate danger and sat back on his haunches.

Jar'ek stood with feet planted firmly, shoulder width apart and raised his arms spread wide, palms up towards the compartment ceiling. When he began to speak, his voice was augmented with the public-address system and reverberated around the shuttle bay, bringing a look of surprise from Kathy and Kira.

Jar'ek spoke the ancient words of ritual: "Vishluht – Kah'tash — Almatesh — Q'blahant!" (Stand and be judged for your crimes against the Empire!) As he spoke those words in Takeshi, a blue glow spread from his tattoo, down his arms and extended from his fingertips. Jar'ek swung both arms up sharply until his palms met in a loud clap. Thunder rolled through the shuttle bay and shook the deck plates. Behind Jar'ek the blue Takesh Avatar for Celestia appeared. But this time, it was three times the height of any Pythanon warrior, and it was ***angry***.

The entire Pythanon delegation gaped up at the apparition and then scrambled to their feet; heads bowed low on their chests. Jar'ek's voice boomed: "Celestia, read the list of charges for the accused."

Celestia's oversized avatar spoke in Terran Standard, its voice just as overpowering: "The accused, Golgaht, Elite Guard Commander is charged as follows: 1. In a display of extreme incompetence, the Guard Commander allowed a mutiny under his very snout. 2. Said rebellion resulted in significant loss of life and Imperial Assets, including the lives of the entire command staff of the Warship Alacrity. 3. Through gross dereliction of duty, said officer also allowed a single mutineer to steal an assault shuttle and use it to attack a vessel carrying a Meld of the Harmonic SEED resulting in serious injury to said Meld and the Celestia's Terran Executive Officer. 4. Said officer has through continued incompetence been unable to root out the rest of the mutineers on Alacrity with any degree of confidence."

Jar'ek: "Golgaht, has any misdeed been left out of this reading of charges?"

Golgaht, still staring down at the deck plates said in a small voice: "No, Highness. The charges are accurate in all specifications."

Jar'ek: "Why, I believe you requested permission to commit an even graver offense against the Empire, just a moment ago!"

Golgaht's snout jerked up so that he could look directly into his Emperor's eyes, startled he said: "Highness, I beg your indulgence, but I do not understand what you speak of."

Jar'ek: "What were Alacrity's orders when you left for this system?"

Golgaht: "To make all haste to transit to this star system. To render aid and protection until relieved by greater forces."

Jar'ek: "And have you accomplished your mission?"

Golgaht lowering his head once more: "No, Highness. I have failed."

Jar'ek: "Yet, you petition me for a quick death for you and your surviving crew, do you not?! How can the Empire not see this as ***DERELICTION of Duty***??! How can it not be considered ***DESERTION*** in the face of adversity!?"

Again, Golgaht and his entire delegation gaped in utter surprise, at Jar'ek and the menacing Avatar behind him. They must think him mad... yet, was the logic escapable??

Jar'ek: "Celestia, what is our judgment ?"

The giant avatar boomed: "***G U I L T Y !***"

Golgaht looked as if his eyes were about to pop out of his head and one of the older members of his delegation looked as if they were about to pass out. Surely, the Emperor wouldn't sentence them to a long, slow death of torture…it was his right….

Celestia Avatar: "No quick death for you, or your guardsmen, Golgaht!" Sweat broke out on Golgaht's forehead, and he began to pant. His greatest fears began flashing before his eyes…

Jar'ek held his hand out towards Captain Lao and said: "Captain! Give me your sidearm!"

Kathy Lao glanced at Kira To'Torat as a cloud of dread moved across her features that matched her own expression. She turned back and looked directly into Jar'ek's eyes, expecting to see anger reflected there. But there was no anger, only calm assurance. The captain reflected for a moment and then unholstered her weapon and handed it butt first to her Admiral. Jar'ek took the deadly firearm and examined it. It was same deadly sidearm he carried with a few design differences. It had a manual power slider instead of a psionic interface created for the Terrans and other non-psionic soldiers. And the maximum firepower was limited to something more appropriate for everyday use by guardsmen.

Jar'ek turned to face Golghat.

Jar'ek: "And the only possible sentence for such charges?"

Jar'ek began to slowly extend the arm that held the captain's blaster towards Golghat. And Golghat breathed a sigh of relief. The new Emperor and Admiral might be merciful after all and provide him with a quick, honorable death. He could ask for nothing better—his wife and cubs would miss him, no doubt. But this was for the best. But something was wrong with the way the Admiral was aiming the weapon. He wasn't aiming it at all.

Celestia Avatar: "No, you and your guardsmen are sentenced to life-long service to the Empire. You must earn redemption by fulfilling your mission. You must prove your worthiness through action. You must wash the stain from your honor with bravery and faithfulness. No…no quick and easy death for such as ***YOU***! A much worse fate awaits you…you and your guardsmen will become the Emperor's Personal Guard."

Jar'ek completed the movement of his right arm, handing the captain's sidearm to Golghat, butt first.

Captain Lao and Dr. To'Torat visibly relaxed. What they thought was going to be an execution, was a gesture of redemption and trust. The captain squared her shoulders and gazed at Jar'ek with a new appreciation. This young man had grown into quite a natural leader—a leader she could follow proudly. She couldn't speak for the rest of the crew, but her decision was made.

Jar'ek: {"Celestia, you don't think you laid it on a bit thick regarding it being such a punishment serving under me, are you???"}

Celestia: {"Artistic license, Highness. I was just drawing upon my personal experience."}

Plato burst out in the psionic equivalent of raucous laughter.

Chapter 57—INQUISITORS

Imperial Destroyer Celestia—Jaden-325-4—Orbit

Jar'ek: {"Celestia, Attend me"}

Celestia: {"Attending, Highness"}

Jar'ek: {"Is Kallehn awake, yet? Does he appear well?"}

Celestia: {"Affirmative, Highness. He woke not long after you left your quarters. Biometric sensors indicate he has returned to near normal, if still a bit fatigued. Dr. To'Torat saw him this morning and has approved his return to limited duty as of today."}

Jar'ek: {"Excellent! Thank you, please connect us over our armor's psionic links."}

Celestia: {"Connection complete."}
Jar'ek: {"Good morning, Kallehn. I hear you've been released from your medical prison…"}

Kallehn: {"Yes, Sir! And I am ready for something to do. Have any Supernovas you need to be wrangled?"}

Jar'ek: {"Errr…not exactly. But I do need you to participate in some planning. Can you meet Golgaht and me in the Command Deck Conference Room in five centifractions? Full Dress Uniform."}

Imperial Destroyer Celestia—Admiral's Quarters

Kallehn paused for a moment and then responded: {"On my way."} Kallehn slowly slid his hand over left shoulder and chest, revealing the changes the embedded nanites made to the appearance of the armor. Silver braided epaulet and the glyphs over his heart indicating his rank as Knight Lord Commander. Kallehn shook his head at the mixed feelings of embarrassment and pride, he felt wearing such markings. His extended memories had shown him the bravery and integrity shared by those *predecessors who had worn these very same emblems in the distant past. He felt shame that he had done nothing to deserve these symbols of such honor.*

*Atlas: {"Not True! You **ARE** young, and new to this role. And the burden you carry is a heavy one. It is normal to feel you are inadequate to do all that must be done. But you **are** a Meld. You hold this authority by virtue of who you are right now. Still, I believe in you, Kallehn Frix! You have great promise. And I have no doubt that your achievements will outshine those of all who came before you. What's more, your Emperor believes in you with unmitigated fervor. I, for one, trust his judgment…"}*

Kallehn stood a little straighter, adjusted his light armor dress uniform, inhaled slowly and exhaled. *{"Thanks, Atlas. I needed that. Let's go help Jar'ek build an Empire from space dust!"}*

Imperial Destroyer Celestia—Forward Conference Room

Jar'ek paced back and forth, looking down at his feet and then raised his gaze back to Kallehn, Golgaht and his adjutant, Guard Captain Frajmaht—who had all been sitting patiently while their Admiral had been allowing his thoughts to coalesce: "As you know, Kallehn is my Knight Lord Commandor. And as such, has direct command over all imperial military assets. His authority is only second to mine. When Kallehn speaks, he speaks in my name." The two Pythanon's bowed in somber recognition of Kallehn's presence and authority.

Jar'ek continued: "But, I stand before you as not only your Emperor but as the Imperial Fleet Admiral. I wear this standard so that you will understand that I am not ***that*** Emperor who would stand above the fray and issue proclamations. I will lead the new Empire directly. And you will address me and, see me as your Fleet Admiral first and, your Emperor second. I believe this to be necessary for the Empire's survival. Is that understood?"

Golgaht: "I will follow your orders without question, Highness…***Admiral***. But I cannot claim to understand your wishes."

Jar'ek: "That will be sufficient for the time being. I only want to make it clear to all Imperial Assets that the Emperor sits at the top of the chain of command, not outside of it. There has been no Meld to lead the Empire for 2,000 SSOs. Some of our subjects may have become accustomed to the current status quo. There must be no doubt where authority lies in the Empire, for even one moment more. Now, I want to inspect the surviving crew onboard the Alacrity. It is my belief that they must all see that the Meld is real and lives, as soon as possible. It is not only an expedient way to end any confusion but these, our Guardsmen, have sacrificed much and deserve to receive my personal thanks."

Golgaht sat across the conference room table flicking his ears—the Pythanon equivalent of shaking his head.

Golgaht: "Lord Fleet Admiral, we have not yet devised a way to guarantee the loyalty of the remaining crew aboard the Alacrity. We must wait for the Alexicon to arrive with reinforcements."

Jar'ek: "And what makes you think the guardsmen and crew coming on the Alexicon will not have been infiltrated with more of the Brotherhood? "

Golgaht: "It is my hope that my superiors will be wiser and have an answer to this dilemma."

Jar'ek spoke privately with Plato: {"Plato, any suggestions?"}

Plato: {"I was afraid you were going to ask me. I have only one suggestion and hesitate to suggest it. It is onerous to the Melds."}

Jar'ek: {"Well, you have my full attention, now."}

Plato: {"Query your extended memories regarding Inquisitor Nanites."}

Jar'ek did as Plato asked. He saw and felt what happened when the Inquisitors were used. It wasn't pleasant. The inquisitors infiltrated the subject's nervous system and looked for even the slightest signs of deception and delivered unbearable jolts of pain to the pain centers of the brain. Over time, the pain centers became even more sensitive—if the subject persisted in deceptive behavior or responses, the pain increased to the point where death was possible. Never before had the Inquisitors been used to test the veracity of any Pythanon. It was inconceivable that a Pythanon could ever be anything but loyal to the Empire. But now, things had changed.

Jar'ek: "Golgaht, I must ask a further act of penance from you and your crew. I do not ask this lightly. But I ***MUST*** ask it of you all. Will you submit to the Inquisitors?"

Golgaht's skin and mucous membranes around his nose, ears, and eyes, where it was not hidden by fur, noticeably lost their color and faded to a pale gray. In his eyes showed the pain and humiliation, he felt at being asked this question. But he looked directly into his Emperor's eyes and clicked his teeth together twice, hard—an emphatic "YES!"

Jar'ek: "I am sorry I must subject you to this further humiliation, Golgaht. Let us hope that all under your command are as loyal and honest as I trust they will be. Otherwise, it is best we find out now, regardless of the cost. Perhaps the founders of the Terran colonies were wise in their decision to ban organized religion. Religion can be a powerful tool for deception, manipulation, and oppression. I would think that most of the insurgents have been duped and-and manipulated in just such a way. This was a widespread practice on old Earth. It was the source of much conflict and violence on the Terran home planet. Only by shining the light of Truth on this false religion can the Empire prevail."

Jar'ek continued: "We will start with the Pythanon delegation onboard Celestia. Then we will order your men to attend me in small groups until we have sufficient numbers to provide adequate security for our inspection of the Alacrity. The rest of the crew can be isolated and tested until this distasteful matter has been settled. I hope, in time, the Guard can find a way to forgive me for this regrettable, if necessary insult to Pythanon honor and pride."

Golgaht: "Admiral, would it not be expedient to bring a phalanx of Mechs to augment your personal guard during your inspection? Mechs cannot be manipulated or corrupted..."

Jar'ek glanced over to Kallehn and their eyes locked. Jar'ek sensed that they were of one mind in this matter. Kallehn, for his part, recognized the deep compassion in Jar'ek's eyes and understood what Jar'ek wanted to say. Jar'ek nodded, and Kallehn answered Golgaht's question

Kallehn: "Since the beginning of Imperial Rule, no Mech has ever been used in the personal guard of the Emperor. Until contact was reestablished with Pythanon, the Emperor was left with no choice but to use Mechs for such duty. That time has passed. If the Emperor did not place his trust in Pythanons to protect him, it would create a schism of trust—of faith. The Pythanons have served the Empire with honor, and with blood for millennia. The Emperor, ***and I*** believe that the current situation is an anomaly caused by the long absence of a Meld. We will not abandon our Pythanon brothers and sisters in this time of crisis. He must take a small risk to show all that his faith in the Guardsmen will never waiver."

Both Pythanons in the room raised their snouts and roared as their emotions overcame them.

"Golgaht, will you be the first to submit to the Inquisitor Nanites?"

Golgaht clicked jaws twice again, then moved to kneel before Jar'ek. Plato had provided the relevant procedures for producing and releasing the Inquisitor Nanites a moment before. The Inquisitors were one of the Restricted Technologies of the Empire. To enable this ability in a new Meld, another ***ritual*** was required, lest this ability fall into the hands of an unintended recipient of the SEED without benefit of ***Judgment***.

Once again, Jar'ek brought his hands together over his head and spoke the ancient words—drew the complex glyphs in an orange mist. Jar'ek reflected that less sophisticated civilizations might consider this a magical incantation. In fact, many of the Terran Colonist would assume as much.

Jar'ek: "Sish'Tak — Frahakti — Pushishu"

Translation: ("Release the Inquisition")

Jar'ek touched his right hand to Golghat's forecrest and a subdued blue light moved from his face, tracing the tattoos until they moved from his fingertips and spread like water over Golghat's entire body. The Pythanon stiffened involuntarily as the nanites began to infiltrate his nervous system. He knew of the nanites from Imperial history, but knowing of such a thing and experiencing it were entirely different.

Jar'ek removed his hand from Golghat's forecrest and took a step back.

Jar'ek: "Golghat, Elite Guard Commander, Trusted Protector. Are you ready for the Inquisition?"

With head still bowed, kneeling on one Knee, Golghat produced two rapid and loud jaw-clicks.

Jar'ek: "Answer truthfully in all things—hide nothing. The inquisitors do not differentiate between relevant and irrelevant deception."

Jar'ek began the questioning: "Do you believe that I am a Meld of the Harmonic SEED?

Golgaht clicked his jaws twice, without hesitation.

Jar'ek: "Are you a member of the Brotherhood?"

Golgaht: "No, Highness!"

Jar'ek: "Will you honor your duty as Imperial Protector?"

Golgaht again clicked his jaws twice in quick succession.

Jar'ek: "Do you have sympathies for the Brotherhood or anyone you suspect of being a member?"

Golgath began to answer in the negative with a flutter of his ears when he suddenly began writhing in pain and fell to the floor. Guard Captain Frajmaht jumped back with a look of disbelief on his face and reached for his sidearm.

Jar'ek raised his hand to stop and yelled: "HOLD!"

Jar'ek kneeled beside the proud Elite Guard Commander as he writhed on the ground and drooled frothy purple blood from where he bit through his own lip. Jar'ek looked deeply into the Pythanon's pain filled eyes and spoke gently. "Golgaht, you must speak the whole truth, even if you doubt your own feeling in this matter. Subconscious or conscious, self-deception will be punished by the Inquisitors. I cannot prevent your pain. I wish I could change it, but I cannot. Together, we must find what conflict is in your heart, and you must speak it, now. The inquisitors are relentless in their search for the truth."

The struggling seemed to subside a bit, and Golgaht swallowed slowly. When he spoke, there was a growl deep in his shuddering voice—a groan of pain that was not only physical but also emotional.

Golgaht: "Highness, I meant no deception! I have had no prior knowledge of the insurrection. But I have had to fight and kill many good Guardsmen who have been seduced by the false profits of the Brotherhood. And upon reflection, I fear that my own son may have some covert connection to the Order, as well. He is very young and has just entered his first term in the Guard Academy. I have no evidence of his involvement! But Officer 5th Zik'Ruthat was his mentor and his patron for acceptance to the Imperial Academy. I fear he may have had undue influence on my young idealist son. I beg you do not punish him for sins he has yet to commit, Highness."

Jar'ek: "I am sorry this caused you pain, my friend. There will be much of this kind of pain as the Inquisition continues. But trust in me, Golgaht, as I trust in you. I am an unwilling ruler, but I will rule from compassion, not vengefulness. No one will be punished for falling prey to false profits."

Jar'ek extended his hand and helped Golgaht back to an upright position, then stood.

Jar'ek continued: "Golgaht, would you protect your Emperor and the Empire from harm even if it cost you the life of your son—your whole family—your own life?"

Golgaht raised his snout and Jar'ek saw the mix pain and determination in his eyes when he spoke plainly: "I would, Highness. It would cause unbearable pain to lose my family, but I could never again fail my Emperor. That dishonor would stain my entire family for all time. They understand my duty."

Jar'ek: "Stand, Golgaht—Elite Guard Commander."

Golgaht stood, shakily. Jar'ek held him steady with his right hand and issued a Psionic Command: {"Inquisitors, deactivate."}

Jar'ek: "Golgaht, you are redeemed. You have been found loyal, and your honor is intact. And rest assured that as you protect me and..." Jar'ek glanced meaningfully at Kallehn, then continued: "...***My Family***, I will consider your family as my own."

Golgaht was at a loss for words. His duty was to protect this being. His honor demanded it regardless of his personal feelings. But the Elite Commander felt a swelling of emotion from deep inside. This Meld was not only worthy of his loyalty and obedience but his admiration and affection. The Judgment of the SEED had been wise indeed with this new human Emperor. He felt a great pride in serving this youngling Prince—this human cub—this great leader.

Promise Space Transport Fleet(PSTF)—Armed Merchantman Achilles

Though spartan by TCDF standards, the officer's lounge aboard the armed merchant cruiser Achilles had a spectacular view. One entire wall was transparent armor-glass. Council Observer Qualtish was relaxing with a cup of hot tea, admiring the rare spectacle of the gray, green and ice-white planet below. Promise was his home. It was a harsh mistress—bitterly cold most of the time, but it had its own beauty, and its own sort of people—those who struggled to eke out an existence, if not some small degree of prosperity from soil that was frozen most of every planetary rotation. But the wealthy robber-barons of the TCDF Council skimmed every hard-earned credit into their own fat pockets. They thought that he—the Promise Observer—had been cowed by bribes and threats over the SSOs, but not so. He took the bribe money and invested it—into the rebellion. The blood money bought weapons and access…access to resources and information that no Promiser would ever have gained through regular channels. And finally, after decades of deliberate and persistent manipulations, an opportunity had arisen that would bring meaning to the hiding, the sacrifices, all of the Machiavellian efforts.

Some had sacrificed their lives and families without hesitation. Others had been sacrificed for the cause, without their consent. Qualtish felt guilt and shame for some of the actions he had undertaken or coerced others to undertake. It seemed unbearable, at times. Then he remembered what he was fighting for. Sallyia, his own daughter, had been used and murdered by the Council just to show him where his place was—how utterly powerless he was. He remembered her beautiful red hair flowing behind her as she ran and laughed in the fields—her startling azure blue eyes that smiled along with her laugh—and the blood running down her porcelain face and neck—the broken nails where she had fought against her attackers. And he remembered the anguished primal cry that came from deep within his soul as he held her limp body in his arms. He remembered it ***all***.

And Sallyia wasn't the only one he fought for. There were many, many others—some known to him, others just photos, data, and names. There would be a reckoning! Those who sought power for power's sake with no regard to any others didn't deserve to live as part of a civilized society. They were a cancer within it. And like a cancer, the body would fight to reject them. Ultimately, they must be excised and destroyed.

Qualtish was startled from his reverie by the sound of approaching ship boots. He stood as the tall, athletic young man approached. His jet-black hair framed his well-chiseled features while his emerald green eyes set off the dark green jerkin and trousers of the Promiser Merchant Fleet he wore. Promise wasn't allowed to have military vessels or even armed merchantmen, according to the TCDF treaty. And if the Council knew of this ship, let alone the other 20 that had been armed, they would have sent overwhelming forces to punish Promise—again. But since the TCDF had pulled out all of their warships and redirected them to Jaden-325, Promise had been quietly arming all of its merchant fleet. A merchant ship wasn't built to take punishment like a warship. But with the element of surprise, these seemingly defenseless ships could deal out a significant amount of damage. The particle beam broadcasters and missile launchers were well disguised, and only a close inspection might discover the fire-control systems hidden behind newly painted wall panels.

Captain Marcus Galfren came to a halt and snapped to attention in front of the Observer. "Honored Observer, please forgive my delay in welcoming you aboard the PSTF. My crew and I are proud to host you."

Qualtish: "The honor is mine, Marcus. You favor your mother!"

Galfren: "Have you news of her, my Lord?"

Qualtish: "Indeed, I do! I saw her and spoke with her not 30

SPRs ago! She is in good health and high spirits.

Galfren: "Thank you, Sir. That ***is*** good news. When next you see her, please express my fondness for her."

Qualtish: "Of course, my boy! But now, I am afraid we must speak of other things—not so pleasant things."

Galfren: "Our efforts at infiltration have succeeded, my Lord!"

Qualtish: "Truly? We have effective control of one of the Taskforce warships?"

Galfren grinned wickedly. It was odd for Qualtish to see the young officer with ghoulish anticipation marring his perfect face. It seemed so incongruous. The last time they had seen each other, Marcus had been only five SSOs of age. The Observer recalled the boy sitting on his lap and smiling up at him. No fear, no hatred, none of the bloodlust that Marcus the man now wore like a cloak to warm his soul. But that child had not seen his own father slaughtered in front of him—beaten then executed because he had spoken out against TCDF cruelties. The war had not yet begun yet the casualty lists were full of such youthful victims. Soon—soon he would have his revenge.

Galfren: "A Fast Destroyer, Observer. And not just ***ANY*** Fast Destroyer. No, our forces have infiltrated the Fast Destroyer ***Necromancer***—the very same ship chosen to transport their intended victim—the former Ranger, now young Emperor, Jar'ek Constandor. We do not have complete control of the ship, yet. But when the time is right, I am confident that our forces will dispense with the few crewmembers that remain loyal to the TCDF. We have planned very carefully."

Qualtish: "This is more than we could have hoped for, Marcus! You and your team have exceeded our expectations. This could well seal the fate of the TCDF on Promise! If we could forge an alliance with this young man...even if nothing more than a single warship survives of that ancient empire...Promise could be free of the New Hope yoke forever!"

Galfren: "Observer, I mean no disrespect, but if we wish to garner favor with this young Prince, why do we not simply release him back to his own warship?"

Qualtish: "You are smart. That is good. I will tell you why. There are two reasons. Firstly, we need more than a friend. We need Jar'ek Constandor to SEE and FEEL the injustice that is inflicted on his own people. He must become an active participant in our emancipation, or I fear we may fail.

Galfren nodded his head in understanding and then asked: "And the second reason?"

Qualtish: "We dare not allow the TCDF to target him when they see their kidnapping attempt has failed. Promise is beginning a civil war with New Hope and the Treech may find us any day, now. Can we afford to fight off the remnants of an ancient empire, as well?! No, we must get him out of that system to safety, show him our plight and plead our case, then ensure he gets back safely to his own forces."

Galfren nodded slowly as he assimilated everything that had just been said: "But what of the rumors we have heard of a new plague, Observer? Surely we cannot risk bringing him back to Promise."

Qualtish: "Agreed, Marcus, agreed. Others have been preparing bases within the asteroid belt that surrounds this system. One of these bases is nearly completed. Few know of its existence. It should serve perfectly to house our guest and allow for a team of scientists and physicians to examine him before we have any real contact. You will need to keep him and anyone he comes in contact with, in quarantine—you understand?"

Galfren: "Of course, Observer. Such instructions have already been issued as a precaution."

Qualtish reached out his hand towards the PSTF Captain and offered a small computer chip: "Good, then take this data chip. It includes the coordinates of the Asteroid Base and identification protocols that will allow you through the defenses. See that it gets into the proper hands aboard Achilles. And give them the heartfelt thanks of all Promisers, for me!"

Galfren took the chip and then snapped to attention one more time.

Qualtish took the young officer's hand in his and held it tightly for a moment. Much passed between them at that moment without a word being said. When Qualtish finally released his hand, Captain Galfren nodded, then turned sharply and walked away. Staring at the captain's back as he left, Qualtish mused if even the death of every man, woman, and child on New Hope could bring back the happy, carefree smile of the little boy that Marcus used to be.

Chapter 58 — A NEW MISSION

Imperial Destroyer Celestia — Jaden-325-4 Orbit

No light shone in the cavernous room. A lone dark-haired human male slowly navigated around the edges of a circle drawn on the deck. His stance was low, arms outstretched in front of his chest holding a long metallic pike—a dim blue sprite of light pulsed through the runes and glyphs which were etched deeply into the metal of the fighting rod. Kallehn focused on his breathing, his center of gravity, his slow, deliberate movements—left foot crossing right, right foot crossing left, always facing toward the far side of the circle—watching—waiting—listening. His hearing, sight, and other sense had been improving noticeably since the melding. Now he concentrated on detecting any hint of sound—anything that would give away his opponent's location or provide a clue to his intentions. He heard the ***sssshhh-sssshhh*** of his own quiet movements as he slid his feet carefully across the deck. He heard the soft susurrations of the shallow breathing of their audience and his own. Then...***Click-click***...was that the tap of an unsheathed foot claw on the decking...Kallehn turned his head to the right sharply and braced himself.

With astonishing speed, another dark shape leaped across the intervening space between itself and its intended target. Furred and clawed hands swung mightily, bringing down a matching pike aimed directly at Kallehn's face. Kallehn dropped to one knee, pushed his own pike up to block and parry the blow. A loud ***CLANG*** echoed through the chamber as the charged metal fighting rods showered the darkened space with bright blue sparks. Without pause, and in one fluid motion, Kallehn twisted and spun in place to bring his extended weapon around in a speeding arc designed to sweep the feet from under his opponent. But the swing struck only empty air as the Pythanon Guardsman had vanished again, just in time. Kallehn stood, continuing the swing of his pike, overhead until it returned to its rest position in both hands, in front of his chest.

Two vertical pupils within pools of dark green stared intently at the two combatants. J'Uhr knew this was training and that his mind-mate would not be seriously injured, but it made little difference to her instinctive drive to ***protect***. The fur down her neck and spine was raised high, and a deep, partially suppressed growl was heard clearly in the sudden silence and her long tail twitched as she moved. J'Uhr paced, never letting her eyes leave Kallehn's simulated opponent. But she also sensed Kallehn's movements—and his thoughts. Their psionic bond had continued to grow in strength, and new abilities had been brought to the surface for both. Just as Jar'ek and S'Fah had discovered, they were now able to share the senses and experiences, in addition to their conscious thoughts. Through the psionic link, J'Uhr could FEEL the tightness of Kallehn's grip as his fingers gripped and shifted position on the powered-pike, again and again. She could feel the sweat running down his face, felt how he kept his body low to enhance stability, saw the scene through his own eyes. These new skills took some getting used to. They could be distracting. And in battle, that could be disastrous.

J'Uhr forced her thoughts to calm. She focused on her own breathing and made herself sit and then lie down, still watching the training session, tail still twitching with anxiety. Well, no one was perfect.

Golgaht growled quietly in appreciation. This young cub almost took him off his feet in that last engagement. He was quick—and smart. Training with the Pythanon Guardsmen had been painful and challenging for the Lord Commander, but he had not once complained. Each time he was knocked to the ground in humiliation he simply got back up, dusted off the dirt and went right back at it. He had gained the respect of the entire Elite Guard Phalanx. And that was no easy thing to attain… The two sparring partners continued to circle each other in the dark.

Kallehn: "So, I understand that all of the remaining Elite Guardsmen have completed the inquisition without incident."

Golgaht: "That is true, Lord Commander. The inquisitors have vindicated all 52 who survived the mutiny. The Admiral is now impatient to inspect the Alacrity and clear the rest of the crew. We should have more than sufficient numbers to ensure his safety. All critical areas have been secured, and random patrols continue. Nothing out of the ordinary has been found."

Kallehn: "Very well, I'm afraid we are going to have to quit stalling and get this over with."

Golgaht: "It is a good thing he does for the crew. It has been a difficult mission for many reasons. His gesture carries significant meaning for us."

Kallehn: "You are right, of course."

Kallehn stood slowly and tapped the tip of his pike on the hard deck. It was a symbol that the practice session had ended. The lights scaled up to their full measure, and dozens of guardsmen could be seen sitting cross-legged on the deck surrounding them, showing keen interest.

Kallehn and Golgaht bowed sharply to each other and walked forward to clasp arms and hands.

Golgaht: "You are getting too good to fight old furballs like me, my Lord."

Kallehn started to smile, then carefully closed his lips, remembering that baring one's teeth at a Pythanon might be considered a threat, or at least rude. He chuckled while returning the pike to a stand for storing practice weapons. "I cannot count the aches and pains that have been inflicted upon my poor body by just such an old fur-ball in recent times. I feel I would have to surrender to any younger, stronger Guardsman before he even lifted a single claw!"

Golgaht: "You have done very well, Lord Commander. I believe you could hold your own against most of the Elite Guard. There have been very few melds in our long history that have shown such promise in the martial arts. You are to be commended."

Kallehn nodded his appreciation for the compliment and began walking back towards the hatch and main passageway. Kallehn: "I'm certain Jar'ek will push us to start the inspection tomorrow morning. I suggest we get a good night's rest. The double staccato clicks of Golgaht's concurrence echoed through the chamber as Kallehn walked through the hatch, thinking to himself—*I need a masseuse*—

Imperial Gunship Alacrity — Jaden-325-4 Orbit

The docking bay of the Alacrity was cleared of all personnel except for Jar'ek's own security detail and those few members of Alacrity's crew who had already been cleared by use of the Inquisitor nanites. As Jar'ek followed Golgaht down the landing ramp of the Vehement, he heard the resounding clap of his security detail and crew representatives coming to attention. This was soon followed by compressed string of staccato drum beats that was the Imperial equivalent of boatswain's pipes. Jar'ek was surprised as the bright emerald green light of a security scanner swept over Golgaht first and then his own body, head to foot. S'Fah, surprised as well, hunkered down in an aggressive posture and rumbled a nearly silent growl of displeasure.

Jar'ek glanced quickly at Golgaht and received a reassuring 'clack, clack' from the Pythanon's teeth. The strong back and shoulder muscles of the big cat rippled and relaxed as Jar'ek caressed S'Fah's neck and ears. Just then Jar'ek was surprised again when he heard loudspeakers blaring honors from some hidden locations throughout the cavernous bay:

"Imperial Guard Command — Arriving."

"His Royal Highness, Jar'ek Constandor — Arriving.
Fleet Admiral of the Harmonic Empire
Primary Meld of the Harmonic Empire
Primary Seed Authority

Emperor of Known Space."

Jar'ek was still uncomfortable with all of the pomp and ceremony required of him, but he realized that it was critical that the rest of the crew, indeed the rest of Pythanon, recognized him as the legitimate leader of the Empire. He would have to endure it until he could get used to it. That didn't prevent him from blushing.

Jar'ek stepped forward on the prepared dais and saluted the waiting crew members, who immediately swung up their right fists to strike their left pectorals in return.

Jar'ek: "Stand at ease!" Even as he spoke those words, he knew that no Pythanon in his service would ever relax in his presence. He still wanted to extend the courtesy.

Jar'ek: "Alacrity, Attend me!"

Alacrity AI: "Alacrity, Attending — Highness."

Jar'ek: "Alacrity, recognize me and report publicly throughout this ship and across this system."

Alacrity: "Broadcasting, now. I, Alacrity, Imperial AI serial number: TZD-321478-E currently serving as ship's AI aboard the IDF Gunship Alacrity do certify that using Psionic and DNA scans I have verified the identity and designation of the being before me who calls himself 'Jar'ek Constandor.' I certify that he bears the authentic Mark-of-the-SEED. I attest that his DNA contains the triple-helix modifications of a Harmonic Meld. I further certify through Psionic Scan and exchange of encoded Psionic Keys that this 'Jar'ek Constandor' is a qualified Harmonic Meld in direct succession to the Imperial Throne. Final communications from Imperial Center, centuries ago, confirmed that all Harmonic Melds were deceased."

Jar'ek: "Very well."

Jar'ek walked forward and extended his hand and grasped the forearm of each member of the crew's remaining command staff.

Jar'ek: "Officer 8th, K'Traketh, step forward!"

K'Traketh was tall even for a Pythanon. The slight graying of his jet-black fur around ear tips and lips belied his youthful appearance and gave him an air of competence and confidence. As he stopped a few paces in front of Jar'ek, he saluted and came to attention, once more.

Jar'ek reached forward with his right hand and placed it on K'Traketh's chest. A blue spark flowed down the tattoo on Jar'ek's arm until it leaped from his fingertips and spread across the front of the crewmember's light armor uniform. When Jar'ek removed his hand, glyphs of Imperial rank and authority glowed on the Pythanon's chest.

Jar'ek: "K'Traketh of Pythanon, I promote you to Commander of this Vessel. In so doing, I entrust you with authority to speak for me in all things relating to this vessel and such other things as may be necessary to protect the Empire. So long as you follow Imperial Law and Edicts, I will support you. Promote those you know and trust to help you fulfill the responsibilities that I've have bestowed upon you along with your rank. Do you accept this challenge?"

K'Traketh's deep rattling voice approximated a Terran accent as best it could when he spoke in Terran Standard: "I accept your Challenge, Highness. May the nuclear fire of Pythanon's sun consume me, body and soul, before I fail you, my Emperor!"

Jar'ek slapped K'Traketh's shoulder and said: "Congratulations, Ships Commander, K'Traketh! I'm sure you will make us all proud. Now, please escort the rest of the crew into the landing bay so that we can get this unpleasant business of the inquisitors finished and behind us.

Imperial Destroyer Celestia — Jaden-325-4 Orbit

Jar'ek sat in the observer's seat, quietly watching the subdued activity on Celestia's bridge. He marveled at the efficiency of motion demonstrated by the Pythanon's. Some of the Elites had been assigned to help cover bridge positions. They now had three full shifts. Jar'ek, strictly speaking, wasn't expected to work a shift anywhere. But he enjoyed the quiet of night shifts on the command deck. It gave him time to think.

The last of the inquisitions was complete. The crew of the Alacrity had passed with flying colors. Once they had heard the Alacrity AI confirm the identity and authenticity of the new Emperor, any thought of insurrection disappeared. There had been a handful of crewmen who had been members of the Brotherhood. These had come forward and were furious with their former religious leaders for manipulating them. Just as Golgaht had asked in the past, these former rebels begged for their own execution to satisfy their honor.

Jar'ek again refused all of these requests. He explained that being misled by corrupt leaders was not a crime. Now was a time for them to serve with honor and put those honest mistakes behind them. Jar'ek had every confidence that the future service of these Guardsmen would be a source of pride for their families and their entire species.

Celestia: "Sire, can I interrupt your introspection for a moment?"

Jar'ek: "If you must. Is it something urgent?

Celestia: "Well, it's not exactly urgent, but it may be time-sensitive."

Jar'ek: "Okay, give me the bad news…"

Celestia: "NOT Bad News…"

Jar'ek: "Really? Then give it to me! We could all use some good news."

Celestia: "Yes, hmm…well, it has yet to be determined whether it is actually good news… but here goes. During the battle for Alacrity, one of our comm probes reentered the system and docked with the Celestia. It had an interesting encounter with some Imperial Military Units and has returned post-haste with a message from them—for your eyes only."

Jar'ek sat up straight in the seat: "WHAT!? Why didn't you tell me earlier? What sort of Military Units? How many? Are they sending some here? Were there any sentients on the base?"

Celestia: "The message wasn't marked urgent, and we've been a little busy. Based on the information in the message header, it is time sensitive, but not urgent—thus my messaging queue assigned it a lower priority. But I think it must be very important, so I wanted to bring it to your attention now that you have a bit of breathing space."

Jar'ek: "Fair enough. Now, answer my other questions and play the message privately for me on my ARDisplay."

Celestia: "The details were classified beyond my security clearance, Sire. You'll have to listen to the message or query the comm probe directly to get your other answers, I'm afraid."

Jar'ek: "What? You are an AI assigned to a Diplomatic SEED Vessel—is there a security clearance above Imperial Red Level?"

Celestia: "Evidently there is one now. It is called Imperial Ultra Blue Level, at least according to the Comm Probe."

Jar'ek: "This sounds interesting… play the message."

Celestia: "I'm afraid I cannot. I do not have sufficient clearance to decrypt it. I'll have to forward it to your personal ARDisplay. You should have it in your message queue, now."

Jar'ek focused on the blinking cobalt blue message icon in his ARDisplay, and it immediately opened.

—Message From: T'ash Tantra — Imperial AI and Base commander — K'nesthus Base — Sector Z-57QA-452G.

Imperial comm probe has been successfully authenticated and upgraded with new security protocols.

Classification Level Ultra Blue – SEED/Meld Eyes Only.

1,873 SSOs ago, the last known remaining Meld died at this

station having contracted the plague. The Meld carried up-to-date intelligence about the state of the Empire, as well as the latest engineering designs and scientific research. This base does not house a SEED repository. As the Meld was dying, he needed to devise a mechanism to secure this vital information before his death. A stasis unit was constructed to sustain the SEED fragment until it could be recovered and installed in a SEED Repository.

If the memories of this Meld are to be salvaged, a living Meld must collect them as soon as possible. Due to the sensitivity of the information stored, all Imperial Military Assets stationed in System Z982 were ordered to remain here until relieved or until an Imperial Override has been issued to countermanded these orders. Message Ends—

Imperial Destroyer Celestia — Jaden-325-4 Orbit

Jar'ek sat in the observer's seat rubbing his chin thoughtfully as he soaked in the vista of surrounding space provided by his ARDisplay—another technological marvel provided as a benefit of the Melding. Plato was becoming more attuned to Jar'ek's moods and his occasional need for solitude. So, he waited patiently, sorting through extended memories of the Sector Base in Z-57QA-452G. This information could be out of date, but the last base commander assigned to the Imperial Shipyard K'nesthus was an ancient Takesh Admiral named Brithat Shi'hakt. And according to related memories, his expertise was in engineering—and he was a Meld!

Jar'ek: {"Plato, what do you make of this eyes-only message? And why institute a new, higher level of security—Ultra Blue?"}

Plato: {"Yes, Interesting, isn't it? The base commander was a Meld! If the Admiral survived in quarantine for a hundred years, the information he accumulated could be vital to the rebuilding of the Empire—base locations, plague research, disposition of military assets to name a few possibilities. It is possible that some systems were not infected and flourish to this day!"}

Jar'ek: {"He was an engineer, wasn't he? K'nesthus was only one of many large shipyards across the Empire. But wasn't it rumored to be the center for Research and Development for the Fleet?"}

Plato: {"Although engineering designs may be stored in multiple locations in the old Empire, few of your predecessors were engineers or scientists. Brithat Shi'hakt was both. So, adding the extended memories of a brilliant engineer to the SEED Repository on Celestia would be of enormous value. And we certainly couldn't afford for that knowledge to fall into the wrong hands. I would recommend we send an envoy to retrieve the SEED Fragment and see what else can be salvaged from the Shipyard."}

Jar'ek: {"You don't think I should lead the recovery mission?"}

Plato: {"I think Kallehn is perfectly capable of completing this mission and I suspect you will be needed elsewhere very soon"}

Jar'ek: {"Pythanon?"}

Plato: {"Precisely! The Alexicon should arrive in this system any day, now. Only the Primary Harmonic Meld can dispel the myths and half-truths of the Brotherhood. And haste is required. It is possible the entire Pythanos system could be consumed in a religious war."}

Jar'ek: {"You're right, of course. Millions of innocent Pythanons could die. Stopping that must be my first priority. Very well."}

Jar'ek: "Celestia, attend me."

Celestia: "Attending, Highness."

Jar'ek: "Schedule a meeting with senior officers and guardsmen for 08:00 tomorrow morning, run diagnostics on the FTL drive and plot a least-time hyperdrive course for System Z-57QA-452G"

Celestia: "Orders confirmed."

ABOUT THE AUTHOR

C. Arthur Shuey was born in Panama City Beach, Florida in the early 1960's. In the early 1970's he moved with his family to Atlanta, Georgia, where he's lived ever since. Mr. Shuey has a degree in Chemical Environmental Technology from DeKalb College, and now works in Information Technology for a national non-profit.

His interests include Soccer, Martial Arts, Science, Science Fiction, Social Justice and learning as much as he can from people with diverse backgrounds.

His favorite authors include: Andre Norton, David Weber, Robert Heinlein, Isaac Asimov, Gene Roddenberry, Lawrence White and

Favorite podcasts include: Anything NPR, Science Friday, All Things Considered, OnPoint and, Wait, Wait…Don't Tell Me

Follow this author on Facebook "fb.me/HarmonicEmpireBooks", on twitter @HarmonicEmpire and on the web at www.HarmonicEmpire.com (Where you can register for immediate immigration.)

Glossary of Terms

Units of Distance (Based on Speed of Light c)

Useful distances are measured in nL or mL

Quanty	Unit	Conversion	Unit
1	nL(Nano-Light Second)	1	Foot
1	nL(Nano-Light Second)	30.48	cm
3.1	nL(Nano-Light Second)	1	m
3100	nL(Nano-Light Second)	1	km
3.1	µL(Micro-Light Second)	1	km
5280	nL(Nano-Light Second)	1	mile
5.28	µL(Micro-Light Second)	1	mile
1	µL(Micro-Light Second)	1000	Feet
1	µL(Micro-Light Second)	30480	cm
1	µL(Micro-Light Second)	305	m
1	µL(Micro-Light Second)	0.305	km
1	mL(Mili-Light Second)	1000000	Feet
1	mL(Mili-Light Second)	304800	m
1	mL(Mili-Light Second)	304.8	km
1	mL(Mili-Light Second)	189.4	miles

Acronyms

IAISA	Imperial Artificially Intelligent SEED Agent
FTL	Faster Than Light

Colloquialisms

Hygiene Facility	Restroom, Bathroom
Fresher	Contemporary version of a smart shower
X'Ah	Genetically Enhanced (Extra)
Empath	
Telepath	
Psionic	Extrasensory perception and abilities, including telepathy, empathy, precognition, telekinesis and transmutation.
Phalanx	Military unit consisting of 50 guardsmen or mechs.

Character background

Character Name	Origin	Description	First introduced
Jar'ek Constandor	Planet: Promise, Terran	TCDF Ranger 26yo, Psi rating Level 5 – emotional telepath with matched X'Ah-Panth, only.	Chapter 3, Section 2
Kallehn Frix	Planet: New Hope, Terran	TCDF Ranger 26yo, Psi rating Level 4 – emotional telepath with matched X'Ah-Panth, only.	Chapter 3, Section 2
S'Fah	Planet: New Hope, Species: X'Ah-Panth	Genetically engineered from Terran Panther. Enhancements include improved intelligence, heightened strength and senses, improved Psi.	Chapter 4, Section 1
J'Uhr	Planet: New Hope, Species: X'Ah-Panth	Genetically engineered from Terran Panther. Enhancements include improved intelligence, heightened strength and senses, improved Psi.	Chapter 4, Section 1
Captain Kathy Xiang Lao	Planet: New Hope, Terran	Commanding Officer of the TCDF Dragon Eye.	Chapter 3, Section 1
Tactical Officer Sasha Conner	Planet: Promise, Terran	TCDF Lt., Tactical Officer, TCDF Dragon Eye	Chapter 3, Section 1
Medical Officer Kira To'Torat	Planet: Promise, Terran	TCDF Ranger 26yo, Psi rating Level 5 – emotional telepath with matched X'Ah-Panth, only.	Chapter 30, Section 3

Character Name	Origin	Description	First introduced
Helm Officer Rico De Lucena	Planet: New Hope, Terran	TCDF Lt., Helm Officer, TCDF Dragon Eye	Chapter 3, Section 1
Chief Frost Vermanderly	Planet: New Hope, Terran	TCDF Master Chief, Operations, TCDF Dragon Eye	Chapter 27, Section 1
Chief Russ Taylor	Planet: New Hope, Terran	TCDF Master Chief, Engineering, TCDF Dragon Eye	Chapter 23, Section 1
Chief Sheridan T'Kathrad	Planet: New Hope, Terran	TCDF Senior Chief, TCDF Dragon Eye	Chapter 28, Section 3
Admiral Kirkland Heidrect	Planet: New Hope Species: Terran	TCDF Admiral, former Military Governor of Planet Promise, Candidate for Terran Council membership	Chapter 51, Section 4
Captain Kyle D'Sai	Planet: New Hope Species: Terran	TCDF, Commanding Officer of TCDF Battlecruiser Shashtavich	Chapter 51, section 4
Lt. Cmdr. Jenn Casey	Planet: New Hope Species: Terran	TCDF, Executive Officer of TCDF Battlecruiser Shashtavich	Chapter 51, section 4

Made in the USA
Monee, IL
19 March 2020

23511489R00223